THE GHOSTS OF DANDY CROSSING

PRAISE FOR KATIE LEE

"She knows the good country from the ground up. In a lifetime of song and acting and writing Katie has fought to preserve the ground we live on and hardly seem to know. Now she goes into the heart of the matter where good feelings rise like the river itself and roar us back to better days."

—Charles Bowden, *Killing the Hidden Waters, Blue Desert,* and *Black Orchid.*

"Katie Lee was the first person with the guts to record my "Gallo del Cielo" song. She is an un-equaled storyteller, one of our most important folk singers for the last seventy years, and a writer-activist who has always been on the front lines of the vanishing West. She rode the rivers, and has lived what others only dream of. To read Katie Lee is to read great and true history not besotted with the bullshit of academic historians. There ought to be a statue of her in front of the Cowboy Hall of Fame. And, hell, the Smithsonian."

—Tom Russell, *'120 Songs of Tom Russell',* www.tomrussell.com

"Your passion and connection to the canyon is visceral and contagious; brings it to life and helps people realize what beauty was lost. The Glen Canyon scene is literally the best of the entire film and often brings people to tears."

—Beda Calhoun, Associate Producer of the documentary film, *DamNation.*

"Katie Lee is a lovely lady whose lust for adventure, music, and life in the canyon country of the North American Southwest remains untamed even after over 90 years of hardcore experience. Katie's writing clearly reveals her relentless passion for Glen Canyon, both past and present, and reflects the crystal clear perspective of this great heroine of the modern environmental movement."

—Jack Loeffler, author of *Adventures With Ed, Headed Upstream*

"If you want to know what Glen Canyon was before it was flooded, if you want to know the people who settled the last part of the West, and if you want your heart to be touched, then Katie's words will do just that. Her books are like a fine wine, they just keep getting better."

—Richard J. Ingebretsen, MD, PhD, founder of Glen Canyon Institute.

"Katie Lee speaks for the canyons and the sweet desert recesses. She is our foul-mouthed, lightning-eyed, boot-stomping baladeer, a character Louis L'Amour never could have invented. Born from the rock itself, she is a lifetime of experience on this wild, restless, cradling ground. If you want to know this place, you need to know Katie."

—Craig Childs, *Apocalyptic Planet, The Animal Dialogues, The Way Out,* and *The Secret Knowledge of Water*

THE GHOSTS OF DANDY CROSSING

BY KATIE LEE

Dream Garden Press
2014

Cover photographs by Katie Lee

First Edition
ISBN: 978-0-942688-87-0

Dream Garden Press
268 South 200 East
Salt Lake City, UT 84111
http://www.dreamgarden.com/
phone: (801) 521-3819
e-mail: books@dreamgarden.com

๛ ๛

BOOKS BY KATIE LEE

Ten Thousand Goddam Cattle
Published by Northland Press, Flagstaff, Arizona
Copyright © 1976 by Katie Lee
Revised edition 1980
Third printing (revised) 1985 by Katydid Books & Music
University of New Mexico Press edition reprinted 2001

All My Rivers Are Gone
Published by Johnson Books, Boulder, Colorado
Copyright © 1998 by Katie Lee

Glen Canyon Betrayed
Published by Fretwater Press, Flagstaff, Arizona
Copyright © 2006 by Katie Lee
A reprint of *All My Rivers Are Gone* with added
photographs, index, and afterword

The Ballad of Gutless Ditch
Published by Katydid Books & Music
Copyright © 1964, 2012 by Katie Lee
Limited edition of 500, signed by author and illustrator

All books available from Katydid Books & Music
Excluding *All My Rivers Are Gone*
www.katydoodit.com— or the publishers

Katie Lee books and music are also available from Kensandersbooks.com

In memory of
Slim Williams
For many good reasons...
through sad and glad seasons.

THE GHOSTS OF DANDY CROSSING

CHAPTER 1

September 1, 1962 — Dandy Crossing

'*Where is that woman anyway?*'

Jason squinted against the early morning sun. He spoke loud enough to startle himself and send a multitude of possibilities clicking through the turnstile of his mind.

She's pert'near always on schedule. Step's the one we mostly have to wait for. He looked upriver. Sand in large clumps gave to the river's tugging and fell from the banks and bars with soft slaps. To a riverman the sound spoke one word: *Rising*.

He looked downriver. Silt-ladened water frothed over rocks at the head of Trachyte Creek, sending small pink plumes into the air beneath a gage station cable stretched bank to bank. From the left side, where he stood on a sandstone ledge one hundred feet above the water, he watched the end of the ferry swing out into the downstream current and thought he'd better tell Windy, the Ferryman, that Annabell was starting to pull at her cables. He felt uneasy for the old girl with her bridge pontoons, oil drums and planks.

Uneasy for some other things as well.

Standing back, he reached for his binoculars and searched the horizon for a dust plume. Pushing the straw hat farther back on his head, he sat down on the shaded stones and leaned against the cool wall of an ancient ruin.

Yesterday he'd driven to Dandy with the crew to pick up his boats from a Cataract run, and instead of returning home to

Blanding he'd elected to wait for Shan and Step at the river. The three of them were to leave later that afternoon on their annual river trip through Glen Canyon. Step had written that he'd be flying in on the mail plane—due around noon. Shan was driving in from San Francisco. *Hope she didn't try to call me after I left home....* *No phones here but the store-to-ferry Peanut Can.* Removing his hat, he looked up and caught a jet's snowy track drawn boldly across the blue southwestern sky. He followed the chalk marks eastward to the horizon, a canyon and the road snaking out of it toward the river....

A dust plume!

Jason grabbed his binoculars and focused on the road. It was Windy Short's truck bouncing down to the ferry, sun glaring off the windshield.

Dernit! Can't see who's inside. Now why the deuce did I climb all the way up here when she could arrive any minute? Fine welcome after almost a year!

He watched the truck reach the landing, saw Windy get out alone, walk down to the outboard, untie the bow rope, hop in, pull the motor cord and swing the tiller in a series of smoothly linked motions. The boat floated gently up the eddy; when it hit the fast current its little tail dug down and spewed a frothy red 'V' out the stern. It drew a graceful arc upstream, and like a rocket slowly burning out, landed on what was left of the sandbar below the ferry. Windy inspected the landing, got on the ferry, cranked up the old Chevy engine and started back, leaving the outboard beached.

Bradley must have called from the gaging station to warn him. The left bank was out of the main current now, and holding, so Annabell's bulkiness would rest easier there. Through the binoculars he saw Windy jump ashore and sight Jason's boat, the *Tickaboo*, bedroll and gear beyond the willows; saw him look around, upstream then down, like watching a movie he'd seen a hundred times. *Now he's going to turn around and look across river.... Now he'll look up here but he won't see me.... Now he'll put his hands up to his mouth....*

'Ja-a-y-son!'

He chuckled, reached for his hat and stood, waving it in a slow arc above his head. 'Up here, Windy.'

The man hollered in return, but a twisty canyon breeze garbled his words beyond deciphering.

Now Jason knew why he'd climbed to the ruin: he didn't want to talk to anyone. He had things to think about—alone. Windy talked too much, usually about the wrong subjects and almost always at the wrong times—didn't mean anything by it, of course, did it to keep away the silence he claimed to love so much. His wife had left him, and with nobody around to jabber at, he hardly let his tongue rest a minute when there was.

Jason stepped away from the edge and sat, again, with his back against the ruin. The truck started and a few seconds later dust curled up over the cliff from Windy's passing. Using the glasses he checked the willow branch he'd stuck at the water's edge about dawn. *Hmmm, water's up to the fork... still rising. We'll have a lively run down to the Rincon if this keeps up—over twenty-five thousand second-feet.*

For a man who did considerable sitting, there wasn't equal time to think quietly on subjects of his own choosing. Fifteen years as an oarsman down the rapids of the Colorado, through Grand Canyon, down the Green, San Juan, Salmon, Snake and Yampa rivers, doesn't leave a man much cogitating time—most is taken up answering questions and catering to the comforts and whims of paying passengers. It was good, looking down at the river now and seeing no one there. All summer the wild, wary and adventurous had 'run the Glen' in their rubber rafts, aluminum boats, fiberglass and fold-boats, kayaks, and yes, even inner tubes, air mattresses, log rafts and pontoons. Here at Dandy Crossing they loaded supplies and disappeared into the—to them—unknown. *Windy says a thousand took off from the landing this season—that means about a hundred—glad I spent my time on the Grand and San Juan runs.... Guess I don't care for this part any more, without Step and Shan.*

Three years ago, and quite unexpectedly, Glen Canyon had become a new, almost magical world for Jason. His two dear friends Shan and Step had made it so by showing him the canyon through their eyes. Before it had only been a job, guiding others through a canyon he'd had no time to absorb because of his responsibility to his passengers. Learning Shan's songs, Step's photographic techniques and their reverence for the splendor of Glen Canyon had brought a bleary, everyday experience into sharp, pleasing, minute-to-minute focus. On these trips: no baby-sitting the fifteen to twenty-five passengers, no hurt feelings to salve, no complaints to address. A chance to do as he pleased! If a jarring thought occurred, it sifted through their togetherness and was diluted to nonsense by the river. Best of all, at the end of each day, Shan would take out her guitar and sing all his favorite songs. It was hard to contain the joy he felt being a part of this threesome; easy to fear the magic might fade. Apprehension at the start of each trip churned his stomach— someone would detain him, or it wouldn't be as heart-warming as last time.

So far... I've been wrong.... Sure hope it stays that way.

Sunlight munched its way into the ragged outline of Jason's shade, swallowing his reverie. He secured his hat, pulled his heels against his butt and rose in one easy motion; six-foot-one, of slender build, straight and supple as bamboo, sure-footed, hard-muscled and suntanned—to the collar and wrists; from there down, pale as flour. He stretched, jabbed his thumbs into the small of his back and braced backward. Today, his fifty-four years felt like forty. It was a clear, bright, warm, autumn day, with a random breeze to tickle the sweat on his forehead.

Step is due on the mail plane at noon.... Guess I'd better start for the landing strip.... We can load up and get on the river tonight.... Won't matter if we camp a couple miles downriver, just so we get where nobody can catch us.

He climbed down the cliff using some Moki steps chipped ten centuries ago by some rock-crawler intent upon a shortcut to the river—erosion had barely left room for his fingertips, let alone the toes of his boots. Reaching the last step, he leaped from the wall and rammed his boot heels into the soft sandy slope beside the road.

He headed upriver for the strip. *Windy'll come down from the store when he hears the mail plane, then Step and I can get a ride back to the landing.... He'll want a beer... maybe Windy'll bring him one, but I doubt it, not that thoughtful.*

He was nearing the strip when he heard the plane. It came

on the downwind leg, made its turn and dropped lower, but still seemed high to Jason, who'd flown in here many times himself. Coming over the runway, it stayed a good forty feet from the ground. The pilot opened the door of the Cessna and kicked out the mailbag, teetered his wings and gained altitude.

The jettisoned bag bombed a rabbit-brush on landing, sending the feathery seeds skyward in a dusty cloud. Jason's pessimism also took wing.

Oh no! Now where the devil is that guy…? And Shan's had plenty time to get here from San Francisco. Head down, he walked to the mailbag, slung it over his shoulder and started back for the ferry, kicking at the dirt with each step—his disappointment, along with worry and apprehension, skyrocketing. He was half way back when Windy came rattling dustily along. Jason threw the mailbag into the truck bed and climbed into the cab.

'So where's Step?' cracked Windy, jittering the gas pedal.

'Unless he's in that bag, he isn't here.'

'Where the hell ya s'pose he's at?'

'Lord only knows. Maybe there's a letter in there telling us he had to go back to Tangier or someplace,' offered Jason, grumpily.

'Tangiers! What the hell! I figured he'd be pantin' like a gopher—brought 'um a cold beer.'

Jason looked down sheepishly. 'Thoughtful of you, Windy.'

Windy spun a U-e and asked, 'Wanna come up t'the store with me, or ya wanna go back down t'the ferry?' Not waiting for an answer he continued, 'I kin fix us up some lunch—when Shan gets here she can leave 'er car at the store and I'll take ya both down in this.'

'I've got some work to do on the motor yet, Windy. Maybe I'd better…' but looking up he saw the man's eyes full of hope for a few minutes of company. 'Okay, that's a good idea. I'll walk down later if she doesn't come soon. Guess I'm hungry at that—about sunrise since I ate.'

They clattered up Farley Creek a half mile, slid to park and went into the store. Windy, very importantly and methodically, sorted the mail into little pigeon holes behind the wired window which represented the Post Office. There were about eight letters and cards, a few newspapers and a tin of boat parts for the six inhabitants of Dandy Crossing.

White and Farley canyons entering together on the left bank of the river comprised one settlement; Cass Hite's ranch and orchard on the right bank, the other. Old Cass had named his crossing 'A Dandy' and the river people kept it that way. To the rest of the world it was Hite… if you could find it on a map. Jason walked to the freezer and got an ice cream bar. He laid a quarter on the counter and leaned there, looking out at the only gas pump within a hundred miles. A hum from the generator and a creaking of roof beams in the midday heat were all that broke the silence.

It hadn't always been this tranquil at Dandy Crossing. Windy's had been the Upper Store, Fred Bennett's, the Lower Store. There'd been some fifty families living at the confluence, where a copper processing mill had run full tilt in the forties. The sound of little kids screeching at play, the *thrugging* of big trucks in low gear, the banging of tailgates and the thumping of the mill had echoed through the canyon all day long. After dark, the cottonwood trees rustled, a steady spring gurgled beside the cliff wall and a lively river sang its song up-canyon.

Jason snapped his mind away from something he didn't want to think of—a thing the three of them had written about during the winter. On this, their last trip down the Glen—while it was still a living river canyon—they were going to proceed as if nothing about it would ever change. Nothing was to mar this final adventure. No talking about the river's misbegotten future.

Windy's voice pulled him from his thoughts. 'Ain't nuthin' here from Step; reckon he's comin' with Shan?'

'I don't see how,' Jason said, taking half the ice cream in one bite. 'They're coming from different directions. Oh say, before I forget, I need a couple more cans of oil. I'll toss them in the back of the truck. Don't let me go off without them.'

'Okay.' Windy came from behind the Post Office cage, put Jason's quarter in the register and yelled, 'Sale! I'll go slap up some lunch—sam'itch okay?'

'Sure, anything's fine, Windy.' He licked the ice cream stick clean, stuck it in his shirt pocket and walked out of the store. At the foot of the steps he picked up two cans of oil and tossed them over the tailgate—the clatter echoing down canyon. Windy, in his trailer next to the store, slammed the icebox door and started to whistle. Each sound seemed isolated, pointing up the fact that all sound here would soon be terminated.

Jason walked the grassy plot, entered the trailer and crossed the threshold with caution. Since the flood, a loose board, when stepped on, made loud, bawdy sounds and he was sure it hadn't been fixed. Windy set peanut butter and jam sandwiches on the booth table, uncapped the pickle jar and poured cold milk into jelly glasses. Sliding in opposite Jason, he bit right into his sandwich and the subject Jason and friends had elected not to discuss.

'Who ya think's gonna git the concession at Rainbow? They shore by God better give this'n here to me—I run this goddamn ferry fer more'n six years.' He took a big gulp of milk and followed it with a generous burp. 'I ain't seen no indication the one down to Wahweep's goin' to nobody but ol' Art. You still workin' on the one down t' Hoxie Crossin'?'

Jason chewed slowly. 'The County commissioners and BuRec will decide. I'm involved only because the law says a river man must run the marina.'

'Naw, it's the Park Service that'll have the final say, an' I gotta lotta pull with them guys. I been takin' damn good care of the tourists here at Dandy—the Bureau boys too. They know goddamn well I kin handle 'er.'

Jason reached into the pickle jar, avoiding the man's eyes. It depended on which day you listened, what Windy was for and what he was against. He'd been cursing the Bureau along with the rest of them for the past seven years, but now that the dam was nearing completion and flooding a reality, he was kissing up to them for a concession on the reservoir.

Jason altered the subject. 'What's Buck going to do with his cabin?'

'He ain't figured it out yet—whatever'll giv'um the most trouble. They offered t'pay him for it, y'know—wanna use it fer some kinda storage shed up to the new Hite Marina—gonna name it after Cass, I guess—said they'd come an' git it when the water starts backin' up.'

'I would have thought they'd do it the easy way: just let the cabin get buried in silt and water.'

'Naw. Nelson says they got some preference 'bout the build-ings.' Snorting, he added, 'Tough titty. Buck'll do what he wants with that place; took'um a long time g'ttin' the gas heater 'n stove in there and then buildin' onto the back. He ain't jist gonna quietly move out and let'um take over.'

Licking milk from his upper lip, Jason asked, 'Where'll he move to, do you know?'

'Prob'ly to the mine. Says he don't know fer sure yet; might move up t'his claim on the Green, or mebbe he'll stick around here t'work on the White Canyon bridge when they start it.'

Jason looked Windy in the eye, pert-near sure Buck had not even *thought* about working on the bridge, and said, in view of the man's integrity, 'Unless he's thinking sabotage, I doubt he'd do that.'

Jason felt a twinge of conscience. If he wanted to stay any-where near his hard-earned profession as guide, boatman and owner of Glen Canyon Expeditions, he'd have to do the sort of things Buck didn't. He had a big family—six kids and a wife—a house, responsibility, things he couldn't neglect. How far would his conscience let him go? Swallowing the last of his milk he smacked his lips and stood, wishing he were Buck, a loner, a younger man; one that local gossip held to be a man who did *what* he wanted, *when* he wanted and *how* he wanted to do it.

Windy was breezing: 'Ol' Bennett's lots more philosophical 'bout it than Buck. Hell, he's been minin' here fer goddamn near thirty years. His boat dock goes, his house, his mines, the whole shootin' match goes. Know what he said t'other day when the BuRec tol'um how much they was givin' him fer his house n'land? Tol'um, 'Well, that's fine, fellers, never thought I'd make so much off a defunct operation. Think I'll pick out the next place you bastards is gonna build a dam and get some more property that don't cost nuthin'—that way I can go to m'grave makin' a buck offa you, instead of the other way around!' Windy shook his head. 'Boy, they must have a special breed of rat comes 'round t'places like this for the cleanup job. S'a wonder some of 'em don't git kilt'!'

'They're a special breed, all right.' Jason wrinkled his nose.

'Can't wait till Shan gits here t' tell 'er what Bennett said 'bout them Bureau dimwits.'

Jason wanted to ask him not to mention things like that, but instead he said, 'It's time I got down to the boat and finished with my tinkering on the Johnson.'

The two stepped out of the trailer with toothpicks working at their gums, and cottonwoods *whis-s-shing* in the early afternoon breeze.

'What'cha tinkerin' with?'

'Nothing much, just sputters a little on the high-speed jet.'

'I'll take ya down.'

Before Jason could say he'd rather walk, Windy ambushed him with a practicality. 'What about yer oil? Gonna leave it in my truck?'

'Whoa! Thanks for reminding me.' He reached for his wallet, but before he could take it from his back pocket, Windy pulled open the cab door. 'Aw, fergit it, Jason—you spend more money here 'n anybody 'n you never even let me buy ya a beer.'

Jason grinned. 'Next time try ice cream.'

꙰

CHAPTER 2

Afternoon — Same Day

It was creeping up on two o'clock before Windy returned to the store and Jason got to work. Moving his tools to the back deck, he removed the spark plugs and cleaned them while the stern of the *Tickaboo* corked gently in the surge.

Guess I better clean the carburetor while I'm waiting. If we have to hang around for another day, or if Step doesn't come at all... God forbid...! that could change things... If Shan and I went alone, my wife'd have kittens and Windy'd have us eloped, no matter I'm old enough to be her dad!

He replaced his tools in the ammo can and pulled the starter cable. Taking the boat upstream about two miles, he adjusted the jets until it hummed like a purr-cat. Making a few figure eights, he swung back toward the ferry. The prop's sound of thick chocolate in a blender told him the river carried half its weight in silt; told him to check his shear pin supply—there'd be more drift than usual. As he passed Buck's cabin and Fred Bennett's dock he turned away, trying not to visualize them under water. Satisfied with his adjustments he beached on a sandbank above the ferry, cut the motor and tied her up.

Standing on the sand beside his gas containers, he gazed a long time at the two-hundred-foot stretch of moving water. Raising his eyes to the far bank he saw the river stand still and the shore move upstream. For a few seconds the world turned at his will and he was the center.

'Jason!'

Startled, he spun around, out of balance.

'Hi, Jason!'

He looked down by his bedroll... nothing... the road by the ferry phone... nobody. 'Where the dickens are you?'

He heard her giggle. 'Up here, silly.'

Looking skyward he spotted Shan perched atop the ferry cable rigging, camera in hand, hair blowing in the wind. She had one leg wrapped around the post, the other over a guy-wire and was laughing fit to fall off.

'Gosh, how'd you get up there?'

'Suction cups. You took a couple of good swipes at that sandbar, Mr. Boatman—you tryin' to knock out *Tickaboo* before we have a chance to use her?'

'Naw-w-w, spark plugs were dirty, thought I'd best tune up before we got underway. You look good on that pole; you gonna stay there while we run the canyon?'

'Where's Step?'

'Not here yet.'

'You're kidding!' she exploded—then sighing, said, 'No, of course you're not.' She swung her leg over and started down the pole stirrups. 'What's happened this time?'

'Dunno—he didn't come on the mail plane like he said and there wasn't a letter from him—I thought maybe you'd had the last word and could tell me.'

'How? Last I heard he was in Santa Fe, and I've been on the road since San Francisco. I thought you'd both be waiting here like Washington at the Delaware.'

'You know Step.' He turned palms up and shrugged.

'Boy, do I know Step!'

Shan dropped to the ground and came running down the sand. With an end-of-the-trail sigh, she threw her arms around him and squeezed.

'Oh-h-h, Jason... it's *so good* to be here!'

He crushed her in a bear hug that locked their ears together, letting pulse beats speak the words between them for a long minute. When he answered, 'Ah-h-h yes, Shan Lu,' his voice rippled with relief.

She pushed away to arm's length, holding his shoulders and looking up at him appraisingly; then, snapping her middle finger on the brim of his hat, grinned, and said, 'I see you finally got yourself a good cowboy straw. I hate those bill caps, Jason—they'd make Einstein look like an idiot—now this one gives you real class. You look right smart!'

'My eyes aren't sore any more either.' He gave her a playful slap on the rump, asking, 'How'd you get by Windy?'

'Quickly. I know how long it takes to shake Windy—didn't see your outfit so I came on down—my Bird's up there behind the willows. You been waiting long?'

'Came in with one of the boat trucks yesterday and decided not to go back to Blanding. Been kinda nice having some spare time—got to see Buck when he came in from the mine yesterday.'

'Ah-h-h, the Man from Missouri! So he's off work. Super! He said he'd try to fix his schedule to match our take-off. Can't wait to see that blond, river-buckin' cowboy.'

'He feels the same about you, I bet.'

'So, once again we wait for Step-n-Fetch-it.' She rolled her eyes upward, releasing a sigh of agitation; then her eyes moved past his shoulder to the river. She walked to its edge and stood still, watching. He kept silent and waited for the ritual he knew would follow—couldn't hear her words but knew they were talking.

'Hello, Colly Raddy,' she whispered. Slowly, she pulled the leather strap over her head, grounded the camera, toed off her tennis shoes and removed her jeans. Still staring at the water she walked onto the soft mudbank where small waves slapped and curled.

Jason saw her sink waist deep in the eddy, her yellow shirt billow momentarily above the red swirl before she pushed off into the swift current that caught her, ready to take her along with everything else, but found instead a resistance. She swam with strong, even strokes, remaining stationary, moving neither back nor forward for four or five minutes.

Ah-ha, pretty boy, not so fast.... You can't take me yet... I have my own direction, something I learned from you—set a goal and go for it... maybe around a rock instead of over... remove that bank or make a new channel... that's where I am.... New channel... fruits of success are giving me a bellyache.... Got a bunch of questions.... Need

some answers, Mr. River. Gonna ditch the ratrace and hitch a ride...
just go where you go for a while.

Kicking up a froth she surged briefly upstream, then, slowing her strokes, ducked under and let the river carry her down before striking for the bank. She splashed across the bar with sinking steps, flopped on the warm sand breathing hard, then lay back with eyes closed, a smile of fulfillment on her flushed face.

Jason came to place his shadow over her head in one of their many forms of communication—of touches without touching, speaking without talking, knowing without asking.

Wet lashes parted instantly. 'He's high, Jason, high and silty. I can feel his mustache drying on my lip. I'll bet he's twenty-thousand or more.'

'You're close. I checked with Bradley last night when he took the measure. It was twenty-five then, been rising ever since—couple of good storms this week—and I 'spect another on the way.'

'Okay by me, I could use a good storm-cleansing.' She rolled over on her stomach, shook out her hair, propped her forehead on crossed arms and rested.

Jason made use of these rare, quiet moments to look at her and wonder: *What's a year done for you, or to you, Shan Lu...? Your hair's darker... guess you don't bleach it anymore... longer too, almost to your shoulders.... You're pale now, before the river gets to work on you.* She wasn't a tall woman, or skinny—about five-five with strong legs and broad shoulders—did a lot of swimming, even in winter at the YMCAs, with snow falling in the streets of Chicago, or New York, or St. Louis, wherever she happened to be. But he and Step had noted a change in her these last couple years—she'd bring her discontent to the river and it took her longer to uncoil—often a day or two would pass before it was drowned in the river's Dispose-All. She had always called the river 'He,' and though he'd never before given a thought to gender, he went along with her, because he knew the Colorado wasn't a she-type river—not at all. His eyes moved down the length of her body.... *How can you stand those filthy cities...? In the bars and clubs all night—singing through the noise and smoke?*

He'd once gone to her performance at the Ski Cellar in Aspen, Colorado, and it had shocked him to see two different people in that same body—the Shan lying there on the sand at Dandy Crossing, and the one standing before the microphone in a sleek gold dress and high heels.... *I wonder, river girl-folksinger-actress, what is it you really want...? In place of your sureness there seems to be a nagging itch about where to go... what to do.... Only the river stays constant with you, and what happens when...*

Sand from her up-flung toes scattered his thoughts and sprayed them both. She stood, brushed herself off and came to stand in front of him. Hooking her fingers into his front pockets, she asked in low, even tones, 'If Steps doesn't show by five and we don't hear from him, what do we do?'

He had to smile because she was so serious, and he knew why: She was thinking of him, not Step. When she only considered herself there was a stubborn tilt to her jaw. 'We-l-l-l, I haven't worried too much about it. I'll cross that bridge when it gets here,' he said, so lightly it surprised even him. 'If it'll ease your mind any, I don't intend going back to Blanding, he comes or doesn't.'

'It'll ease my mind, you know damn well it will. I didn't come all this way to make a trip by myself, but if put to the test, I might.' Her tone had the biting challenge he recognized each time she had to take a step back into a fighting corner.

To tease her out, he wiggled his ears up and down in one of his characteristic funny-faces. 'What'll you use for a boat?'

'Why, I'll build a raft out of driftwood and lash it together with rope and rawhide; get myself a crate of chickens and ducks, like those whackos Windy told us about last summer, lose the whole razzoo in the first riffle and *swim* the rest of the way—or take an air mattress maybe.'

They started laughing. Shan doubled over and slapped her thighs so hard the sound was heard clear across the river, where Bradley Nelson had come down to the gaging station to take the water measurement.

He called across, 'What's so funny? I ain't fallen in yet.'

She wheeled around and shouted, 'Bradley... Hi!'

'That you, Shan?'

'Me-e-ee, all me!'

'Gol dern! Swim over and I'll give ya a ride back in the *Silver Bucket.*' He spaced his holler so she could understand.

Shan started for the bank, turned and looked back at Jason. 'Not too fast, is it? I can make the willows, can't I?' she asked, legs apart, ready for the dash.

His heart lunged. She always asked him for questionable decisions about the water and he had to give the answer. He balanced the odds—protection for her on one side, letting her freedom ride, the other—always torn because the final burden turned out to be his, not hers.... *What sort of condition is she in...? Is she strong enough to get across...? She was breathing hard after that swim a few minutes ago... fastest water's on the other side... she'll have to make the willows before she's pulled onto the rocks below....* All this had to be juggled in a moment then tossed off with a casual, 'Sure, if you start upstream about half a mile—it's running five- or six miles-per.'

She relaxed from the stance of a starter and waved over to Brad, 'Too fast, buddy. I'm pooped.'

Well... didn't expect that.... Every time I think I know what she'll do, she turns a cat's-ass.

She called to Brad again. 'Wheel the *Silver Bucket* over and I'll ride back with you,' then bent over and wiggled into her jeans.

Talking about Brad Nelson, they walked downstream a few hundred feet to the gaging cable crossing. With his wife, Myrna, and little girl, Tammy, Brad had come three years ago to take over the U.S. Government weather and gaging station. Brad and Shan shared a fascination with Anasazi ruins and old placer mines that scarred the river banks. They swapped discoveries about the men who mined a century ago then simply disappeared, leaving their cumbersome machines, water wheels, sluices and narrow gauge tracks to crumble and rust beside the wandering waterway. The government job, which paid a modest sum, left Brad time to pursue his hobbies of collecting and exploring, and growing apples, peaches and apricots in the fertile soil of Cass's old orchard.

Operation Silver Bucket was the name Brad had given the tram. A painted silver box, hardley enough to seat two people, was suspended by a series of four overhead wheels that rolled across a cable stretched bank to bank. While Shan and Jason were walking downstream, Brad had climbed his tower to the platform where the box was tied. He got in, released the brake and let it roll about a quarter of the way down the cable where he stopped, dangling some twenty feet above the water. He lowered a gyro into the current there, and two other places, measuring the cubic feet per second and marking the numbers on a pad. From the center of the cable, where momentum ceased, he hauled the cart to the left bank tower by means of a cable grip.

Shan, waiting on the left landing, reached for and steadied the *Bucket*.

'S'matter,' teased Brad, getting soft in your old age? Thought you were getting in shape to swim the Grand.'

'Our Leader *here*, says our river *there*, is running above twenty-five thou and that's pretty stiff swimming, even for Weissmuller; besides, me Jane—been sittin' on derriere all year, very soft.'

'Looks solid enough to me, Jane. C'mon sit down so we can get this wheeler rollin'. You got t'come up to the house and say hello to Myrna and Tammy—she's four now, would'ya believe?' He turned and called, 'Jason, crank up the *Tickaboo* and meet us over there.'

'Beat ya!' Shan hollered over noise of the down-stream rapid.

There were two small boards at each end of the *Silver Bucket* about a foot from the bottom, serving as seats. The box itself was less than three by five and was enclosed only with rails of two-by-fours; the top one touched Shan at mid-thigh, Brad, just above his knees. Supports of steel made a cradle for the structure, coming around the ends above head level and beneath the pulleys to form an inverted 'V', through which he unclamped the brake and didn't have to set it again until they were past center. He stood then, and using both hands, tugged on the hand grip.

As they inched toward the platform, he shouted over his shoulder, 'Hey, I found out who the fella is that's buried in the grave next to Cass, down at Tickaboo.'

'What? Can't hear you, Brad.'

He gave a strong pull, turning to tell her again, lost his balance and let go of the grip. As they rolled back down the cable Shan grabbed the rail and held up her hand to steady him. She saw his legs stiffen, his face go white, hands flail for a hold on something. Lashing out with her arm, she slammed it behind his knees, reaching for his belt as he crumpled to the floor of the swaying car. It rolled past center—up—back again—bouncing on the agitated cable above the throaty gurgle of the water.

'My God, Bradley! What happened?'

His face broke into a sweat. 'I dunno. Never did a dumb thing like that b'fore. You all right?—didn't hurt you when I flopped down like a hooked fish, did I?'

'Not me, but look at your knee; it's shaking the whole *Bucket.*'

His leg thumped like a rabbit's foot against the sideboards. A relieved peal of laughter reformed his tense face. 'Maybe I better learn to swim; Myrna said I was gonna fall outta this thing one day. Course, it ain't exactly made for two.'

'Holy Christ, Bradley! You mean you can't swim? You're out of your bloody mind fooling around this river without a life jacket!'

'Never was afraid... but then, I never come so close to falling,' he said sheepishly. 'Maybe I better get a jacket one of these days.'

'One of these days damn quick, I'd say! S'pose the cable broke, or you fell off the ferry?—what'd Myrna and Tammy do then?'

'Aw-w-w...'

'You listen to me, Bradley Nelson! Get a jacket, you hear Jason's got dozens of them. Does he know you can't swim?' She looked upstream to see if he'd crossed the river, and saw *Tickaboo* beached on the right bank.

'I dunno—never went up and said, 'Jason, did'ya know I can't swim?'' He smiled, stood up and gave his full attention to hauling the *Bucket* up to its mooring. As she started down the ladder, he asked her please not to say anything to Myrna. 'I'll get a life jacket all right, I promise.'

'Okay, Brad, but if I come back to find you soloing this thing with no water wings, I'm going to write the Jesus School of Water Walkers and get you a manual!'

The delayed reaction hit, making her heart thump in her throat—*Godalmighty, what if he'd fallen over! Even with a jacket, that's no damn Sunday picnic down by that rapid. I couldn't have saved him... even if I'd had the guts.... Hell, I'd probably have screamed for Jason.* She shuddered, walking up the path to their house.

Jason, who'd been walking through the willows on his way up to the house, hadn't seen the episode, but as they stood over Brad's artifacts—arrowheads and pot shards—eating Myrna's cookies and drinking cider, he noticed her tension. *City nerves—she'll loosen up in a day or so,* he decided.

The Peanut Can rang.

Shan and Jason did a quick heads-up—ferry passenger, or word from Step? Myrna went to see if Windy had answered from the store and returned with the news that one of Jason's boatmen had come with a message.

Shan put down a thousand-year-old stone *scraping* knife and turned from the table saying, 'Come on, Jason, it's got to be news about Step.'

'Sure hope you're right,' he replied, but was also thinking— *The hook to play me to shore.* Thanking Myrna for the refreshments, he picked up Tammy, hugged her, and said, 'We'll see you again, honey, before we go.'

As they were leaving, Shan advised, 'You better hide these arrowheads from the Buck or there'll be a swapping party one of these days, and I'm bettin' you won't be the winner, ol' buddy.' When Myrna turned her back to wipe off Tammy's face, Shan pantomimed life-jacket-buckling to Brad, toughened her mouth and thumbed over to Jason, mouthing the word.

Saying no more, they almost ran to the boat. When Jason pulled the starter she shoved the nose out and boarded in one motion. *Tickaboo* swung to the current and whined into deep water, whipping her shirt tail, blowing wind-tears through crows-feet, forcing that fresh earthen smell of silted water up her nose. She opened her mouth—drinking the air, smelling the taste, tasting the smell.

As they beached and Shan tied up, one of Jason's young boatmen pulled up in his truck, ambled down the bank, handed him a piece of paper and said, 'Lona sent this down 'n told me you'd decide what t'do about it. Hi, Shan,' he called, then, looking at the color and flow of the river, smiled. 'Y'all are gonna have ya a mud-bath b'fore your trip's over.'

'Still too thin to plow, Bill,' she said, and laughed, but her tone had a cutting edge she hoped he hadn't noticed…. *He's only the bearer, not the cause…. If Step can't make it, we've got a knotty problem.*

'Jason, I got some parts to take t' Buck for his Jeep, so I'll be seein' y'all in a bit.' He ground the starter to submission and drove upriver to the Missouri Man's cabin.

Shan walked to her T-Bird for a pair of Levis. She changed slowly, giving Jason time to mull over the note. Some minutes later, with bedroll over her shoulder, she came to where he stood toeing the sand, thumbs hooked into rear pockets. She poked him in the ribs, set her weight on one hip and asked, 'Where does this go? On the raft I'm building or down there on the beach?'

He took it from her, walked over and threw it down by his own. 'It goes right there... for now.'

'What's that mean, *for now*?'

He handed her the note.

'I don't want to read it, I just want to know what you're going do about it—obviously Step's not going be here tonight.'

'He called to say he's tied up in Santa Fe until tomorrow noon...'

'Oh shi... nuts!'

'Ocean Nuts what kind of nuts are those?' She'd almost said one of his least favorite words so he tried to look severe, but the corners of his mouth wouldn't turn down. 'He'll get a charter, be here tomorrow afternoon... pending instructions. Lona thinks we ought to come back to Blanding tonight with Bill and wait till...'

'Oh, sure! What's two hundred miles just to sleep for a night in stuffy rooms instead of here under the stars in our *separate* bed-rolls? You go right ahead.'

Now he smiled—sorry for having allowed her temper to rise. 'Like I told you, Shan, I'm not going anywhere—let's get your duffle and stack it here with mine.' Gently he put an arm around her and steered her up the bank.

'Careful, you might start the scandal of the year—we both know how different I'm supposed to be in the eyes of the know-nothing...'

'I'll say!' he laughed, wiggling his ears.

When they reached her car he pulled out a stubby pencil and using the shiny white hood of the Bird he wrote:

Call Step Immediately. Tell him—take charter to Dandy tomorrow afternoon. We'll wait here. Have someone from Wahweep pick us up at Kane, Sunday noon, Sept. 30. We'll fly to Dandy Oct. 1 & drive her car to Blanding. J.

The sun, starting to tell of evening, turned the water from its gaudy sequin sparkle to iridescent blue and pink. As Shan pulled things from the trunk, irritation fading, she eyed Jason thought-fully. 'You know, Mr. Leader, maybe I should take my stuff to Buck's for the night—that way you won't have Windy's breezing to cope with.'

'Want to cause a *real* scandal and make me sore to boot?— hustle Buck out of his nice warm bed and leave me here to freeze beside the river?'

'Don't be smart. I'll sleep outside on one of the cots. Anyway, we won't have the whole State of Utah chewing cud about me leading one of the LDS Elders astray—they'll just pair me off with a good looking miner who knows how to handle that kind of scene, and will give Windy a good squash when he starts mouthing off.'

Too late! She saw Jason wince from the barb not intended for him—never for those she cared about, only for the no-nothing gossips.

Forcing a smile to soothe the sting, he reminded her, 'All I'd have to do to pull Windy's stopper would be to defend our friendship, you know that.'

'Oh-h-h… Jason, I'm so sorry.' She dropped her hands to her sides, trailing clothes in the dirt. 'Of course I know,' she shook her head. 'Don't mind me, I'm still uptight. I just want out of here before somebody hangs us up and ruins our trip….'

'I know, I know.'

'…Step, late as usual…. God, why can't that man ever get anywhere on time…! Lona wants you home…. Windy's got a runny lip…. Brad can't swim…'

'What?'

'He damn near fell out of the *Silver Bucket* this afternoon. He can't *swim*, the crazy fool.'

Jason's eyes flared. 'Good Lord, I didn't know that!'

'Well, you do now. Give him a lifejacket, ferchristsake, and make him wear it. I don't know what I could have done if…'

He gripped her shoulders, forcing her blinking eyes to meet his steady ones. 'You couldn't have done a thing. I'll take him a jacket before we leave here and I'll *insist* that he wear it every time he gets in that box or on the ferry. Now... it's time you stop worrying... and unwind!' He then slid a happy thought under her nose. 'We've got time to do some exploring tomorrow while we wait for Step, and I bet Buck'll want to come along.'

'Oh wow, terrific! Let's go right now and see if he can.' She grabbed the loose ends of her clothing, jammed them into a watertight bag and toted them to the camping spot. On her way back for a second load, she heard the clatter of Bill's truck.

Jason spoke quickly, to get everything out before Bill reappeared. 'I know you'd like to see Buck right away, but look, Windy's invited us for supper and it's best we go—he's been waiting all day to jabber at you. We'll leave your Bird here so we can pick up Step tomorrow.'

'But after supper we gotta go see Buck.'

'Without Windy? Fat chance.'

Bill pulled into the turn-around and yelled, 'Hey, you two, ya 'bout ready t'go?'

Shan shot Jason a look, raised her brows and with a painted-on smile muttered, 'Uh-huh, thought so—got a message from dear wife, Lona, that we're supposed to come back to Blanding.'

'Too bad—looks like a lonesome trip for him.' He stepped into the cab and gave Bill the note, motioning her to follow. 'We'll ride up to the store with you, Bill, but from there on you're solo. Step's flying in tomorrow afternoon and we'll shove off soon as he arrives.'

Bill shot a quick glance down at their duffle, nodded to Jason and said, 'Sure thing.'—and to Shan with a knowing smile— 'Bet'cha can't wait t'git on that river.'

As they drove up Farley, a lowering sun turned the Organ Rock to deep, flaring red, giving her the feeling they paralleled a wall of fire. Hooking an arm over the door, she leaned out to catch the wind, saw a blue heron take off from the ridge above, swoop and land, deep purple, on a bar mid-river. The men's voices droned away at company business as Bill drove slowly, seeming not to notice anything around him. *Would I get carelessly blind like that after living here a while...? Probably... nature of the beast.... No-o-o, surely I could never do that.*

'Everybody out,' she heard Bill say. 'If I don't dawdle I might get home in time to grab sum'thin my kids ain't gobbled already.'

She opened the cab's door and they exited in front of the store. 'Shan, ya have a good trip now,' and eyeing Jason, added, 'I know *he* will.'

'He ought to—doesn't have to cook, build fires or guide tou-rons, only take orders from Step and me.... See ya, Bill, take it easy.'

∾∾

'We-e-e-l-l-l, if'n it ain't the Canary herself,' came Windy's adenoidal twang from behind.

'Hi, man, what's up? Last time I saw you, you were sopping three inches of mud off the floor of the store.'

'Yeah, and last time I saw you, you'uz hung up t'other side of Farley Wash 'n couldn't git down t' the river.'

'But that's why I've got friends like you with trucks.'

'Goddamn lucky ya have, too. Hell, you'd-a been settin' there yet if I hadn't hauled about forty boulders outta the stream 'n trucked all yer gear down t' Bucks.'

'You're a blessing, Windy, a real blessing.'

'Christ, Jason, that ol' trailer would'a ended up clean t' Kane Crick if I hadn't had 'er tied to a cottonwood with a hunk of mine cable. The back end went clean off the ground in the flood and swung off them blocks. Water come up t'the bottom of the chairs.'

Shan and Jason exchanged winks over his head as he leaned over to measure the water level. She raised her thumb and fore-finger before her eyes and spread them apart about three inches, quickly rubbing her nose when Windy stood up.

'I hear you're feeding us tonight, Windo, that's real nice of you. Guess I'd better not get you drunk if I don't want to be exer-cising the business end of a can opener, but I think the beer should be on me. I could use one right now, how about you?'

'Sure. Celebrate the return of the Singin'-Lady Boatman-River Rat-Geeter Player...'

'Okay, you can quit now, or I'll call you a *Fairy* Boatman.'

'Tha-a-ay....'

Jason smiled as they went about their routine, happy that Shan showed no outward trace of her impatience to be off with small talk and on with the trip. They walked into the store, and as Windy went to the fridge for beer he burbled, 'Hey, wait'll ya hear what ol' Bennett tol' the...'

'Why is it every time I come in here I think of ice cream?' interrupted Jason loudly and firmly, opening the freezer and digging down in the frosty contents. 'Sure do miss this on the river.'

'I'm buying,' Shan said, 'but don't spoil your dinner.'

She roamed outside, dissatisfied to be under any roof that shielded her from the sky, the breeze and the flow of vital smells, leaving Windy to rummage through the freezer, get what he needed and go about locking up the store. Jason finished his ice cream leaning against the big cottonwood trunk; she came to hook an arm through his and whispered, 'It's best I sleep on Buck's cot tonight, really, Jason. Keeping Windy's rattle-mouth stopped is important to you and we've got a whole month — all of us sleeping wherever we damn well please on our private beaches.'

Before he could respond, she joined Windy crossing to his trailer. 'I just wanna be forewarned—does this old thing still fart every time you go in and out the door, or have you fixed it?'

'Fixed it! Why would I fix it? I'm still waitin' fer the Bishop to come pay me a visit. *That* reaction'll be worth a pot of *gold*!'

They followed him into the trailer.

From outside one could hear the sounds of supper in preparation. Stomping feet and scraping chairs on the wheezing old floor echoed to the trickling spring beyond the cottonwoods where birds made their sleepy *peeps* and rustling sounds of settling for the night. The wind changed from up-canyon to down. Every few minutes Shan came out and stood in the cool grass to watch the colors fade and to breathe the river-scented air. Bats careened through soft coral twilight, silent of wing. Nocturnal sounds slipped in to replace those of day. Stars began to arrange and concentrate their battalions in the eastern sky, sending out a few to reconnoiter before the troops advanced. The new moon, a golden eyelash awash in a sea of turquoise, drifted to the cliffs and disappeared.

Down along the river, beaver slapped at their work as sand-banks fell to the shameless advances of the water. From the shallows, where the river cuddled with rocks smooth as velvet, came their intimate night whispers. Flecks of black played twilight tag—driftwood floating to the next resting place—to the fire of some camper, the lone hogan of a Navajo, backed up a side canyon, high-watered in the fork of a tree, eddyed or shelved on a sandstone ledge. The surface turned from bronze to silver-gray, in streaks and swirls, in circles and ruffles, an ever-changing pattern, pulsing, breathing, throbbing, alive and moving; strong, gravid with his burden of silt.

The current's fingers tugged at *Tickaboo*'s stern, swinging her gently up and back. Little waves patted her gunwales and sand tickled her stern as it whispered past, muttering...

> *Not much time...*
> *not much time...*
> *not much time.*

A mile away, under cottonwood trees by the river's edge, a Coleman lantern blazed on in the cabin of the Man from Missouri.

ॐ∽ॐ

CHAPTER 3

Early Evening — Same Day

Buck Watson put a match to the mantle of the Coleman lantern and cocked an ear toward the open door. The faint sound of an engine arguing for traction in a sandy wash drifted upriver. He stood motionless, waiting for the intonations to inform him *whose* engine.

Tick of a loose tappet and a carbon knock.

Bennett.

He took the lid from the coffee pot, smelled, threw the grounds out the door and started a new batch. He then lit the oven and stood back. *Puffh!* Two potatoes dipped in bacon grease went in, and from the Servel, a frozen pie and some leftover venison stew in an old bean pot.

His bronzed body, bare to the waist, was smeared here and there with grease from an afternoon of working on the Jeep. Lifting an arm to see if it was possible to forego the application of soap and water, he wrinkled his nose and said aloud, 'Little whiffy. Maybe I better have a shower.'

Again he heard a motor and froze to unscramble the sound for clues to its owner.

Across the river—banging tailgate and slick manipulation of double clutching.

Nelson.

Twilight thickened.

Buck jammed bare feet into tennis shoes, slung a towel over his shoulder and went outside to the shower. A five-hundred-gallon tank stood on a wooden scaffolding thirty feet from his shack sheltered from the wind by a sandstone cliff. Water piped from a spring trickled into its top; at the bottom a hose with lawn sprinkler attached made up the shower. A section of old Jeep tire nailed to the scaffolding served as a soap dish, and underfoot, liberated from an abandoned canoe, was a duckboard. When he removed his jeans he was unaware that his appearance in the afterglow resembled a man moving about missing a torso.

Hand on the tap, he heard another sound.

Bennett's dog barking down by the river.

He gave the handle a hard twist, and as water hit the boards, stepped aside to test it with his foot. Though it had been heated all day by the sun, he shivered. He'd have shivered if the water was scalding. Buck hated cold, cool, even tepid water... getting in and out of it raised his goose bumps to the texture of sandpaper. He grumped for twisting the tap so hard, but as yet hadn't admitted his reason for grumping. Had anyone told him he was edgy, he'd have said they were nuts.

Warm water covered him now, dissolving the goose bumps. He knew she was here because she'd written him the dates of her annual river trip with Jason and Step, emphasizing a hope that his days off from the mine would coincide with her days at Dandy.

She doesn't usually wait this long to come by... but hell, Windy could still be bending her ear; maybe she had to go back to Blanding with Jason.... Nah, not like Shan to leave once she gets here... or she plans to come later, after supper, and bunk.... Ah-ha...! Or maybe it'll be the sink again...

He turned off the water and soaped himself down, smiling as his eyes strayed to the kitchen window, recalling how she'd looked—like a bird in a little bitty plate—her tan skin glistening in the light of the kerosene lamp, wet hair dripping on the floor as she tried reaching for an escaped hunk of soap, totally unselfconscious.

The air had cooled, so he let warm rinse water dissolve his second crop of goose bumps. Sniffing the rich smell of perking coffee he dried quickly and walked back to the house.

A flash of headlights on the cliffs across river made him stop to listen once again for the sound of an engine. Light crossed the tops of Bennett's poplars.

A brake drum squealed as a truck bumped into the dry wash. *Windy. Damn…! Unless he isn't alone.*

Inside he yanked the coffee pot from the flame, checked the oven, pulled on a clean pair of jeans and rubbed some Wildroot into his damp crew cut.

The brakes squawked again in front of the cabin. Voices.

'Hey, Buck!' Shan yelled from outside.

Before he could get from his bedroom porch to mid-kitchen she shot through the front door and took a flying leap at him, arms entwining his neck, legs scissoring his waist in a crotch-hop. He grabbed her bottom and braced against the jamb—after five or six years of such greetings he'd learned that a doorjamb was a good place to be when this maneuver came off.

In the doorway, Jason stood grinning, and behind him was Windy, mouth flapping as usual.

'I 'member the first time she done that to ya—ya went ass over teakettle inta the road out front'a the store. 'Course, she weighed more then, 'n ya had more r'grab.'

They ignored him while he speculated on whether Buck's lean, brown hands had ever held that fanny under more personal and private conditions. Rumor had it that—*Soon's she gets past Dorothy Bar, outta sight, she shucks all her clothes and don't put 'em on again till she gets near Kane Creek Landing*—and when rumor had something, it was true, far as Windy was concerned. From there he let his omnivorous appetite gorge itself on the private doings of others, stirring the delectable again and again—women were mighty scarce at Dandy Crossing.

Buck's thoughts couldn't have been farther from Windy's horny meditations. Shan's happy face, freckles and dancing eyes, with traces of wrinkles at their corners and the deep furrow in the middle of her brow that led his eyes to her pulled back hair, were sights that pleased him. He wanted to ask: *Has it been a rough season…? How was Chicago…? And New York…? Did you make enough money to quit for a few months and enjoy the canyons…?* A thousand questions he didn't even know he wanted to ask came tumbling up, only to be pushed back in the recesses of his mind where two years later he would find them—tangled, unwoven threads, still dangling from the whole cloth of his consciousness.

'Dammit, Shan, you look ugly as ever. How'd you get so white? About time you started studying for another B.A. degree.'

Shan pushed back, legs still locked around Buck's waist, fingers interlaced behind his neck. 'My God, Buck! What's happened to you? Your hair's wet and *you smell like soap!*'

He pinched the muscles above her knees, hard, making her legs spring open in reflex, dropping her to the floor as a sudden warmth mounted to his face. He *had* taken that shower for a purpose. Covering his discomfort with silence, a direct stare and the boyish grin that got him over most hurdles, he turned a host's attention to the others. Pulling chairs from under the table he offered seats and inquired of Jason, 'Get your Johnson tuned...? Thought I heard you revving her up this afternoon.'

'Yup, ready to go,' Jason nodded. 'Just waiting for Step.'

With Windy, he dropped into the idle talk of men who've spent hours together in a lonely place rehashing the same topics every day. To Buck, Windy was the same as having a radio blaring. To Windy, taciturn Buck was like talking in a huge amphitheater, his own voice returning without reproach or interruption. Not that Buck didn't have many and complex thoughts—he simply let them incubate before he loosed them to a carefully selected few. In an idle tone he asked Windy, 'Did you set any fish lines today?'

'Naw, water's too dirty—gonna wait till it quits rainin' up north. You get anything this afternoon?'

'Yeah, one.' He turned to the others. 'Say, have y'all had supper? That big ol' catfish'll make a good bunch of steaks, and I've got coffee...'

'We ate down t'my place,' Windy interrupted. 'I thought she'us too pooped t' have a party 'er we'd a come gotcha—then she says she wants t'say hello b'fore hittin' the sack. Dunno what she'd do without my taxi service.'

Shan leaned back, both hands on the edge of the sink as though positioning herself for the kickoff, and in a cool, level tone said, 'Well, Windo, my car's at the ferry, Buck's got his truck and Jeep, Bennett's got a Land Rover. I think between all those vehicles we could manage and won't have to use your taxi—then of course, I've also got two good legs.'

A couple seconds passed while Windy decided whether this was for jokes or malice, chose jokes, and quipped: 'Oh, yeah—hoo-ee! I'll say ya have.'

Jason could tell she was going to have at him soon if he wasn't removed from her presence. To her rising tremolo he offered his moderato: 'Windy, I hope you don't mind if I use that taxi service— kinda tired, think I'll hit my sleeping bag. Shan wants to have a jaw with Buck, but you won't mind taking me down to the ferry, will you?'

Goddammit! Backed myself into that one, now how the hell am I gonna get out? He threw Buck an envious look, swallowed and said, 'Sure, Jason, I'll take ya.'

As Jason rose, Buck went to the stove and poured Shan a cup of coffee.

But Windy hadn't tossed in the towel yet—he turned in the doorway. 'Hey, Buck, I'll bring ya back them cigarettes ya wanted.'

'Huh-uh. Remember? I started rolling my own again. Got no use for those cotton-stuffed gaffers anymore. See ya tomorrow, Windy,' and to grease the wheels a bit, added, 'I'll take Shan to the ferry when she's ready to go, or let her sleep on the cot outside and play with the rattlesnakes tonight.'

Defeated, Windy croaked a barely audible, 'Okay,' shuffled out the door and followed Jason to the truck. *I'm gonna miss something, goddammit, jist know I am!*

Shan barely suppressed her laughter until the truck started, then she roared. 'Great God, he's something else! Harder to get rid of than a tick.' Then, feeling a bit shamefaced at her display of relief, she muttered, 'I shouldn't be so hard on him, poor lonesome dude. Is he like that all the time?'

Buck shrugged, not wanting to talk about Windy any more than he talked to him. He changed the subject by poking the steaming cup of coffee under her nose. 'Now sit down and tell me where you been for the last two months. Haven't heard a word about New York or…'

'Aw, Buck, I'm here now. I don't want to talk about those stinkin' places when I'm in paradise.'

'I got you, Shan Lu—not another word.' He returned to the stove to pour coffee for himself, thinking how good it felt to say her name while he was looking right at her.

She looked around the familiar room, at the worn linoleum, plastic curtains, the teetering old driftwood lamp with a snakeskin shade that someone had given him; at the bookcases!—old fashioned Birds-eye maple with tilting glass fronts that covered most of the wall space and held his mining, geology and engineering books, novels and philosophy—books, books, books—everything from *Nietzsche* to *The Little Prince*. The eye-level cases were full of pots, arrowheads, shards, knives and scrapers, stone axes and pieces of woven sandals; the bottom ones, crammed with rolls of USGS maps and ore samples. On the remaining wall space the Colorado River snaked across a series of 15-minute topographic quads. A small corner table was stacked with disheveled magazines—*National Geographic, Western Horseman, Playboy*. The only feminine touch was a braided rug, probably made by his mother, that formed an oval between two strong leather chairs. Yet in no way was it a typical bachelor's quarters.

She loved this room—kitchen, dining table and living room all in one. Since her first Glen Canyon trip, it had become a kind of sanctuary, part of the river experience. Throughout her private guiding, exploring years— nearly ten—she'd brought maybe six friends to the river, and if the weather was unsettled Buck would offer the floor of this room; if it was fair, one of the cots outside— also the use of his outdoor shower and the privy out back; even food if anyone was hungry and, in her case, the kitchen sink for a warm sitz-bath on cold nights. Often she'd come to Buck's a day or night before put-in, to be alone and relax or yak with him when he was there; if not, and for some wild reason this cabin was locked, he'd told her where to find the key.

This spot on the river appealed to her for its history, the old Dandy Crossing, where they'd swum their stock and rafted their supplies across—the one crossing in hundreds of river miles, up and down, that Chief Hoskininni had shown Cass Hite; the place where the Robbers' Roost gang slid out of sight; the one the Mormons missed when they picked that sorry Hole-in-the-Rock crossing—all of it long, long before there was a ferry.

Buck set his cup of coffee beside hers, shattering her reverie. She planted her elbows on the table and stared up at him. 'You're tan, Cowboy, been Moki hunting lately?'

'Not lately. Last Spring Leo and I went. We're walkin' along California Bar and he pulls this stone knife right out of the ground like it'd been waiting for him there a thousand years—only 'bout half an inch showing, y'know.'

'Jay-zus! Where does our old hiking buddy get eyes like that? What did you find?'

He went to the window sill, returned with a small box—placing it in front of her. She stared at it so long that he nudged her. 'Go on, open it—it's not a scorpion, it won't bite, just something I saved for you; not like it's your birthday.' He knew that was in October, wasn't sure when, or even how many she'd had... maybe thirty-five or -six.

With mounting excitement she removed the lid. On a bed of cotton, glistening like a precious jewel, was a rose quartz bird point less than an inch long, a quarter-inch wide. A thousand years ago it had lain in the hands of the artisan who'd chipped its perfection away from the rough rock—now his proud spirit rested in her hand.

'Oh, Buck... it's so beautiful... like a piece of jewelry!' She looked up, eyes glistening with gratitude.

Oh-oh. She's going to tear up.... Maybe I should have just handed it to her, instead of getting it all fancied up in a box like it was something special. But the minute he'd found it he'd known where it was going; his excuse being that, he wasn't going to part with other pieces in his collection he knew she wanted, so the bird point would make up for it.

Shan was touching his arm. 'Thank you, Buck. It's too lovely to keep in a box. I'm going have a jeweler fix it to wear on a gold chain.'

A bit embarrassed he turned away from her and mumbled, 'S'cuse me a minute, gotta... got to get the potatoes out.' He reached in the oven with bare hands, pulled out the potatoes, gave a quick whistle and threw them on the drain board. 'Damn things are hot!'

'Sure they are, nitwit,' she laughed. 'They've been in the oven.'

He got the rest of his dinner on the table and sat down—not really hungry, wanting to talk but not knowing how to start. This was her last trip with her two close and dear friends before the dam drowned Glen Canyon, and for the first time since he'd known her, almost nine years, she seemed overly restless.

'Hey, I got an idea. Would you have time, after you come off your trip, to take a run up to Wolverton Mill—four or five days maybe. We keep sayin' we're gonna do it, why not then?'

Her eyes went full round and lit up. 'Gee, why not? I've got six weeks before I have to go back to work. Think we'll make it before the snows?—all I got's my socks, ya know.'

'Socks'll do,' he laughed. Her remark was in reference to a nude swim and hike they'd been forced to make a couple years ago up a side canyon over rough terrain without footwear, and Buck had remarked: *'Now that I've got my Bare-Assed Degree, sure wish I at least had my socks.'*

'We got a nice long Indian Summer comin' up, I just ordered it. I'll even help you carry the small bellows down if they're still there...'

'My, my, what's got into you? You said you'd never be a pack-horse for no dame.' He watched a smirk spread to her eyes that crinkled with delight.

'...and soon as I do my dishes you can have a bath in the sink. It's gettin' too cold outside.'

She smiled appreciatively and wondered why he was trying so hard to please her. His next remark clued her.

'You look tired, Shan Lu, better sleep in my bed tonight. Jason knows you're not coming down to the landing, and Windy...'

'*Phuff!* Windy's the least of my worries.' And as if she knew his thoughts, added sadly, 'Probably won't be many more times I'll get to conk out here at the Missouri Man's Bunkhouse.' She turned her full gaze on him and asked the one question he wanted to avoid and didn't really have an answer for. 'Where will you go when they take all this away?'

'Gonna go fishin' on the Green,' he quipped, lightly as possible.

'Come on, level with me—what'll you do with all this?' She made a sweeping gesture with her arm and swung her feet from under the table.

'Hell, I *am* goin' fishin' on the Green. I've got a claim up there that might turn out to be worth something—anyhow, I'll go work the sucker till I find out.'

She nodded. 'Okay, what about the cabin?'

'What about it?'

'Are they going to tear it down, or just leave it here for the...'

'Oh, *they* are doing *nothing* with it... I'll take care of that.' Abruptly, he rose for another cup of coffee, tossing the remains of his cold one, along with the subject, in the sink.

'Hey, I went berry-pickin' yesterday; how about a nice piece of pucker-berry pie with ice cream sloshin' and meltin' all over it?'

'Sure'... staring at the floor, not really hearing him... 'When, Buck?'

'When what?'... knowing full well.

'When'll the reservoir be up here?'

'Shan Lu will you quit thinkin' about it? We got a trip to plan. Let's have a look at the maps.'

She rubbed her bare foot over a bubble in the linoleum, still looking down. 'Guess we'll have to forget about the Baja trip next winter. You'll be busy moving, maybe working at another mine.'—Then, before he could get to that one, she added—'But I'll probably have to work anyway, back in Shitcago or some other gruesome place.'—thus confirming his suspicion about her disenchantment with her job.

The nightclub life is getting to her. He brought a large slice of pie to the table, saying, 'There, that oughta pucker yer elbow—it's good for freckles, coughs and colds, fits, farts and sore holes.' His eyes softened. 'You don't sound like yourself, Shan. What's the matter?'

Looking up she sighed. 'Like you said, I guess, tired. Tired of pouring all my woes into my guitar, tired of singing for people who don't care what a song is any more. I can't wait to get on the river and forget all about *people*.... If that dear, damned fool Step doesn't get his slow ass in gear by tomorrow afternoon I'm going to remove his gonads!' She looked at the pie. 'Hey, where the heck's my ice cream?'

He pulled on his ear and grinned. 'Waiter says they just ran out.'

They discussed the Wolverton trip. Buck brought the topos and she began tracing their route while he washed dishes, coming to the table now and again to point out something with his wet finger.

'These maps blow me away.' She smiled with a mouthful of pie, dribbling some juice on the table. 'We've hiked a few miles, haven't we…? And there isn't a straight line anywhere but the sections and the borders. Yum-m, your mama taught you good—this is *great* pie!'

As her eyes slid over the quads, she saw that he had marked—with red dotted lines—all the canyons, mesas and streams they'd hiked; notations in other colors, of mines and places where he'd worked; camping and meeting places, with dates alongside. He often took provisions to the uranium miners downstream; would climb into his supply boat with a 25-hp Johnson on the back, deliver the stuff and come back upriver; just like old Bert Loper a century before him—only Bert didn't have a motor. Since they'd known each other she'd found him in some damnably strange places—even for an itinerant miner, jack-of-all-trades.

The memories gushed up:

Came on him one day two hundred miles south of here, working on a state highway; doing what, I don't know… Found him again a hundred or more miles in the opposite direction, stacking chunks of petrified wood into his truck bed for an old rock hound friend of his who sold them in his store…. Once drove down a twisty, dusty, Chinle Shale back road and met him working with a survey crew…. Couple years ago he wrote that he was 'employed, assaying ore at Shitamaring Mine on the backside of the Henry Mountains,' should I happen to be near…. Then, there was the time I met him herding cattle off Elk Ridge, down toward Fart-knocker Canyon for the winter—that's where I gave him the name 'Cowboy'…. But I could forget about hiking late in the Fall—he'd always be in Missouri, visiting his Mom…. The Man's like a leaf in a dust devil!

She hadn't noticed her pie plate gone off the corner of the table until Buck said, 'You can take these maps with you—get your Map-O-Meter on them and tell me how many miles we got to walk, and if we're going for another B.A. degree—might be kinda cool and we'll need more than our socks.'

She rolled up the maps while he lit the kerosene lamp, turned off the harsh glare of the Coleman lantern and went to his screened-in porch-bedroom, calling back to her, 'Sure am glad you came tonight. I haven't changed my sheets for a month.'

'Buck, I don't want to chase you out of your nice big bed, you only get to sleep in it every ten days or so. I can sleep outside on the cot.'

'Nothing doing—this bed smells like ramblin' roses 'n lilac sachet fer a month after you leave. It improves my dreaming considerable.'

'Yeah, I'll bet.'

She'd never asked about his private business—an unwritten law in these parts—but her curiosity rode on a hunch that at least once in the long-ago, some woman had severely trounced him. He had jumped that law once by asking how she handled fresh guys in nightclubs and she'd wised off: *I kick 'em in the balls.* But at the moment, since he was making the bed and she didn't have to look him in the eye, her Dutch courage allowed...

'Buck... don't you have a girl at the mine? Good-lookin' dude like you; bet they're all over you like a mess of monkeys.'

Silence.

Oh-oh...

Then came a springboard answer, 'Oh, yeah!—got so many I can hardly bat 'em off with a stick.' She thought that was all he was going to offer but his tone and next words were serious. 'A tougher lot of dames you never saw, Shan, and most of them uglier than the underside of a barstool. If a guy woke up in the middle of the night 'n found one beside him, he'd make a new door gettin' the hell away. *No...! No* girl at the mine.'

She smiled at her artlessness—wrong question for the answer she was after: *Does he have a lover...? I doubt he ever pays for it, nor can I see him accepting whatever comes along... .Got a feeling that if a woman wanted to go to bed with him, she'd be the one to do the asking— something in his body language... pride...? wounded vanity...? fear of falling? Can't tell. If he really doesn't care for a woman, bet he can be blunt as hell....* She looked at the little pink bird point lying on its cotton pillow, and slowly shook her head. *He's like a little kid sometimes.*

'Hey, church mouse, what're you thinking about?' He stood in the doorway, crew cut nearly touching the lintel.

'You'd laugh like hell if I told you.'

'Go ahead, I can use a good laugh.'

'Just wondering… uh,' she hesitated… 'what you do for nookie.'

'Oh, *I* charge *them*, chicken, and you ain't got enough money. C'mon, it's getting nigh onto my bedtime and I want to find out if you still fit in that sink; y'look a little blubbery around the edges to me.'

'Is that so!' she squalled, too stymied by his quip to say more.

She stood up from the table, stretched and walked to the sleeping porch where she stripped for her warm sitz-bath bath, and thought about how well she'd carved her niche with Buck. Solid, as with Jason, Step and other men she'd wanted as friends without becoming entangled in the sex mesh. Sex was such an easy caper to pull off, the other deal more difficult; its rewards not so ephemeral. *To anyone else my question would've been a direct come-on.*

Wrapped in a towel she returned to the kitchen, thinking how impossibly lucky she was to have met these river people through Step; how they cared about her, how they'd changed her life, and how grateful she was.

'Hey, Cowboy, I wonder if you have any idea how much I love—even depend, now—on the piñon gum you send to me in your letters. Hadn't been for you, I'd probably not even know about it; how to pick the hard resin, get it past the sawdust stage, then chew it down to an everlasting taste of the whole Southwest.'

'Somebody had t' learn you about the important things in life.' He smiled and dribbled his lower lip. 'You slobbered all over yourself first try, as I remember.'

'Still do, only not on myself. There'll be days in some gunky city, out walking or backstage getting ready for a show, when I just pull it outta my pocket and start chewing, and… *wh-h-ish!* I'm back in piñon country.'

'No better place.'

Buck drew water in the sink, moved a short stool over beside it, handed her a bar of soap and said, 'Don't drop it, sloppy—last time I had to move the fridge to find it.'

'So what?—you hardly ever use it.'

Starting for the back door, heading for the privy, he turned. 'I forgot your history lesson. Heard an interesting thing about Chief Hoskininni from one of the Navajos at the mine.' He talked as she soaped herself down, her bottom in the warm water, legs stretched out on the drain board.

'What about him?' she asked.

'Well, you know he had two sons.'

'Only two? Thought there were more.'

'Not when he died, just two—twins, as a matter of fact.'

'I don't remember hearing that.' From a dipper she poured water over her shoulders.

He leaned against the door jamb. 'That's what Honoshay told me—their names were Flying Cloud and Falling Rock. When he was sick and old, the Chief called them to his hogan... had to decide which one would succeed him as Chief, and he knew the only fair way was to make a contest: They were to go on a big hunt, range as far as they chose, and return before the end of two moons— whichever brought back the most magnificent animal would be chief.'

'Sounds more legend than history.' She stopped soaping her legs and listened intently, her eyes like fireflies, blinking in the lamplight.

Buck tucked his thumbs in his pockets and went on. 'Days went by, then weeks, and the old man got weaker. The tribe was scared he wouldn't live to see which of his sons succeeded him. Then one day, toward the end of the fifth week, Flying Cloud returns with a giant elk. The tribe couldn't imagine a finer trophy than that, but they had to wait for the other son. Two moons passed and still nothing. Finally, they sent runners out to look for him 'cause Hoskininni was nearly gone. They never found him, you know... and you can still see signs along the road that say:

WATCH FOR FALLING ROCK.

'You sonofabitch!' she screamed. 'I ought to brain you!' She flung the soap at him, catching him on the shoulder as he ducked out the back door howling with laughter.

'Why do I always fall for those crappy stories of yours? Just wait till I get outta here, you bastard!'

He came around to the kitchen window outside and banged on the glass, then stuck out his tongue, thumbed his ears and disappeared.

Half growling, half chortling, she poured warm water from the dipper over herself, climbed down and dried off with Buck's stolen motel towel. Wrapping it around herself, she went to the front door and called, 'Buck?'

No answer.

Probably in the privy.

She stepped outside, listening to the night sounds, the smell and gurgle of the river, while feeling its surge against the bank fifty yards away. The air was cool. Stars covered the sky and the jagged outline of cliffs across the river looked like the giant jawbone of some Jurassic beast.

'Buck?'

Still no answer. She walked around the end of the cabin to the cots under the cottonwood trees. He wasn't there—wasn't anywhere near the shower tank, and the door to the privy was open so he wasn't there either.

Returning to the screened porch she found the covers on the big bed turned down, all clean and ready for her. Fatigue enveloped her almost to the point of blackout as she sat on the edge wiping her feet on the towel. Sinking in the bed's softness, she pulled up the covers, closed her eyes and whispered, 'I'll get you for that one, Buck Watson.'

ॐ◦ॐ

CHAPTER 4

September 2, 1962 — Dandy Crossing

The Cessna 180 touched down on wet sandy ground. Step automatically glanced at his watch to see how long the flight had taken—bit over an hour.

'That's good time, Willie,' he said as they rolled to a stop at the end of the deserted runway.

'Look what's north of us!' The pilot pointed to furious blue-grey clouds rolling in like breakers. 'Lucky it's a ways off; we might not have made it.'

Step got out, feet touching ground before he left the seat. 'Looks like it's caught up,' he called, holding out a hand to feel the heavy droplets.

Willie shouted over the engine noise, 'I'd better get out of here if I don't want to fly with the angels.'

'Are you taking off in this? Why not wait till it passes over?'

'Got to move on, Step—have a late afternoon charter to Los Alamos waiting for me… maybe. Anyhow, I can beat this, it's only local.'

Step reached back of the seat for his gear, stacked it a few feet from the plane and returned, shouting his thanks. 'Good flight, Willie, I enjoyed it…. See you on the thirtieth at Wahweep.' Closing the door firmly he stepped away from the prop wash and made a lazy salute.

The little red plane turned, taxied up the runway, turned again, paused, gunned to full throttle and lifted easily in the air.

It banked left toward Mexican Hat to avoid the steel blue advancing curtain upstream. Step opened his duffle and got a poncho, then, tucking bag, camera cases and ammo cans beneath his arms, waddled to the oil drums beside the road to await his friends.

Wind-slanted rain drove down, whipping the oilcloth about his legs. He set his gear on one of the oil drums, himself on the other, covered all with the yellow poncho, pulled his knees up under his chin, tightened the cord that held his rain-cover in place and sighed. All this was performed with meticulous precision, after which he permitted himself a wry smile.

I would present an uncommonly queer picture to anyone looking on. Man sitting on barrel in the middle of nowhere, covered with oiled canvas and… ah…! oh yes, picking his nose. Extricating his hand with some difficulty, he reached with a long supple finger to wiggle it in his left nostril…

Rivulets formed in the rutted road. These drew his attention to the high cliffs across river, down which streams of red water would soon be pouring. As he scanned the stone outline around him, the rain stopped and the backdrop, which had sealed off all vision upstream, now appeared downstream. To the north, bits of blue shown through elongated wisps of grey. The cliffs glowed, reds deepened, oranges unfurled like banners across the rock, as if the sandstone had opened its pores to suck in the diffused light and taken color from the water. Should the sun come out, the walls would glisten and reflect its light, but the color density would lessen.

Step saw bubbles perking around him—the earth drinking up the moisture it so needed. Lowering his feet he watched a shivering sego lily, her cup brimming with crystal drops. He shook his head—*Poor little thing, how you'll come to hate water—soon you'll drown.* He thought of getting his camera but, looking at the sky, decided there wasn't enough light.

Shan had a name for this trait so deeply ingrained in her photographer-friend's personality: pushing the Procrastinating Button. 'You're lazy, and you have to give yourself excuses so laziness will lose its identity.'

On cue The Button spoke: *By the time you assemble camera, tripod, proper angle, etc., the wind will dump the water from the lily's bowl and...* he looked down at it again. *There...! told you so.* A breeze had done the job!

His watch said one-thirty.

Cascades spilled from the cliffs and the clean air prickled with a clarity that seemed to magnify everything. Mother earth was drinking her fill, and the music to his ears was a peaceful symphony of muffled sounds with an occasional *ping* from the timpani on his poncho.

BEEP!

He flapped skyward, a startled yellow parrot, tangling himself in his gear and nearly tipping over the barrel. Turning, he saw Windy's grinning face poking out of the truck cab, his lips moving.

'Hello there, Windy—what did you say?'

'I said, take that goddamn thing off your head so's you kin hear me. It quit rainin' ten minutes ago.'

'Oh.' He grinned sheepishly, removing the hood. 'Guess that's why I didn't hear you drive up. Where are Shan and Jason?'

'Upriver to Dark Canyon with Buck; Ought'a be back less'n an hour. Shan figured you wouldn't make it b'fore two'clock. Them guys is all packed ready t' go, so if ya want I'll take ya down t' the *Tickaboo*.'

'No hurry, Windy. Why don't I go up to the store with you and have a beer?'

Windy snapped his fingers. 'Shit! You'uz due here yesterday an' I carried a cold beer with me half the day, jist so's ya could quench yer ravin' thirst the minute ya hit the ground. I'uz down t' the ferry when ya flew over or I'da had one on me now.'

'That was good thinking, Windy.'

'C'mon, Professor, we'll go git the beer then I'll take ya to the landin'; then I got t' git t' Blanding fer some supplies, 'er I'd hang around 'n see ya off.'

Step placed his gear in back and climbed in beside Windy, wet poncho squishing under him as he sat.

'I thought Shan'uz gonna bust a gut yesterday when she heard you wasn't comin'.' He turned the truck, spinning the tires and shifting into a jumpy second. 'Lona sent Bill down t'git her and Jason, but Jason sent 'm back alone. Guess she's 'fraid Shan's gonna rape him without you around, huh?' He giggled wickedly.

'Oh no, I don't think so,' Step said in a detached tone—he spoke in a slow, rich voice, almost sensuously, each word having the faintest clip of an English accent.

'Hell, I wouldn't mind gettin' raped by 'er. Course m' wife might not like it.' He still pretended to himself and everyone else that she was coming back, that she'd just taken a vacation. 'You ever get any of that, Step?'

'Hmm?' he asked absently, watching the canyon wrens dart from tree, to cliff, to stream, as they sang their taunting, cascading song.

'I said, did ya ever lay Shan?'

'*Lay* her?'

'Yeah. Shack up with her. Get in the sack. Screw 'er.'

'Me?' He backed away to get a better look at Windy, not willing to believe the question.

'Yeah, *you*. Who the hell ya think I'm talkin' to?'

'Heavens no, Windy—whatever gave you such an idea?'

'Boy, she's really got all you guys trained—'er else it's the goddamn truth. Buck clams up like an oyster with a pearl whenever I try talkin' t' him. Ain't never met nobody who'd admit t'layin' 'er an' I know damn well she ain't no virgin.'

'Hardly. She's been married.'

'Yeah, I fergit about that.'

'Did you ever happen to consider you might not have met all the men she's known?' Step offered with a touch of sarcasm. 'Not many of them show up here.'

'Well, hell, you've knowed 'er a long time, you ought know *somebody* who got in 'er pants. I don't see how come *you* never made it.'

'Well, old man, it isn't a question of *making it*, you see, even should I find the desire'—using his lectern voice now, heavy on the clipped English—'I've known the woman for so many years it would seem like incest. Why is it so important that you know this about Shan, one way or another?' He pressed the top of the cab with palm and elbow to keep himself from rising off the seat as they banged up the bottom of Farley Canyon.

Windy mulled that for a second, then, altering the subject only slightly he asked, 'You get'ny in Tangiers?'

'In Tangiers?' As if trying to remember, he pursed his lips and ran his thumb back and forth across them in a gesture of long habit, deciding to let Windy's imagination wing it. 'No, not in Tangiers, as I recall, but I met a very pretty Italian girl in Tieback, Saudi Arabia, and we went off into the desert on camels for three or four days—had a delightful time.'

Windy's eyes lit gleefully. 'Hoo-eee! Them Eye-talians are good 'n hot, I hears. Did ya rip up the sleeping bag?'

'Oh, we didn't have sleeping bags, old man! We slept on huge beds in pointy-domed buildings, and once in a very fancy tent owned by the Maharaja who backed the expedition—soft Persian rugs all over the sand with incense burning in ornate brass pots. Ah yes, delightful!' he teased.

Windy squirmed for room in his jeans, vicariously experiencing the scene as they crashed into the stream, throwing water up on the windshield and through the windows. Step held firmly to the door and pressed his feet hard to the floorboards.

'Great balls, Windy! Chap needs his own set of brakes when he rides with you!' He shook water from his hair and continued, 'No, I don't believe the Italian women are any warmer-blooded than, say, the Spanish—all Latin blood, you know. Greek girls, for example, have an austere quality about them, but they look to be smoldering much more than the others— like the deeper you plumbed the more intense it would be, and to me, old man, the more frightening.'

'Hot shit, it wouldn't scare me none!' Windy shouted. 'I'd love it! I'd get so deep I couldn't get it out! I'd like t'go down into some volcano that looked at me like she'uz smolderin'. Yipes!' He slammed up to the store and smashed down the brakes, nearly skidding into the corner of the building. 'Let's drink to the Greek girls!' he whooped.

He's probably like a rabbit. Step untangled his damp poncho, got out and followed Windy inside.

Sunlight filtered through the thick grayness overhead, moving it aside like a magnifying glass burning holes in silk. The cottonwoods shook themselves free of raindrops, letting loose a sudden barrage on the tin roof—appropriate accompaniment to a church key biting open two cans of beer and a toast from Southern Utah to the smoldering beauties of the Mediterranean.

❧

The cave was dry, the fire warm. Rain spread a great sparkling curtain across the entrance. Periodically, the wind tore a cold veil of mist from the curtain and flung it under the overhang, making the fire spit back. Shan leaned against one end of the arch close to the entrance where she could feel the spray, see the wind tear the clouds apart in strips of grey and white, an occasional ribbon of blue rippling in-between. As she watched, the rain suddenly vanished, seeming to leap back up into the cloud-strips as quickly as it had come. Across the arch, the water-curtain split into torn pieces.

She moved to the center of the arch. 'Boy, that one came like a bunch of fire hoses all at once; bet we have to bail out *Rintintin* before we start back.' She was looking down at Buck's aluminum canoe bobbing in the swirl of a tiny eddy—'Your water bottle's floating in the stern, Buck.' She turned and asked Jason, 'Was that the storm you said was on the way, yesterday?'

'Guess it was. But you didn't get much of a cleaning—your hair hardly got wet.'

'Thanks to Buck, we made it up the scree just before the sky's bucket tipped over.'

'It's real cozy in here,' said Jason.

'Yeah, nice,' agreed Buck. 'I bring up driftwood sometimes, to wait out gushers like this when I'm setting my fishing lines. Good thing you can't see the ruins from the river or there wouldn't be a stick in here now.'

'For sure,' Jason agreed. 'Wouldn't be much left of the ruin either if everyone that rows by here climbed up for a look.'

They stood on the cave's lip, looking up at the rusty-dusty flood waters that gushed from a narrow hanging canyon two hundred feet above them. A dark stain of desert varnish below the lip made it look as if the mouth was dribbling tobacco juice. Fortunately, the cave was midway up on the V-shaped canyon wall, closer to the river and free of the storm-born red spout. Shan nudged Buck with her elbow and pointed upward, a Cheshire smile sliding over her face. 'That's the canyon we hiked last year, huh-m…? The one with all the nice, long potholes… and the…'

'That's it.' He gave her a squint-eyed glance and pulled in the corners of his mouth. 'Please tell me you don't still keep that picture?'

'Oh, but I do. It's a great conversation piece.'

'Crap! I should learn never to go along with your dingy ideas.'

'It wasn't a dingy idea—I had to have proof.'

'Did anyone ever tell you, you have a sadistic sense of humor?'

∽∾

Sometimes before, sometimes after her river trips, and according to the time each had before returning to work, she and Buck would plan a one- or two-day hike. They'd pick a canyon upland, on the Colorado Plateau, in the river drainage, off the Glen or the Maze country—any canyon or water hole that piqued their curiosity. Last year their intent was to hike a 'hanger' from the top down, to where it hung above the river, since they couldn't hike it from the bottom up. There are hundreds of such canyons in the slick-rock country, always tantalizing for the sheer mystery of how they were formed and what might lie inside them; like why would one canyon enter the main channel at river level, and the one right next to it exit the cliff face anywhere from fifty to five hundred feet above?

Planning a day hike, they packed a lunch, and with approximately fifty road miles to cover, they left just after sun-up, Buck driving the Jeep up Farley Canyon to the main road, then northwest toward a well-known Moenkopi landmark called the Sewing Machine. By mid-morning they were parked under a cottonwood where they could easily find their way into the mystery canyon. It was a day graced with unveiled sun, no wind and warm for that time of year.

Shan had never seen Buck with a backpack—this day he was shirtless in jeans. She wore his shirt, her tennies and nothing more than a camera strapped across her shoulder. He hiked with three items, always; his 0.22 Ruger Bearcat pistol, Bowie knife and the quarter-size, flip-out magnifying glass he wore on a string around his neck. There were a couple other items she knew about that he packed in his pocket and had put to use more than once on their many hikes: ten yards of stout string and a few fishhooks. In the

Glen they never carried water because it was always there—today it was there because it had rained a few days ago.

They were looker-hikers, not talker-hikers, therefore no chit-chat as they slipped between the creamy breasts of Cedar Mesa sandstone. The farther they descended, the deeper the potholes became, Shan stopping to plop into most of them.

'Hey, water ousel, supposing I want a drink out of one of those? I'd like one or two left in pristine condition and not all stirred up by your butt.'

'I'll save you a couple. Meanwhile, turn around and look what's next to the cliff there on the sand about ten feet behind you.'

One of the Glen's small pink rattlers was slowly making for the wedge of sunlight just ahead of it. Buck took a side step and reached for the Ruger.

'NO!' she shouted. 'It's not bothering you. You aren't sleeping here tonight. Let it be.'

Buck was in the habit of shooting anything that wiggled, bit, leaped or stung, something Shan had done when she was a kid growing up in the desert, but the Glen had given her an entirely different outlook, and it was one of the things she and Buck had serious disagreements about. *Okay to shoot to eat, not okay if some varmint just happens to be in your way—it was here first.* Jason and Step would fork-stick the rattlers behind their heads, pick them up there and loose them many yards away. One time she'd gone so far as to call Buck a misguided Redneck and he hadn't spoken to her the rest of the day. Usually he'd capitulate when she was around, but she was convinced he reverted to his old habits when she wasn't.

He holstered the gun and they kept heading down.

Half an hour later they came to some serious drops. As long as the intrusion of Cedar Mesa sandstone held out, the drops were negotiable, but they were coming to the underlying layer of crumbling, Moenkopi mud-stone, less easy to negotiate. Above them, the upper layer dripped red over the smooth fleshy sandstone like jagged knife cuts into soft, vulnerable flesh.

The canyon deepened.

A drop they couldn't negotiate sent them along its upper side as it narrowed even more, until.... A bend or two farther the sandstone gave out entirely and they looked down fifty feet into a crevasse with a muddy snake of captured water at the bottom. Where they stood on the lip of the pour-over it was only thirty feet across—above, the walls rose another fifty. Shan danced from side to side trying to look around abutments that zigzagged to the river, which they could hear, but not see.

'Damn it,' said Buck, 'we're close!' He leaned over the drop to see any possible hand- and footholds and shook his head. 'No way down *that!*'

Shan let go a sigh. 'Fine... Canyon just said, *'No!'*'

'Looks that way.'

'Sometimes, I like it when they do. Oh, I'd like to see the hanger and the wildness that has to be around that bend; but the fact that *no* human prints, or animals either, have *touched* that turf kinda pleases me.' She took off the shirt and tied it around her waist.

'I wouldn't be so sure—those guys with ropes and...'

'Don't spoil my illusions. C'mon, let's get back to the potholes. I've got an idea for a photo to illustrate a story I'm writing about cowboys.' She'd noticed one lengthy pothole, fed by a side drainage as well as the main, where she'd be able to set up her camera and run in for the shot.

When they approached it she stared at it for a long minute, then looked at Buck. 'Time for a bath,' she said.

'Is that your fifth or tenth? Be my guest.'

'No, *you*. It's real warm today... you're all sweaty... you could get cooled off.' She leaned over, put her hand in the water and smiled. 'Just right for the likes of you; not cold, not scalding.'

'Just call me Cucumber. I'm fine.'

They argued for five minutes before Buck, in a truly benevolent mood that day, agreed to humor her. The camera had a timer, and what she wanted was a photo of him in the pothole, with her sitting on the shelf above pointing the Ruger at him. In picture words: *The only way to get a cowboy to take a bath.*

'I bet it isn't for a story at all; you must have something else in that rattled head of yours.'

'Maybe I'll tack it on the inside of my closet door, like the one you have of me dressed in my guitar, inside your outhouse door.'

After a couple tries, she got her picture, with Buck grumbling all the time, which made it perfect, as far as she was concerned.

He rolled out of the pothole and dressed. She handed him the Bearcat and put her camera back in the case. Over the years, she'd watched him bring down rabbits on the run, and even ducks in the water, when they needed a meal. She was a fair shot herself, and the little gun fit her hand nicely. It was light weight for a chunk of steel, which is why Buck chose to carry it on hiking trips, in preference to others he had.

Instead of holstering it, he aimed for the skyline a couple-hundred feet away, took a potshot at a small steeple of rock with a perfect ball of stone balanced on its tip… and missed.

She was surprised. 'Can I try?' she asked, reaching out a hand.

'Be my guest… safety's on.'

Shan laid her camera down, took the Ruger, turned sideways to the target and took a firm stance on the sandstone, feet slightly apart. Raising her gun hand high, she pushed the safety off, slowly brought it down toward the target… and shot.

The ball disappeared and the steeple beneath it crumbled.

She looked at him and smirked… pushed the safety on, blew into the barrel like some hot gunslinger and handed him the Ruger, grip first.

He looked at the gun as if contemplating its betrayal—looked at her satisfied grin, tucked in the corners of his mouth and said, 'Keep it!'

'Wh—what d'you mean? I can't carry it… got no pants on.'

'I mean *keep* it. It's yours. You now own a Ruger Bearcat 0.22 caliber pistola, complete with Bucheimer-made leather, snap-strap holster. I'll carry it for now.'

∽∾

'Hey, look who's on the ferry!' Shan yelled to Jason. 'Kinda looks like the old beanpole, doesn't it, Buck?' she called, crawling back over gas cans, tackle and bait, to where he sat at the tiller of *Rintintin.* 'See who's there?'

'Don Quixote hisself, I'll bet.'

'Ol' Step'n'fetchit, for sure,' she said, moving back to the bow. They waved to the lanky figure, who toyed absently with the hair at his crown. He raised his hand, spreading fingers wide in greeting. All of Step's facial features were large and, when animated, appeared even larger. A half-moon grin split open his face, his strong aquiline nose wrinkled and flared, and his deep-set, amber eyes sparkled. 'Where've you been? I've been here for hours,' he stated convincingly.

'Like hell you have!' erupted Shan. 'We heard your plane before the storm hit.' She threw him the bow rope. 'Here, tie us up.'

Buck stepped out of *Rintintin* onto the ferry, extending a hand to Step. 'Yeah, we heard you come in. I hit the backlash of a haystack in Sheep Rapid about when the storm hit, so we climbed into a cave 'til she blew over. How the hell are ya, Professor? Heard you been over in the *real* desert. Find any arrowheads?'

'No, but we saw a canyon similar to this one—same red sandstone, same erosion pattern, little different culture, more advanced but active at the same time—place called Petra. They carved pillared temples out of the walls and the only access to the place is through a crevasse about as wide as the one in Dungeon Canyon. You'd like that, Buck.'

'When they gonna dam it?'

'Funny thing, I asked them that question and they thought I was crazy, wanted to know why I asked such a thing.'

'Maybe we can ship 'em some Bureau guys; they'd soon find out why.'

'No,' Step replied, taking him seriously. 'I wouldn't want them to ruin both places. That Aswan Dam... gads, what an incredible mistake!'

'Hey, knock it off, you guys.' Shan bounded between them and gave Step a hug. 'What were you hung on *this* time Stephen Atien de la Torre—get locked in somebody's darkroom?'

'Hi, sweetie.' He smiled down at her, returning the hug. 'I'll tell you about it later.'

Jason, last out of the canoe, joined the circle and shook Step's hand, though they were much closer than a handshake would indicate; their former trips, with the hikes, conversations and discoveries they shared had made them a tight trio. Both he and Shan looked to Step for their best camera shots, and Jason could hardly wait for the talk about shutter speed-aperture-*f*stops, low angle light and many other things.

At three o'clock, with shadows pushing into the canyon turning the water a mottled blue, the *Tickaboo* and passengers departed. The shower had cooled the air and both men wore jackets. Shan's yellow shirt was tied in a knot between her breasts. As they slid into the main current she loosened it impatiently and waved to Buck, calling, 'See you on the first, Cowboy. Don't forget—Wolverton!'

He watched the boat bob through the first riffle. For a few moments it disappeared, then, rounding the bend of the Dorothy Bar, popped up on a silvery flash of waves.

He saw the yellow shirt flutter like a sail and a shiny object arc over the boat into the river—her Timex watch—Shan's final kiss-off to civilization.

He laughed and waved once more. Then they were gone.

る✧

CHAPTER 5

September 2 — Evening — On the River

TICKABOO's occupants heaved a sigh. At the tiller, Jason removed his hat and sat flat on the back deck, legs stretched out, steering. Step pulled out his tobacco and lit a pipe. Shan lay full length on the foredeck, chin in hands, breathing in the earth-smell of the water. No one spoke.

About an hour after departure they made camp near Tickaboo Creek. Jason and Shan unloaded gear, Step gathered wood and started a fire. Then Jason set up the kitchen while a barefoot Shan spread bedrolls across the ground tarp. She looked at the sky to see if she should secure the beds for a wet night; pale and clear overhead, the storm hadn't come this far down canyon, but to the north, high cumulus rolled over the Henrys, boiling up in the brilliant mauve and red of a setting sun. She fixed the rain tarp in place to be pulled up if needed.

They were tacit in their new freedom, not wanting to speak because the silence alone was beautiful and they were reluctant to shatter it. Shan put on her shirt. Step removed his socks and tennis shoes to feel the clean, rippled sand between his toes. Jason went to the river's edge and stood with hands behind his back, looking, breathing deeply, trying to push out what was inside him by taking in all he could of the outside. A sense of relief flooded through him, his throat constricted, and he felt a wetness fill his eyes. Even with her back to him and her foot working the air mattress pump Shan sensed Jason's emotional release and went to stand beside him. She put her arm around his waist and they looked out across the silted water. 'We made it,' she said, and sighed.

He squeezed her and answered softly, 'Yes, thank the Lord.'

She turned to see Step, pipe in hand, also gazing over the river. 'Did you think we wouldn't?' he asked, as if it weren't possible.

'I *always* think we might not,' Jason countered.

'You threw the fear of God into us this time, Steps. I was sure they'd grab Jason off before you got here. We told Windy to tell everyone but you that we'd already gone.'

'I'm sorry—came as quickly as I could.... I...'

'Everything's fine now.' Jason assured, 'We're here.'

It wasn't exactly tension strung between them, more like a quivering awareness waiting for their communication system to be free of static. They lived in separate worlds when they weren't here, but each knew what the other was thinking, what the other had escaped and what they all had to go back to. Their sensitivity made them a little sharp with one another in their impatience to be cleansed of civilization—aware that if they weren't careful their unity could be muddied by an exchange of words that still had clinging to them some nugatory trash better left unspoken.

Sunlight reflecting off the cliffs across river turned their complexions a dusky bronze as they went about getting water, pumping up mattresses, stacking wood and preparing a dinner of soup, thick steaks, fried potatoes and canned peas. Shan, facing Jason over the cook fire, propped the spatula against a stone, then stood and shoved him backward into the woodpile. He shot her a look of hurt surprise before he saw the devilish glee on her face.

'There now! The Wee People are at work here, and let's have no more of this silence—all evil thoughts out in the open!'

Jason came after her with the fork, chasing her around the fire. 'I'm thinking some pretty evil thoughts all right,' he growled, 'and you'll know what they are pretty darn quick.'

Step backed away, shaggy brows twitching with amusement, and as Shan dashed by, stuck out a leg, sending her sprawling and laughing in the sand. Jason pounced on her legs, pinned her down and pricked her bottom with the long fork, saying, 'Mmm, I think it's tender enough to serve, don't you, Step?'

'Give it another poke and let me see.'

'Ouch… dammit, I have to sit on that!' she howled.

'You should have thought of that before you stashed me in the woodpile, little Miss Vixen.'

'Yes,' Step nodded, 'I think it's about ready to serve. Maybe it should be tenderized a bit more before you salt and pepper it— Irish Bitch is tough, you know.'

'Ah-ha! I think you're right.' And with a few good whacks on her rump Jason got up and went back to the fire to turn the steaks.

Shan rubbed her tail, rolled into sitting position and screwed her face into a mock frown. 'Yer a coupla bullies, pickin' on a purr defenseless lass.'

'Oh sure,' Step said. 'You're about as defenseless as a she mountain lion in heat.'

'Who says I'm in heat?'

'Windy wants you to let him know when you are.'

'Ohferkrissake!'

The tension was gone. Shadows topped the cliffs and Shan went to trade shorts for jeans.

౭౿ఞ

Dinner was over, pots scoured with fine river silt and stacked. Step lit his pipe and lay back against his duffel bag. Coals glowed under the coffee pot and the river's dispute with the rocks that tumbled out of Tickaboo Creek became louder as night settled over the canyon.

Jason went to the boat to shave. Shan took her guitar from the case and came to sit with Step, who reached a hand and said, 'I was hoping you'd feel like playing tonight, sweetie—it'll be good to hear you again.'

'It'll feel good to play where there's no noise and no drunks,' she responded, splaying her fingers across the strings in a *rasquea-do*. She tuned with harmonics and began to pick a melodic line against the minor chords that Step recognized as one she'd written a few years ago, *The Tale of the Tickaboo*.

'Ah-h-h,' he breathed, 'the right place for the right song—what could be more perfect?'

Singing: '…They say at midnight when the winds from out the canyon blow, and Colorado's foamy waves dash on the rocks below...' Her voice curled around the notes with so much pleasure the sound became almost sensuous. 'That a horse of solid silver comes, whose feet are shod with gold, and dashing over canyon walls in reined by rider bold...'

Jason came back from the boat, silently put his shaving things away, and stretched out on the sand, propping his head on one arm to listen. No one appreciated Shan's voice more. He could close his eyes and be somewhere else, be some*one* else in a suspended state—he was Cass Hite, or Hoskininni, he was the River, a silver horse—or here, where he loved to hear her sing the most, with the bass boom of the big river accentuating the drama of her song. It wasn't a common voice nor a big one, but natural. It expressed all shades of feeling—sorrow, joy, anger, bitterness, love—but for him, stronger than anything, it expressed nostalgia. Because he was a lover of music and had been a music teacher in his younger days, he responded to whatever mood the music wrapped him in, to the memories it called up... reliving... rejoicing... regretting... remembering.

Her song ended with a plaintive echo drifting off upstream.

'I've felt almost too many sensations today,' she confided. 'Makes me marvel at what a unique container we earthlings live in—the pleasure/pain, high/low we can tolerate, register and respond to.'

Jason placed a marshmallow on the end of a willow stick and lowered it toward the coals around the fire. 'You're one of those who feel very high highs, and very low lows, Shan Lu. I hope you don't sink too far when you go back to work in the clubs.'

'You're one too, my boatman. Watching all this disappear in front of your eyes is going to hurt you a lot.'

Jason watched a meteorite explode over the rim of the canyon and saw their days exploding with it.

Step, leaning on his duffel, looking at the yellow flames, said lazily, 'Some people never feel enough to know what's high and what's low. They have to go to a psychiatrist to find out.'

'Sometimes I wish I could be like that.'—She noodled a few notes on the guitar—'It'd save me buckets of trouble.'

Step blew out a puff of smoke. 'You don't wish that. You wouldn't be here if you did.'

'I said 'sometimes.' What's different about today is that every sensation has registered *so strongly*, so completely filled my mind and body that I'm satiated. That's new for me. I always want more. But I feel as if there are enough mental and physical sensations *right here* to keep me going forever. My river is trying to tell me something... that sensations are the *real food*, not just heady wine... that I could live here like Bradley and Myrna, Fred and Helen, and... Buck,'—She said his name again, slowly, almost a whisper—'Yeah, Buck,' as yet another sensation flowed over her with the realization that Buck felt what she was feeling tonight, and had for a long time.

Step turned to her, burbling his lips, '*Bm-m-p!* You wouldn't last six months, cookie. You've been part of the high concentrate—excitement, artistry, creativity—that's your field.'

'Steph-en,' she answered, low and measured, 'each artist has a time, an era, when their art, their performance, is popular and means something to others—audiences are nothing but fickle. I think my time is passing.'

'Phooey,' said Jason. 'A talented person like you never goes stale.... You'll think of something to keep your audience interested.'

'And whatever it is, she'll need a response, she'll need that audience.'

'Wrong.' She closed her eyes and heard the river clapping over the stones lining Tickaboo creek.

☙❧

The two men and the woman camping beside the river this September night are as separated in their social lives as they are together on this river. They are not children. Jason is almost sixty, Shan in her early forties, Step, half a decade ahead of her. Over the years on this river, Step has bed-rolled a few women—in that other world, several more. Jason, father of six, none—other world the same. Shan on the other hand, has taken the *river* for her true love—other world, several easy-come-easy-goes, and two marriages. Each has lived a far from ordinary life—active, productive, rewarding, exciting—and between them, there has grown a fond love in which sexual relations play no part. She and Step run naked whenever they feel like it; Jason, only to bathe, or if he must, swim—dry clothing on his head for the other side of a pothole. Shan's trips with Buck and his Moki hunting buddy, Leo, have been the same, full of the same unselfconscious frivolity, and Shan well remembers how, years ago, that all fell into place:

She had agreed to take two 'greenies' with her through the canyon, only to find her usual store of Jason's boats were already in use. So, to keep her promise she borrowed a friend's rubber raft—not her preferred or well-known craft—and adding injury to insult, the river flipped its wig and ran high that fall. Buck saw instantly her two companions would be as balsam to the iron of the river when they had to help her get that hunk of blubber ashore... or launch it... or get it unstuck from the mud and rocks. With no small measure of concern, he and Leo helped her pump the thing up and load supplies for a ten-day run. Buck loaned her an extra 7-hp. motor, because just looking at the one she had gave him the shivers. After she'd gone, and the river boiled even higher overnight, they felt bound to follow and see how she was doing, or even *if* she was.

No sign of them next day after poking into a dozen or more canyons, and only one indication of prints where they'd might have camped overnight.

Late afternoon of the second day Buck and Leo were about to give up and press up to Dandy—only so much gas remaining— when they heard shouting from an island downstream. Leo pulled out his binoculars. 'That's them... wavin' an' dancin' up and down like pistons... an' they ain't got no clothes on.'

'Figures,' said Buck.

Nor did they run for cover when the two men pulled ashore and joined them. Shan was in tears she was so glad to see them. In over her head and scared, the last thing on her mind was her naked body. Her rescuers had come to save her.... The two men accepted the situation as if it happened every day, and from then on, that's how it stayed with them.

⤵⤴

At the fireside Shan sniffed the air and stood, laying the guitar on its case. 'Smell that, Fetchit? We're downwind of something— what is it, Jason?'

He rose from the fire with a marshmallow half roasted and went toward the creek out of the ring of firelight. Back within seconds and smiling, he returned to the fine art of marshmallow roasting and told them they could have venison for breakfast if either had a slingshot.

A beaver slapped water near the bank, the fire crackled, the river swished and gurgled. Shan felt her senses changing guard. The wind's shift after twilight and darkness... its whisper in her ear... brush on her skin... cool, or damp, or warm off the land... all sifted through her senses to evince the kind of night they would sleep peacefully through. She could almost feel her sense of smell accumulating—freed from smoke, smog and asphalt it would soon be able to decipher the lineage of a piece of driftwood by its odor when tossed on the fire, and be able to separate and identify the animal scents she'd had to ask Jason for.

He handed her a perfect marshmallow, crisp and round. 'Dessert. Be careful, it's still hot in the middle.'

She pulled it from the stick and bit cautiously, looking over at Step. 'What were you up to in Santa Fe that took you so long?'

Lengthy pause.

'I don't think you want to hear about it now. Our agreement said we weren't to discuss such things.'

'We might as well get it over so we can enjoy the rest of the trip,' she pressed.

Jason felt his back muscles ripple like a cat's and said apprehensively, 'Or spoil it before we get started.'

More silence.

'There's that too,' Shan agreed, surprising the others. She was usually ready to go tooth and nail into whatever was on her mind.

Still not unwound... thought Jason.

Now she's considering Jason, Step observed.

'I just heard my river say—*later,*' she muttered through a mouthful of marshmallow, then bent to pick up her guitar again.

She sang for almost an hour, while the fire faded to coals and Step fell asleep. As she put her guitar in the case and prepared for bed, Jason rolled three large stones from the fire ring's edge to the foot of their bedrolls. Nearby in the quiet, eddy mist swirled and rose into the willows, as if the river'd gone out on a cold night and this was its breath, vaporizing. Shan called it 'witch's breath' and stared long. Step, the other desert rat, sneezed in it, and Jason, when nobody was looking, stoically reached for the small of his back and pressed hard.

Step woke, then wandered downstream to the willows beside the river to relieve himself and listen to what the water had to say. He checked Polaris for north, sniffed the breeze for rain and smelled instead a strong metallic scent from his stream of urine against the cool air. *Asparagus! Jesus, that was way back in Santa Fe.* He zipped up and returned to see Jason's long-handles disappear into the sack. He didn't have to look to see where Shan was, the scent of her soap told him things were back to river norm—*She'd take a bath no matter what, before hitting the sack with or without two gentlemen.* He rubbed his chin, felt stubble, scratched, wished it was past the itching stage and banked the coals for the night.

Gentlemen.... He laughed at that, but it was the first word that came to mind. Their sleeping arrangement was more like Victorian, or Quaker to be exact, since they operated on an invisible bundling-board system. He thought of Windy—the impossibility of making him believe such a thing—and recalled the few abortive attempts he'd made to explain their relationship before he gave up and let people think whatever they damn pleased. He wasn't sure himself how they came to be so free with each other. Shan never pushed her sex at them; it was natural, not lewd, for her to be nude whenever she felt like it. If she'd ever shown any desire to 'get laid' (as Windy so crudely put it) he felt their friendship put him far past any desire to rise to the occasion—they'd been neighbors in the same southern Arizona town, forever it seemed—and Jason, a religious man, a family man, could hardly be corrupted even if she'd set out to do so. Her honesty and outspokenness belied any female tricks. Everyone knew where they stood with her. Step even accepted the fact that he was lazy, labeled by her: *A little boy who loved to be mothered, slower than molasses in January, a procrastinator—Old Two-Step.*

She came from the river, a towel wrapped around her goose-pimples. Hugging it to her front she turned her back to the glowing coals and looked at him. 'Aren't you going to take a bath, Steps? Nice clean creek nearby.'

'Me? Get in that ice water? You crazy?'

'Coward,' she snickered, and bounced off to the sack.

He gazed after her. 'I'll accept that,' he nodded, and went to brush his teeth.

Shan wiggled into her pajamas and crawled into her bedroll beside Jason's, her teeth chattering, mumbling, 'Where's the rock? My feet are cold.'

'Shoot, you're cold all over—that ice water'll stop your heart one of these times. Quit squirming and I'll get you warm.'

She felt for the hot rock. 'Oh-h-h, that's loverly,' she sighed, pulling her head down into the bedroll, spooning against him. After a few shivery convulsions she poked it out again and said, 'I checked the boat, it'll be all right even if the water should come up'—then, rolling flat on her back and peering at the stars, added—'Hope it doesn't cloud up and rain on us.'

Saturated with the warmth and happiness he felt in the company of these two people, Jason looked at clouds still bunched over the distant mountains, their dark bottoms scraping the peaks, and said dreamily, 'I doubt it'll fall tonight, Little One.'

Step's head appeared before the backdrop of stars. He dropped his pants at the head of the roll and stood shivering in his shorts. 'Which side am I on?'

'Over here by me—I'll try you once again. I should know better by now, because I say that every time we start. But I suppose we should give him the benefit of the doubt, huh, Jason? See if he's learned anything.'

'Am I really as bad as she says?' Step asked, poking his feet in.

'Pretty bad.' Jason's teeth caught the glow from the starlight as he smiled.

'I could put up with the one if he didn't do the other,' she prissed.

'Yeah,' Jason agreed. 'I wouldn't mind the snoring if he wouldn't let all that cold air in.'

'And the hot air out!' she huffed.

'There ought to be some sort of invention, a scientific apparatus to keep things under control when a person's asleep,' Step observed, 'like a cork.'

'Jesus!' protested Shan, 'that'd be like popping a bottle of champagne in the middle of the night with none of the rewards. No thanks!'

Step threaded himself in beside her and backed up for warmth, the head and shoulders of his six-three frame sticking out the top. 'You guys needn't worry about your uppers freezing, you fit these damn things.... Say... maybe that's the cause of my ailment, my thunder-gusts, so to speak. I contract from the cold up here and subsequently it squeezes out below.'

'In that case, Professor, try sleeping with your ass outside.'

'You're unkind.'

'You're inconsiderate.'

'I'm helpless.'

'Oh, always that, yew pore leetle thang. Is that what you say when you bed some fair damsel...? I'm...'

Jason gave her a stifling hug around the middle, cutting off air for the rest of her sentence, and yawned. 'G'nite, you two chatterboxes.'

Step scrunched down, reached around and gave her an affectionate pat. 'Goodnight, cookie. I'll try to be good.... Night, Jason.'

❧❦

CHAPTER 6

September 2 — Late Afternoon —Dandy Crossing

Buck backed into the turnaround and pushed the gas pedal harder than he meant to as he slewed onto the double track to return to his shack, splashing mud on his khakis through the doorless Jeep in the process.

Whoa, horsy! What's the big hurry?

If he'd thought to analyze his actions he'd have known he was still hyped from the company of his just-departed friends. He might be what some would call a 'loner,' but one of his greatest pleasures was doing things for people he cared about—or even didn't care that much about if the effort brought worthwhile results. Raised on a Missouri farm, there was almost nothing he couldn't fix, tear down, build up, patch, re-make or rid himself of if necessary, one way or another—nor was he enticed by the almighty dollar. If the job went lopsided, he'd quit, find another— in other words, he was an adaptable creature, mostly at ease with himself and others. Mostly.

He lifted his foot and slowed the Jeep to its usual bump-glide-crawl. *That's better.... Got three more days before I go back to the mine... no need to whirlwind it.*

As he crossed Farley Creek, he heard a motor and the sharp squeak of brakes, along with a rev that meant someone was coming down to the landing who didn't know how to drive the country. He was familiar with the sound of every engine that lived at the Crossing and this wasn't one of them. A dark green truck with a

Park Service logo on the door came into view. *Oh, shit.* It crossed the creek and drew up behind him. The man got out and ran quickly to the Jeep, as if he thought it would pull away.

'Hello, sir,' the man said, nearly out of breath. 'You're Mr. Watson, Buck Watson, aren't you? We've met before, but only once, and I wasn't sure...'

'Which one are you?' Buck looked over the top of his sunglasses, frowned and switched off the ignition.

'Which...? Oh, yes, I understand. I'm Jock Henderson. I'm here to get a couple signatures, you know, for the purchase of your home... uh, cabin, here at Dandy Crossing; the one we plan to use at the Hite Marina, when the lake comes up.'

'Reservoir.'

'Uh... yes, Mr. Watson. You've already completed the formal contract, and we just need...'

Buck cut him off. 'Do I have to sign my life away on a bunch more government papers, and wait for twenty years to get paid for drowning me out of here?'

'Ah-h no, sir, it's very simple, really. This is the payment form—we pay you and deliver the amount already agreed upon when the lake... uh reservoir, reaches Farley Canyon's confluence with the Colorado River. Your cabin is almost a mile upstream, and several feet higher, Mr. Watson, so you'll have several more days...'

'Yeah, well.... Henderson, let's get on with it, give me the papers. If it isn't a boatload of Governmentese-gobble-de-gook, and I can understand it, I'll sign here and now and you can be on your way.' *Next time one of these assholes comes snooping around my place, I think I'll shoot him!*

'Fine. Just one second.' He ran to the Park Service truck and returned with a clipboard, papers and pen. While Buck read over the now familiar lingo to make sure nothing had been changed, Henderson had the good sense to wander off.

When he ambled back to the Jeep about five minutes later, Buck handed him the clipboard. 'I noticed a slight change in what-all's included in the original property contract. I thought you guys didn't want the water tank along with the cabin and fencing.'

'The boss said you didn't care one way or another, and we've found a very good use for it, but I can...'

'Nah, that's okay. I don't want to haul it out of here—got no need for it anyhow, not where I'm going.' He started the Jeep.

There was a moment of awkward silence as the man tucked the clipboard under his arm and said, 'Uh... well, thanks, Mr. Watson. I appreciate your cooperation; I know it isn't easy to...'

'No need to thank me, Henderson, I'm just glad I don't have a job like yours, or anything close to it. So long.' He revved the motor so the Park Service guy would move off... but sat, idling, waiting for him to get in his truck, turn and head out Farley, making sure he was gone and the air clear once more. He shook his head, amazed at a single day's turn of events—so fine a beginning with great friends, and so sour an ending with Henderson wading in. He took a deep breath and looked toward the river, then up at the cliffs on the far side.

Must be after four. The sun had dropped behind the rim, igniting the bottom of a huge cloud blown westward by the squall; willows lining the bank rocked one way, then another, as evening began to change an up-stream wind to down-. He looked up river toward Fred and Helen Bennett's cabin, the cottonwoods beside it, the boat dock and ramp that Fred had so carefully planned and painstakingly built—all to be taken away to some other place where it didn't belong—the cottonwoods, everything, drowned. He ground his teeth and slammed the butt of his hand against the steering wheel in anger and frustration. *Fucking Henderson...! Why in hell did he have to show up and ruin my day?*

About to shift into low and start for his cabin, another sound turned his ear back toward Farley—familiar? Not familiar. *Somebody wantin' to cross on the ferry.*

Pr-r-r, put-put, pr-r-r... a slight sputter.

No-o-o... couldn't be... I wonder if...? He braked.

Around the last bend, where a single shadow followed along beside him against the red canyon wall, rode his good friend Leo on his quiet little BMW motorcycle. Buck, in a blink, cut the motor and got out as Leo coasted up beside the Jeep.

'Hey there, ol' buddy, welcome to the wilderness!' He threw his arm around Leo's shoulder, then stood back, tilted his head and smiled. 'I am truly glad to see you.'

'How-dy, Buck,' came Leo's slow, Midwestern drawl. 'How's it goin'?'

'Better, now that you're here. Your timing's almost perfect—I said almost, because you just missed Shan, Jason 'n Step by a couple hours.'

'Aw, dang…. Goin' down or comin' out?'

'Down—their last trip together on the river. Flying back in about three weeks. She left her Bird here 'cause we're doing a Wolverton trip soon's she gets back. How long can you stay? You could come…'

'Huh-uh,' Leo shook his head, 'only got a few days—gotta be to m' little sister's weddin' end'a this month—maybe we can plan for next spring.'

'Well… maybe, who knows; depends on when the goddamn reservoir arrives.'

'Yeah.' Leo looked down toward the river. 'I try t' fergit about that.'

'Well, let's. I got a very large catfish needs eating and three more days to do whatever suits our fancy—we can go digging, crawling, rowing, hunting—about anything but flying.' He nodded toward the cabin. 'You ride on up, Leo—it rained some this afternoon and I like to check on Bennett's boat dock when they're away. I'll be along right soon.'

Leo drove away very slowly, his legs straight down, almost walking the bike, dodging a puddle here and there, taking time to savor a place that was like a second home to him. Glancing to his left at the airstrip, he thought of the many times he'd set the Paper Piper down there, or come on the BMW, like today. Now that he knew there wouldn't be many more such times, he felt an urge to soak it all into his memory—the Moki and critter hunting, the hiking, rock hounding and river running with Buck, Shan and Jason… so much more.

Tall and lean as the stalks of corn that grew on the family farm in Kansas beside the Big Blue River, Leo Waller, a man of many trades and talents, let his brothers grow the corn while he spent his time inside one motor or another, keeping the farm's machinery in tiptop shape—and half of Marshall County's as well. Inside the barn, built for his workshop and hangar, he had cussed and glued the Paper Piper Cub together, then, not satisfied, built from a kit what he called his Speedy-Beedy Biplane—had to lengthen the landing strip he'd dozed beside the corn field for that one. Shan, on her many trips cross-country, often made Leo's farm a pit stop. She'd met all his family, flown with him, seen his basement 'museum' full of ancient pottery and once she actually rode to a trail head with him on the BMW! Threatened to run the Ol' Missou and yank him along too, but it never happened.

He shut the motor and coasted into the yard beside the cabin—sat a moment before he flipped the kickstand and heard the crack of his hip as he swung his leg over the seat. He stood and stretched, listening to the soft clatter of the cottonwoods, a canyon wren calling down the night. *Best little bird there is—bet it still has a nest in the cliff over there by the water tank. I'll have a look in the mornin'.* He unhooked and shouldered his pack, walked across the grass to the other side of the cabin, chose his bed for the night and dropped the pack on it, watching raindrops jump and sparkle off the springs. Next, he made a trip to the outhouse, sat... and chuckled. *Buck's still got Shan's picture here; what'd she say when she first saw it?—'Can't imagine what kind of 'movement' this inspires!'—sumpthin' like that.* He took a look behind him to make sure the lye can was not there, but sitting on the floor. *Dang glad he left off that goofy hook-up with the lye can—I 'member plenty good when he had it sprung so's it'ud dump lye into the hole as ya got up off the seat!—almost burned m'tail off one time, before I made clear.*

Leo heard the Jeep start up down at Fred's place and wandered back to the front yard fence—one that he and Buck had put up together to keep the varmints out of his vegetable garden. Sometimes he'd been there to help with the planting. There were still dah-dit-dah rows of onions, carrots and beets, and even some collard greens. *Gonna have some of them tonight, bet'cha.* They both loved collard greens; that made him think about the two farm boys from the Midwest, Buck landing here for keeps, and him whenever he could. Not that he wouldn't have moved West for good, but he had a mother, sister and brothers to look out for since his pa died—he was the oldest, so couldn't just pull anchor and leave Kansas.

Leaning on the gate under the elk horns, he looked up and grinned. Buck had constructed a typical Western entrance to his abode: two eight-inch-diameter tree trunks, near eight feet tall and forked at the top, were buried in the ground, one each side of the gate; another across in the forks—*All smooth as a baby's butt with river silt.* Top center, Buck had mounted the skull and rack of a six-point elk. From one antler dangled a petrified rattlesnake, a kit fox tail hung from another, and beneath the elk's jawbone, a javelina skull swung from wires through its eye-holes. Leo smacked his lips. *Yum, I kin still taste that pig.... Buck marinated the bastard fer a whole week last fall, in a tub of beer under the water tank, with a bunch'a other stuff I never knew nuthin' about, prob'ly just as well.... Dunno where he learned to cook, but man, oh man!*

Buck pulled up and parked under a big cottonwood that almost framed the front yard. He came to stand beside Leo. 'Garden gets kinda thin and scraggly this time of year, but we've still got plenty to eat. That was a good crop you and me put in— Fred tends it while I'm working, and he and Helen help me eat it.'

'I seen ya still got our door stoop,' said Leo, pointing toward the front door.

'You didn't think it could go anywhere, did you?—even in a strong flood. As I recall, it took us both to rope and haul it out of the river, it was so waterlogged.'

About five feet long, three wide, and three inches thick, it had come floating down the river one day and lodged itself against some cottonwood roots along the bank. They never did figure what it had been in its former life—an old mine door maybe, or part of a sluice box—anyway, it was old and scarred and what made it intriguing to both men was that it had ten square-headed, hand-forged nails sticking out from different places. Buck pulled them all and saved them, half for Leo, half for himself.

'You still tell folks it was the backboard from yer old privy?' asked Leo.

'Sure... when I don't want'um sittin' there too long.'

Buck opened the gate, reached for his Bowie knife and slashed off several good-sized collard leaves. They scraped the mud and leaves from their boots on an old andiron Buck had fastened to one end of the steps and went inside. From old habit, Leo reached up and slapped the lintel, six or more inches above his head. They had learned to step cautiously through doors of average height, since both were over six feet tall; so, when Buck moved into the cabin one of his first improvements was boosting all three doorways. The privy he left squat.

After a dinner of baked spuds, greens and catfish, they went outside on the stoop. Leo cut a chaw, and Buck, who didn't chew or even smoke anymore, took a toothpick to his teeth. From their perch they could see the bank-to-bank roll of the river through the trees and hear its soft gurgle where it tugged at exposed roots along the shore. For many minutes they just sat, chewed, spat and picked without saying anything. Leo aimed a glob of tar at a stinkbug crawling through the grass, missed, and asked, 'How are Fred 'n Helen takin' to the comin' of the rez?'

Buck flipped his toothpick at the same bug, also missed, and said, 'He *sounds* philosophical about it, but I know it's biting him deeper than he's letting on. Their kids asked them to come live with them at Dove Creek, but of course they don't want to do that; they're real independent folks; it'd never work.'

'What about ol' Windy? Where's he goin', ya know?'

'Oh, hellfire! Who can guess? One day it's the Hite Marina: *'I'm gonna git the concession there,' he says. Next day: 'Gonna buy me some land along the highway, build a store and gas station and grab the tourists.'* Next thing, he's moving to Alaska.... Never can tell what's coming next.'

'You kin mimic him real good,' Leo says through his laughter. 'At least he's got more'n one idea.'

'Oh, yeah, they come thicker'n turds 'round a country schoolhouse. Last night I thought Shan was going to de-nut him before Jason led him outta here. Half the time I feel sorry for him, he tries so hard—other times, I'd like to bust his jaw.'

'Speaking of de-nuttin'—didn't I meet one of yer victims comin' out Farley when I was comin' in?—the guy in the Park Service truck? Simpleton almost run me off the road.'

'Aw, he's just an errand-running flunky, brought me some papers t' sign. Trouble is, you can't ever get to the *real* bastards; they hide in bureaucratic towers where they pull up the ladders and throw their shit down on us. I told the last guy I found snooping 'round my cabin, that if I ever saw another one there, I'd blow a hole through him.'

'I got a more pleasant idea,' mused Leo. 'When you was talkin' about Shan, I'uz thinkin'... mebe we could take *Rintintin*, do a quick run down, find'um and spend a night with 'um. You said you had three more...'

'No, Leo, I don't believe we oughta. This is their last trip together—sort of feel like we'd be intruding—besides, ol' buddy, you came to go Moki hunting, right? I know just the place where, with *your* eyes, we might even find something as u-nee-que, and un-find-able as a... *chamahia*.'

꙰

CHAPTER 7

September 30, 1962 — Kane Creek to Dandy Crossing

Slipping like a grain of sand to the bottom of an ant-lion's den, their last day in Glen Canyon began.

Morning flashed a sky so blue it hurt the eyes. The river's surface picked it up and faked a clear stream—Navajo pinks were tinged purple, greens seemed bluer. There was frost on the yucca spears and brittle stars of it turned to strings of water beads in the grass. What air stirred was kissing-gentle as it warmed in the rising sun.

The travelers moved slowly about their tasks in various stages of dress and undress, laughed and joked, ate heartily of Jason's famous pancakes and touched each other often in their coming and going. The river still had a lot to say, whipping around the point, *burbling, grumbling*, and occasionally giving off what sounded like a cat's low *yowl*, followed by a *burp*.

'I think he's got a stomachache,' said Jason.

'Poor baby,' Shan sympathized. 'He'll have more than that when the Wreckers give him their famous high-colonic kill-all.... But that's okay,' she smirked. 'Someday he'll open up and poop all over them!'

The *Tickaboo* was snubbed in a tiny half-moon cove at the mouth of Dangling Rope Canyon. They packed the boat slowly and without much care, knowing all would be removed a few hours hence.

'Give me the life jackets,' said Jason. 'They stay with the boat, so I'll stick them down under the back deck.'

Shan pulled on the back of his belt as he passed, before she handed hers over, and said, 'Whoa… you *did* give one to Bradley before we left, didn't you?'

'No-o-o,' he drawled.

'WHAT! I thought you…'

'I gave him *two*—one for Myrna, in case they ever want to get in the *Silver Bucket* together.'

'Ah-h, you! Who are you going to tease when I'm far, far away and you don't have anyone around, like me, who bites every time you pull a smarty?'

'I may lose the knack; you're the best sucker I know.' He smiled and gave her a playful slap on the rump.

At first they didn't use the motor, preferring to saturate themselves in nature, to creep up slowly on a less attractive place and cushion the shock of re-entry. Shan rowed, singing with the rhythmic dip and push on the oars—her body free of surplus fat, an even brown, showing no marks of secrecy. Jason lay up front across the bedrolls in his trunks, singing with her, hands behind his head, tanned from top to toe. Step was stretched across the stern face down, like a brown log protruding over the water, stroking a full, soft beard and thinking: *At least Kane is an easy first step after these idyllic days on the river…. Aside from whoever comes to meet us, no one will be there this time of year.* It was nineteen miles from Kane to Wahweap over a primitive road, and when they got to Art's place there'd be friends to talk with who felt much as they did about the river. He put aside the thought that now there could well be workmen from the dam staying at the lodge, eating and drinking there as well, and how Shan might likely tear into them. But Willie, the ever faithful pilot, would be there for sure to take him to Moab for his photo shoot and drop Shan and Jason back at Dandy on return. The trick would be to leave from Art's quickly— like as soon as they arrived.

At Rock Creek Shan pulled in the oars, switched places with Step on the back deck and started the motor. Jason was feeling a heaviness he could not explain, a kind of foreboding. Sadness? When his thoughts had wandered to the end of the trip he'd blocked them, now they began filling his head. *Will we ever take a river trip together again...? When I suggested we run Gray and Deso next year, Shan seemed disinterested and Step thought he'd probably have an assignment somewhere in Australia.* He saw Step sitting on the oar-seat reloading his Rollei and came to join him.

On the right they were passing Cattails Canyon. Step, recalling the photos they'd once gotten in there, pulled Jason from his reverie. '...with that fuzz all over her, she looked like a plucked duck.'

'Huh?'

'Shan, when she greased down and we broke the cattails over her. I got some back-lit shots that were superb.'

Coming around, he said, 'Oh sure, I remember... the wind was up that day—we had trouble getting them to stick—whose idea was that, anyhow?'

'Whose do you think?' Step gave his head a tilt toward the stern where Shan sat steering.

'Don't you ever wonder what she's going to do next?'

'Always! But that's what makes it interesting.'

'Sometimes a little too interesting.' Jason worked with his knife, making a willow whistle. 'Remember when she used the ski rope for climbing? If that handle had worked loose from where it just *happened* to anchor when I threw it up, she could have fallen thirty feet! I'd never have tossed it if I thought it would stay!'

'I've said before, you worry too much, Jason. Remember the time she disappeared off the stern? If she hadn't been laughing so hard, we'd never have found her up in the tree. Bloody monkey! She just grabbed the limb as we went under it in the boat.'

'But that wasn't dangerous,' he chuckled in recall. 'How does she think up things like that in the blink of an eye?'

'I wouldn't call it thinking, more like impulse, almost a reflex—she likes to experiment and, of course, she's completely uninhibited.'

Jason nodded, tapping the willow stick with his knife handle, slipping the bark free. 'That's right. I guess I never was, or could be.'

'You're improving,' smiled his friend.

'Last Chance Creek,' called Shan over the motor's *gurgle*.

'Last chance, *indeed,*' said Step.

Shan ground her teeth and let her thoughts take wing: *Ten miles to the end of freedom… to civilization, the ingrown toenail… to revving up the process of retaining one's identity in the swarming masses…. No more uncivilized practices like sleeping three in a bundle of warmth and friendship… no more swimming, playing, hiking, living naturally with the elements! Put on the makeup, the fancy gowns, the high heels and shore up those protective walls…. Adios, Last Chance…. Hello, Trail Spring…. Toodle-oo, Meskin Bar….* She turned off the engine, lifted the prop from the water and lay face down, chin resting on one hand, the other trailing in the river. *Tickaboo* turned lazily in the current as they absorbed the stillness—high contrast to motor noise, even higher to what would come all too soon. They breathed deeply, relaxed in their special places, each one's thoughts mingling with the wavelets gently slapping at the sides of the boat. It was a kind of ritual they always performed at the end of their trips—a silent salute to the Canyon, opening to it with every pore, taking it all inside and locking it up for recall, when nothing else would appease the anger and frustration that sometimes comes with daily living.

At Face Canyon they entered a long forgotten zone of self-consciousness. Shan and Step reached to cover themselves. Shan punched into shirt and shorts, saying as she did, 'Well, on they go; mustn't corrupt the young and innocent. Yuk! Feel like my wings have been clipped.'

'They have,' said Step, zipping his pants and adding philosophically, 'I actually don't mind trading my sacred nudity for something worthwhile—say a cold beer…. Hope somebody remembers the rules and brings some.' He turned to Jason and said, 'Wish I didn't have to go to Moab right away for that photo shoot. I like to hang around the canyon for a day or two and relax, before I step back into our busy world.'

Jason nodded, and tooted on his willow whistle.

The whistle was another kind of ritual. Each trip he'd make one for Shan to keep as a reminder for their next trip. Whenever she blew its notes, memories of the Glen would play back. Even when it could toot no more, she would roll it in her hands and dream river dreams.

Jason stood, pulled khakis over his trunks and took the oars for the last few miles to Kane Creek.

Bill, having driven from Blanding with the boat trailer, met them at Kane Landing. After initial greetings, no beer and business talk, they were silent, riding over the bumpy, gravel track to Art's place in the van, trailing the *Tickaboo*. Bill took off for Blanding as soon as the three, with their gear, left their seats.

Art wasn't at the Lodge. They looked for familiar faces, for boatmen who knew about other trips with friends of theirs, but found no one. Neither were the dam workmen about, it being near two in the afternoon, everyone working. Step and Jason were silently relieved. They needn't have worried—Shan was in no mood to talk to anyone, let alone a dim-dumb-dam-worker, as she called them. Her thoughts were on Buck and their trip to the Mill.... *We're gonna have a bundle of fun.... Sure am glad I signed that Playboy Club contract for the end of the month, instead of next week!*

'Yoo-hoo,' she called across the lobby. 'Willie's in the bar, so all we need to do is grab a sandwich and go! Yippee!'

They all were friends of Willie, the pilot who ferried them throughout the canyon country. He knew every used and unused strip on the Four Corners map where he could, with luck, set his Cessna down, plus a few that he'd made himself out of necessity and wouldn't likely try again. Willie had brought Step to Dandy, and Step had arranged for him to meet them at Wahweap after the trip and take them where they needed to go.

❧

Communicating was difficult above the engine noise of Willie's small plane, but Jason knew there was little time to go over the plans for his annual fall trip to the Midwest where he showed films of his river trips to potential buyers. This would be the last of those showings. Even the latter part of the movie would not be available to his passengers—after January the reservoir would be steadily eating up miles of the lower section, and Kane Creek Landing would be a thing of the past.

Shan was looking out the window, as always, tracing places they'd been, seeking others she wanted to explore. He tapped her on the shoulder, leaned over the armrest close to her ear, and said, 'Hey, Little One, when's the best time for me to come to Chicago?

How long will you be there?' He could see she didn't want to discuss this right now, but he had to start making plans.

'Oh, Jason,' she half shouted, 'let's talk about it when we land. I don't want to think about that stuff now—wanna look at my favorite country.'

He pinched his lips shut and nodded.

After saying goodbye to Step in Moab, while idling and taxiing, she did tell him that the best time would be late October— she'd still be at the Hugh Hefner's Playboy Club—he could come to one of her shows. *Hm-m... I don't know about that... better to hear her on a river. As* soon as they were airborne for Dandy, she again had her nose glued to the window glass where it stayed until Willie buzzed the Crossing.

Buck met them at the airstrip (before Windy could cover the distance from the store) and whisked them off to the cabin. As they drove up, the first thing she saw was her Thunderbird stashed beneath a tarp, and once again she was grateful for his care and thoughtfulness. By the time they got their gear untangled, sunlight was walking up the canyon walls.

Jason, looking skyward said, 'Better take this fine car and head for home, Little One, while I've still got plenty of light.'

Shan hugged him hard, then, taking him by the shoulders, looked deep into his eyes and smiled. 'See... we had the trip of trips after all, and nobody, *but nobody,* can take that away from us.'

'No, my Little One, nobody can.' Reaching into his shirt pocket, he pulled out the willow whistle, gave it two toots and handed it to her, barely managing a return smile. Swallowing hard and bending double to get into the seat, he started her car.

She leaned in through the open window and kissed him softly on the cheek. 'I thought for sure you'd forgotten—I should know by now, you never have—thank you so much, Sweetie.' She backed out, gave two toots on the whistle and saluted him. 'Watch the high centers; this little baby ain't no truck. See ya in a week or so.'

Buck watched and listened intently to this interchange, feeling the vibrations between them like a connecting rod, sensing that Jason's feelings for Shan were way beyond mere fond affection. When he called her 'Little One' his voice changed tone and timbre, closer to a caress than any physical embrace might be, and far beyond what his Mormon upbringing would allow him to admit. He'd seen and heard them together over the years, watched appreciation and understanding grow between them, and learned, at least from Jason's side, there was far more to their relationship than met the eye.

Jason reached out to shake Buck's hand. 'You two watch out for the bears up there at the Mill. I hear they like…'

'I'll be the only bare up there, if it's not too cold, and well you know it! Take care, Jason.'

They waved and turned for the cabin.

Supper with Buck was elk steak and ice cream from the freezer—carrots, potatoes and salad from the garden. Conversation was about Leo's visit.

'Damn near got my nuts cracked riding that BMW with Leo at the helm. No matter how smooth that littler bugger is, the turf beneath is Marble Town, USA.' He got up from the table, went to the glassed-in cases that held most of his treasured artifacts and took one out. Returning, he pushed the dishes aside and laid what looked like a blade down in front of her. 'What d'you think of that?'

She stared… gently touched its deep yellow-gold color and ran her hand across cold, smooth silk. It was wedge-shaped, near a foot long, with a fan-shaped head, like a spatula… and smoothed down, from about half an inch thick in the middle, to thin edges all around the upper half… the other end round, like a handle, about an inch thick. If it had been polished on a jeweler's wheel, it couldn't have been any smoother or shinier. She lifted it from the table, nearly dropping it… heavy, over a pound… turned it over, held the broad end up to her cheek and looked up at Buck.

'My god, what is it?' she asked in a whisper.

'A *chamahia*. Leo stepped over the big end sticking out, turned around and bent down just when I saw it through his legs and stooped to pick it up. We banged noggins so hard we near fell over backwards!'

He would paint it like a Laurel and Hardy show, that's Buck, but I've got goose bumps on my arms just holding it, and the back of my neck tingles. Aloud, she asked, 'But… but what would they have used it for…? Too fine and chip-less for digging or chopping. It feels like a hundred different hands, over many years, had lovingly caressed this stone!'

'It's a ceremonial object, for sure… maybe used as an altar piece inside the kiva… polished for harvest ceremonies… something like that—nobody really knows.'

'What's the stone?'

'Probably jasper—it's heavy enough.'

'Where'd you find it?'

'Now, Miss Shan Lu, you know better'n to ask a dumb question like that.'

'Yeah… couldn't help myself.' With a slight frown, she laid it gently down on the table. 'How come *you* have it? Didn't Leo see it first? I know how you guys are about stuff like that.'

'Well… to be truthful, we couldn't decide, so Leo says he doesn't want to chance taking it back home on the BMW. Besides, he likes seeing it out here where it came from; says it won't be happy in Kansas.'

'He's probably right. There's something about it that makes me think it belongs here and wants to stay.'

She picked it up again and put it against her cheek, feeling the cold velvet stone… and again, the tingles on the back of her neck.

৵৽

CHAPTER 8

Wolverton Mill - October, 1962

The weather wasn't any colder for that time of year, but we were up a bunch higher than the river—Mill's about eight thousand feet, stuck up on the side of Mount Pennell, and Shan was doin' what comes naturally, wearing nothing but her tennis shoes.

There's a little creek runs down a crease in the pines, Straight Creek, it's called—'bout as straight as the back leg of a lame dog—and she was hankerin' to get into it, as usual. The morning was perfect, warm as toast, like I promised her. Indian Summer. Up here, sun shines full into the canyon 'till it gets to Pennell Peak, then things cool off rapidly. We left the Jeep a mile or so back and walked up the canyon 'cause the road to the Mill's been pretty bad washed out over the years.

Not in any big hurry, we just moseyed along at an easy pace, sometimes me first, sometimes her, climbing over rocks where we had to, nothin' steep, and crossin' the stream every now and then. We could've walked an old trail, but she likes to stay down near the water; so do I, if I'm looking for arrowheads, 'cause they wash down the natural watersheds.

Finally, we come to this pool, layin' like a hunk of jade, sparklin' in the sun with big, flat-top boulders all around it. She takes one look, toes off her tennies and slips in, swimming up and down with long, lazy strokes. Pisses me I can't swim like that—I'd like to have gone in with her—which is damned unusual for *me*. Hell, I can't count the times she's dragged me through long canyon trenches, to say nothing about Step and Jason, and every time I've hated doin' it. Now, for the first time, I had the feeling I'd like t'see how her skin felt all slippery next to me... and damn me, if standing there on those rocks above her, I didn't get a hard-on you could'a clubbed a cat with! Well... it came so unexpected I almost fell offa the rock backin' up, for fear she'd see my jeans poking out like the handle of a billiard cue. I climbed down the opposite side and went for a piss to convince myself that was all I needed—drained the lizard, and after snooping around for pot shards and stuff, went back to the pool.

Shan was stretched full length on a big warm boulder, drying—she was a whole lot darker than the rocks, except for her hair—not a mark on her body. Reckon she and Step stayed bare the whole time they were on the river. Well, I got no such reaction to her bareassedness again, I'm happy to say, so I sat down b'side her and hauled out the lunch. She sighs, lying with her head cradled on her folded arms, and we commenced talkin'.

'It's gonna to be extra hard getting back to work this year, Buck. Gawd! We had such a *great* trip—each time it's harder to tear myself away. It's okay after a bit, but that first step's a sonofabitch—the blab, the smoke, the smell of booze…. It's bad for an entertainer to feel that way; means there's something wrong with them.'

'Hell, Shan Lu,' I says—ain't nothing wrong with you. I never could figure out how you worked in those gin mills anyway.' (I wondered if she knew I was speakin' from experience. I used to tend bar and put it away like water over Niagara, but I've got it down to a nip for nasty weather now.)

She says, 'My job is to entertain people, make them forget their worries, relax them. Hellalmighty, I can't do it if *I* feel lousy.'

I hand her a watercress sandwich and tell her: 'There's a cross-purpose somewhere if y'ask me—you relax 'em and the booze tightens 'em up again like an eight-day spring clock.'

'Ah-h-h, they don't come just for booze, Buck. City folks go to night-spots for companionship, because they're lonely or bored and want diversion... entertainment. It's not like the Miner's Bar in Cortez with a row of booths and Billy Gutierrez singing cowboy songs.'

I nod, 'cause I know that already, but I also know that no matter where it's at, when someone like her crawls up on a stool or
stands in front of a microphone all dressed up sexy, the thoughts
in the minds of the guys watchin' her are the same—Miner's Bar
or Monte Carlo.

She raises up on her elbows and reaches for an apple, looking
down into the pool as if tryin' to stencil it into her memory, then
she says: 'I like to think I'm bringing them something they've
forgotten, a bit of heritage maybe—that's kinda what folk songs
are about—and I have faith that even if they don't know *why* they
feel a response, they'll go away a bit warmed. But here's the crux
of that—there aren't a lot of listeners anymore. People are jittery
nowadays. They live in noise, shell-shocked by rock and roll, hear
music all pushed out of shape by electronics. They're pummeled
in markets and workplaces with Muzak, and they don't seem to
care about the *story* in a song... So, where's my place in all this
cacophony?'

Well, what was I gonna say to a complicated harangue like
that? I knew what she was talkin' about, but what she might
want to do about it and what I might want to help her do, were
undoubtedly two different things. So, I say nothing.

She goes on: 'I almost feel sorry for them. Ninety percent have
never seen a virgin pool like this, much less a wild place, and the
way it's going they won't have a chance to know what it can do for
them, because most of the beautiful places will be gone... all of
mine, long before that.'

I must'a had my head up my butt, 'cause it seemed the most
natural thing in the world for me to say, 'You could stay here, Shan
Lu...' and I came so close to finishing that sentence... *'with me....'*
I took a chunk outta my tongue! She missed my near slip, thank
Christ (and I'm not even sure I meant what I almost said).

'Yeah, Buck, but who'd bring in the bacon? As long as I can
be in places like this and paint them in songs, I have to try—can't
just up and quit. Besides, where else can I work for three hours a
night and make five hundred a week or more?'

'Jesus! Really?'

'Comes out about like that,' she says.

'Mama Mia, what d'ya do with all that money?'

'I spend it, making it... traveling, clothes, gas, motels, hotels.... If I were to settle down, I'd spend half that.' Then, kinda sad-like she adds: 'But money isn't worth a whole lot if there's not someone waiting for you somewhere, sort of looking out for you...'

...Which sounded kinda strange t'me—her thinking about somebody waiting for her—'cause I know she's been married and divorced couple of times, and must'a had at least two guys lookin' out for her, for a spell anyhow.

Trying to get her spirits back up, I suggested, 'You could hang around Dandy running river trips like Jason'—before I remembered there wasn't going to be any river after next year. She just looked at me, shaking her head. We both knew what the other was thinking.

Nibbling on her apple, she stood, stretched and said, 'At the bottom of all our troubles are just too damn many people. That and the lack of regard for this land as something to protect, rather than plunder.' She tossed the apple at me, hollering, 'Apple core!' pushed off the rock backwards and cannon-balled into the pool.

I wasn't takin' any more chances with my anatomy so I left her to swim in peace.... Decided I'd better watch what I said, too. Hell, I must'a et loco weed, even *imagining* a woman 'round my place all the time! It was then I knew I wasn't thinking about her in the old way—but I still don't know how it got changed over.

We spent most of that first afternoon at the Mill. Lemme tell you, that's a piece of work! Shan couldn't believe how anyone could figure out, *and build,* something as huge and complicated as the twenty-foot overshot waterwheel and lumber saw, with pulleys, belts and gears attached, to say nothing of the *arrastra* that grinds the ore. After nearly fifty years of wind and weather, you could still move the perfectly balanced wheel with one finger. Even parts of the belt around the drums were there, and the shed that holds it all had a shingled roof mostly intact, though much of the siding was gone. The flume that shoots the water from Straight Creek to the waterwheel's paddles was all busted up and falling apart, being the most weathered part of the equipment. Old man Wolverton's cabin and workshop were kinda slumped into the mountainside, but his summertime bed springs, strung on wire between four trees, would still hold a mattress and looked mighty inviting t'me after all that hiking around. Somebody had snitched the big bellows—it figures. Not many people get up here, but if and when they do, there won't be a nut, bolt or nail left in this place. B'sides I'd have needed the truck to take it home; and the small one I said I'd carry down for Shan, that was gone too. Just as well.

The rest of the trip didn't bear any incidents of importance. I cooked elk hamburgers over a grated fire for dinner and Shan played her guitar for a little while b'fore we hit our separate sacks, like always when we camp out; only that night, I wondered how it came to be? *Why,* I wondered. I still don't know.

I didn't find any arrowheads, no pot shards either, but I came away with something else—a feeling that Shan Lu was reachin' for something she was afraid to take hold of, like a trapeze artist just startin' to hang on with her teeth but not ready t'let go with her hands. She was happy and light and funny in her conversation until we talked about the river, then she got cynical.

I know she feels like the Glen belongs to her—everyone does who's had a snoot-full of it. And when you spend affection on a place, as well as time, that's the same as stakin' a claim. Look who's talkin'! But I've had more rivers taken away from me—among other things—than she has, and maybe I've learned not to take it so hard. She's got some special link with the old Colorado—different from other people's. No matter what the river's doin', she feels it, like it's part of her body. Flash floods down the canyons are like blood surging through her veins. Standing bare in a wild rainstorm under a waterfall with lightnin' flashing all around her is a kind of spiritual thing between her and the river. Even the goddamned dust storms! I've watched her, and it's almost like she's being made love to by the elements.

She says the river humbles her. Well, I don't figure it does much good to be humbled by another person; that'll just make you feel unsure of yourself or resentful, but being humbled by nature can sure give a fella an idea of his limitations. I think she was starting to get thrown off balance because a threat to the river is a threat to her person and her position in the world. And I thought she was tired of doing what she does all by herself, because she's in her forties. That can make a gal sniff into the future. But hell, I should'a known I was out of my depth. What women *say* they want and what they *really* want is never the same, and I was tryin' to make her the exception to that little rule.

Well… she ain't.

We spent the next couple days fooling around the west side of the Henry Mountains, down past the Mine near Shitamaring Creek where I've worked some, and along the Waterpocket Fold— Shan calls it the Watch-pocket Fob, don't ask me why. But there's lots of *real* names on the land around here all fancied-up on the maps… like Fort Knocker. Balls! It's *Fart* Knocker… you take that canyon on a horse like the cowboys around here do, you'll get more than farts knocked out of you! I worked roundup with them one fall, and I *know*. Furthermore, *Shitamaring* is a Paiute word, having nothing to do with shitting, but the Mormon State of Utah even had to fiddle with that, calling it something else on the road maps.

We stopped a couple days in Hanksville visiting my friend Ernie, who has a rock shop there—she wanted to hike some side canyons off the Dirty Devil, but by then my feet were starting to ache. Instead I gathered up a batch of blackberries and made a pie for Ernie our last night there. Next morning we spent an hour in Goblin Valley on the long way around to Jason's house, where Shan's car was stashed.

I'm just as glad I didn't have to take the North Wash route back to Dandy. After that shower we had the day before we took off for the Mill, I'd half considered going around the long way, even in the Jeep. But, of course, Shan wanted to go up the Wash. I could tell you stories about that trail you wouldn't believe—like people being stuck in there for days until a bulldozer got there to dig them, and the road, out. You have to know how to drive a ten-mile road with seventy-five or more stream crossings. Half the time it's impassable because the bugger's full of running water and sand traps, to say nothing of the big dunes at the head of the canyon where you go in. I always have pictures in my head about wagons going through there a hundred years or more ago. Must'a been real fun! True, there aren't any big drop-offs, but there are places where you have to roll up out of the bed and over a hill, where it narrows down between high gravel banks and cliffs. I know why they don't call it North Stream or North Canyon, because you could get *washed* outta there in a heartbeat when the water rises! Just thinking about it makes my arms ache.

Jason was on his way to some sort of meeting when we got to Blanding, so with just a few words between them about his going to Chicago, and a few goodbye hugs, we went our separate ways—me west, her east; back to singing in places she's not sure she wants to be.

There wasn't much sense in going to Dandy, since I was due back at work in the morning. I decided to have something to eat at Fry Canyon and go on to the mine—wouldn't have to get up so early that way, and I could get a full night's sleep at the good ol' Happy Jack.

I had to figure out a plan—was thinking about it on the drive from Hanksville to Blanding, and wasn't doin' a whole lot of talking on that long ride. I needed to back off a little from this relationship with Shan. It's true she hadn't taken up much of my *physical* time, maybe only three to six weeks a year since I met her eight years ago, but a newer and larger problem had risen—Yeah, that one, the one at Wolverton beside the pool... And a bit before that, if I was gonna be honest about it, she started invading my *thoughts,* even when she was many miles away.

I'd thought about her while she was on the river this last time... after Leo'd gone back to Kansas and I was at the mine... but mostly when I was alone at Dandy.... I'd find her tangled up in my fishing lines... or squirming in the sink when I washed dishes... standing over my Moki collection... looking at my maps. Worst of all, her blond head would be poking out from my bed-covers whenever I came in or out the back door of the shack.

Well... it's gotta stop...! Been there once, and I'm never going there again. Not ever!

The new plan. Before I got in any deeper, it was going to start with the letter writing. Usually I wrote to her at least once a month. From now on, I'll cut back to just a few times before she returns in the spring, and leave the heavy letter-writing to Jason, who'll keep her informed about the river and its fight with the reservoir. I know Helen or Fred write to her now and then, and I guess Brad or Myrna do too, so there's really no need for me to add more. Cutting back on our correspondence will also curb my natural inclination to tell her stuff that seems to draw us closer together each time she comes to the river. Maybe I'll be at Dandy when that time comes… maybe I won't.

ॐॐ

Shan had indeed wondered why Buck was so quiet the last few hours of their trip. The farthest thing from her mind was the very one nagging at his. First, she thought he was more subdued than usual because he was tired from all the driving, or maybe he'd eaten something that didn't like him. But in the end she suspected he was just bored. Their usual trips together never lasted more than three days, so being in the company of a woman for almost six was probably more than he was used to, or wanted. Yet, what did she really know about him outside of the hiking and boating they'd done together, or with Leo and Jason? They never spoke about his life at the mine, how he came to be living at Dandy, what family he had in Missouri, other than his mom, where he got his degree in metallurgy—she'd learned that from Fred Bennett. But then, she'd never asked any of those questions; figured he'd tell her whatever he wanted her to know.

They talked about the river, the ruins they'd been to, and others they wanted to see, about rocks, back roads, pot-shards and arrowheads, boats, and gold mining and hidden trails. They discussed the history of the country, what it was like long before they came, who to talk to if they wanted to know more; and if something unforeseen happened that left them stranded, what to do about it, how to find their way out. They talked from time to time about going to Mexico, the Sea of Cortez, Baja. He'd told her, if she ever had enough time to spend a month down there, he'd quit whatever job he had at the time, and get another when he came back.

As far as she knew, he'd never seen her perform, or even knew what she sang when it wasn't about the river. She'd told him that his letters, and Jason's, saved her sanity when she was away during those winter months, through cold, slushy, windy weather in the east or Midwest; even when she was on the West coast, it amounted to the same thing—standing in front of a microphone before a crowd, or recording a song, a radio show, an interview. She'd go back to her lodgings well after midnight, sometimes as late as two AM after having breakfast, and before turning out the light, she'd read those letters over and over again while she chewed on the piñon gum he's sent her... putting herself back where she really would rather be.

৵৽

CHAPTER 9

Winter, 1963 — Chicago

The Library of the Playboy Club lies in ceiling-zero smoke—smoke blown from tarred lungs over coated tongues through stained teeth. The tongues babble. The Key-holding members of Hugh Hefner's famous Hutch twitch, squirm and jet plumes of smoke into each other's faces over chimneyed candles that sit on tiny, round tables, nearly every one occupied. Ash trays are filled with half-smoked butts, lipstick- and spit-smeared.

A few cigar-smoking conventioneers sit as close to the small, raised stage as possible, blowing thick blue clouds into the dimmed spotlight's beam to where the singer will sit, eventually curing her like a kipper. Ice rattles, glasses clink. Bronze liquid flows, liberating inhibitions, dissolving insecurities, healing suspicion. The booze odor permeates the room.

Shanna Farran stands at the back of The Library (so called to indicate that the entertainment here is intimate). She wears a gown of white French fringe that hangs, unbroken, from a Directoire line below her breasts, over silk crepe to just below her knees. Her shoes are white satin slings with gold straps—hair coiffed high, eyes heavily lined. A gold chain, dangling a small, pink, quartz arrowhead, encircles her neck. Over one shoulder she holds a guitar. She speaks to the big-boobed cottontail standing beside her. 'We aren't very busy tonight; wonder what's going on?'

Boobs answers, 'You seen the weather outside?'

'I don't have to see the weather in Chicago, it's always bad, but it doesn't stop conventioneers.'

The room's manager walks up. 'Say, darlin', we'd better hold the show for another fifteen minutes, till they break downstairs. Go have a drink with your friend.'

'Will do, Mike—I can wait all night to start this show.'

At this hour she's usually bored and impatient to 'get the show on the road,' but tonight is far different. She's antsy, listening intently to the buzz of the room, the mood of the Keyholders—trying to anticipate what she can sing, or not sing, on this special occasion. She takes her guitar to the checkroom girl and returns, inching her way between tables to a man seated on the other side of the room. His double-breasted suit, tanned face and close-cropped hair look alien in this setting—eyes darting about with the interest of an awestruck child. He is neither talking nor squirming, and the lemonade before him is choked with fruit. Shan slides down opposite him, making him start.

'Gosh! Where'd you come from? It's so dark here I can hardly see my hands.'

'I'll bet you never dreamed you'd be inside a Playboy Club, did you, Jason?'

'Can't say as I wanted to. How do you breathe in this place?'

'Very little.'

'I thought you were going to sing.'

'I am, but we have to wait for the show downstairs to break. They want to fill the room.'

'You mean fuller than it is now?' Astonished, he looks around.

She emits a low throaty laugh. 'I can see you don't understand the economics of the gin mill. The point is to fill it so full they can't move; that way they're sure of getting more for their money.'

'Doesn't seem practical.'

A fuzzy bunny tail suddenly rears itself to within inches of Jason's face. He pulls back, staring in wonder, head touching the curtained wall behind him.

Again Shan laughs. 'A tall one, ain't she? The fellow at the next table is most likely getting the 'Boob' Treatment.'

'The... huh?'

'She leans over while she's making change until they nearly fall out. It usually induces the men to leave a bigger tip.'

Jason digests this inside dope with eyes glued to the fuzzy ball. It tips away, slightly, as the girl relaxes on one mesh-stockinged leg.

'For your edification, Jason, those tails are fireproof. Some of the bigger nerds try to light them—they think it's one helluva joke—so Hefner had them fireproofed. Wasn't that clever?'

The tail departs. Jason shakes his head, and after trying to un-cramp his legs, turns his attention back to Shan. 'Are you gonna be able to sing a song for me, Little One?'

'I'll try, but it probably won't be too good—no time to set it up, to get them in the mood. I'm only on about forty min-utes... but, if they're quiet, maybe it'll work.' She reaches out to stroke his hand. 'I wish you didn't have to leave tomorrow, Jason; tonight's only the second time I've seen you—that damned Johnson Outboard School took up all your time.'

'I know, sweetie. It's not like the old days when we showed the Glen movie, made new friends and talked all night. Nobody's looking after the boats, the tourists and construction at the new marina but me... so I have to be at Hoxie Crossing tomorrow.'

Here was the most recent thorn in her heart. None of them had expected the head of the reservoir to reach Hoxie so soon—only forty miles downstream from Dandy. But even while they were on the river last year, things were in motion that Jason knew nothing about and had no control over. The Park Service had awarded the concession at Hoxie to the Mayor of Blanding, who'd placed Jason on his committee—in compliance with a Park Service ruling that one of them must be an experienced river man. Without warning they had sent Jason there to take charge. Not that he *wanted* to run the marina—far from it—they just knew he'd do whatever they, and the Church, asked. That's how he was.

'Sorry.' She relaxes a bit. 'Seems we never get to talk any-more... but maybe it's best that way, and I don't have the good sense to know it.'

'Golly, I hope it isn't.' He holds tightly to her hand and in a soft, deeply affectionate voice adds, 'It's so good to be with you again, Shan Lu, even here—*real* good. I can't write what I'm thinking in letters, you know that.'

'You used to, Jason.'

'Not really.'

'Well, I got the message nonetheless.'

'When you're through tonight, we'll have time for you to get the message again, won't we?'

'Jason, it's tomorrow morning already... but yes,' she said smiling, 'we will if you don't fall asleep.'

One of the band members inches through the crowd toward the stand and, in passing, leans over asking, 'You ready, doll?'

'Yeah, Harry, let's hit it.' Jason releases her hand.

'You'll stay here till I get back?' she jokes.

'Heck yes! How would I ever get out from under this thing?' He sips his fruity lemonade, watching her move as she balances easily atop precarious heels. *What a shame she has to walk on stilts and sing her songs in a place like this—gives me the jimjams.*

The room takes on the high *whine* of a comb of bees. Two women sitting behind him screech a glass shattering laugh. He ducks. A voice says, 'Can we have this chair?' Before he can respond, the chair and the voice are gone.

With a fanfare from the trio, the MC brings her to the stage where she sits on a high stool. She crosses her legs to wolf whistles, takes the guitar across her lap and strums, waiting for the din to quiet. To Jason's amazement, it does.

She sings... a song about Rovin' Gamblers.

Is that Shan? Her voice is plenty loud, but gee whiz... it sounds so... so kind of mushy over this sound system.... Midway through the song the audience starts to buzz again. At the end they clap loudly, puffing like pigeons, whistling and calling, 'Bravo! Bravo!' The cigar smokers at the front table shout up at her, 'Sing somethin' sexy, honey!'

She stares down through the pink spotlight—a bemused smile frozen on her lips. Jason holds his breath.

'Aren't you gentlemen horny enough already, without my adding to your discomfort?'

The Key-holders erupt with the sort of laughter they most enjoy—laughter at someone else's expense. 'Atta girl, you tell'um!'

'Now that I know the intellectual level of your preference, I just happen to have a little ditty I wrote for such occasions...'

Last night I got laid on the prairie,
As I nestled down deep in the burrs—
I wondered why this here young cowboy
Had failed to remove his spurs!

The room explodes with laughter. The conventioneers slap their legs and knock over a drink. Jason stares down at his hands, face turning russet under his tan. He swallows hard, neither hearing her next introduction, nor recognizing the song; he sits amid the strangeness trying to contain the turmoil of his emotions. *Golly, what's happened to her?*

He hears her speaking with great sincerity, and the room has quieted once again—he recalls her use of this technique on river trips. It makes her listeners feel as if her personal longings are theirs as well, and is very convincing.

'...friend who's come all the way from Utah to hear his favorite song, and I was hoping you'd be real quiet so I could sing it for him. Sorry, it isn't sexy.' She smiles down at the men in front of her, whose laughter has become less boisterous and more self-conscious.

Now this other Shan starts telling the audience about the Wreck-the-Nation Bureau trying to dam Grand Canyon; how people are sheep to let these things happen... and something about flooding the Sistine Chapel to get nearer the ceiling. Jason could slap himself for asking her to sing a river song in this atmosphere— even wishes he was back at Hoxie Crossing on the darned *reservoir.*

'...Glen Canyon was called *The Place No One Knew...* Well, *I* knew it, and my friend here tonight knew it. I'm sorry there weren't more—it might have been saved from a watery grave. And so, for Jason...

Three jeers for the Wreck-the-Nation Bureau
Free-loaders with souls so pure-o,
Wiped out the good Lord's work in six short years...

This isn't Jason's favorite song. He wants to chuckle and cry at the same time. His ulcer is starting to give him fits. He hates what the dam has done to their canyons, the fluctuation, the choking drift, the new couldn't-care-less class of people. But he's now having to make his living on the backed up water at Hoxie Crossing Marina, guiding trips over what is now called Lake Powell... and it's easier on a man whose hiking legs are giving out, easier cooking and sleeping on a big boat than on a sandbank. He hardly ever gets to go upstream to Dandy on what's left of the river, and deep inside he feels a kind of betrayal about the comparative ease of reservoir camping.

'...I'll tell you now of their latest whimsy,
To fill Grand Canyon to the brimsy,
While Rainbow Bridge comes crashing to the ground...'

The words and their truths penetrate only slightly here in this smoke-filled room, but he does recognize and is grateful for the humor in the song. *I wonder how these folks could care at all about such things, as far removed they are from anything, any place, like the Colorado...*

Substantial applause signifies the end of her song. The audience seems to have sobered somewhat and she thanks them for being attentive. They ply her for an encore, making Jason wonder about his embarrassment for her. He wishes to hell he was out of here, with the person he knows Shan *really* is instead of this lacquered—he searches for another word before reluctantly using... sexy doll. His eyes sting from the density of smoke in the small Hutch. He'd like to breathe some fresh Utah air.

಄ೋ

Two-thirty AM finds them in her white Bird mushing through blackened slush toward Lincoln Park. Streets are far from deserted and Jason wonders what on earth people find to do at this hour. He has a room at her hotel but plans to spend the remainder of his all too short time with her—telling her about all the changes, and somehow try to prepare her for the heartbreak he knows will come when she actually sees it.

She's been circling the block for a parking place and brakes suddenly, sliding to a stop. 'Thank God! Somebody finally got up and went home!'

'Huh?'

'A parking place!' She sees bewilderment on his face and laughs. 'Never mind, it's not worth explaining. C'mon, let's get upstairs and have some hot chocolate like you used to make on the river.'

They go, knowing it won't taste the same.

Across from him at a wee kitchen nook table, robed in red velvet, she sips the chocolate. The makeup is gone, her unbound hair makes a soft frame for her face, complimenting the green of her eyes. This looks like the Shan he knows, and it feels like the time to ask, 'When are you coming to the lake, Little One?'

'Reservoir. I told you in my letters—when we three can go together.'

So she still holds the dream. There's no use explaining why this can't be. The fact that Step spends a good deal of his time out of the country these days, and Jason has very little time to himself for such trips, is incidental. She claims that people can do whatever they want, *if they want to do it badly enough.* Truth is, the other two *don't* want to—watching her go through it would tear them apart as well.

He sighs. 'I hoped you'd changed your mind by now. I'm sure you'd get *some* enjoyment out of a look at the upper parts of the side canyons, like...'

'It's not my mind I have to change, Jason, it's my *soul.*'

Her voice is a knife probing an old wound. Another subject maybe. 'That song you sang tonight, when did you write it?'

'I started it on our last river trip; wrote some more after I left you in Blanding, finished it when I stopped at Leo's in Kansas.' She gets up to pour more chocolate. 'I'd have sung the Boatman's Song tonight, but it was tough enough holding them with something more trenchant.'

His eyes light. 'You could sing it for me now without all that confusion—it'd be mighty nice to hear your real voice again; that sound system...'

'Jason, you wouldn't ask if you knew how much I hate playing here—and singing to those insensitive slobs night after night.'

A lump comes in his throat without warning and he has to gulp some hot chocolate to get it down, pretending to choke as an excuse for the wetness in his eyes. How he longs for those nights when her river music filled their world, longs to hold her in the big sleeping bag, to bring the warm rocks for their feet, turn in the night and touch her, feeling the response of a hand or foot against him.... And, oh Lord, how he aches for her laughter, that free hilarious laughter echoing through the canyons—a testimony to their happiness. But he cannot reach her now. She's gone... far away. He tries to blame it on the place. Taking her hand he rises, saying, 'Let's go to sleep, Little One. You're tired and I have to be at the airport by noon. It must be near four o'clock.'

She nods, offering a weak smile. 'I'm taking you to the airport, you know—thank the he-Jesus it's not before noon.'

Something's troubling her, but he can't put a finger on what it might be. When he comes from the bathroom in his long-handles, he finds her in flannel pajamas, opening a window. A puff of wind blows soot into her face.

'Oo fff, smell that shit! It's like being gassed!'

A wan smile crosses his face, and he thinks... *True, but I wish you wouldn't let it spoil what few pleasures we still have...* He says, 'I see now why you call it Shit-cago.'

She crawls into the double bed, switches off the bed light, and pulls the covers up in darkness. The room feels like a black box, but Jason slides in with a soft moan of pleasure at just being beside her again. Reaching over he pulls her close to spoon against him, feeling sleepiness and contentment as he blots out the room and lets memory transport him to happier ground.

Shan stiffens in his arms.

He's so surprised he doesn't know what to do but hold on, thinking she'll relax in a minute. Instead she rolls over, saying something about having to be on her stomach or she can't sleep. He turns away, lying on his back, staring into the folds of blackness. She shifts and bounces, turns and flops, mumbles about a drink, turns on the light, gets up, brings a glass, puts it down on the nightstand, turns off the light and crawls in again—this time, so far to her side that Jason thinks she must be nearly falling out.

He turns his back to her and tries to sleep, but is no longer sleepy. She moves restlessly, sighing heavily at intervals until his nerves are on pins and he's ready to throw off the covers and leap to his feet.

At five o'clock he can take no more. He gets up quietly and puts on his clothes. For a moment he thinks she's asleep, lying for the first time so still, but her breathing is uneven and there's a slight movement.

About to slip out the door and go to his room he hears her say in a wide-awake voice, 'What's wrong, Jason?'

'That's what I wanted to ask you, Shan.' He is heavy with sadness. 'Are you afraid of me after all these years?'

'No!'

'Then what is it? So many things about you have changed, I don't know what to say or do anymore.'

'*I've* changed! Good Lord, what about *you?*'

'Well, I probably have, but not toward you. I'll always feel the same about you, Little One. You're very special in my life. You know I'll always love you even if I can't show it every time I want to.'

He can hear muffled sobs in the pillow and longs again to hold her in his arms, because he knows she needs him badly at this moment, but he's at a loss to know how to act. 'I wish you'd tell me what I've done wrong. I want to help you if I can…. But maybe the best thing is for me to go, and let you get some sleep.'

She moves… probably sits up since her voice is closer to him now. 'Oh, Jason, I don't know how to tell you… it's so different here in a hotel room in the lousy city. All of a sudden being here together is *wrong*. We don't belong *here*. We belong out under stars and moonlight by our talking river in our own place. This dump isn't *ours!*'

'I understand, Shan Lu, dear Little One. You needn't say any more. I wanted to be close to you so much that I put all other things aside, even your own feelings, when I should have been more aware.'

Sobs catch in her throat and what she says comes in spurts. 'I wish… I wish… Step were here… and, and we had our sleeping bags and could all sleep on the floor… or there was another bed in this lousy room… so you could stay with me… close… or there were enough blankets for you to sleep… sleep on the couch… so I could at least feel your presence…. I don't want you to go, dear Jason… I love you too, but we've lost so much by losing the one thing we both loved…'

He leans over the bed feeling for her shoulder, very glad the room is in darkness. She takes his hand and kisses it. He takes both of hers, kissing them.

With a calmness that amazes him in view of the crashing tumult inside, he says, 'We can't replace our river, dear Little One, but we can keep those things the river taught us, and what we built ourselves—our faith in each other, our love, our friendship... if... *if we really want to.* You try to come to Hoxie in the spring. I'll be waiting there for you.'

He opens the door and steps into the lighted, empty hall. Tears streak his face and drop on his shoes as he stands alone in the creaking elevator.

৯৯

CHAPTER 10

Early Spring, 1964 — Dandy Crossing

In wild country, without phones, very little radio contact, and native runners long gone—if you needed to get a message to someone near this place you'd best have someone drop it with a heavy stone from a light, low-flying plane and hope, with the wind drift, that it came at least close to its intended mark. Or, if *you* were flying the plane, had the guts and the knowledge, you could put down on a pick-and-shovel runway, squeezed between high canyon walls, beside the snaky river.

As he'd done many times before, Leo set the Paper Piper down almost gently and taxied to the far end of the Dandy strip. He and Shan got out, saw no living soul at Bennett's place and walked an expectant quarter mile to Buck's cabin… to find him gone. His Jeep was there, but the truck he used to haul his small house-trailer and to travel to and from his mine job, was not, nor was the key to the cabin in its hiding place.

Since yesterday, at several different locations, they'd hunted for him without success. Although both knew he wasn't exactly the type to leave a trail, they figured with Leo's plane and the truck Shan had borrowed from Jason—left at the Fry Canyon airstrip— it wouldn't be all that hard to track him down, or at the very least catch a scent. Leo had written him that he was coming to go Moki hunting, and Shan, who had stopped off at Leo's farm in Kansas on her way West from her Chicago base, had opted to join him for a few days of canyon hiking, and maybe a short trip on the river—what was left of it—with Buck.

At the river bank in front of his shack she stared down at the red Moenkopi water swirling beneath her feet, feeling as fretful and flummoxed as it looked—acting like it was the victim of a bad stomach ache as it burped and crepitated along the banks, making gaseous sounds, tearing at tree roots, belching and spitting from beneath a huge ledge rock. The water wasn't all that high, just in a hurried runoff and deeply colored. With hardly any imagination, she could believe the patches of drift that bobbed on the surface were large cow pies. Perhaps that was just her shitty mood: *Come all this way for nothing.... Naw, not nothing—this place is never nothing, in fact, it is 'everything'—but to come all this way for only half of everything is why I'm pissed.... Because he's not here.*

As the sound, smell and knowledge of this place tugged at her heart, she swallowed over a stinging throat and gritted her teeth to hold back tears. *Only another year and everything here will be gone—the shack, the store, the ferry, the river—drowned behind a goddamn dam one hundred and eighty miles downstream.*

She shook her head and said to the river, 'Hi, muddy old friend. Tell me... where the hell is Buck?'

She and Leo had once jumped into *Rintintin* and followed him downriver after Windy told them Buck had left an hour before in his supply boat with a load of provisions for some uranium miners. This he did on his ten days off from whatever mine job he was working at the time. *Hey, he's not downriver is he? Nah-h... not doing that anymore, since the rez is on the rise... so his letter to Leo said.*

Until recently, she'd been one of a few to know of his whereabouts—he'd write every month or so—but no word had come from him in over three months. *Why? Did I do or say something to piss him off...? Doesn't seem likely... but now that I think about it... he acted kinda strange that last day of the Wolverton trip... sort of like his guard was up.*

The few letters she'd received since then were mostly about the weather; no jokes, no telling her what he was doing, planning or thinking, and nothing of Windy or the other Dandy folks that were usually included with his news. In other words, more strange behavior. No phoning him of course, but from her river friends, like the Bennetts and Nelsons, who would see him every now and then—there at Dandy, on his way up or down river, or at the closest town market—she knew he wasn't sick or buried in a pile of yellow-cake. He'd often joked about 'glowing in the dark,' but she didn't think it was funny at all, and told him so. It spooked her even during the early fifties river trips when the boatmen would point out the formation that contained uranium and loudly sing: '*Shinarump, shinarump, shinar-rump-rump-rump,*' as in *Charge of the Light Brigade.*

She stared at the river, then turned away and went looking for Leo, who was wandering around somewhere. She found him on the cabin door stoop.

'Hey, Leo, I know we didn't see his truck or any sign of life when we flew over, but let's walk up Farley to the store, see if maybe Windy is back, and find out if he knows where Buck is... or was... or will be.'

'Yup, bound to be one of those, if I know Windy.'

On their way past the landing strip, they stopped by Fred Bennett's dock to see if Buck's two boats were there. They were. 'I'd hoped Fred would be around,' said Shan. 'He's the only one who'd know where to find our evasive friend for sure—the only one.'

Turned out Windy *was* at the store, and *absolutely*, he knew where Buck was. They were so bent on finding him that they listened when he told them, 'He's workin' at the Happy Jack'—they'd already checked there—'Tol' me he was done at the Hideout Mine, wouldn't go back there if they begged him on bended knees—said they was so...'

Quick as a whip, Shan caught the twist in Buck's reasoning. She poked Leo. 'Ah-ha! We haven't checked the Hideout.... Let's go.'

Windy raised his eyebrows at her. 'I jist tol' ya; he ain't there. He left.'

'Uh-huh, heard you, Windy—thanks for your help; we'll run him down even if we have to chase him all the way back to Missouri.'

Before he could launch into a diatribe about whatever came into his mind next, Leo picked up the vibe and headed for the door. 'We best take off before the wind changes,' he said. 'That strip's bumpy as an alligator's back, 'n I need all the help I can get.'

Walking back to the Paper Piper, they discussed Buck's penchant for clamming up around Windy—like not telling him anything he didn't want broadcast over the entire Southwest. Buck would either go mum, or, short of an outright lie, change dates, times, places—anything to confuse. When she heard 'Hideout,' Shan knew right away why he'd told Windy he'd already left. Because he hadn't.

'But why now?' she asked Leo. 'Especially after you wrote him you were coming to go Moki hunting with him. Jesus…! All the way from Kansas in the Paper Piper, and he does a disappearing act. I think it's damned snotty of him!'

As they neared the plane, Leo just shook his head. 'I dunno. Don't seem like him, does it?'

Gentle, unassuming Leo. Tall, lean, with a stride like a camel—sure and steady over rocky terrain, up Moki steps, through sand and gravel, through brush, cacti and mine tailings. Shan had hiked and rivered many a mile with their mutual friend, at least as many as she'd hiked with Buck, and would hike many more after the river's demise. Leo had once slept in her tent when their backpack trip got stormed on and he had only his sleeping bag. She well remembered that hike—he snored like a Kansas thresher.

The take-off was bumpy, but buoyant enough; they cleared the cliffs and turned east under a mid-morning sun. While bouncing around in the air, Shan fished out her journals looking for directions to the Hideout from the Fry Canyon landing strip—*if* she wrote them down. She always carried her journal's notes into the Canyonlands—notes she'd begun taking since her first river trip in the early fifties. Flipping the pages her eye settled on something else… her first meeting with Buck:

Glen Canyon Trip — Spring, 1954

There were a couple fellows at Dandy Crossing this afternoon who had lived and prospected this area for years. One was with Endicott Copper Company. He said the Happy Jack mine was a copper mine, not uranium, back in the early 1900s, and that he used to hear the Hoskininni dredge from clear atop South mountain; told me there were three or four dredges in Glen Canyon in the late 1800s. The other man, Buck Watson, told of Charlie Gibbons—a one-time character around Dandy. Said he'd made plenty of money from the yellow cake and with it bought a ranch in Idaho—wouldn't have anything on it that wasn't white—horse, house, fence, everything white. But he spent all the money and after the White Horse went kaput he started freighting on the Hoskininni Trail and running a pool hall in Green River. Most of his 'freighting' was done for the Robbers' Roost gang. Ollie Pilchard, another colorful character was, in Mr. Watson's words, 'A hijacker, or more to the point, stinking crooked; would lift anything that was loose and some things that were tied down, once in a while things that were chained, bolted and locked down.' The easy, quiet way he talks reminds me of cowboys I've known all my life who will open the loop for a story, twirl it lazily overhead, then let it out ever so smoothly to lasso the punch line. I could tell right away, this guy is a born storyteller.

She smiled, hearing his voice through the Piper's engine... but found no directions to the Hideout in her notes.

Over the years, Buck had worked every mine in the immediate area plus several on the periphery, and was well-known as a steady, reliable hand at whatever they put him to. When one mine closed and another opened, he was usually first on the list to be hired by the new company. He could do anything from simply removing rock—work that called for setting dynamite charges—to drilling, driving heavy equipment or assaying, which allowed him to play with toxic chemicals. How he might be employed at the Hideout was anyone's guess.

They would find out

The little plane skirted the Mossbacks and banked toward the Fry Canyon landing strip. It settled easily on the runway, writing a dusty trail as it rolled alongside the main road and taxied to where the truck she'd borrowed from Jason waited. Leo got his sleeping bag from the Paper Piper and threw it in the truck bed with hers—they had no idea where they'd end up that night if they didn't find The Man. Both knew, vaguely, where the road to the mine was, but Shan had only been part way up it, and Leo not at all. They had the whole afternoon to find it, but would need to figure in some 'getting lost' time. For sure they didn't want to be stuck on a two-track drop-off, trying to find the way out of a maze of side roads, dead-ends and other cliff-hangers while they hunted for a solid mine road, especially in the dark.

The whole country was a big Swiss cheese. You'd have thought that during the uranium boom everybody who could swing a pick or lift a shovel had been digging into the mountain, along the ledges and into the cliffs. Talus mounds looked like pup tents stuck to the sides of inclines where no tent should be. The Hideout was one of those cliff-hanger mines, cut into a lengthy ledge that separated two different rock formations, dumping its innards over the rim to form several such tents. This early in the afternoon they could actually see where the mine was, but the road, or roads to it, were woven into a tapestry of dribbled, blending colors.

After two or three false starts, they learned from a man at Natural Bridges National Monument that they should take the switchback road up between the Bear's Ears, cut off from that and find the right ledge. No sign was going to point the way, and there were other mines up there. He gave them an *approximate* countdown of turnoffs before the Hideout and wished them luck.

Well, he was wrong. There *was* a sign leading to the mine, two in fact, and they made it just as the setting sun was turning cliffs across the way a shocking waterfall of colors—from soft yellow to orange and crimson, through violet and maroon—washing over terraces and caves, down the two-thousand-foot walls into the deep purple bottom of White Canyon.

On their side, a road had been dozed along the bottom of the Wingate sandstone into the softer Chinle formation. To the right, the Wingate wall rose a couple hundred feet straight up before it met the Kayenta ridge, rising many more above that. The ledge they drove on was about thirty feet wide from cliff to open space—barely enough for heavy equipment.

They bounced toward a blown-out core on the ridge and up to what looked like the mine's office trailer protruding from a nest of tarpaper shacks and house trailers. Shan looked amid the clutter for Buck's, but didn't spot it. A bare light globe, probably never unlit, hung over the office door—nearby, a generator *put-put-putted*.

After tromping up two milled lumber steps, Leo rapped on the door and they went inside.

A man with a growth of reddish stubble scratched his cheek. 'Buck? Naw... he left early this mornin'.... Be ten days afore he comes back—his time off, ya know.'

'Shit!' followed by a long, tired sigh from Shan—the nice lady in jeans and t-shirt.

Leo, always the gentleman, shoved his bill-cap up to his hairline and gave the guy a hopeful glance, 'Did he mebe say where he was headin'?'

Shit again—I know the answer to that before we get it.

'Nope, din't mention nuthin'... t'me, that is. Collected his pay 'n took off. He might'a said sumpthin' t'one of them other fellers he works with.'

Leo thanked the man and they went out the way they came in.

'Like bloody hell,' Shan mumbled as she stomped down the steps, too grumpy to even offer red-beard a half-hearted thanks. 'And shit some more, Leo. You know Buck's not about to lip off to anybody about where he's going, so there's no use trying to find somebody to ask....'

'Naw... I 'spect not.'

'...Besides, we gotta leave here. If we hurry, we can get back to the main forest road while we've still got some light; then we can camp up there for the night. You want to drive? I'm not overly eager to hug those switchback muthahs in the gloming.'

'Sure thing. Let's do that.'

'Dammit! You realize the only thing we know now that we didn't know before we drove our butts all the way up here, is that he hasn't quit. But whether he's diggin, assaying, driving heavy equipment or pooping on the tomatoes, nobody knows.'

"Er Moki huntin' neither, I guess,' he added sadly.

༄◦✄

Leo turned the truck around and crawled slowly along the serpentine ridge. The walls of fire across canyon they'd seen on their way in, were now awash in bands of bruised mauve and purple, with only the tailings from the tents standing out against them.

'Hey! Look!' Leo's hand sprung off the wheel and pointed to an alcove they hadn't seen coming in. 'Ain't that Buck's trailer?'

Shan's head swiveled from the velvet depths of White Canyon to where Leo pointed—her heart skipping a couple of beats as she squinted into the aperture.

'Mama, mia, I think it is…. And that looks like what could be his truck right beside it.' She looked down at her hands, fingers tightly interlocked.

'…inside, just now,' she heard Leo say, unclenching her hands.

'What?'

'There's a light just went on inside. See?' He pointed again with one hand while spinning the wheel in the direction of the alcove with the other.

Shan's heart was thumping much faster than it was supposed to. *Cool it…! All this be-bop because we've finally caught up with Mister Elusive? How many damned times have I gone looking for him before… without all this flutter?*

As they parked beside his truck and got out of theirs, Shan said quietly, 'Leo, you go bang on the door. I'll wait here—you know, make sure he doesn't have company, or might be getting ready to leave.'

'Aw-w, Shan, what'cha mean? He'd open the door for you b'fore he would the US Mint, 'er anybody.' He was thinking of the many times he'd seen her crotch-hop him while he stood laughing at their enjoyment.

She hadn't told Leo about the lack of communication between her and the Man from Missouri, or her suspicion that he might not want to see her, because even she didn't know if this was true.

'Go on—just being polite. You know how moody he gets sometimes. He might not feel like company this late in the day—it's almost dinner time, ya know.' She motioned him toward the door with a wave of her hand.

Leo shook his head, walked up two metal steps and banged on the door.

'Yeah, yeah… just a minute, Mack,' came Buck's voice from inside. The door swung open, and with the light behind him he looked like a giant standing two feet taller than his friend below.

His eyes popped open wide… then were squinted by the spreading of a clown-faced grin. 'Leo! I don't believe it! Sumbitch,

man, where did you come from? Haul your skinny ass in here!
Gets cold this high up in the springtime.'

Shan still hung back beside the truck, heart sounding like a
timpani in her ears.

'Gotta friend o' yers with me.' Leo smiled, and expecting
another explosive greeting, backed off the steps.

She walked to the bottom of them, looked up, and said, 'Hello,
Buck, how's it going? Haven't heard from you in quite a while.'

Pure vacuum for five seconds.

'Shan,' he breathed, started to step down, then backed up,
held out his right hand, pulled it back, looked over at Leo, then
reached out with his left hand to assist her up the steps and into
the trailer. 'This is... is more than a surprise,' he said, slowly.
'Kinda like a shock.... Never expected...'

'Didn't ya get m' letter, Buck?' asked Leo, who'd come up
behind her and closed the door. 'Told ya all about our plans t'come
visit; Shan, t'see what's happenin' to the river, you 'n me t'go Moki
huntin'.'

Buck just shook his head and stood there, his arms folded.
Again, there were wordless seconds—no one knowing what to say,
each not wanting to be the first to speak. Shan looked long and
hard at Buck's strange stance. One side of his body seemed to be
protecting the other. Her eyes traced the familiar widow's peak
that framed his usually tanned face, now very pale, then dropped
to blond hair curled at the opening of his shirt and some reddish
abrasions on his right collarbone.

'You've been hurt, Buck,' she stated flatly, positively.

Silence.

Buck looked down, swallowed, and tucked in his lips. Letting
go with a sigh, he dropped his arms to his side and looking at
Leo, said, 'It's eating time. I've got some elk stew on the stove over
there, plenty for us all.' Still looking only at Leo, he added, 'I'm
really glad to see you.' To Shan he directed, 'We'll eat... then we'll
talk about... about... other things.' Holding her gaze, he added,
'Not now,' and limped to the stove.

All during dinner Buck took almost no notice of her, direct-
ing all his attention and conversation to Leo. They talked about
hunting artifacts and game, and about guns. They rehashed the

finding of the *chamahia*, and how it was time for him to take it to Kansas for a spell; bring it back next time he came hunting. If Leo was aware of the strangeness between them, he said nothing, and she didn't push into the talk; instead, she watched as he favored his right arm and shoulder while he ate, trying to make it look like there was nothing amiss. All her plans for spending a day or two with him on the river or hiking some side canyons before they were drowned, faded like ripples 'round a drop of water.

Buck was speaking again. 'Don't even think of going anywhere else to spend the night. Me and you will sleep in the bunks right there, and Shan can sleep in the trailer next door. The guy is on leave—I've got the key and permission to use it whenever I need it.'

Well, at least his hospitality hasn't changed.... Wonder what he'd do, or say, if I were here alone. Unable to corral her thoughts any longer, she cleared her throat and spoke. 'Windy told us you were working at the Happy Jack, said you'd quit here...'

He glanced over at her. 'You know I always give Windy information that's slightly altered.'

'Shan figured that out right away,' said Leo. 'We'd already checked the Happy Jack, that's why we come up here... but...' he wrinkled his brow... 'why'd the feller up to the office yonder say you was gone? Sure am glad I seen your trailer on the way out, or me and Shan 'ud be sleepin' up on Elk Ridge tonight.'

'I was going to the cabin, but it took me longer than I thought to get all my shit together. I'll be heading down in the morning. That's who I thought was at the door when you came—Mack was maybe going to help me. What are you guys driving?'

'Shan borrowed one a Jason's ol' trucks, 'n I come in the Paper Piper—it's down to the Fry landin' strip.'

'Good, that gives me an idea... tell you when we finish our meal.'

Buck, who was sitting at the end of the small booth where they'd eaten—Shan on one side, Leo on the other—turned sideways in his chair and rested his right arm on the table.

'Nothing much to tell you, really... happened here about a week ago.... I'm not hurt bad... just plenty sore with a few scrapes here and there... but if I'd been standing where I was standing ten seconds before this two-thousand-pound boulder came loose and rolled down, I'd have been very dead, very fast. When it rolled, I was back in a crevasse and it shoved me farther in, grazed my shoulder and sent some more unattached rocks down my front, buried my boots clear to their tops in boulders and crunched a few toes.' He smiled his tight little smile and took a sip of coffee. 'But I was still standing.'

Shan closed her eyes, rested her elbows on the table and dropped her head into her hands. She heard Leo gulp.

'Some of the guys dug me out and the boss drove me to the Blanding Clinic right smart! My shoulder was a bit outta whack; Doc adjusted it and did a tape job. Can't lift things too easy right now, and the scrapes are nothing... Band-Aid types. I can drive, but it ain't the easiest thing I ever did on these roads, even as good as I know 'em. You're a blessing in disguise, Leo. You can wheel my truck and me, and Shan can take some of my tools in Jason's outfit, if she will. That's the good idea I had awhile ago.'

Shan had raised her head when she heard her name, and Leo saw tears in her eyes. His big hands reached out, like he wanted to help Buck get up, or clear the table, or something... anything.... As if in shock, he muttered, 'Ss-ure thing, Buck, we'd be glad to do whatever... however we kin.'

Shan blinked the wetness away and said, 'I'll be happy to take your stuff down to the cabin, Buck. I only hope it means you're leaving the Hideout.'

'As a matter of fact, I'm not.' Buck turned his coffee cup upside-down on the table. 'Funny thing... I was about to tell them I was going to quit *before* the accident. When I *did* say I was getting the hell out of here before I ended up dead, the boss *begged* me to stay and put me in charge of the assay office,'—with a tucked-in grin he added—'at considerable more pay. So I'm staying... at least for now.'

৵৵

In her sleeping bag that night, in the tight little bunk of a strange house trailer, Shan floated back in time; half dreaming, half awake, clicking through the times and places she'd hiked, hunted, explored, jeeped, boated, swum or just sat and talked with Buck—talked about the Glen and all its hidden, mysterious glory. She tried to place their intermittent meetings end-to-end to get a clear picture of what others might call a strange, if not impossible, relationship with a man of his nature—one that had given her much pleasure, many adventures and hundreds of stories told with a sparkling sense of humor, insight to the surrounding country and the small, tight little group of friends that lived at Dandy Crossing. A man who'd always allowed her the freedom to say whatever she felt, to act naturally and be in tune with nature, clothed or unclothed, without the intrusion of sex to compromise their easygoing friendship. Figuring into that equation, of course, was the river. It was the river that had brought them together and their love for the river had kept them there... so far. Could something be happening to their friendship because the river wouldn't be there anymore?

Is that why he's acting so distant...? Thinks I'm only friendly with him because he can take me on river and hiking trips...? Does he care if I go away and never come back...? I don't know... surely he must... we've often talked about going to Baja together.

Then, a guilty little thought entered her very tired brain. She well knew Step and Jason didn't want to be with her when she got her first look at the reservoir. Even when she'd picked up the truck in Blanding, Jason had been on his way to Hoxie Marina, and told her he was too busy to show her around. In the back of her mind she'd been toying with the thought of asking Buck to take her in *Rintintin. Not now.... I know we can't do it now... we've lost so much time looking for him, I have to leave tomorrow, and he's hurting... but when I come back in the fall... he'll be okay by then... That's what I'll do... ask him if he'll take me for a look at some of our side canyons.*

She still could not say, 'For a ride on the reservoir...' or even imagine it.

෪෬

CHAPTER 11

Summer, 1964 — On the Road Again

Shan took the three steps down from the small stage at the Pigalle Restaurant as the spots faded and the applause died down. This was her last night in St. Louis.

Jason had been there and gone. He'd come, not to show the river movie this time, but to see old friends and let them know that if they came to Blanding or Hoxi Crossing next spring he would take them, still, to hike the side canyons off the reservoir before all were drowned. In truth, he'd come to say goodbye to those who'd loved the river trips and who wouldn't be the least bit happy to even *see* a dead-water reservoir, much less boat on it—and to give Shan her 'hit' of the Glen while she was working many miles away from it. They'd spent two days together eating, walking through Forest Park and talk, talk, talking about past trips and the folks at Dandy Crossing. She swore that Jason even smelled like the river when he came east to bring her news—words and stories that sustained her through the months she spent singing her songs on many different stages, and easing the hundreds of miles she drove from one end of the country to another…. That plus his wonderful letters with more news that somehow reached her, no matter how far or how often she traveled.

The morning after closing she spent packing the Bird, making calls to her agent in Chicago, getting instructions and directions to her next gigs four nights away in Miami, Florida, where she'd be for a full month working two different rooms and bunking with friends who lived nearby in Coral Gables. This made it possible for her to ease off the hotel-motel circuit that got very old very fast.

I'm so lucky to have loving friends scattered all over the map who welcome me with open arms, give me a bed, offer me great food and can't wait to talk about the rivers and canyons we both love—like Leo, in Kansas—and here her thoughts jammed against a wall—unlike Buck, right here in Missouri... *I don't even know what town.... Oh, yeah, Rushville...* where his letters came from when he went to visit his mother every fall or Christmas. She'd forgotten where it was in Missouri, and the fact that it wasn't home to him anymore—he lived at Dandy—was the reason she'd never thought of his hometown as a stop-over, with or without him.

She would stop in Ft. Lauderdale for a short visit with Lillie, her sister-in-law, who'd told her on the phone that morning she had a surprise waiting for her there. Often driving six hundred miles a day put her in Chattanooga that night, Tallahassee the next, and finally, Ft. Lauderdale.

The surprise rested beneath a waterproof cover on a trailer in Lillie's driveway. It was 16 feet long, made of fiberglass, had a steering wheel, gears and an unbroken boat seat behind a stout windshield—all familiar to Shan, who'd taught Lillie to water ski years ago on Lake Mead. Now Lillie owned and operated a water-ski school with several ski boats, mostly inboards, and a few older outboards—this was one of those, and Shan could mount any kind and size horsepower motor on the rear that she chose.

'It's a *lake* boat, baby,' said her sister-in-law, 'but you can run it wherever you want to. I wouldn't advise rocky rapids though.'

'I get the message, smarty-pants, but I do love you for thinking about me in my time of need. I'll have a trailer hitch installed on the Bird while I'm in Miami and pick the boat up next month on my way out. How much do I owe you for all this? I can pay you when I come back...'

'Hey, shut up about that. I might wanna come ski one of these days on that lake... uh, reservoir, or Utah's Urinal, whatever it is you call it. That'll be payment enough!'

'Fat chance, honey, unless somebody else is doing the driving.'

ॐ∞ॐ

From Miami it's a long, long way to Tinseltown, but it only took her five days. She stopped to show Leo her boat, which she'd already named in her mind—*screwdriver*. Leo helped her paint it on the sides, leaving a space after the *d*, then capitalizing the *R*: *Screwd River*. He advised her to buy a 25-horse Johnson motor for it and offered to go with her to test it out whenever she felt enough slack in her schedule, and he in his. She'd phoned Jason—actually found him at home—and asked him if she could leave it in Blanding for him to take to Hoxie Crossing Marina at his convenience, store it there until she could bring the motor, and with luck they might try it out together. She hoped desperately for a chance to see him, even briefly, before she pressed on to Hollywood, where she'd be making her first recording. He promised to try to be there when she came through, but of course that didn't happen. *All this forethought and planning—am I truly thinking of boating that reservoir in lieu of Buck not taking me in* Rintintin *to what remains of the river? Maybe so.*

She unhitched the boat and left it in Jason's driveway for Bill to take care of... lighter, but sadder for missing him. With Bill, she left her itinerary, including addresses where Jason could write to her for the next few months. When he got a chance to read it, he felt tears forming and shook his head, even knowing how much ground she often covered: '...Chicago... (her base of operation)... Detroit, Michigan... Ogden Dunes, Indiana... Chicago... Boone, Iowa... Dayton, Ohio... Duluth, Minnesota... Cooper, Wyoming... Sedona, Arizona... Prescott, Arizona... Las Vegas, Nevada... Hollywood... San Francisco... The Ranch, Tucson, Arizona... Lake Forest, Illinois... Louisville, Kentucky... Biloxi, Mississippi. It'll be early fall when this gig is finished, Jason, then I'll be on my way to Dandy. Hopefully.'

Instead of the average couple-a-month letters from Buck coming to her Chicago base, she had received two. They were flat as a salt pan and just as dry—no jokes, no information, no stories, no questions, no answers. She could almost read between the few lines—*Hello Shan, goodbye Shan, kiss my ass*—or thought she could. He no longer even addressed her as Shan Lu.

That last meeting at the Hideout mine when he was hurt seemed eons away. He'd been inexplicit, certainly, though not as blunt as his letters were now. It had taken her many months to face the fact that she didn't really know that much about him—nothing of what he did or who he was before he came to Dandy, because he never told her, nor had she asked.

I haven't been paying attention... always had so much laid back fun in such incredible surroundings... took it all for granted, never questioned if my actions, my words, ideas, or perhaps my attitude might have been offensive, since it never seemed to be.... I only know what this man feels about the canyon... and the river... and a few people, nothing more. The tide of our coming and going, our hikes, exploration, river and jeep trips all seem to have backed up at Wolverton Mill.... And yet, I can't think of a thing that was differ-ent about it than all the other places he's enjoyed showing me.... And I'm sick of tootin' all over the country... especially the east—a head of broccoli compared to a Western century plant ... I'm tired of people saying, 'What an incredible life you lead...' The key word is not 'incredible,' but 'lead'.... Haven't I guided my life where I wanted it to go, and used my intuition and curiosity to help me along the way...? So...! Get off your slow ass, Miss Shan Lu, and point your sights in a new direction!

❦

CHAPTER 12

August, 1964 — Dandy Crossing

'Your phone's ringing, Windy.'

'I know, I kin hear it. Let the sum'bitch ring. Jesus Christ, Bennett, I'll never get the wheels under this goddamn trailer if I stay down there all day waitin' fer them idiot campers t'make up their minds about whether Annabell'l git 'em across 'er not. That goddamn ferry's only been runnin' fer twenty years; what the hell them stupid people think she's gonna do, sink 'er sump-thin?'

'Eighteen... and she's been known to founder a little.'

'Shit, they don't know that!' he spits, setting more blocks beside the jack. 'This crop what's comin' in here now waitin' fer the lake t'come up, half 'em ain't never been off the pavement in their lives, an' the other half thinks a ferry's somethin' with wings!'

'It's a reservoir, Windy, and your phone's still ringing.' Fred Bennett's eyes twinkle in his thin, handsome face. 'Want me to go down and take 'em across?'

'Hell no, I don't! Want ya t'help me t'git these damn wheels under here. Nelson's down there—if it's anything worth botherin' about he'll crank 'er up.'

Bennett pokes his long slender fingers into a shirt pocket and draws out a cigarette. 'The water's coming up so fast you might not be able to run the ferry more than a few days. Down at the mine yesterday the drift was already log-jammed in still water.' Bennett's voice is like the pronouncement of a sage. 'That means we got a big puddle nearly in our front yard.'

'Yeah, 'n a goddam dirty one too with the runoff bringin' down alla that crap.' Windy wedges another block in the space made by the raised jack.

'Say…' Bennett needles, 'maybe it's one of the Bunglers of Resource boys ringing your bell. They're liable to tattle to the President and the President will jab the Department of the Inferior, and the Inferior Department might squeal to the Park Service and the Park Service'll find a way to dispense with your services as a ferry operator—all because you won't answer the phone.'

'Oh balls, Bennett!'

Fred's pale blue eyes shine with mischief. He sits cross-legged on a camp stool smoking a cigarette. Leaf shadows play over his sharply chiseled features and his large Adam's apple slides up and down as he snickers.

Windy steps back from the jack and stands on the handle, trying for another notch. It slips and he falls backward as the handle zings past his ear and flips, imbedding itself in the loose bark of the cottonwood trunk behind him. The trailer drops down a few inches onto the blocks he's placed under the rear end.

'There…! You goddamn sum'bitch!' he yells, triumphantly. 'Thought you was gonna fall down again, didn't cha? Well, o' Windy don't git smart very fast, but when he does…. That goddam jack slipped on me three times already this mornin'…. Damn near tore m'arm off the first time.'

Bennett, pointing to the jack handle still quivering in the cottonwood bark, says quietly, 'You're safe, almost hit you in the head, and that would'na bothered you none.'

Windy removes the handle with a grunt and a poisonous look at Bennett. 'Now, let's try 'er again. Every time I git it up a couple inches you jam another block under there so she don't fall again. Say…' he pauses in thought, 'maybe you're right about them Bureau boys. There's still a couple of 'um here. Guess I better find out.' He hands the jack handle to Bennett and walks into the store. Before cranking the handle he picks up the receiver to hear if anyone's talking—only static, so he rings. In a moment Bradley Nelson says, 'Hello…' but before Windy can answer, another voice terse with the inconvenience of waiting shouts, 'Where ah y'all? I bin ringin' this thing for twenny minits. Is this ferry still in operation?'

Bradley answers: 'Yes it is, sir, but the ferryman must be busy at the store. I was just taking the water measurement and heard you ringing. If you like, I'll take you across. We're sorry.'

'Well, I *have't* cross or go back all the way around. Will this thing hold mah campah?'

'Oh yes, sir.'

'It don' look safe t'me....'

Windy snorts, bangs down the receiver and returns to the trailer.

'You fired yet?' asks Bennett, flipping his cigarette into the fishpond.

'No... and I ain't about t'be, until I'm ready t'go. It's another one of them goddamn tourists; probably some Texan, don't know shit from Shinola—*'Will this thang hold mah campah? It don' look safe t'me,'* he mimics.

'Here-here now, don't be maligning your own state,' says Fred—punching Windy's instant reflex button like a vending machine, knowing exactly what will come out.

'Texas ain't *my* state,' he yelps. 'I was born in *Arizona*.'

'There's a difference?'

'Goddamn right there's a difference! I...'

Windy's routine protests trail off down Farley Canyon.

❧

For twelve years the canyon, the spring and the stream have known Windy Short and Windy has known them. But twelve years is only an instant in the lives of these natural things. What the canyon remembers is the violent surges of heavy, red, silt-ladened water that periodically scoured its bedrock. Maybe in the twelve years of Windy's occupation the stream has cut a few millimeters into the soft sandstone bottom. The spring remembers dry times when it had to go underground to keep from dying, but when things got better, Big Water pushed it up again.

Some hundreds, or even thousands of years ago, there were other Two-Feet living in the canyon, mingling voices with the spring and stream. They trod with softer steps, moved less earth about and didn't get the stream dirty with oil and gas and parts of old cars, as Windy did. While the soft-treading voices were here, the stream's bedrock wore down a few more inches. The voices left, came back and left again, and in-between would be long periods of silence, except for the nature folk—the animals, the birds, the fish and insects. The only loud sounds were thunder, the roar of floods and the splitting and falling of rocks.

Time passed.

The stream conversed pleasantly with the low hollow whistle of wind, or worked carefully removing and repacking sand, chewing away at roots and reeds, finding its way around or carrying down whatever fell into its bed.

Now... another change.

The voices are leaving, as before. Is another dry time coming? Will the spring have to go underground again? The animals are acting queerly—especially the beaver. They come chattering up close to the voices, cutting trees, and are frantically engaged in storing things they never needed before.

The stream meanders... and wonders.

ॐॐ

Fred Bennett wanders down Farley Canyon from the store where he's been helping Windy jack up his trailer. His cabin is just around the bend from Farley's confluence with the Colorado, at the southern tip of the Dandy Crossing airstrip. His steps are slow and his arms swing easily at his side—the stride of a slender man used to many miles of walking, climbing, bending, stooping, carrying loads and knowing exactly how much, how far and when to stop and relax his muscles. Years of being a superintendent of the White Canyon Uranium Mill has taught him what his body can tolerate. Before that, as a hard-rock miner on his own, measuring his steps with the uneven country he traveled, he eased into it, followed its rules, did not try to get anyplace quickly, or find a rich mineral vein before anyone else. One could liken him to a giraffe ambling up to the juiciest part of the highest tree, taking what suited him, leaving the rest.

His cabin had once been the general store at White Canyon, the Lower Store it was called by those who lived and traded there. Many voices and memories echo through the rooms where he and Helen now spend many of their days—Helen in her late seventies,

Fred, his early eighties. They have another home in Dove Creek—a long day's drive over mostly dirt roads—and if it weren't for age and the need to be nearer facilities like drugstores and hospitals, he'd spend all his time at Dandy, where he reads a lot… if he isn't repairing, replacing, reducing or rearranging things around his house and boat dock. Like Buck, he loves tinkering, until he gets what he calls 'over-tinkered.'

Fred is still a very strong man of muscle for his age. He has a beautiful five-foot bow that he made for himself—of Osage wood he found along the San Juan River in Bluff—and will shoot the arrows he made and feathered for it half the length of the Dandy airstrip, where he often practices just before hunting season. He and Buck have an on-going game-hunter's wrangle over sportsmanship tools. Fred: *'When you gonna hunt like a real Westerner… 'sted of walking around loaded down with lead in your pants and shinny objects that make a lot of noise?'* Buck: *'When are you going to quit waiting for a deer to come sit in your lap before you can take a shot at it?'*

Fred hasn't quite figured out why his place here at Dandy, where he's breathed enough uranium dust to wreck his health, means more to him and his peace of mind than any other place on earth—including his more-than-comfortable home in Dove Creek. He suspects it's the river, but isn't sure why a river should make any difference. Sure… the sound of it, except during flood times, lulls him to sleep, insuring dreams far more pleasant than the sounds of traffic off Route 90. And feeling its flow beneath his boat, gently rocking, even pushing upstream or dodging rock and sandbars, is far more satisfying than walking or driving almost anywhere. He has read enough to understand there are others like him who have felt such a pull, and not always in later life, like his own circumstance— Shan, for instance, who fights her way upstream for this river every day—he doesn't remember being attracted to the water and its flow all those years he worked at the mill. Maybe because he didn't have the time then.

Maybe he wasn't paying attention.

❧

Bradley Nelson stands at the wheel of his aluminum outboard, the better to see and dodge the springtide of drift coming down the big river as he crosses over to the White Canyon side. One end of the ferry rests on a freshly-dozed ramp that slants toward the river from the road, the other end bobs in an eddy above willows bent low in the heavy current. Nosing upstream to avoid hitting a tree trunk, he is splashed with spray. He looks down to see how much water he's shipped and smiles at the faded orange life jacket covering his chest.

'This doggone thing comes in handy for more'n just floatin',' he says to the wet jacket—his faith in it now so firm he thinks he can swim. Twice since the day Jason gave it to him it has kept him alive, telling him never to struggle against the current, to just hold his breath and he'd come up soon enough. More than ever now he thanks Shan, because Myrna is with child number two. Aside from being much loved, he is a much needed father. He pushes into quiet water beside the ferry, coasting to the tie-up. The man beside the camper and his two children watch—his wife leans out the window.

'Howdy folks,' Brad calls. 'Sorry to keep you waiting. Now you just roll your camper right up on the ramp here and we'll get underway. Can't say as I blame you for being concerned, sir, that's a mighty beautiful outfit you got there.'

The man swells with pride beside his turtle shell with the flashing chrome, then nods at the ferry. 'Ah had a look at it like y'all said—seems sturdy enough. Them look like landin' barges undah there, the kind we used in the wah.'

'That's right, three of 'em. They'll hold just about anything.' Bradley goes up the ramp and unhooks the log chain across the entrance. 'Your kiddies can get on board and stand over there by the railing if they like.'

The two little boys squeal with delight. Jumping up and down like small pistons, they skip up the gangplank and peer eagerly over the side. As the man cautiously drives his camper up and the big pontoons bounce slightly in the water, the kids fake little noises of terror. Brad chocks the tires then begins conversing with his passengers.

He notes the license plates. 'You folks are a long way from home. Are you staying around these parts for a spell, or are you on your way to California?'

'We camped ovah there last night, by them trees. Come t'see that big recreation lake your state is so proud of, with great campin' and fishin' all the foldas say. But so far I ain't seen hide n'hair of it. Guess we'll go on to California.'

'Well,' Brad laughs, 'you're just a few days too early. The head of the reservoir is around the corner about five miles downstream. We didn't think it'd be up here this quick, to tell the truth, but with all the snow melt from Colorado and Wyoming this year we'll be ferrying across on still water pretty soon with just a couple of outboards, instead of these landing barges.' At this point the man's wife, who has extricated herself from the cab, waddles over to the conversing men. In a glance Brad understands why the man wondered if the ferry could hold his camper. *Great guns, she must weigh three hundred pounds!*

'Ah don' see how y'all could move this big thing 'cross that rushin' rivah with just two little bitty outboards.' She speaks in a thick perfunctory twang that sounds used to disagreement.

'Oh, ma'am, there won't be a river here then, Just still water, and two seventy-five horsepower motors can move this very easily, even when it's fully loaded.'

She gives him a look of total disbelief and ripples over to her children beside the railing. For a minute Brad expects the ferry to tilt to that side.

Poor lady, it's rough on her, camping out.... She'd a whole lot rather be where she didn't have to haul all that weight up and down. He looks back at her husband and smiles, blessing the good luck to have his little Myrna, not nearly as gross even with a new baby inside her. 'Guess we can get started,' he says lightly, walking over to Annabell.

Annabell is the engine—the ghost of an old Dodge truck—not the name of the ferry as some think. Before her there were other distinguished relics of horsepower from the Ford and Chevrolet stables, and when Cass Hite lived at the Dandy Crossing in the 1880s it was *real* horsepower that got him, the Indians before him, the miners and the Wild Bunch from Robbers' Roost across the river.

Brad proudly explains: 'This is the engine that runs the ferry. The cable that pulls her across is attached to the rear axle here around this wheel. As she goes forward the cable pulls us across, then I put 'er in reverse to come back and the cable wraps the other way. Annabell is probably the only truck that goes backward as many miles as she goes forward.' He turns the key, releases the brake, pushes the clutch in with his hand and slips the engine into low gear.

The man from Tennessee recognizes the gear knob as an original—a small black, Bakelite ball. For some obscure reason he longs to touch it, is old enough to feel wistful about his lost youth and the times he tinkered with old engines like this one. 'How long y'all had a ferry here at this crossin'?' he asks.

'The first auto ferry was built by Mr. Arth Chaffin and dedicated in September of 1946. Looks as though its last ride will be around the same time of year, but reversing the last two numbers... 64.'

As the ferry moves out into heavy current the kids strain at the railing, their mother holding each one firmly by his belt. They can bounce all they like but they're definitely anchored.

'Ah see y'all are wearin' a life jacket—any significance in that?'

'Well, no, not really. I wear it out of habit now. I was able to pull the wool over everybody's eyes until a friend of mine discovered I couldn't swim. She made me promise to wear this pincushion at all times, so I've come to feel naked without it. There's more jackets over on that post if you feel like putting them on, but there's no law says you have to.'

'No, mah kids can swim all right, even the little one, an' mah wife...' he drawls, pulling at his ear, his eyes crinkling wryly... 'she floats. Couldn't sink huh if I tried.'

About a quarter of the distance across large chunks of driftwood detonate against the sides of the landing barges, sending his kids into a duet of jangled shrieks. The man asks, 'Do y'all evah git stuff comin' down big enough t'give the ferry trouble? Looks t'me like a whole forest cut loose out there.'

'No sir, not with this new one. Back in 1957 though, the old ferry went out on us—river rose and brought down a complete log jam—you could barely see the water. She was made mostly of oil drums then; pulled 'er right off the cable, flipped 'er and scattered chunks downstream about twenty miles.'

'Hoo-ee!'

'Good thing it happened, in a way. Folks've been coming in here the last few years with heavier rigs. Mostly we just took Jeeps and power wagons across before. The road you're taking out on the other side wasn't anything to crow about—washed out a lot of the time, used mostly by miners and hunters. Then people heard that a reservoir was coming and they wanted to see this part of the canyon before it got drowned. Fact is, there's a good deal of sentiment about it right now. Some of the locals and the conservationists don't like the idea even a little bit.'

'Mah gosh, ah kain't see why. Nice purdy blue lake in here could dress up this place considerable—shorely be better'n this mess. B'sides, looks t'me like y'all could use a little water in this desert. *Our* dam supplies the whole valley with water an' power too.'

'Yes sir, yours probably does, but this one won't. It's just here for storage purposes, and millions of gallons will evaporate or seep into the porous sandstone every day. The power the dam will generate is going to cost a lot of money, more than the Bureau says it will now, and what this reservoir will cover can't be found anywhere else in all the world—it's a very magnificent canyon, the Glen…. Well, here we are folks.'

He noses in close to the gravel bank and turns Annabell off. The man, his massive wife and kids, squeeze into the camper and slowly roll down the planks to solid ground where he stops.

'Got t' talkin' so much I forgot t'pay y'all… and y'all forgot t'ask me—Never git this nice new ferry paid for thataway.' He hands Brad seven dollars.

'Say, that's right. I get such a kick out of runnin' this thing I plumb forget the most important part of the job. Well, thanks folks, have a good trip now. Stop on your way back to Tennessee and we'll have a nice blue reservoir here for you.' He waves as they gain the level road and teeter off to North Wash.

અનુ

Slowly, like lava flowing, immured between the high canyon walls, the dead water creeps up six to eight inches a day. But the river, born a million years ago, works assiduously, carrying the silt eroded from Earth's pockets down his contoured bed to the sea. With these fine cutting tools he flushes winter's deposits. Changing color he percolates to a vigorous state of motion and power, surging, rolling, laughing in his vernal orgy, probing the rock's fissures—fecund, virile, *wild*.

Coming hard onto the rapids at Dorothy Bar, scouring the bottom, shifting sandbanks, grinding boulders, growling with glee, he feels an ominous pressure—as if Earth had shifted again, making another pocket for him to hone and fill. With the Herculean weight of driftwood on his shoulders, he ignores it and rushes on.... But there is an insidious change.

Is this the time to start a new bed? He has done it before, many times. Rivers have shaped the planet, have spread, moved, reformed and joined. They have changed climates, fed the seas, the land, the animals... and the people. They have pointed the way, ended the search and delivered the message.

Carry... carry... carry on... a million years toiling. An artery transporting the life blood of Earth... the living pulse of the planet... his reward not merely getting there, but shouldering the burden required of him, as it has been forever.

Rivers   true gods of this earth—have been betrayed!

There is a welling up... heartbeat slowing. Suddenly, the river is treading on himself! Under-waters roll back against his forward thrust like a runner tripping over his own feet. Like in a dream, he's unable to run or lift his limbs... impotent against the invisible restraint.... Everything is in slow motion.... He is heavy with sleep... powerless...

HE CANNOT GET AWAY!

Searching frantically for the drop in his bed, he falters, the floating cargo enmeshes his shoulders... presses down.... His feet slip from under him... he drops his cutting tools, the grinding boulders, the fine polishing silt...

The artery clots...

He departs his soul...

...and DROWNS!

৯৩~৶৲

The pressure on Bradley Nelson is even greater than on Windy Short—he has to leave for high ground sooner because he's at the river's edge. He and Myrna have already packed their belongings in boxes and put them in a trailer behind the Jeep, but there's much yet to be done. It's true, if Brad wasn't the sort of person he is, more tasks would be completed, but he's one who lets others impose on him. Many friends, like Shan for instance, have left things at his house to be picked up later. Somehow those things are still there, and now there is no 'later.' Next week, if not sooner, the BuRec men will be there to tear down the house. He really hasn't time to run the ferry and jaw with tourists, but he likes to do these things. Reality doesn't strike until he looks at Myrna, whose face is thin and tired from hours of packing, shifting, taking care of Tammy and worrying about where to put everything— then he resolves: *I got to take the bull by the horns and get these chores done.*

As he turns to take the ferry back to Windy's side, Myrna comes from the house, calling. She holds something up and he climbs the bank to meet her.

She gives him a paper bag full of chippings—little stones and pot shards.

'Honey, don't these belong to Shan?'

'Golly, I dunno, I guess they do.'

'Well, I don't think we're going to see her before we leave, do you?'

'I doubt it. What'll we do with them meanwhile?'

'Why not give them to Buck and let him keep them for her. If he doesn't see her before he leaves, he can give them to Jason.'

'Okay, baby.' He smiles, kisses her lips with lingering tenderness and, rubbing her tummy softly with the back of his hand, adds, 'I mean my *two* babies. Go feed that new boy, woman. It's nigh onto noon.'

Bradley's thoughts are in reverse, as is Annabell, backing across to the left bank. He thinks of other days, recalling the change in people when their environment is altered, and here considers himself—the apprehension he feels bordering on terror when forced to move to a another station. There have been three since his acceptance by the USGS. Each time it has taken almost half a year to inter his trauma and live with ease in the new surroundings. One would think he'd have no qualms since there are relatively few people at these stations, but it isn't the people he finds disturbing, it's the place. First he must meet it, then understand it. From understanding comes compassion, following that, respect. On the heels of respect, trust—and in the wake of trust, behold...! Love. As with Shan, this last step is his undoing. He becomes a prisoner of love—of the canyons, of the side streams, of the river whose mood, weight, speed and density he measures. Meet-understand-empathize-respect-trust-love.

Isn't there a weak link in this chain?

Can ever a love be trusted?

᷾᷾᷾

The gigantic old willow that for one hundred and twenty years has draped its slender leaves over the banks of Stillwater Canyon now crashes violently through the angry red turmoil of Dark Canyon rapid and swirls momentarily in a whirlpool below, its branches holding to the eddy. But the old trunk, finally liberated, wishes to go on. One hundred twenty years a sentinel... watching, wondering, wanting to go where the river took the men who'd carved their names in her trunk when she was younger. So... struck by lightning in last winter's storm, she'd leaned toward the water, dipped her branches in and waited for the tug of spring flood-tide.

Through the millrace of Cataract she's come, banged and scarred, minus two of her larger limbs, but with her huge trunk still intact. She whirls out of the eddy into Narrow Canyon and toward the Glen.

The water smoothes.

Bobbing along in mainstream, she makes a ridiculous silhouette against the sunny side of the canyon. From the bank she is a horse floating on her back, four feet pawing the air, neck arched, rocking playfully from side to side... her twisted branches concealed below the surface. Look! She's been resurrected as a kelpie in the river's flow... rejoicing with new life and motion in her second world.

There is a clang! A rumbling of many drums beneath the water.

The gay kelpie's ride is halted midstream and water rushes over her upturned belly... surging... pushing... submerging her as the drums roll on.

A patch of faded orange leaps upon the old tree's trunk as she flops and splashes in the roiling waters under the drums. She bellies up again. The drums stop. She emerges.

Victory!

But don't you notice something there, Kelpie? Is there not the faintest struggle when you slide beneath the ferry? Does he not give call for help or cry for life as he's caught and held by the strap of that faded jacket beneath your prancing willow hooves? Will you alone know his thoughts as water enters his breathing?

Oh, Myrna…

Oh, my baby…

രൗඔ

CHAPTER 13

August, 1964 — Dandy Crossing

Fred Bennett hears the throttle cut back on Buck's supply boat. The prop idles, cavitates, then churns forward, pushing its way through a thicket of half-submerged willow and eddying driftwood at the reservoir's edge. Sun on the aluminum sends signals flashing through the growth.

He walks down the road to where his cabin used to be and stands on all that remains: the front porch—now acting as a boat ramp.

It is early afternoon. He waits, arms folded, watching an open sego lily drown in the lapping tide. Between the gunning of the motor and banging of drift against the chine, he hears the steady punctuation of Buck's swearing. After several minutes the prow wedges through the willows and comes to dock. Buck throws him the rope and cuts the switch. Fred looks toward the back of the boat where a canvas had been folded with a coil of rope on top. It is gone. 'You found him,' he says, almost in a sigh.

Buck nods, looking at his hands. 'Yeah, and I wish I hadn't.'

'Where was he?'

'His life jacket was caught on a half-submerged tree that he probably tried to stave off, thinking it was smaller. Must have slipped. Got dragged under when it rolled.'

'Christ almighty!'

'Nothing much left of him. We put him in the government truck and they're taking him to Blanding. I told Myrna after they left—no need for her to see him that way.'

'Christ, no!'

They step over the foundations of the cabin, hands in their pockets, heads down, and automatically turn up the old path to Buck's shanty.

'Water'll be up to the road in a couple more days,' Bennett says. 'Come up faster'n anybody reckoned—sure you don't want me to stay and help you get the rest of your stuff loaded?'

'Naw, she's all done, the heavy stuff—Jeep's at Fry already. Thanks anyway. Windy helped me load the Servel last night. All that's left is a bunch of books, maps, Indian junk and clothes— be finished by tonight. In a way I'm glad we found Bradley, now I can clear the hell outta here fast. Too bad those goddamn BuRec idiots couldn't'uv spent more of their precious time on the search.'

'Yeah, since it's probably their fault anyhow. You know, I'll bet he'd still be around if it wasn't fer this fuckin' puddle. The river's velocity would carry a log, or even a tree, right on past the ferry.'

'We'll never know. I wouldn't'uv found him at all if I hadn't seen his shirt. It ballooned to the surface.'

'Did you tell Myrna about the jacket?'

'Windy will.'

'Yeah. Has she calmed down any?'

'Not so's you can notice it.'

'I think Jason's coming after her and Tammy tomorrow to take them to Blanding.' Fred's voice is tinged with weary sadness, thinking how Shan is going to take the news about Bradley, and when she hears about the jacket, oh, lordy! 'Best get Myrna out of here b'fore she jumps off a cliff.'

'Damn right. She's gonna lose that baby if she doesn't quit carrying on like she is.' Buck shakes his head and runs an index finger back and forth beneath his nose.

'I don't think she cares,' says Fred, kicking aside a small rock.

'She will later.'

'Jesus, Buck, I never heard *you* talk like that—you sound like a father.'

'Who says I ain't?'

'Nobody says you ain't, but nobody ever said ya was neither... 'specially you.'

Buck's eyes glint as he grins at his friend. 'Shucks, I prob'ly got sixteen little buttons runnin' round various and sundry Mexican villages who'd call me 'Papa' if I ever went back t'find out.'

But Bennett is not deceived. The statement is too unguarded, too unlike any heard before, and he knows there's more back of it than mere joking. He also knows that's all Buck is going to say about it.

They reach the road and Fred stops. The moment has come that they can well do without. They've never had to speak of their friendship—weeks can pass without them seeing one another—but when they come home there's more to asking, *Is Fred down at the house?* or, *Buck back from the mine?* than just wanting to know the answer. Bennett came to White Canyon thirty years ago, Buck fifteen, and they were rolled from the same dough. Though Bennett is married and twenty years older with kids and grandkids, he's still a loner like Buck. Neither knows a whole lot of the other's past... yet they know it all. They've fished together, mined and ousted claim jumpers together, gotten drunk, argued philosophy, politics and religion together, and fought the dam and the Wreck-the-Nation Bureau. The last count they lost. Bennett knew all along they would—he was once a state congressman—but Buck had convinced himself he couldn't lose... again. In Buck, Bennett sees himself reflected in a youthful mirror—in Bennett, Buck sees the calm waters of acceptance and wishes he could be like that instead of churned up over the way things are. 'Well, old Mucker, if there's nothing I can do, Helen and me will be gettin' on to Dove Creek.' Then Fred allows himself one feeler. 'D'ya know where you'll be goin'?'

'Yup. Goin' up to my claim on the Green. I'll dig around till I find something.... Stay if I do, if not, probably come back and work at the Hideout.'

'Mind if I come see you sometime?'

'Hell no, Fred, be glad to have you, you know that. B'sides you might need a place to hide now'n then from all the women in your family.... And anytime you want to help me work that claim, you know half of it is yours.'

They shake hands—both wondering if there isn't something earth-shaking they should say at this ending of an era. In lieu,

Buck says: 'You know the Park Service nearly lost a diver when they were looking for Brad this morning.' He looks down, toeing the dirt, pondering some mystery.

'You don't say? How? Dumb luck?'

'Typical of their blunderin' ways, they're looking for him down around Tickaboo. One of the three doesn't come up at the appointed time 'n place and they know his tanks are gettin' low.'

Fred removes his hat, wipes his forehead on a shirtsleeve. 'Why in hell were they so far downstream—they got some imbecilic idea this is still a *river*?' As he looks up, Buck's brows knit in puzzlement.

'Funny thing… maybe it is. The diver comes up about *four miles* down canyon, no air left at all—says he was caught in a current on the bottom so strong he couldn't pull out.'—storyteller's pause, thumbs hooked in pockets—'What d'you make of that?'

A low whistle from Fred and a barely audible, 'I'll be damned!'

'And maybe the river won't!' concludes Buck with a sardonic grin.

Fred throws back his head and laughs, Adam's apple bouncing like a golf ball. 'Jesus Christ! Wouldn't that be something… if…. Ah, well, does my ol' soul good to know it takes more'n a goddamn hunk of cement to kill this ol' devil.'

Buck's eyes twinkle with delight. 'That little bit of information could reactivate my belief in the super-unnatural.'

Sharing their faith in the river's secret has made the parting easier. Fred replaces his hat and offers, 'If you need lumber for your sluices—the Bureau stacked the boards from my shack over by the slag heap—help yourself, it's theirs now…. Windy says they're planning to build a tool shed with it.'

Buck squints toward the water, saying with quiet emphasis, 'I don't think they'll build a tool shed, Fred.'

Bennett feels the impulsiveness of his youth feeding back to him, sees in Buck's rippling chest muscles and the clenched fists inside his pockets the excitement of anticipation. His smile makes a full crescent beneath his hawkish nose. 'Good luck to you, Buck. Whatever the hell it's gonna be, I'll bet it's a gut-buster!'

'So long, Fred.'

Buck turns and heads up the dusty road to his cabin.

At the inside it could be forty-eight hours before the river, at its present flow, reaches the road—at the outside, maybe sixty. He has already bought and loaded Windy's old house trailer with the more important things, put *Rintintin* on top and taken it back to the store, where he'll hook on his fishing boat. The Bureau has paid for his intact house, and through some arrangement he doesn't care to fathom, will move it from its foundations to the newly located Hite Marina upstream.

What's to be done he must do tonight. He runs up the road.

Bounding over the ripple-rock steps on his front stoop, he leaps for the deer antlers above the door, brings them down with his hundred and eighty pounds and takes them inside. The cabin is empty but for a rickety bench and table, several orange crates of books and magazines, a dresser full of clothes and a section of the glass-front bookcases with his Indian relics.

He begins throwing it all, papers, maps, old letters, into cartons, whistling softly. As he transfers a sheaf of papers from the scarred old table to the boxes a letter scoots across the floor and sticks in a crack of the linoleum. Fifteen minutes later, after all the boxes are packed, he notices it.

Typed. Return address: Shanna Farran, Lincoln Park West Hotel, Chicago, Ill. Postmark: Nov. 23, 1962.

'I thought I threw all these away,' he says aloud, turning around, surprised to hear his voice echo where it never did before. 'Goddammit,' he mutters, starting to tear it in half, then realizing he wants to leave no shred of evidence, reaches for a match—at the same time feeling something inside the envelope besides the paper. He tips it on end letting a strong silver chain, dark with oxidation, slide into his hand. Poking it in his pocket he unfolds the letter and reads:

Dear Buckle...

I barely made it in time for my first concert at Lake Forest. Got caught in a blizzard outside Valentine, Neb. The Bird spun around twice in the middle of the highway and I thought I'd run my last rapid for sure. I'd give everything I own to be at Dandy Crossing instead of this miserable, cold, slushy place. It's supposed to be Thanksgiving. The only thing I give thanks for is that a hangin' don't last forever. God love ya for sending me the Piñon gum! Every time I chew it I think of you and that gorgeous place full of sun. You can bet I've been wearing something besides my socks in this deep freeze. You didn't say if Fred or Leo was going Moki hunting with you this spring, but even if one of them does, I hope we can go upstream and spend a few days in Dark Canyon—I sure ain't about to go down-river, or whatever it's called now—might get there in time to see the redbuds blooming. Buck, every time you mention Baja, I think what a good idea it would be to see those lovely, lonely beaches before the Nation-Wreckers get there and dam up the ocean, which seems like a project befitting their mentality. Just let me know how serious you are. I'll order the maps and arrange my schedule. We can try for our M.A. degrees! By the way, Cowboy, it's time you changed that string around your neck you hang your rock-hound glass and compass on. I hope you're not so full of meanness this new one turns your neck black. Merry Christmas! Happy (belated) Birthday!

OOdles, Shan Lu

'Damn women!' He stuffs the letter in his pocket, thinking bitterly, *I don't care who they are, always got a noose out somewhere.* He squints narrowly, congratulating himself on the fact that he's hasn't written to her for several months or seen her since the Hideout. It was after Wolverton that he made up his mind what to do about Shan.

"Nuffa that crap, I got work t'do.'

He goes out under the clothesline to the privy and opens the door. American Heritage Smell Number Two permeates the dark interior. Out of habit he dumps a can of lye from the bucket into the hole and steps up on the seat. From an overhead shelf he takes a box the size of a salmon crate and carries it back to the house. Removing a loose piece of linoleum from the floor, he opens a trap door that allows access to the plumbing beneath his sink and takes from the sawdust-packed crate three sticks of dynamite. With the experienced hands and deft movements of a man who has spent a good part of his life setting charges, he makes a hole in the end of one stick with his knife, takes a string from his hip pocket and ties all three together. He inserts a short fuse into an explosive cap and the cap into the stick of dynamite, then goes to his truck for a long timer fuse to attach to the short one.

So intent is he upon this operation, rummaging under the seat of the truck, he fails to hear the squeal of Windy's brakes in the dry wash. Before he gets the timer fuse out of the truck, Windy charges over the rise and skids to a halt in his personal dust-storm. 'Balls!' he growls.

His front door is open, the dynamite exposed on the floor. Before Windy can dismount he tosses the timer back in the cab, goes to him and stands beside the cab door.

'Hey,' squawks Windy, 'I got a little surprise for ya that's gonna make ya turn up the corners of yer mouth an' smile with delight and pleasure.'

'What happened? One of the Bureau guys drowned?'

'Naw, better'n that—fer you anyway. Here's a letter for ya from Shan.' He eyes it lasciviously as he hands it over.

Buck is about to say, *'Send it back to the return address,'* savvys it would just be bait and cools it. 'Thanks. I could've picked it up on the way out.'

'Thought ya might need some help. Bennett left while ago fer Dove Creek, says yer pullin' out t'night.'

'I'd better, don't you think? Water'll be up here in about forty-eight hours.'

'Yup, guess it will. I took Bennett on what I wish could be the last trip across on the Ferry—that goddamn driftwood's gettin' too much to handle.'

'What about Jason? He's coming down in the morning for Myrna, Tammy and all their stuff, so you'll have to bring them over.'

'I will. Left it over t' their side and come back in the outboard. Once I get that sum-bitch back here I ain't makin' no more trips till summa that crap sinks—or you'll be lookin' fer *me* like we was fer Brad an' I...'

'Hey, Windy, want to do something for me?' Buck pulls the runaway mouth to a halt.

'Yeah, sure, that's what I come fer.'

'I need that pipe wrench of yours; guess mine's already at Fry. I want to get those plumbing joints off under my kitchen sink.'

'I got two sizes. Lemme see the fittin's so I can tell which one ya need.' He starts to get out of the truck, but Buck stands fast against the door. 'Need them both—the sooner the quicker. I'm all done with everything else... almost.'

'Okay, I'll go git'um.' He starts the truck. 'Ya wanna eat supper with me? 'Ya got no place t' cook no more an' my bottle gas is still hooked up to my house trailer.'

'Sorry, but I said I'd meet a couple guys at Fry Canyon tonight—told 'um I'd be there by dark. By the time I get those fittings off, check my fish lines and get the boat on the trailer, I'm gonna be later'n a castrated man to his own wedding.'

'Awright,' says a disappointed Windy. 'I'll be back in a few minutes.' He spins up more dust, backs to the end of the fence and turns around.

Jesus! That guy is a fuckin' genius for picking the wrong time to show! He runs a hand through his brush-cut, takes the timer from his truck seat and goes inside. Laying the dynamite and long coiled fuse under the floorboards, he closes the trap door, replaces the linoleum and walks to his fishing boat.

If I'm not here when he comes he'll go back to the store. If I am he'll sit around and jaw for another half hour.

Buck doesn't actually care about the fish lines, especially now, having to work up to them through the drift, but he unties and starts upstream. Hugging the bank, he threads his way to the end of the old river where there is a marked velocity to push against. He noses through tail waves into the turbulence of North Wash riffle and finds his thoughts to be no quieter than the water—difference is he can *read* the water. He doesn't go *fishin'*, he snags fish. Doesn't go for the reasons most folks do either, doesn't revel in deep thought, read, snooze or write, so why fish? If you asked he might say he fishes after a boyhood habit on the Missouri, but that's not quite right. He doesn't even like to eat fish much of the time—a steak man. What he snags he mostly gives away or stuffs in the freezing compartment of his Servel until nothing else will go in, then he takes them to Windy to sell to the tourists who don't know how to catch catfish.

He has about four lines in the eddies where large channel cat lurk and if he doesn't look to them twice a day he'll find a big one hooked to his line half eaten by another. He recalls Shan asking him once why he bothered chugging those few miles upstream for what looked like bait. His reflex answer was probably the closest he came to revealing his reasons, plus something of himself.

'I like t' see the pore fish dangling from the end of my line as a gentle reminder never to let it happen to *me*.'

She had fixed smiling green eyes on him, and said, 'You mean a *second* time,' then said no more.

After that he began to feel less at ease around her. He had the feeling she knew what she didn't know, couldn't guess and wasn't about to find out.

'Whoa! Goddammit, look out!' The current has forced the nose into an explosion wave that turns it to starboard, then clear around, heading downstream. *That's what I get for not minding what I'm doing. I need to get my thinker tangled up with her right now like I need Windy for my brother!* He goes for an eddy and starts fighting back upstream, as well as fighting back his thoughts.

Buck is a true loner in spite of the time he spends in the company of other people. When he's with his fellow miners, lounging around the store, watching the tourists, talking to Windy, he still feels basically alone. Lost in reflection, he neither hears them nor answers most of the time. A few, yes—Bennett, Jason, Leo... and Brad Nelson, when he was alive—shared one common interest, or common love, the river, and somehow Shan slips into that niche.

He gathers in the lines, damning the whole illogical pattern that's taking away his hermitage at age forty-eight, making him change his whole approach to life. Privacy is what keeps the balance, privacy and what a man is used to. He can take ten days at the mine so long as he has the next five or ten on the river or in the sanctity of his cabin, alone or with companions of his choosing. This uprooting. It's happened before—reclaimed land taken from him after ten years labor—the cabin he built for his mother to spend the rest of her days in. The Bureau decided to put in a storage dam there; *they* determined what to pay him and when he was to get out; *they* traded him a hunk of land a two-toed sloth would sniff at.... *Makes a fella wonder why he comes to a place it all might happen again. Because I'm a rotten gambler, that's why.... And after looking around I discover there's not a fifty-mile stretch on any river in the U.S. that the BuRec or the turdacious Army Corps of Engineers hasn't located a mess of dam sites, where they won't someday plunk a dam.*

Had Buck been a violent man he long ago would have shot some employee of those government branches. When he came to Dandy, Windy fanned a rumor that he'd done just that. How close he came, no one knows. Beneath the calm voice and slow easy movements seethes an unsuspected rage—rage at power systems beyond the control of a society that fostered them to serve, but now enslave. Whoever makes a living in this system is no friend of Buck's—the evidence is nailed to his front door:

> NOTICE: ANYONE WITH THE BU REC WHO HAS
> ANYTHING TO SAY TO ME, WRITE IT.
> I DON'T WANT ANY OF YOU ON MY LAND UNTIL
> THE DAY AFTER I LEAVE.
>
> Buck Watson, legal owner.

On the end of one line is an unmolested seven-pound big-whiskered cat, which he guts, throws in the boat, then turns downstream. When he reaches his small cove, he ties up and looks at his watch. Three o'clock.

As he surmised, Windy is gone from the cabin.

Two pipe wrenches lie on the stoop with a couple of cans of cold beer. Buck sucks in the corners of his mouth, shakes his head and mutters, 'That poor lonesome polecat... tries so hard.... He should live in the city.'

His next move is to take truck and trailer to Bennett's landing, then run back up the airstrip to the fishing boat and bring it down to the landing. Maneuvering the boat around Bennett's old foundations is a frustrating process, but he manages to winch it onto the trailer and drive back to the cabin. There, he fills both truck and boat with the crates and cartons already packed, along with his tools, deer antlers and fishing gear. With a boat trailer behind the house trailer it'll make a long rig, but he only has fifteen miles to go over a road he can drive blindfolded. Last are the two outboard motors. When he hoists the bigger one into the boat, the twinge he feels near his collarbone reminds him of the mine accident—it healed nicely, but always tells him when it's overworked.

It is near five, and the sun has crawled behind the cliffs when, sweaty and winded, he remembers Windy's beers. As he pulls out his bandana, the letter Windy brought him drops to the ground.

He picks it up with the beers and goes inside, stepping over the pipe wrenches. Opening one with a church key still hanging beside the drain board, he takes a big swig and stands contemplating the empty room.

'You were a pretty damn good shack for an old river rat,' he says to it. He downs another swallow, spilling some and wiping the dribble with the back of his hand. 'Wait till they see you tomorrow! Hah!' His laugh rings through the emptiness and settles bluntly on the silence. He chug-a-lugs the beer, opens the second and peers at Shan's letter. Postmark: Detroit, Michigan. 'That's good. She's a long way off.' He leans back against the sink, tears off the end and reads:

Dear Buck...

By now it's kinda obvious I'm not going to hear from you. After six letters with no answer I can take a hint— only I can't figure why? What did I do to make you mad?—talk too much? Say the wrong thing? Well, whatever it is, Buck, I'm sure sorry. I've missed your letters keeping me in touch with Dandy, and find myself wondering where you're going and how you'll make out... You told me once you might go to your claim up on the Green. Guess you don't care, but my plans are indefinite. I hate to face coming out there to find all of you gone—yes, even Windy—and since I've heard nothing about you taking me in *Rintintin* I'd best figure out some other way to see what's left of our river. Some kind of fate has pushed me in that direction—I fell heir to a 16-ft. ski boat! I've named it *screwdriver*—with a space after the *d* and capitalizing the *R*—*Screwd River* (heh-heh). I left it with Jason to store at Hoxie Crossing until I can get an outboard for it. Should you change your mind about companionship, please let me know. Funny thing. I found a pair of your socks in my duffle. I would've sent them back but sorta had the feeling you wouldn't need them anymore.

So long, Cowboy. Stay well.

OOdles, Shan Lu

P.S. I see the Indians are still looking for him.

He turns the paper over. Pasted on the back is a color photo of a road sign:

WATCH FOR FALLING ROCK.

The room darkens and swims in blue-green light. Buck shivers. In and out of windows come huge grey catfish, mouths *awp-awping* as they swim in the drowned stillness of the cabin... turning... twisting to the ceiling, down to the dark floor with sporadic bursts of speed... whiskers raking the wall boards. Nelson's pale body wafts into the cool green depths, carried gently in the arms of a mermaid with streaming yellow hair... Shan. He seems merely asleep and she's come to lay him on the couch until he wakes.... Only the couch is gone. On his face is a smile and in her eyes are pools welling to spillways that he has seen once or twice before....

'Shan Lu,' he cries, 'I'm not mad at you, but our place is dead... DEAD...! And there's nowhere for us to go! We don't belong in this century. It isn't our world anymore. It's been invaded by greedy bastards who want to turn every inch of it into a dollar... and to the slobs who let them. Our kind of people are gone! I once had a crazy idea... wanted to build another room on this cabin and move you into it—take you out of those lousy gin mills where guys are always trying to get you in the sack. I wanted you to come here and explore the canyons, write, play, hike, run the river, sing, any goddamn thing you pleased—wanted to live here the rest of my days with someone who'd stand and fight for their beliefs. Hell, people don't believe in anything anymore, let alone move for it—bunch of wishy-washy weasels. Chicken-shits...! The whole fuckin' lot... liars and cheats and cowards! SHEEP! Go anywhere so long as they don't have to do anything for themselves. They come pushing the system ahead of them like a steamroller, smashing everything in sight, us runnin' ahead trying to stay out of the way. Well, I ain't gonna be like 'em! And this time I'm taking with me what's mine.'

He spins away from the drain board, slinging his half-empty can to the far side of the room, shattering the watery image and the windowpane.

The cry of a wounded animal accompanies the sound of falling glass. It's a moment before he realizes the cry has come from him. He kneels, takes the other letter from his pocket, wads them together... strikes a match... watches them burn.

'You ain't ready, Shan Lu. They don't have you against the wall yet—anyhow you *think* they don't. One of these days maybe you'll be ready, but I'd go off my rocker waiting and hoping for that. I almost asked you once, before I remembered we live in different worlds. This is only your part-time world. I'll be an old man before you give up all that applause for the care and keeping of just one guy.'

He stands, scattering the ashes with his sneakers.

The after-sundown bluish light settling in the canyon makes him aware that he hasn't much time to get his fuse strung. He opens the trap, carefully lifts the charges and attaches the timer. As shadows deepen he uncoils it across the kitchen and the back porch, out the screen door and into the yard, cutting it off at what he knows will be near three hours.

While he works he's vaguely aware of something missing. A sound, that's it. There's no river sound. Only the *lap-lap-lap* of dead water pushing and sucking at driftwood in his cove. Furtively it seeps into the red Moenkopi, staining it a deeper red, its advance revealed by a ring of leached-out salts.

From the seat of his truck he takes a .44 Magnum Smith & Wesson revolver. He un-holsters it, walks to his shower tank and shoots five holes, watching with satisfaction as water squirts rakishly in all directions. The last bullet he fires at the end of the fuse.

It lights.

He bounds into the truck and drives down the road without looking back. When he reaches Fred's stack of lumber he pulls a bit past it and stops, goes to the boat, removes a can and pours gas on both ends of the pile.

He strikes a match on his jeans and tosses it. *Fwoomp!* Flames reach for the sky, followed by a curl of black smoke. Gas can replaced, he drives to Windy's store.

Windy comes to the door gnawing a chicken leg. 'Hey, I heard some shots up the canyon. That you?'

'Nope, that was Buffalo Bill.'

'What the hell was ya doin'?'

'Shot a few holes in my water tank.'

'Ho ho! You mean the *Bureau's* water tank.' He slaps his leg with such glee the chicken leg drops in the dirt.

'No, mine, tonight... theirs tomorrow. You want to help me get the house trailer hooked to my truck? I'll put the boat back of it—she'll ride okay to Fry Canyon. Here's your wrenches, and thanks for the beer, Windy... it came in handy.' In the boat he has what he hopes will keep Windy busy for a while and stave off his curiosity. 'How about a nice cat?' he says, handing him the fish.

'Sure thing. Wow, he's a big sum'bitch, ain't he...? Almost like the one in m' pond. Figured I'd give poor fish a break, just leave 'um there, let him swim out when the lake comes up.'

'Reservoir.'

'Yeah, Utah's Piss-pot, like Shan calls it... sum-thin' like that.'

As they work, hitching-unhitching, assembling the rig, Windy babbles on. What he most wants to know is where Buck's going, and if possible what Shan said in her letter. To the first question Buck answers, 'Up on the Green, where I've got a half-assed claim.' To the second, 'I ain't had time to open it yet.'

Buck knows something he hasn't told anybody: there's no ore rich enough on that claim to pay for the work of mining it. But instinct tells him he needs that interval of quiet to prepare for living again with people in a community where his next neighbor is twenty yards away. Eventually, he'll come back and work at the Hideout... unless he decides to go to Mexico.

The canyon blue has turned deep purple when he holds out a goodbye hand to Windy, climbs in his truck and drives out of Farley Canyon.

A woebegone Windy stands in the road, head inclined to one side, watching him weave out of sight. When Jason comes for Myrna and Tammy tomorrow, that's the last of the Dandy Crossing residents—only Windy will be left to run the ferry until the North Wash road goes under. He didn't get the concession for the Hite Marina after all—instead, bought a piece of land on the highway near the Happy Jack where he plans to build a store and gas station that'll catch the miners and tourists going to and from the reservoir.

In the dusk, as the wind changes he smells something, looks down Farley and sees an odd red glow fanning the walls.

'Sum'bitch! What's that?'

For a second he stands scratching his head, then leaps in his truck, splashes through the creek and zooms down the road.

Coming closer he sees sparks rising into the air and smoke blowing downwind. When he gets to the woodpile he's grinning from ear to ear.

'Good thing them Bureau-rats is up t' Blanding 'er they'd be over here with little buckets of water tryin' t' put it out.'

He's about to turn the wheel and go back when an impulse jars him—not one of curiosity or meddlesomeness, but of sentiment. He has an urge to look just once more at Buck's cabin before they take it away. Windy's not able to put words to this feeling, but he's caught up in nostalgia for the good times there, and more importantly, for the serious times.

Never talked serious with nobody but Buck, 'cause he'd listen. When I brought muh new bride to Dandy everybody kidded me and made cracks about how I'd wear 'er out in two weeks screwing her to death—oh, I remember awright—fellas at the mill called me Horny-toad. But Buck was real nice to both of us. And when she left me two years later, because she couldn't stand the isolation, I 'member sum-thin' else.... After she done went, I spent the first nights at Buck's place, sleeping outside under the cottonwoods so's I wouldn't feel so bad bein' alone in the bed we'd shared.

Yup. I wanna go have a last look at the place. Buck I'll see again, but not that cabin by the river.

He bumps over the road, noting each rock, curve and sandy spot with the tenderness of a child. He knows the noise of his brakes is a kind of warning signal that he's coming, that's why he's never had them fixed. He likes to be with friends and talk. Also wants to give some warning—that way they treat him better. Windy is more sensitive than he's given credit for, but his curiosity he just can't smother.

This time when they squeal in the wash he's sadly aware there's no one to hear, but he humps the rise and slams to a skidding halt in the yard his same old way. Turning out the lights he sits listening to the sounds of the night. All quiet but the *slurping* reservoir and a breeze *shuffling* the cottonwood leaves. An almost-full moon clears the rim, an opal jewel that lights up his sad and lonesome world.

As he steps from the truck he hears water running. Walking around back he spies the tank's new fountains pissing the ground, catching moonlight like the whiskers of some big cat. He shakes his head.

'That was the best goddamn shower at the Crossing.' He sniffs the air and wrinkles his nose, smelling something unusual. Glancing at the outhouse, he notes the open door, and mutters, 'Nope, that's not it.'

Around front again he steps into the cabin… stops… stands looking at the empty room, painting his own pictures of how it used to be. Moonlight beams through the window, casting a brilliance on the linoleum that is reflected back to the ceiling. He notices the glass is shattered. The plastic curtain makes a light scraping noise as it brushes the sill in the night breeze.

'Hmmm, wonder how he did that? Prolly smacked it with a table leg 'er somethin'.'

Windy's nose wrinkles once again in response to the familiar but misplaced odor. He walks to the screened porch where half the floor is bathed in fluorescence and spots a rope-like thing snaking across and out the door… where a tiny blue flame moves slowly along it.

For a moment he's completely nonplussed. The sight doesn't connect with the image he has floating before him—Buck's big double bed and Shan's blond head poking out the covers, then…

'Yipes!' He leaps in the air falling backward against the doorjamb.

Out the door he goes at a dead run, skids to a halt and spins into a squaw-berry bush. Recovers. 'Whoa!' Recalling the length of the fuse as it crossed the porch, he cautiously returns to check the speed of its burning. He hasn't lived around mines most of his life not to know what Buck has done. Following the timer into the kitchen where it disappears, he opens the trap door and peers into the darkness. Dimly, he can see three sticks of dynamite tied together. He closes the trap and moves again to the porch.

"Bout an hour I make out… Buck, y'ol sumbitch, *good fer you!* Wisht I'da knowed this, I'da *helped* ya!'

Like a man putting dreams away, he shuts the front door gently, and stands a minute smiling. A stronger breeze has risen and the cottonwoods are chortling. Again the odor of the outhouse wafts around the corner.

'Wonder why he didn't do nothin' to the ol' privy? Thought the blast'd take care of it, prolly. Well… just in case it don't…'

He runs for the truck, boots the starter, skids around the corner of the cabin, through the clothesline and up to the one-holer.

'Eee-hah! Here I come, dam builders of the world! You bulldozers of bat-shit, you ain't got nuthin' on me! There!'

He slams his grill-bar into the side of the privy and bowls it half off its foundations—backs up and gives it another go from the front.

'There! You fuckers of mothers! You rapers of rivers!' The boards rip, splinter and fall in a heap around the hole and into it—one jagged two-by-four protrudes from the seat.

'There, you cock-suckers! Go crap in your hardhats and pull 'um down over your deaf ears!'

Another cowboy yell rends the air, echoing up and down the grave of Glen Canyon as Windy prongs through the barbwire fence and slues down the road.

CHAPTER 14

September, 1964 — Green River

Buck sits up in bed reaching for his .44.

All still… no wind… moonless dark. He has no idea of the time. Silently, he swings his legs off the bunk, sticks feet in sneakers and rises. *If it's that damn bear, this is his last go-round. If it's some sonofabitch snoopin' my claim, I'll take care of that too.*

The sound that woke him, the soft crunching of gravel underfoot, comes again. He slowly pushes the curtain aside with the muzzle of the gun and peers into nothing.

'Blacker'n the inside of a cow,' he mutters.

Someone calls his name—the voice makes his stomach contract—then silence again, except for a very loud *thumping* inside his chest. 'Jesus Christ, I better take a trip t'town. I'm gettin' jumpier than a chute full of shoats.' He turns toward the door, still not believing his name was called, believing less the voice that called it. 'How in the hell could…'

The gravel crunches again—this time around the opposite side of the trailer. Once more the voice calls softly, questioning, as if the caller isn't sure this is the right place. 'Buck?'—then louder, in a near desperate tone—'Buck, are you there?'

His first impulse after realizing he's fully awake is to crawl back in bed and not answer. If the caller decides to come in uninvited he can say he was asleep. But the note of desperation hits him in the gut again, so he grabs for his flashlight and opens the door, stepping on the linoleum blister, making it wheeze like always.

The strong beam reveals nothing but the swirling patterns on the surface of the Green River.

'Who's there?' he calls abruptly, though he damned sure knows.

'Oh, Buck, it's Shan,' comes the relieved answer. A beam of light shoots crossways from the corner of the trailer to illuminate him in his jockey shorts and sneakers. He swings his light and for an instant they blind and reveal each other, frozen. Shan turns off her flash and comes to the stoop uttering a relieved sigh.

'God, I'm glad it's you. I wasn't sure this was the right place even after I found your Jeep, it's so damned dark. That's why I kept my flash off. I was afraid I might get a shot taken at me.'

'You just might, sneakin' up on a lone prospector at such an unsociable hour—good way t'get windows installed in your skull.'

'I know. That's why I kept calling. I thought if you weren't here, whoever was would know I was looking for you.'

'Come on, get inside—it's cool standin' here in my under-duds.'

The obvious irritation in his voice relaxes to polite indifference, studied and practiced. It is an impersonal tone that he intends to keep no matter where or when they are together. To her it doesn't sound rehearsed, only different. She blames it on the 'unsociable hour' and follows him inside, remembering other meetings in vivid contrast to the awkwardness of this moment—times of joyful excitement, a promise of adventure and a feeling that he awaited her coming. Why he hasn't answered her letters is beyond her, but she knows it won't be easy prying an answer out of him—he isn't the kind to float his emotions like oil on water, and if she were the kind to back off and let sleeping tigers lie, she wouldn't be here. She has neither talent nor patience for subtlety, but right now, she's scared… unsure of herself… baffled over the change in a friendship she cherishes.

He lights the Coleman and turns on the wall heater. While he puts on pants and a sweatshirt and begins making coffee, she explains, with difficulty because he's not making it easy for her, why this visit in the middle of the night.

'Buck, I'm sorry I had to wake you but I got the Bird stuck in one of the washes. I thought I could get it out with a shovel and letting some air out of the tires but nothing worked. I figured from the directions Fred gave me it wasn't too far to walk but it took longer than I thought.'

All he says is, 'Uh-huh.'

'Sorry,' she says again, hoping for some response—hypersensitive to a chill beyond the temperature of the fall night.

'S'all right. I get up every night about this time to see if the rain has rot the rhubarb.' His back is to her so his face doesn't help explain this new flatness in his tone—usually he'd set up his wry witticisms with a comic's instinct for a laugh. She watches the back of his neck intently. The crew cut is longer than she's ever seen it. *Bet he hasn't been to town for over a month.* She pulls a piece of Kleenex from her jeans and blows her nose.

'You got a cold?' he asks, not sounding really concerned.

'Just getting over one—don't worry,' she adds quickly, 'it's past the contagious stage. A few days in this wonderful sun and I'll knock it completely.'

'*A few days!*' He hears this in an echo chamber and thinks: *Got to find an excuse to get her out of here…. Didn't think she'd find where I was…. Should have warned Fred…. Why would she come when I didn't answer her letters? Damn women anyway!*

Turning from the coffee pot he sees her hovering by the stove, eyes dark with confusion, her face pale and tired, the furrow between her brows deeper and creases at the corners of her mouth that weren't there before. Though he can't say why, he notes with satisfaction that she's beginning to show her age.

He watches her scan the contents of the trailer and stop at the two bunk beds. Many nights they've slept close together on the ground beside a river or in a canyon, but that was then, and Buck knows he can't bed down in the same room with her now. He steps on the asthmatic spot in the floor as he walks toward the bunks to begin remaking the lower one where he was sleeping.

Shan manages a dispirited laugh when she hears the sound. 'Holy Moses, Buck, that sounds like the one…'

'It's Windy's old trailer, got swamped in the flood—gives off a wheeze when you step on the blister—hit it just right and it'll fart,' he states, as if she didn't know all about it.

The creases at the corners of her mouth turn up in a smile. 'I remember very well,' she states, moving closer to the heater and folding her arms, waiting to find out his plan.

He obliges. 'You can sleep here and I'll go outside on the cot. That upper bunk's fulla junk that's packed to go.'

Well, that part hasn't changed—he still exercises the hospitality that gives her the best bed, but the last of his statement jolts her.

'Packed?—are you moving out, Buck?'

'Yup. Was gonna leave about dawn.' He rubs his chin stubble, right proud of the quick thinking to get her out of here, and glad his truck is always half-packed anyhow. Truth is, he hadn't planned to leave until the end of the month.

'For Dandy Crossing?'

'There is no Dandy Crossing anymore. Ferry's at North Wash.'

There's a long, uncomfortable silence between them. Shan wants to shout: *But you can't leave now because I've come and botched up your plans!* She's aware she's not welcome, that he wishes she'd never come. She does too. She's miserable, frustrated, almost ready to cry, in need of sleep. Above everything else, she knows better than to give vent to her emotions until she can think clearly.

Dropping her head, looking at the floor, she says softly, 'I'm sorry, Buck. I wrote you several times that I wanted to come, and asked you to tell me if it wasn't all right. Guess you never got my letters.' Close to a whisper, she dares to add, 'I had to find out why you haven't answered me, and why you aren't my friend anymore.'

'Hell, I'm your friend. You're inside on this cool night aren't cha? An' there's a hot pot of coffee over there on the stove for you, before you bed down. What greater proof is there than a man giveth up his own bed for a friend?'

She smiles wanly. 'That's right, I appreciate it, really.' Looking over at the sink she's about to say...

...But he reads her and interjects, 'Sorry, can't offer you a sink dip or the shower outside—I already used the warm stuff in the tank.'

'It doesn't matter, Buck, I'm too tired anyhow,' she hedges, wishing with every cold bone she could sit in that sink full of warm water like she'd done in his cabin so many times before.

He throws some blankets on the bunk, gets a sleeping bag from a drawer underneath, walks to the door stepping over the blister, stops on the stoop and turns to her. 'I got to get up early 'cause I plan on takin' a bunch of stuff to Fry Canyon tomorrow. Soon's you wake up we'll get your Bird outta the sand.... G'night,' he says, and walks abruptly into the dark.

For a long time she stands beside the stove, hugging her elbows, her eyes full of tears. She turns off the coffee, sheds her clothes and wraps herself in one of Buck's motel towels, then pours a cup of brew and sits on the bunk, sipping slowly.

Damn! Why is he so set against me? What in hell have I done? The Wolverton trip?—impossible!—we had a great time. Maybe he has a girlfriend and I'm an embarrassment; that's the only thing making any sense.... But surely he'd tell me... wouldn't he?

Of course not.

True, he'd allowed her more of his personal thoughts than he had other women because her beliefs seem to parallel many of his own and she didn't ask a bunch of questions—questions plugged him up like rice in a radiator; but concerning his past life, and especially his present thoughts, she knows nothing. Their mutual regard hasn't grown out of the usual games men and women play— games that tend to widen the gap between the sexes and finally end in open warfare. Their games have been guessing games about how Nature formed this or that place, and what man will do to it to alter that formation in the future; Buck from a geologist and prospector's knowledge, Shan from a leave-it-alone point of view. It would be hard to understand why these two attracted each other at all if it weren't for their mutual love of the land and its many mysteries.

Before Buck had willfully widened the gap between them, he'd dropped a few unguarded phrases that she was smart enough not to ask more about, letting her imagination work on them instead. Now and again a tired brain will run with refreshed rivulets, and wind-whispers will stir up past thoughts and conversations that have escaped:

'...My Pa was a hard man to live with; not much give in him (past tense; he's probably dead)....' 'Mom makes the best blueberry pie in Missouri (loves her—might be a favorite son)....' 'When my sis left, the house grew a little sunshin' (a tyrant? a nag? gave him some kind of trouble?)....' 'Most women are a crafty bunch (one probably got to him along the way)....' 'I was seven when mom and I moved to Rushville (after his pa died maybe, and left him to care for his mother)....' 'Never wanted to kill a man until I ran into him (the Missouri fish and game warden Fred told me about?).'

The coffee has left a bitter taste; she goes to the sink, rinses out her mouth, splashes cold water over her face, turns off the wall heater and the Coleman, drops the towel to the floor and crawls between the blankets. Sighing heavily, she lies back, inviting sleep. The stove crackles as it cools. Water drops sporadically into a pan under the sink spigot. A coyote calls in the night—a lonesome sound she loves—but it fills her now with restless discontent.

'Wish I were a coyote,' she whispers. 'Even if your life is tough at times, it's not complicated, and you can always depend on others in the pack. No living thing is solitary... not even you, Buck Watson!'

She flops on her side.

The faucet drips.

She rises, feeling for her jacket, finds a plastic bottle in the pocket, takes a tranquilizer and inches her way to the sink—running water in her hand she gulps the pill, turns the faucet off, hard, and removes the pan. Fumbling her way back to the bunk she steps on the bulge—just right—it farts, making her jump.

'Jesus...! Just like you, Windy, to haunt this place.'

Lying down again she stares through the blackness vainly fighting for memory of another time when Buck may have spoken to her in this indifferent, semi-irritated voice. None comes. She's heard him use it with Windy, with an occasional tourist, never with her.

Shan hates to see her theory blown, yet is smart enough to know that every male isn't capable of the kind of kinship she has with Jason, Step and Leo. Yet, regarding Buck, she is totally blind. She is unwilling to concede that he may not be in total control where she's concerned—because she wants him to be different—unlike her two ex-husbands and other men she knows, or has known, who insist on displaying their manhood with jealous tantrums or sex marathons that ultimately bore her. This wish is strong enough to blind her to the fact that, in her case, he is still very much a man, and is finding it difficult to just be her friend.

But the Theory:

That men and women should be able to sustain relationships of respect and love without the pressure of having to prove their gender. Being a student of Jungian psychology has taught her ways to control her sexual cravings, making them work to her advantage, instead of pushing her where she doesn't want to go—toward men whose form of companionship is mainly between the sheets. But not everyone is tuned to the workings of the libido, men especially.

'Such crap—the dictates of a society,' she mutters, rolling over on her stomach. 'Can't sanction a man to be a woman's friend without insinuating lover—to have love, and not make it. I want friends and a lover who knows the value of those friends and allows the association to enrich rather than destroy him. Fat chance!'

The chance is indeed fat... but she's not willing to look at it yet. Nor does she sense the truth—that she wouldn't be here if her subconscious hadn't already implanted the notion that Buck might be that very one.

She rolls over, feels cold and draws up her knees. *I'm no closer to the answer now than I was a year ago.... Should have stayed away, but I thought if I could see him he'd loosen up.... Isn't going to give an inch... stubborn Scorpio.... Yeah, well so am I, by damn!* She shivers, pulling the covers up around her neck. *If I can get him to come with me in* Screwd River *on the reservoir, since Jason and Step won't... it's the only way I'll find out anything.... But if he's made up his mind not to go, I'm beat there too.... Still...*

Times past, the river acted as a hypnotist gently relaxing and lulling her to sleep, now her eyelids are on puppet strings, her body tense. In spite of that her head fuzzes. She whispers, 'Thanks, pill,' and turns over into a drugged and dreamless sleep at last.

No one stands over her in the morning with a steaming mug of coffee. No gentle jibes, no china blue eyes smiling into hers.

No Buck.

ðø⁂

Rintintin's chine drums against a rock. Buck pulls the rope aboard and starts its little outboard. As the nose moves around to the current he twists the throttle full on, slicing against the flow, toward the San Rafael. After gaining a steady speed he sits on the corner thwart of the square stern, steering with his foot... thinking:

She ain't kiddin' me with that stuff. They're all alike when it comes to getting something they want—that sad hangdog look, muttering instead of talking so you can hear. She used to always be bouncing around, laughing, goin' her own way, tending to her business. Jesus! She's been following me around all morning, hasn't stopped asking questions since she got up...! All the time we're diggin' her Bird outta the sand.... 'Are you towing the trailer behind the Jeep or the truck...?' 'Can I help you pack anything...?' 'Could you go down canyon with me for a few days?'

Help, hell! And I'm as like t'go with her on that fuckin' puddle as I am to give birth to a bouncing baby cobra. Damn! If the claim was on the other side of the river I'd send her out alone. As it is I'll have to herd her like a newborn calf. She had to be out of her mind coming here in that Bird—don't know how she got as far as she did!

The canoe makes a scraping sound on a sandbar as he cuts the motor, then floats to the bank and leaps out. He knots the rope around a boulder and walks upstream pushing back supple willow saplings that have turned a dusty yellow.

Ya know... I better let her think I'm goin' with her or she'll be here till next spring. The idea calls up a time when he'd have been more than happy with that arrangement. *Humph! A guy can't never be sure when he's gonna change his mind about a dame, or when she's gonna change it for him.* He pulls in three fish lines, finds them empty and begins winding them slowly around a two-by-four, talking to himself.

'Lessee, I'll take the truck and trailer to Fry with the canoe on top. Windy's runnin' the ferry from North Wash across to the new Hite. She's made it through the Wash before in that contraption, guess she can again. When we get to Fry, probably tomorrow evening, I'll make like I have to go to work at the Happy Jack... right away.... That way she's off my back!'

He looks at the sky for the weather report, notes a few thin cirrus bands trailing over the San Rafael Swell and decides it's not going to rain, at least not for another day or two. 'We can leave in a few hours, everything's aboard 'cept the canoe. She can sleep in the trailer where she did last night and I can use the bed of the truck or the ground.'

'Hot potatoes! That settles that! Tellin' her I'll go down the damn reservoir with her will make her move a little faster and wipe the gloomy look off of her. She blames her cold, but I think there's more to it. She's bitter about everything, hates her job and won't even play her guitar anymore.'

He pulls in one more line, finds a sturdy wiggling dinner on the end and elects to give it to Ernie at Hanksville when he stops for gas. He slams the head on a rock and goes back through the willows to the canoe.

The sweet aroma of damp, decaying leaves swirls up from the sun-warmed bank and assails him, stimulating a scene pushed deep in his memory...

Fall.... The canyon floors, soft with the mulch of many seasons, cushioning bare feet as they walk beneath the spectrum of turning leaves that give off an earthy perfume where they lodge in the crotch of a tree, splashing it with color.... Shan turning around, lifting her arms high to shield her eyes, looking up at a wild grape that twines the trunk of an oak in red glory, then grinning devilishly as he picks his tenderfoot way through the woods, saying: 'You Tarzan. Me Jane.' His answer: 'Hell, compared to me Tarzan wears a tux!'

Standing beside the canoe he shakes his head vigorously to shatter the scene, flings the fish angrily into the boat, and says aloud, 'I'll be hanged if I'm gonna go over that crap again!' But as he pushes out into the river he retracts—'No, by God, I *can* think about it now. All of it. I'm over the hump. It's not gonna bother me anymore.'

He can even go back to the Wolverton Mill trip when he first began to notice: ...the smell of her hair—smoky, silty or like soap.... When he began to compare Shan with fall.... Rushville and fall... red and yellow floating on the old Missou.... The cabin.... His mother raking and burning leaves.... Pamela and fall... Pam, with child, calling... calling his name as the rolling indifferent current swept her under then over the spillway of the dam.... Yellow and red leaves tangled in her auburn hair when he picked up her lifeless form.... More leaves on the green soft grass of their love-making place crunching beneath his step as he carried her home, with their unborn, in that Indian Summer.... Pam.... Shan.... Separated by so many seasons, so different in their ways.... Pam, who took with her everything that was love.... Then Shan, who made him wonder if there wasn't more as their friendship ripened; setting his mind adrift again.... Making love with Pam... Shan...? by a river on a bed of leaves in nature's setting... beneath no roof.

Yes, it was the Mill trip that made him decide he couldn't continue. Shan, after all, was *not* Pamela.

It is noon when he docks at the claim, carries the outboard to the truck and looks around for Shan.

A breeze sets the cottonwoods to *shushing* softly—counter to summer's *clacking*—loosing yellow leaves over the clearing as he crosses to the trailer door. Rounding the corner he sees her standing under the shower tank, and notes the rose-quartz bird-point he gave her dangling beneath her chin. Notes too, that her skin is pale, and her legs show slack muscle tone in the noonday sun. She doesn't see him until he makes a sound opening the door. She starts, drops the soap and grabs the towel to cover herself.

'Uh... oh... sorry... didn't know you were back.... I uh...' she stammers, glancing down.

His look has changed from cool indifference to a bemused clinical expression, appraising her, eyes flicking up and down her body like he might consider buying her for his harem. One corner of his mouth tilts up in a cynical smile—then he goes inside closing the door after him.

She stands shivering in the breeze, mistily seeing his look superimposed against the reddish boards beneath her feet. A double image of the fallen soap stares back. Hope curdles in her stomach.

'Oh God, why don't I go! Why do I have to wait for the stabbing!'

She turns off the water and dries herself listlessly; puts on clean panties and struggles into dirty jeans, all the while trying to understand her strange startled reaction to Buck's presence. Was her reaction the cause of his look, or his look the cause of her reaction?

Why on earth should she feel embarrassed in front of Buck?

He looked at me like some of those drooling creeps in the clubs. My God, at this point I'd even be glad if he tried to rape me! Anything would be better than this!

She walks slowly into the trailer.

They eat a quick lunch, rinse the dishes and secure cupboards and drawers.

With the two of them walking back and forth, forgetting about the *wheeze*, the trailer sounds like a farting machine—the only thing that's made Shan laugh throughout the whole morning. Sometimes, she steps there on purpose, until she finds it only pisses Buck off.

One o'clock, they hit the road to Hanksville. Telling her to take the lead, he follows behind in his truck, pulling the trailer.

They travel up from the bottom-lands of the river to the steppes of the mesas, through sandy arroyos, across the eroding Mesozoic formations, inching slowly around dark red buttes, tilting down across slickrock. Winding... bouncing... rolling through the crushed and steepled land of southern Utah.

ॐ

CHAPTER 15

Same Day — Green River to North Wash

High overhead in the jet beads of the young hawk's eyes, two vermilion dust curls reflect their passing.

Dry and wet streamlets vein out from the knuckle-raised fists of the San Rafael Reef across the San Rafael Swell toward the confluence of the Colorado and Green rivers. Vermilion-rust-yellow-pink-buff-magenta-rufous cliffs clutch at dark green alligator bark juniper and piñon pine on top of the Reef like lustful fingers tangled in unruly hair.

For a long time the hawk plays wing tag with the vehicles. Like ants they haul a cumbersome burden through the deep erosions, never leaving their determined route.

A cold air mass suddenly drops the hawk. As he circles back against the wind, pinion feathers spread to steer his turn, he smells rain. This displeases him; rain interferes with hunting.

Leaving the road-ants he banks toward bottomland with wings stretched full and eyes alert for the sight of his afternoon meal. He glides toward the river, away from a storm that is gathering east of the Swell.

The caravan pauses at Hanksville for gas, a few groceries and delivery of the fish to Buck's friend Ernie; afterward, they drive beside the Henry Mountains rising to the west and southward toward the great Colorado Plateau. For several miles the road parallels the Dirty Devil River before it plunges into the heart of deep, red pillars, needles and buttes —a fiery furnace that some call hell, others, heaven.

It is late afternoon when Shan pulls to the side of the road. Buck, lagging half a mile behind to avoid her dust, eventually stops behind her, leans out the window and hollers, 'What's the trouble?'

She comes to his door sipping a beer and smiling. 'Nothing, just wanted to get out and stretch. Isn't that the road we took to Wolverton Mill?' She points to a jeep trail winding up through shale toward the Henrys.

'Yeah, that's it.'

'How about a beer?'

'No thanks,' he answers bluntly. 'Maybe you haven't noticed what's behind us.'

She looks north. A solid steel blue curtain has dropped from sky to desert floor already blocking out part of Mount Ellen. The five-o'clock sun shimmers yellow and unreal through a saddle in the mountains across the front of the coming storm.

'Holy smoke!' she whistles.

'We better get the hell outta here or we'll be smack in the middle of one of those gully-washers and stuck for a week.'

'Right,' she says, thinking: *That might not be such a damn bad idea after all.* She's had a couple beers and feels impervious to his fretfulness. 'Wait a minute, I gotta make a pit stop.'

As she goes to the front of her car and squats beside the wheel, she contemplates what might happen if she had a flat: If *we don't get rained on, if our cars don't break down, we should be at the crossing tonight. Hm-m-m. Looking at the valve cap she decides, Naw, better leave it in the hands of the gods…. Besides, that'd be a really dumb thing t'do… he's no idiot.* She hoists her jeans and returns to the driver's side of the Bird, reaching inside the open window for another beer. Holding it up, she comes to the truck and says lightly, 'You should try one of these, then you wouldn't be so grouchy.' Drumming impatiently on the side of his door he responds, 'If you really want to see a grouch you get us stuck here in a mud-bath, Shan. We won't be able to go forward or back for two or three days if that sonofabitch hits us b'fore we hit the ferry.'

He's used her name!—first time since she got there two days ago. She raises her brows, smiles and says, 'Well, progress!'

'What's that supposed to mean?'

'Nothin', Tarzan. Sure you don't want a beer?'

'No! I want t'get goin!'... but he hears 'Tarzan' and realizes she's teasing him. Up to now he's played it cool—if he gets angry she'll know something's bothering him—he allows the corners of his mouth to tilt up, reaches for the can and adds, 'But if we gotta swim this will help.' The china-blue eyes look straight into hers saying nothing she can translate.

'How much farther is it?'

"Bout twenty-five miles.'

'We can make it before dark, can't we?'

'It'll take us a couple hours with this trailer, *if* North Wash is dry. We sit here chewin' the fat much longer, she's gonna be a bit more than damp.'

'I get the message.' She holds the can to her chest, presses the ends together and tosses it to him. 'Me Jane.' She smirks and jogs to her car.

Ticked off, he slams the can on the truck floor and leans out the window calling, 'Keep in sight from now on—this road is goddamn tricky.'

As she reaches to close the door a strong gust of cold wind wrenches it from her grip, scoops up a barrage of sand and throws it inside. She spits out the grit and looks back into a dark blue bowl that shows no horizon—one brilliant streak of sun spotlights the desert scrub around them. In the distance, Chinle shales pour over muted orange sands like scoops of melting blueberry ice cream. She stands transfixed by the eeriness of it all. Buck waves her ahead impatiently and she pulls the door closed.

They are about a mile into North Wash when the storm breaks.

An unobstructed blast hits and rocks the cars as the sun is deftly snuffed out with dust. Tumbleweeds torn from higher ground roll and bounce like great beach balls through a pink fog. They bunch, separate, then run an obstacle race to the nearest obstruction where they're caught, trembling, in the wind. The road, visible only a few yards ahead, begins to wind and drop. Like veiled ghosts the buttes and spires float past. They seem immutable, but today they'll lose a few more grams to the whirring emery.

Now, through the sand and dust comes rain—shooting against the vehicles like machine gun fire. Shan has slowed to a crawl, thinking it's hail, but drops the size of golf balls spread on the hood, streaking it red. Within seconds the windows steam up and water seeps under the tightly bolted top.

The wind eases, and the rain becomes a ruthless pouring.

She hears a series of muffled staccato notes and turns to see Buck's headlights blinking. As she brakes, the car slides sideways coming to a stop on the right edge of the road. There's a bang on her window and a yellow blur outside. She cracks it open.

Buck, in a nautical slicker, bareheaded, with water streaming from the end of his nose, shouts, 'We picked a hurricane! The stuff on the road has turned to gumbo already. Can you make it to the other side of this wash?'

'Yeah, I think so. Gad, what a deluge!'

'If we can get up to those flat rocks, we'll be above the river. Pull off to the left at the top where you won't sink in. I'll wait to see if you make it.'

'Which way...'

'Hurry up, dammit. I give this wash about five more minutes b'fore it's level with the floorboards.'

'Dammit yourself! Which way are my wheels pointed? I'd prefer to start in the right direction.'

'Turn 'em left. Get going!'

'Aye aye, *Sir*.' She rolls up the window, straightens and goes downhill, splashes through the bottom and up the other side without slipping. Instead of pulling off at the top, however, the car disappears from sight.

'For Christ's sweet eyeballs, what's that damn female doing?' Buck dashes for the truck, yanks the five-speed transmission into second and starts down. He races a wall of water that will tear through moments later, chewing away banks, making the road impassable until the state's heavy equipment comes from Hanksville to reconstruct it. The upgrade is hard packed and, like Shan, he has no difficulty gaining the top, even with a trailer in tow. Immediately he sees why she went ahead: there's a ditch beside the road and she has driven onto bedrock some distance beyond the rise. He pulls up behind her, hands gripping the wheel so tightly that blue veins stand out on his wrists. He takes a deep breath and relaxes.

A wet bat comes running toward him under a flapping army poncho, opens the door and crawls in, trembling.

'This is it,' he says with grudging finality, 'right here in the middle of the goddamn road.... But I don't expect anybody'll come along tryin' to pass, unless he's equipped with a periscope,' he adds with a spark of his old humor.

She is shivering. 'My God, it's really coming down. How long do you think this'll keep up?'

He gives her a disgusted look. 'You sound like a damn tourist. Anywhere from two hours to two days, ma'am—if the florabordgets don't creep up into the hornatrabs and cut off the cobracycles.'

She offers a teeth-chattering smile and sniffs. 'Sounds like the beer improved your disposition even if it muddled your speech. Want another?'

'Nope. I'm hungry. You?'

'Any time, it doesn't matter.' But her thoughts are elsewhere— deep in winding crevices watching potholes fill with thick, red water. Impassable. They won't be able to explore the canyons downriver now like he'd said they might.

Buck's mind is on food and the facilities for preparing it— corn, potatoes, even fresh beef from Hanksville. The beer has mellowed him, so for the moment he's forgotten the reservations placed on his behavior toward Shan. He's wet, it's cold and starting to blow again, but the trailer will be warm once he gets the fires going.

'Ah-ah-ah-chizzz!'

He looks at the wet bat beside him. 'Better get what you'll need from your car while I get the trailer warmed up and some water on for coffee.'

She wipes her nose, opens the door and disappears in the downpour. Buck tightens the slicker around his throat, leaps out and runs for the trailer.

ঌ๛ঌ

Not until he's inside the small confines of Windy's old house-on-wheels, looking at what is now *his* bunk, does he remember where he planned to sleep in case they didn't get to the ferry. 'Hell,' he mutters, 'the cab of the truck's okay.' From the cupboard he grabs a bottle of Jack Daniels, unwraps the dishtowel and slugs a sizable belt. The warmth tingles down his throat. 'Hello, Jack ol' friend, been a while since we tied one on—maybe tonight's the night, huh?'

When Shan comes in with her bag, the wall heater is lit, the coffee pot heating, and the Coleman lantern glares with the intensity of a Kleig light. She leaves her sneakers and poncho by the door, goes to the small toilet nook and changes into dry jeans, soft Navajo boots and a clean shirt.

While Buck is preparing dinner, he hears the trailer's raspberry sound off and turns to see Shan standing by the heater warming her fanny. He hands her the bottle. 'Here, have a snort of this, it'll warm ya up quick.'

'Afraid I've turned sissy in my old age, Buck; got to have water with it.'

'Hell, it won't warm ya up very quick that way.'

'Okay.' She looks at him, searchingly, suspicious of this change of attitude—is it triggered by booze? She takes a small pull at the bottle, determined to keep her own head clear. She's never seen Buck drunk, doesn't want to and wonders how long it takes him to go from happy, to sullen, to mean.

She needn't worry.

Buck knows why he doesn't drink; it costs too much for even a buzz. With the second pint he becomes profoundly analytical and philosophical, a state very boring even to himself, but here with Shan he no longer cares what he might say, since he won't be seeing her after tonight.

Before they eat he pours her a drink, with water. He has started to talk, not carefully guarded talk. She thought they'd probably eat in silence under the pall of his gloom, but Buck is a series of surprises—one of his attractions. As they sit down she winces in the lantern's glare, and taking a chance on this renewed humor, asks him if he has any candles in the place.

'Yeah, guess so—you expectin' t' go outside and have a look at the land?'

'No, smartass. I want to cut the spotlight and eat by candlelight; not trying to be romantic, I just want to aid digestion.'

He shrugs and brings two from the drawer—beat up, half burned and festooned with crumbs and coffee grounds. 'These ain't very fancy and I got no gold candlesticks for the occasion— I'll just stick 'em to the table.' He lights them, turns off the Coleman, sits, says, 'Grace,' and dives in.

Twice during the meal he tips up Jack for a sizable gurgle. Shan watches for stage two, but there's no change. In fact he acts like the Buck she's always known—easygoing, soft-spoken and not drunk. He talks about his claim on the Green, and how nothing has come of it; how Fred helped for a while; how he should have known *that* place, like every other he's picked, is going fast to civilization. 'Hell, when I first filed on it, I could barely get to it with the Jeep; now there's uranium roads all over the goddamn desert. Anyhow, there's no ore there worth bothering about.'

Shan sips her drink. 'If you want to stay clear of the mob you'll have to go to Alaska, or Australia. This country's out of control—the greed syndrome has firmly set in—we're breeding like mosquitoes, we poison everything we set foot on, and our lousy influence spreads like the plague to places we've never been. We can't leave anything primitive or natural alone—we have to cut it down, rip it up, drown it, burn it, develop and pave it from Nome to Nogales or we're not satisfied. Never satisfied!' She stabs viciously at a piece of steak.

Buck stares at her for a while, saying nothing, waiting for the vitriol to cool. 'Nope, don't think I'll try Alaska—too cold. Australia?—too far. Maybe I'll get down to Baja one of these days though.'

'Guess I'm not invited on that trip anymore, huh?'

'*When* I go, *if* I go, I'll be going to stay.'

'I see.' He is staring into some world she can only guess. 'Well, you let me know how it is—supposed to be kinda primitive.'

'That's just fine with me.'

'But what'll you do, Buck? How'll you make a living? Mexico's got a bunch of rules and regulations that you won't go for, like what gringos can and can't do, or own. At least they're on to us.'

'I'll beachcomb, fish, buy an onyx mine or hunt sea turtles maybe.'

'Oh, sure,' she snorts. 'I can see you being a party to that slaughter, even if they'd give you a license—and you've got too much pride to be a beachcomber.'

'How come you know so much about me?'

She watches the shadow of his shaggy head wavering in the candlelight against the wall, and peering into the amber of her glass says sadly, 'Places like the river drew a knot of folks who wanted the beautiful, untamed and lonely. Of those it drew it only kept a few—those who could communicate with it and with each other.' She lifts her eyes to stare directly at him. 'That's why I know about you. That's why a few years back you went with me on a trip as far as the Rincon, because you knew I loved the river and you didn't want me to be hurt by it.'

He tips the bottle again, and licks his lips as though he's just drunk syrup. 'Lotta good it did; you got hurt anyway.'

'*We* got hurt.'

'Not by the river, in another way: by the loss of it.'

'Exactly.'

'By rights the loss ought'a affect me more'n you. I lived there, but I think you've turned sour and bitter against the world. I could tell by your letters....'

'Oh, so you got my letters after all!'

'That's one of the reasons I never answered them. I didn't want to watch what was going to happen to you when you saw the reservoir, any more than Jason and Step.'

'We-l-l!' Shan heaves a great sigh. 'I invented every reason but that one.' She fingers the little pink arrowhead at her throat and continues, 'You're right, I *am* bitter—can even taste the bile myself.' She shakes her head, uttering a heartless little laugh. 'So finally I get to the mystery of your silence. I must say it makes more sense than some of the other things that were theorized.'

'Such as what?' he asks, getting up with a languid flowing motion, still showing no sign of drunkenness. He brings the coffee pot from the stove, pours some into each a mug and adds a *gurgle* of the diminishing sour mash to his own.

'Like Jason thinking you got tired of people when they hung around too long—like Windy, who insisted you were in love with me—like Step, saying you probably weren't used to running around with women in the buff and got horny, then figured you'd best...'

'Never entered my mind.'

'That's what I told him. Told him you were my *friend*, and we were too busy exploring to bother about...'

'...Until now.'

She has been staring into the coffee mug between her hands, elbows on the table. His deliberate emphasis on the last two words startle her. One elbow slips from the table and she spills some of the hot liquid on her hand before she can get the mug settled.

Buck watches her candidly, not with a look of lechery or even desire. If anything his expression is sad, his lips slightly pursed.

Shan's mouth fills with saliva and her heart quickens, its *booming* seems to fill the room. Heat prickles across her forehead, then the whole surprising reaction passes as quickly as it came. She swallows, her eyes fixed on his.

'Why now?'

He is silent, rubbing the stubble on his chin with the back of his hand, not taking his eyes away from hers, and smiling slightly. The only sounds are the creaking of the trailer and rain battering the roof.

She swallows again, loudly. 'You told me once I was never going to find out how you were in the sack, said you sold your body high and I didn't have enough money.' She manages the shadow of a smile. 'I still don't have much money. What changed your mind?'

'Lotta things... you for one.... You're different.'

'How am I different?'

'Your face has changed, there's hard lines around your mouth, and your voice... your voice is sarcastic, like you got your back up all the time.... And I never saw your skin all white, like women in the city. When you were on the river you were brown, healthy and relaxed, looked like you were born there... like maybe Eve looked before she got to palaverin' with the snake and covered herself up—her real self.'

Tears well in Shan's eyes and her voice is low, almost a whisper. 'Pretty astute, Mr. Watson. You're right, of course. We *were* something like Adam and Eve before self-consciousness nailed them.

I suspect the fable lost something in translation and what really happened was that their garden got ripped off first, like ours.'

Buck continues to rub his chin. 'You keep saying *we* all the time. I manage to cope with these changes, it's happened to me before. You're the one seems to be affected.'

'And you're not?' She pours the last of the Jack Daniels into her mug of fresh coffee. 'Somewhere along the line you took a bite of the apple too. How'd that happen? I thought you were incorruptible.'

'Just a natural man, like Step says—got horny.'

'I don't believe that... but I suppose anything's possible. In spite of having been around a bit there's a lot I don't understand about men.'

'Well, you ain't alone. There's practically *nuthin'* I understand about women... and some things I don't want to.'

She nods at the empty bottle. 'I think you needed outside help to get around to this.'

'You might say Mr. Daniels assisted me over a hump, but now I'm strictly on my own.'

'Didn't anyone ever tell you it's a lot better when you're sober?'

'I am sober.'

She gives him a brittle smile and stands up beside the table.

But Buck *is* sober. It's like he says—just to get over the hump. He rests like water in a pond... unhurried... unruffled... and stubborn.

Many times Shan has castrated a man before he could get to her, just by talking. Since Buck's startling revelation she's been trying to divert him. She wants him, all right, but on *her* terms. She's afraid to delve into her feelings if a one-night stand is all he wants from her, because that isn't all she wants from him. She leans against the booth and stretches her legs, stalling for time.

'I can't see why you want me now if I'm so ugly—so pale, with hard lines in my face and all.... D'you just feel sorry for me and think some tender, or maybe un-tender, loving care will...'

'I didn't say you were ugly, I said you were different.'

'I had you figured for the kind of guy who'd prefer making love in the open, on a bed of leaves, or on a riverbank, instead of all cramped up inside a farting house trailer.' With thumbs hooked in her hip pockets she looks around the steamed-up box. 'These things remind me of motels.'

Stretching an arm along the back of the bench, he looks up at her with the shadow of a smile. 'I prefer it wherever it is,' he lies—pushing away thoughts of Pam-Shan and the yellow leaves of fall—'"especially after a long time of not preferring it at all.'

She notices he doesn't say 'I prefer *you*' and it tugs at her pride. Sarcastically she quips, 'They say virility doesn't run too high in the abstemious male.' And with her stinger, adds, 'You sure you're up to this, Cowboy?'

The stinger misses its mark.

He moves to the end of the bench, reaches for her belt and gently pulls her to him. Dropping the bantering tone, he says, quietly, 'Shan Lu, you know goddamn well I'm up to it. You're scared—scared I'm gonna be rough with you. Believe me, I'm not.'

Her heart quickens again, seeming to out-drum the rain. She isn't afraid of that at all, she's afraid of herself, especially now that he's put her on the defensive. She struggles for a matter-of-fact tone of voice. 'I'm not too good at just shacking up with some guy. Love me or not; there are certain preliminaries. But I suppose you're not interested in such trivia, in which case I'll be no better or worse than the girls at the mine.'

Fingers still loosely hooked in her belt, eyes soft and serious, he watches as she stubbornly sets her jaw against trembling.

'You through? Cause I got something t'say.'

She shrugs as if it doesn't matter.

'First of all we ain't shackin' up, because this is going to be the first, the last, and only time. Second, I don't love you—I thought I did once, but that's changed. Third, I'm not just *some guy*. We're doing this because we want to, and probably have for a long time, so the preliminaries, as you call 'em, have been happening for a good number of years. Next—no woman, since I was nineteen, ever got left unsatisfied unless she lied—lotta women think they get even with a man like that but they only hurt themselves—so if you want to come out ahead, I'll go out of my way to make your part of the deal worthwhile. Another point...'

'Suppose I like it—*we* like it—why will it be the only and...'

'Wait a minute, I ain't through. You couldn't be like the women at the mine if you were glued to them. The reason it won't happen again, Shan Lu, is because of you—you want me along with the river, and only when it suits you. I made up my mind years ago to leave the crowd and take the far trail, but you're still half-and-half. Well... the river's gone and you got too many things t'git off your chest. My craw's been full of those things long enough. I'm done with it. But you won't give up even when you've lost the fight.'

He pauses, swings his legs from beneath the table and slides to the edge of the bench. Letting go of her belt, he spreads his legs and wraps his arms around her hips, locking her loosely inside the circle. 'Now, if you want to put up a fight you go ahead, but I'll tell ya right now, I give ya more credit than that. I know you've thought about being with me like this b'fore, so it's not against your grain—at the cabin once, you asked me what I did for nookie... because you wondered how it would be.'

She licks her lips, stares at the candles and once more insists, 'Yeah, and you told me I was never going to find out.'

'Like I said, I've changed my mind. Even a man has a right to do that once in a while. I want you now same as most men want a woman who physically attracts them. What's wrong with that?'

'Nothing. But you don't love me.' She states it as a fact.

'Nope.'

'You didn't like us the other way?'

'It was fine the other way. I got to know a lot about you that I wouldn't know otherwise.'

Of course Shan accepts his 'Nope' as a challenge, failing to figure in his cut-off switch when he realized she wasn't ready for his kind of love. She's certain if he loved her once, she can make him love her again. She hasn't looked at why she cares, nor recognized the fact that she's behaving like the kind of women she abhors.

Buck, on the other hand, is immune; doing this to get her out of his system. For him making love will be a cleansing.

She leans back in the circle of his arms and rests her hands on his shoulders, finding it difficult to be casual in this new role. 'Well then, we might as well end it up proper,' she states blithely.

'I usually prepare and anoint myself for such an occasion but with the lack of water inside and the temperature of it outside, a bird-bath will have to do.'

'You already had one bath today. B'sides you smell like a god-damn rose all the time anyway.' He wrinkles his nose, drops his encircling arms and stands.

'I want to see how it feels to kiss you—I never have, you know.'

'I'm well aware that you never have, because...'

'Because that's the way you wanted it.'

She snaps away from those times and in a sales-pitch tones recites: 'What sort of kisses do you like? I have all kinds—slow simmering sexy ones with my tongue searching around the edges of your mouth and pressing against your tongue—soft, teasing kisses guaranteed to engorge...'

'Never mind, I'll lead the way. Afterward, if you want to put it in some category, feel free.'

Still fighting, she says, 'I don't think you were unhappy with the way we were, Buck. I wish...'

'Quit talking, Shan Lu. I was but I didn't know it.' He raises her chin, looks into her eyes and covers her mouth with soft lips... wrapping her in oblivion. She tries to stay clinically interested but after the first thrill of female power over a man's growing, her mind disengages and her glands take over. She is warm, and wet, from nose to knees. After undetermined minutes she is unable to note the category, is uncertain of her equilibrium, and unconscious of the fact that she no longer stands on the floor. He releases her suddenly. Her feet touch, her knees buckle and she grabs him for support.

'Y'all right?' His eyes are tinsel flickering in the candlelight.

'Yes... yes, of course,' she answers to a spinning room.

With a mocking smile he asks, 'Are you sure *you're* up to this?'

'Don't worry, Cowboy. I can if you can,' comes her brave answer.

'Oh, I most definitely can,' he assures her, looking down at the sizable bulge between his legs.

'Yeah, I see. Strange... I never took much notice of him before.'

'He never thought of performing for you before,' he lies—passing off the incident at Wolverton—picks her up and carries her to the lower bunk.

'Prepare and anoint yourself.'

'You mean I have to take off my own clothes?' she teases. 'Seems t'me you should have the pleasure of undressing the woman you've gone to so much trouble for.'

'No trouble at all, Miss.'

He unbuttons the silver conchos on her Navajo boots, pulls them off and unfastens her belt. Slowly freeing the buttons on her shirt, he takes each arm from its sleeve like a man undressing a small child, then, rocking her hips, he slides off the jeans. He's seen every naked inch of her over the years, in the water, in the wind and rain, in her sleeping bag, sunning on the sand…. Why is blood thumping in his temple…? Why is this different?

Her eyes follow each movement until both hands reach beneath her for the hooks on her bra. 'Whoa. Now it's my turn.' She smiles, reaching for his belt.

Buck backs away quickly. 'Oh no, I can take off my own duds, you just tend to your knitting.' Suddenly he knows if he lets her undress him it will be a total undoing of all the promises to himself—that he will lose control of the advantage he has over the situation at this moment.

Her eyes widen in surprise. 'Why, Buck, I think you're embarrassed. That's half the fun!'

'Not for a lady.'

She drops her feet over the edge of the bunk and takes the offensive. 'Lady? I'm a lady in the living room only, a gourmet in the kitchen and a pro in the boudoir. I'm told that's the best combination you can get.'

Backing toward the wall heater, he responds with an enticing smile and softly says, 'Then come to the living room, little lady, and act proper.'

Shan leaps up, throws her head back and lets out an unbroken laugh.

Ignoring her, Buck removes his pants and shirt and places them neatly over the back of a kitchen bench.

'Look out! You're in gourmet territory!' Her laughter turns to coughing and tears, verging on hysteria.... She can't stop... the whole scene is far beyond ludicrous. She doesn't want Buck this way, yet is trying to convince herself it will turn out all right. Her whole body turns heavy with guilt because she knows this scene, and all that's led up to it, is her fault. She grabs her midriff and doubles over.

A comforter, a blanket and two pillows lie in the middle of the floor. Buck comes to her and folds her weeping, shivering form gently in his arms, kissing her forehead, eyes, neck and shoulders, while he talks in husky tones that fade to whispers.

'Shan Lu, you do and say things that make me want to love you one minute and strangle you the next. Right now those things are so mixed I dunno which is which... and I don't care. I just want to make love to you and make you happy—even if it's only one time. I don't want it to be a three-ring circus or something you'll remember as disgusting. Maybe I'm kinda old-fashioned for your tastes, but there are some things I'd rather *do* than talk about.'

Hysteria subsides to little whimpering sobs as she surrenders, nodding against the curly blond hairs of his chest. He leads her to the comforter and takes off her bra and panties, softly kissing each breast, then kneels and pulls her down beside him, settling her on the pillows. He strips his shorts, lies down next to her and pulls the blanket over them.

'We should have done this years ago,' he sighs, 'when we first thought we might want to. Think of all the fun we could have had all that time.'

She reaches for him, pressing herself into him, entangling her legs with his. 'You're sure right about that, Cowboy.'

Midway into North Wash, atop a mound of slippery red earth that's beaten into eroding rivulets and hemmed in by rushing water, the trailer shudders. Chances are it would slide into the grappling fingers of the flood if it weren't moored to the truck. Rain lashes the window glass, leaving wounds of bloody wetness— gusts of wind rocking it from side to side.

Inside it is warm and dry except for some seepage around the door. The candles burn low, spreading wax over the oilcloth on the table where the dinner dishes lie, forgotten.

For the two lovers, who have ceased talking at last, the sound that rises above the drumming rain and is the most familiar to their ears, makes them feel as if they might be running rapids.

Which, of course, they are.

ళ్ళు

CHAPTER 16

October, 1965 — Fry Canyon and the Crossroads

'For Chrissake, Buck, ain'tcha gonna open the goddamn door? It's *me*, Windy!' A shuffling of feet inside his old trailer and the flatulent greeting of old warped floorboards sets Windy grinning on the stoop.

Buck opens the door, surprised to see his old neighbor. 'Windy! I'll be damned.' Then a look of concern replaces what had started to be a smile.

Windy is dressed in bib overalls, long handles and a hardhat cocked to one side. Where his pixie eyes used to be are two sunken hollows rimmed with soot, his beard a week's stubble, his teeth covered with nicotine stains. The toes of his boots curl up off the ground, heels nearly gone, and a bruised knee pokes through a frayed pant leg. He reeks of gasoline. Yet he grins same as always and his spirits don't seem much worse for the wear.

'Well, come in, ya raunchy ol' sonofabitch. You must of fixed the brakes on that old clunker of yours—didn't hear you drive up. What's doin'?'

'Aw, nuthin' much. Hell, I din't fix them brakes, they plum wore out.'

'You look like you been *workin'*. How'er things going out at the Crossroads?'

Sliding onto the booth beside the old Formica table, Windy gives a twisted grin and shakes his head at the cigarette burns he put there long ago. 'Shit, they ain't goin' a'tall. Nobody out there this time a year, 'specially at that mud and driftwood bog they now call Hite.'

Buck nods, sensing an uncharacteristic aura of defeat. Whatever anyone might say about Windy, they can't call him a quitter. If a steamroller flattened him he'd rise up like Bugs Bunny just to be flattened again. 'How about some coffee,' he offers, heading for the stove.

'Got a drink?'

'Sure,' Buck answers, stifling his surprise—then, detours to the fridge and returns with a beer, setting it on the table in front of him.

'No, I mean a *real* drink. I could use a shot a booze.' He slumps down and takes off the battered hardhat.

'Yeah, I think I got some.' Buck returns the beer to the fridge, goes to the cupboard, unwinds the dishcloth from the Jack Daniels and sets bottle and glass in front of Windy.

Ignoring the glass, Windy tilts up the bottle for a good belt, runs his dirty sleeve across his mouth and releases a loud *Brr-r-r-aaak!* 'Ya still drink the good stuff when ya drink, don'tcha?'

Buck nods. There's something on his old neighbor's mind or he wouldn't be here, for one… or drink hard booze before lunch, for two. They don't see much of each other these days—Buck working and away from Fry Canyon most of the time, and Windy operating what the locals laughingly call 'the junkyard,' about fifteen miles west where the new highway crosses the old road to Dandy.

Windy looks around his old trailer and inquires, 'How's the ol' box holdin' up? Kinda makes me feel like we're down t'the river, settin here. I heerd the ol' fart in the floor when ya come t' the door—ya never fixed it.'

'Nope, keep it to remind me what a jerk I am sometimes, sort of like having someone around to give me the bird.'

'Yeah… well, the only reason I sold it to ya was cuz m'ol' lady din' like that noise.' Windy has forgotten that his wife left him long before the floorboards warped, but the statement, instead of turning Buck off, warms him, making him aware that he's missed Windy's jabber, his insatiable curiosity and tall stories. More than that, he misses the place they experienced it all, but that's not a thing he cares to dwell on.

'What's on your mind?' he asks, pouring himself a cup of coffee.

Windy leans back in the booth, tilts his head to one side and studies his friend. The squint lines make his eyes look like desert watering holes, but Buck thinks he sees a spark of the old mischief.

'I come t' invite ya to a pardy. Saturday night. Supper time. Last gatherin' b'fore I haul ass outta here.'

'Before you...' Buck is genuinely surprised. 'Where the hell ya going?'

"Laska. That goddam Bureau and the ass-suckin' Park Service have fucked things up to a fare-thee-well and I'm gettin' the hell gone!'

'*Alaska?* Christ sake, Windy, you'll freeze your balls off—ol' desert rat like you goin' to Alaska!'

'Freeze 'um 'er not, they won't wither 'n drop off from no use.' He pauses, takes the bottle in both hands and, for Windy, says quietly, 'I sold m' land.' There comes with that statement a deep pulling at the inner man, as the bottle leaves the table for another swallow. 'Sold it fer goddam *nuthin'...* but I sold 'er.'

For Windy, land is all there is. Selling means giving up half a life's battle and going for a new start. In each other's eyes they see years float by, knowing the hurt of leaving something they've claimed for their own and paid for with love, hard work and care. Buck's been leaving gradually, taking off for a while but always coming back, now Windy's taking the bit and doing it all at once. Cutting off an arm would be easier.

'I worked m' goddamn ass off at the Crossroads out there, but I ain't never had 'nuff money t'do what aughta be done. That marina up to Hite is gonna turn out 'zactly like I tol'um it would, but the stupid bastards wu'nt listen t'me. Why hell, in a few years the mud 'n silt's gonna fill them canyons clear up to the bottom of the bridges. That's about the dumbest place for a marina they could think of, there in the Floyd Dominy Memorial Mudflats— that's what *I* calls it.'

Buck smiles, remembering that was Shan's name for it, but he says, 'Yeah, I know. All they had to do was look at Pierce's Ferry [now Pearce's Ferry] to get the picture.'

'*Them* git a picture?' Windy snorts. 'Shit, they got eyeballs lookin' up through their assholes!'

Buck gets up for more coffee.

'I din't git nuthin' what m'land was worth, but I can't hold out no longer. Let somebody else bust their butt.'

Windy is a man who accepts adversity like it was tattooed on him, but keeps plowing ahead anyhow; so Buck is perplexed about the change that's come over him... *Always considered him as full of shit as last year's bird nest, but now he's solemn, almost painfully serious.* Returning to the table, he sits, frowning out the window, not looking at the weary, disillusioned face. 'Maybe we ought to all get out'a here like Fred did,' he mutters.

'Oh by the way, Fred 'n Helen'll be comin' from Dove Creek to the pardy this Saturday. I wrote to 'um. Asked Jason too, but he's too busy with boats and tourists at Hoxie t'git away. Tried t'git Myrna, but she's working s'hard supportin' them kids she can't afford t'make the run.'

Buck looks down at his coffee. 'I was hoping by now to hear she'd found another man to look after her... been almost a year.'

'I tol'er she could come shack up with me if she wanted. I'd kinda like t'have some little bitty house apes running around the place.'

'Windy, ya derned old reprobate, you got no couth t'say a thing like that to her. You know she wouldn't have anything t'do with a friend of Brad's.' He can hardly suppress a smile; that's the old Windy for sure!

Sheepishly Windy admits, 'Aw... I din't say that; I'uz just kiddin'.' He stretches, then squirms out of the booth. 'Well, I gotta git back t'work—ain't nobody there but me, ya know. That goddamn sumbitch water pump give out on me this mornin' and I'll have t'spend a whole shittin' day gittin' it workin' agin.' He takes a last look at what's left of the Jack Daniels, decides against more and grabs his hardhat. 'See ya Saturday night, ol buddy, don't fergit—long about sundown.'

Again Buck thinks he sees that glimmer, but if it's there the dark circles around Windy's bloodshot eyes disguise it. 'Yup, I'll be there,' he says, getting up to open the door. 'If you need any help with your water pump, I can come give you a hand.'

'N-a-ah, thanks anyhow. I'll git 'er goin' okay, she's used t'my tinkerin'—some strange hand a-pokin' round her innard's 'ud prolly set her t'goin' in reverse.' He walks on the floor-fart, goes down the steps and shuffles toward his truck, saying over his shoulder, 'Might bring summa that Mr. Daniels 'long with ya—I 'member Fred likes it too.' He climbs into his old bucket and waves from the cab. 'See ya.'

For the first time since Buck has known the man, Windy pulls out without spinning the wheels or raising a dust cloud. He rattles down the road leaving Buck with a worried frown and an empty feeling in the pit of his gut. He puts the emptiness down to lunch hour... before it gets any closer to meddling with his conscience.

તેન્જી

Deserts lie awake at night in October and November, waiting for winter and what little moisture might come their way. Deserts sleep in the summer daytime because the sun, fierce and strong, holds them in check. But deserts sleep little, night or day, when the seasons of spring and fall move in on them. They dance with the spatter of rain and stinging dust. The freakish wind plays fast and loose with the parched earth, twirling it like a Dervish dancer, and the cold October air can bring anything from sprinkles to snowflakes at the Crossroads by Windy's shacks. Tonight a cold, relentless wind has possession of the territory. It blows from the west, against most of the travelers to Windy's farewell party.

Shan stands in the doorway of the gritty trailer looking into the night. The screen impairs her view so she shoves it open to watch the road.

Windy comes from behind with an amber glow tinkling in his glass and another twinkling in his dark-ringed eyes. 'Can't wait fer him, huh?' he teases, bumping his knees into the backs of hers, making her fall back against him.

'Dammit, Windo, what're you trying to do?'

'Knock ya fer a loop, what else?'

She turns around giving him a scalding look. 'You haven't changed too bloody much, you ol' lecher. I keep wondering how you'll make it up in Alaska with women scarcer than hen's teeth.

That'd be a good place for *me* to go, not a horny old goat like you.'

'Might take a few hen's teeth with me, ya never can tell.' His voice drops to a clandestine whisper. 'He'll be here in a little bit, don't shiver yer shanks about it, ol' gal.'

Shan ignores him and looks to where Fred Bennett sits with his wife on the couch. She walks over and drops down on the floor in front of them. 'Fred, how long since you've seen Buck? Has he changed any? Does he look older? What's he doing these days?'

'Here, here, Chantoozie, not so fast. I have t' take them questions one at a time.'

'Okay,' she laughs. 'Sorry. Helen, have you seen him? I'd like a woman's opinion.'

Helen shakes her small grey head. 'I haven't, Shan, not for over a year, since the last time he came to see us.'

A cynical little smile tips up one corner of Shan's mouth. 'That's about when I last saw him. I'm asking because he never writes anymore—just wonder what's happened to him.'

'Shucks,' Fred snorts, 'he don't write anybody. He ain't been around these parts much this summer, I hear. Helen's sister lives at Fry.... Says he's been working on and off at a mine up north somewhere.'

'He didn't go to work on the bridges, did he?'

'Hell no! That's one thing you can make sure he'd *never* do.'

Windy, standing with his back to the door, a knowing smirk on his face and a glass rotating in his grease-stained hand, looks at Fred and says, 'That ain't the only reason she's askin' all them questions, Bennett. She's got the hots fer 'um.'

Shan looks up, ready to say something quick and mean, but seeing devilment and the old eagerness to be in on things flicker in his wasted eyes— remembering that he's going away, going away hard—smiles instead. 'Windo, you're just one big mine dump of crap.'

'She's goin' down t'Hoxie Crossing fer the first time t'morrow, Fred. Boy, is she ever in fer a surprise! Tell 'er.'

Fred looks down at her, trying to convey the picture he has in mind. His handsome face is pale and he's aged more than Shan expected. His deep, resonant voice used to give listeners assurance that they'd just learned a book-full, even if he talked about dandruff on a gnat's eyelash. Now, that elegant voice is cracked and tired. He seems to have wilted like a wildflower transplanted to a window box. They hold each other's gaze a moment before she lowers hers.

'Oh, I don't think it'll be so bad. I've waited, you know—been sort of preparing myself for the worst—I've seen pictures taken by folks who used to run the river and who got curious about what remains of their favorite places. Lotta stuff I couldn't identify... finally decided to go look for myself.'

Fred wipes his nose on a big red bandana, muttering into its folds, 'Hope you haven't scanned the brochures with the photos by some of your professional friends.'

'No way. I've heard though... oh yes, but there are none of mine, or Step's, or Jason's photos in it, and there won't *ever* be! The traitors and fence-sitters can go to hell....'

'Don't hold 'em in bitterness, Shan, they never felt about it like you. Come t'think on it, I don't know *anybody* who feels as deeply about the Glen as you... even Buck.'

'Don't kid yourself he doesn't. He just can't admit it, or he'd fall apart!'

Fred's gentle voice, not cracking now, answers, 'It'll take more'n a massacered river to make Buck Watson fall apart, Shan. I got a feeling that man's been through more'n any of us knows. He kinda rolls with the punches, Buck does. He's a strong-minded man.'

'Stubborn!' She grits her teeth and takes a large swallow of her drink.

Fred looks at her hair, starting to grey, at the green ribbon tying it back, her shirt and jeans—looks her all the way down and up again to her green eyes and smiles whimsically. 'Yes, I suppose a woman would call him stubborn. I don't think there's many had their way with Buck, so that's the best term they can find to justify their frustrations.'

Shan feels the heat rise from her sternum to her hairline—*He knows! Can't know... Buck would never tell anyone... but Fred's a wise old man.* Her mouth is open but she can't speak.

Helen closes the gap, nodding. 'He's got an aura of mystery about him too, Shan; that's another attractive feature for some women.'

'Oh, for sure! The strong-silent-mystery-man, that's Buck.' She twists up from her cross-legged position and goes for another drink, more than anxious to snip the subject of The Man *off!*

Windy, who's been leaning against the open doorjamb listening for a change, smirks as she passes him, then moves to the stove to stir his spaghetti sauce. Helen gets up from the couch, asking if she can set the table, and Shan returns with her fresh drink to her place on the shag rug.

'Fred, do you know what the USGS did about the names we river people gave the side canyons? They asked us to identify them, so we sent in about twenty-five names…. Wonder which ones they used.'

He rolls his beer can back and forth between pale, lean hands. 'What's the difference what they're *named* now, Shan? They're drowned! And the reason for their names along with them.'

'Oh, don't worry. I've caught the irony of it, but at the time I thought the river people would want to leave their mark on the maps, there being nothing else left.'

'When you come back from that scum pot let me know if you like leaving your mark on Dangling Rope Canyon. They're going to have a Marina there, y'know.' He swallows the last of his beer.

Shan jolts, almost knocking over her glass. 'A *what?*'

'One of them floatin' gas stations…. How's the beer holding out, Windy?' He chucks the empty can to his host and returns his attention to Shan, who is shuddering. 'You *didn't* know.'

She looks directly at him and says, quietly, 'That's the last straw, Fred.'

'So you say, Green Eyes, so you say…. But I think you're going to find a bunch more straws when you get to Hoxie tomorrow. Is Jason going on the reservoir with you?'

'Nope, he's in Blanding for a change, tied up in meetings; says he can't get away for another two or three days.'

'Step. Is he coming?'

'He's in Hawaii.'

'Maybe you can get Buck to go with you… if he's not working.'

'Are you kidding? He doesn't even know I'm here. I made Windy keep that part quiet, or he probably wouldn't be coming tonight—might not yet if he smells the rat… *me.'*

Meditatively Fred pulls on his earlobe. 'Hm-m-m, not like him to treat old friends that way, Shan. You musta got to him somehow… someway.'

'I doubt it,' she replies, casually as possible. 'Besides, I'm tired of guessing about the big Mystery Man and his reasons for doing things. If he doesn't want to say hello when I'm here only once or twice a year, then to hell with him! I've got other friends to hike and run rivers wi…' She stops at the word, trying to toss it off, but it rests heavily, and Fred senses her disappointment.

"Scuse me for being nosey, but you're not going down there all by your lonesome, are you?'

'Looks like it.'

'Not a good idea.'

'So I've been warned, but I'm here now… and I'm not leaving this time until I see it.'

'Now who's stubborn?'

'Another Scorpio!' She flashes a smarmy smirk and adds, 'Hizzhonor, Mr. Watson, was supposed to go with me last year, but when we got to Fry, he had to go to work *immediately*.'

Windy stomps over, plants himself down beside her, and tells Fred, 'Yeah, them two come accrost from North Wash couple days after that big storm we had. They come jist at dark—an this one here wun't even git outta her Bird when I ferried 'um over—she din't wanna see no part of that lake! An' Buck was in one of his no-seeum, no-hearum, no-talkum moods.' He leans into her shoulder and says with mock secrecy, 'Why'nt ya tell *me* ya wanted t' go speedboatin' round the lake last year, Shan? I'd a gone with ya! Me 'n you coulda *screw-driven* in and outta them canyons….'

Laughing, she elbows him away. 'Christamighty, Windy! Don't you ever give up?'

'Why d'you have to go, Chantoozie?' Fred's tone is laced with concern.

'I need to see if anything about him survived.'

'The river? Nothing…. Oh, maybe a side canyon or two has escaped complete destruction, like above Music Temple, but most are under water.'

'I have to see for myself.'

Fred nods, lips compressed. 'Where's your boat?'

'Jason finally took it out to Hoxie—been sitting in his back yard since I towed it from the East last year—I thought maybe he could use an extra boat now and then, but...'

'You don't reckon its *name* has anything to do with his reluctance to take it to the marina, do you, Green Eyes?' He grins broadly.

From the kitchen, Helen snickers and says, 'We heard about your name all the way to Dove Creek.'

'Damn good name if y'ask me,' says Windy, rising from beside Shan. 'Sum'bitch is screwed alright.'

Fred glances up at him, 'And gonna get more screwed.... Dominy wants *two* dams down in Grand Canyon.'

Shan slams her glass down. 'Sure! A mere Wonder of the World that only *he* can improve upon. I could improve on *him* too... if I could get a knife to his gonads! That man is a birth defect!'

Fred chuckles at the fight in her, remembering his own fight before he knew there was no winning against the system. 'Chantoozie, you just keep singin' that Bureau song you sent me—it'll do more good than writing these deaf, senile politicians. They took the fight out of me when they drowned us out at Dandy—we're just ghosts to them now. That was my place to live out m'days... to fish... sit in the shade and die peaceable. I'm too old and tired t'try and find another one like it, even if there was one... which there ain't!'

～⌗～

As Buck showers he feels as if he's preparing for a special occasion, but isn't sure what. It's still hard for him to believe Windy is leaving next week.

'Christ,' he mutters under the little spray, 'I don't know why in hell I don't do the same, there's nuthin' here anymore.'

He turns off the hot water in the newly built stall with a force that could twist off the handle. It drips. 'Fucking stupid thing! The outside tanks never leaked a drop.' Putting on a clean shirt and jeans, he thinks how good it'll be to see Fred and Helen again, and wishes Myrna could be with them too... for old times' sake... to say nothing of Bradley, gone forever.

In his pickup, Buck pushes the wind, trailing sheets of dust, tearing along a part of the road he hardly sees anymore; the same road that for so many years carried him between the mine and home—the shack beside a river that shifted its sandbars every day, giving him a new design in his front yard. A river that talked to him, put him to sleep, earned money for him and fed him food... for thought... for eating.

This last year, living at Fry's trailer camp, has been the worst he can recall. Buck loves the desert, but a riverman without a river is only half a man—flowing water is in his blood.

'This old desert can get along fine without me,' he says aloud, 'but me, I need water. Maybe the time has come to go look up another river.... Yeah, I know... same song, second verse... maybe an ocean. Yup, for once in his mangy life Windy's got the right idea.'

The water tower above the outhouses, shacks, trailers and Windy's junk shows up in Buck's headlights.

He slows, shifting the pickup down into second—sees Fred's Land Rover... Windy's truck... and a... white Thunderbird...

THUNDERBIRD!

'So *that's* the game! I *thought* the ol' bastard had something up his sleeve. Well, some other time, Miss Shan Lu Farran!'

He spins the truck in a half circle, barely missing a gas pump, forming his own dust devil and sending gravel flying in every direction.

As he swerves back onto the road, he stomps the accelerator, leans out the window and beats his left hand against the door, howling into the night...

'*Vamanos!* Here I come! *Viva México!*'

꿍꿍

CHAPTER 17

October, 1965 — Fry Canyon — The Rincon

Shan skids her Bird to a stop in front of Buck's trailer, leaps out, sprints up his steps and bangs on the door with her fists, shouting. 'Open this door, Buck Watson! Right Now! I want to talk to you!'

Silence.

His truck is partly loaded with camping and other gear, indicating that he's planning to go somewhere. She kicks the door and hollers again. 'You open this goddamn door or everybody in this canyon is going to know…'

The door opens and Buck stands there frowning. 'For Chrissake what's wrong?'

She steams past him and in the process shoves him toward the couch, wheels around to face him and hisses, 'You mean what *isn't* wrong, don't you, Mr. Arrogant?'

Open mouthed, palms up, he stands shaking his head.

'My! Aren't we all innocence and light this morning? You're a real sonofabitch, you know that? And damned well you know what's the matter! Who the hell do you think you are?'

He looks her up and down and says, 'Well… I might ask you the same question, since you're the one comes…'

'I'm Shan Farran, once a river-running friend of yours, a casual lay, and now a mere passer-by… here to tell you what I think of you!'

'So this ain't a friendly visit,' he states, controlling a smile.

'You think you can tromp all over people's feelings, no matter *who* they are, don't you? Like some kind of lofty misanthrope who lives by his sacred rules alone, nobody else's feelings matter, right?'

'I don't know what you're talking about, Shan....'

'Bullshit! You ruined a whole evening, probably a whole *year*, with your smartass antics last night—ruined Windy's going away party, shit on Fred's and Helen's expectations of seeing you, especially after their long drive, and as for me... kiss my ass...! I don't give a flying fuck what you do anymore.'

'Well, I was wondering why...'

'Shut up! You never gave a thought about how much Helen and Fred were looking forward to seeing you after a year of your holy absence. Or poor old Windy, who has to leave a place he loves because he can't make it anymore. No! All you could think about was putting distance between you and Shan Lu Farran! Let me tell you, Mr. Watson, you've no idea how much distance you've put between your two-night lay of last year. Yes, two. It was only supposed to be *once*, remember?—*'the first, the last, and the only time'*— said the big man,... but he couldn't quite keep his hands off, could he, when we had to wait another night for them to dig us out?'

Buck sits on the arm of the couch, rubs his hands together, and mumbles, 'I don't see what that has to do with...'

'You don't see anything you don't *want* to see. It has to do with this: Fred and Helen are going back to Dove Creek this afternoon, and if you've got any balls at all, you'll go to the Crossroads, make your apologies and say goodbye to them and Windy. I take it you're leaving for some faraway place or the truck wouldn't be packed.'

'Goin' to Baja,' he mumbles. 'Windy's not as dumb as he looks. There sure ain't nothin' around here any more.'

'Good place for you, Watson. Maybe if you stay down there talking to yourself long enough you might dig up some respect for *decent* folks. As for me, I'm going down to Hoxie to see what's left of my *real* love, the river; and I'm going alone. Just in case you think I want your priceless company, I goddamned well don't!'

'Christ, Shan! Talk about *me*.... I figured after a year you might of wised up enough to not want to see that mess.'

She plunks her hands on her hips. 'Surprise! Since when do you consider my smarts, or lack of them? Anyhow, it's nothing I intend to explain. My affair with a drowned lover is somewhat like another I had awhile back, only this time truer to the promise. It *will* be *the first-last-and-only time.*'

She whirls away, stomps on the fart, slams the door, gets in her '55 Thunderbird and skids off down the road.

The Bird's headlights crawl up rainbow-colored mounds of Chinle Shale as Shan drives, slowly, through the dark, moonless night—a cold, gusty night that resembles a search on another planet. Light is sucked into the sand like pale ink into a blotter, and intermittent blasts of wind sideswipe the car. When she looks back, the faint glow from her tail lights prowls behind in a dusty wake.

Her route twists, then dips into eroded pockets, cuts through streams that meander over slickrock. Periodically a force that isn't wind holds the car to a crawl—orange sand that covers the track and piles in drifts to leeward. She's startled several times by huge yellow arms that loom out of the night like prehistoric monsters— toys of the road construction crew, making it wider.

A sudden rain rushes her when she leaves the protection of a cliff, setting up a din inside her cozy spaceship; when the road veers again to the wall, the rain is sucked back into a black sky. Two red dots flash in the tunnel of her lights and the outline of an animal appears. *A coyote?* They disappear as she approaches, and the shape moves swiftly across the road with feline grace... black and white... striped and spotted... big tufted ears... a question mark for a tail... then gone. *Bobcat!*

'Ah-h-h-h.... Thank you, you wild, beautiful thing!' she sighs.

Sixty miles of winding ends in a clutter of chrome and plastic, pastel trailers, metal buildings and sheds, gas pumps, tanks, chain-link fences and the continuous *put-put-put* of a generator. She stops where a couple of spotlights shine across the area, beside a trailer that Jason has described as his. She is atop Hoxie mesa, several hundred feet above the reservoir. Though she can't see it, its presence is announced by a stale fishy odor.

She gets out of the car and stretches. Starlight filters through fast-moving clouds and the wind warbles in her ears as she turns, trying to get her bearings. North… she decides, facing the wind, and looks up to see Polaris several degrees off from her calculation.

'Hm-m. Just enough to get me lost,' she mumbles, 'if I were afoot instead of horseback.' Looking around for *Screwd River* and not seeing it, she recalls Jason saying it was down the road by the marina in the boatyard.

She opens the trailer door, steps inside and feels for a light switch. The darkness is ripped by a bare globe in the ceiling. When her eyes become accustomed to the glare she senses a vague familiarity about the aluminum rectangle and after a moment places it—the plan is the same as Buck's. She takes a step toward the sink, half expecting the floor to wheeze. It doesn't, but the faucet drips. She turns it off, the thought of Buck along with it, and without lighting the heater or bathing she undresses, brushes her teeth and crawls into Jason's bunk.

ᐒ᠊ᐭ

Shortly after sun-up, people calling, gears grinding, planes landing and taking off wake her. She finds the coffeepot and brews some while dressing, taking care not to look out any windows. When she'd last spoken with Jason, he'd explained why he couldn't join her and told her what to do. Her Johnson motor had been serviced; his former boatman, Bill, would be at the landing to help her launch. Jason's voice had been gentle, as always, and he was glad to hear from her, but the way he rattled off instructions sounded like a record he'd play for someone who'd never been there—*Watch your gas consumption, and don't go too far from the marina without telling someone where you'll be; take a gas stove, there's no driftwood anymore; you can get groceries and frozen meat at the store; there are life jackets in the trailer; if a blow starts, hole up in one of the side canyons. Maybe I can get there by the middle of the week and go out with you a day or so before you have to leave, I hope so*—Jason knew… she'd never been there!

Shan had finally canceled the dream and accepted that she must live with her own misery; hadn't come to Hoxie before now because she was not able to face the agony. Consequently she'd worked clear into September before writing to Windy to find out where everyone was. Before his party she had, once again, entertained the thought of asking Buck to take the trip with her, but this time in her boat, instead of the canoe like she'd once hoped; even though hers would be harder to maneuver in some of the side canyons.

But last night his behavior so infuriated her that even now her hand itched to smack him.

'Bastard!' she mutters. 'Stubborn bastard, what in hell is he trying to prove? You'd think I'd flayed him, not laid him!' She washes her cup and steps out into a brisk, clear day.

At first it's impossible to orient herself. She's almost pleased, because this place is alien, and not hers at all, just an ugly blight on a hilltop. The scattered aluminum houses and junk flung about makes a tenement of what was a once a wild faraway moon-walk. It's so incongruous that she laughs.

'My God, what a ridiculous place to live! Not a shrub or tree to break the monotony.' The reservoir can't be seen from where she is, so she walks to the top of the mound. The horizon widens and the land drops away. She anticipates the shock that's coming, but when it does is not prepared. An invisible force rocks her— she gasps, throws a hand over her mouth, eyes flooding beyond focus.

Spinach-green water lies in a silent trench between the stunted canyon walls—not a sandbar, not a tree, not a talus slope, only wall-to-wall water oozing into every canyon and crevice, lasciviously fingering private nooks, spreading the pink lips, licking at the sandstone, leaving a spittle of salt above the waterline—the present waterline. A white drawdown scar rises twenty feet above, as if someone had pulled the plug in a dirty bathtub, changed their mind and stuck it in again. On the updraft comes a strong mephitic stench.

The tears flow. 'Oh God.... Where are you, Colly Raddy? Where am *I*? Where are *We?*' Somewhere a chain saw answers.... She finds herself on her knees... her shirt is wet, her skin cold... time has left her blissfully unattended for a space she doesn't care to determine. She turns away, clutching her stomach, goes to the Bird and drives down the switchbacks to the marina.

How long does it take to launch a sixteen-foot fiberglass boat with a thirty-five horse motor? Half an hour, maybe. And when launching it over someone's grave? No longer.

Shan drives down to the boatyard where she loads her food and gear into *Screwd River*; then Bill helps her hitch the trailer to the Bird and launch it off the ramp into the reservoir. She parks the Bird back in the yard while Bill drives her boat to the gas pumps, and begins filling two extra five-gallon tanks, plus her feeder tank—enough gas to give her over a hundred-fifty miles of travel... *if* she doesn't go full speed ahead.

At the dock three fishermen are gassing up, themselves already gassed to the eyeballs. One of the anglers tries to draw her into conversation, but she's in no mood for idle chatter. Anxious to be away and into her side canyons, she turns her back, ignoring him.

Tossing his beer can into the water, he comes up behind her and says, 'You all by y'self, li'l girl? You shudd'n go out in this wile canyon by yer self, you liable t'git lost....'

Her stomach flutters and hot saliva comes to her mouth, choking off what she's ready to say, as he blunders on. '...You better come with us, so's nuthin' kin happen to you.'

'Not bloody likely, you insensitive twit,' she hisses through clenched teeth, and turns to face him, her mouth open for the kill... just as Bill steps between.

Standing eye to eye, three inches from the drunk's unshaved whiskers, in a warning voice he says, 'Mister, this lady was here ten years before any of you. She even named a bunch of these canyons you're goin' fishin' in—she ain't gonna git lost!'

Shan steps in behind her steering wheel. Bill unties the bow and stern lines, tosses them to her and winks; she flashes him a look of gratitude and blows him a kiss, again ignoring the big outdoor sportsman, who is still so dense he doesn't know he's been dismissed.

He puts a boot on her deck, and slurs, 'Then mebby she kin show us where the fish are in this damn lake, cause we ain't seen any.'

Her answer is in the form of golden opportunity, so sure it's going to happen she's already choking with laughter. 'Fuck off, ape!' she says, pushing the throttle fast forward, leaving the dock; then looking back to watch the idiot fall butt first into the water.... Instead, she sees Bill grab him by the neck of his jacket and yank him back onto the solid marina walkway.

'N-o-o, Bill, why'd you do that?' she calls, making an arch of spray as she curves away from the marina toward downstream, revealing the lettering on the side of her boat. The drunk somehow gains his balance and pointing asks, 'Whazzat mean?'

'Means just what it says, mister. Unfortunately this ain't a river no more.'

The wind is cold. She pulls up the hood on her parka and looks for familiar landmarks, totally confused by all the fakery and the speed that adds to it when she pushes the throttle forward. Hoxie Crossing, where the tallest trees dipped their branches into the water, their tops whitened by great blue heron rookeries; the gold and green leaves against the immense orange tapestry wall at sundown; the long bar of colorful rocks and fine white sand. *Where is it? Have I turned the corner? Why do the cliffs lean in on me and push me to the center of this stony trench...? Oh... because the talus slopes are gone!* Indeed! They were part of the intricate design of the river, acting as buttresses for the great walls, keeping them safely upright, now they look unsupported and menacing.

She remembers that she'd left Hoxie about ten 'clock, but hadn't told Bill where or how far she was going because she actually didn't know—just that she'd be gone two or three days.... Two or three days... just like those years long ago when she and her friends water-skied on Lake Mead, thinking it such fun, such a wonderful place, and not giving a thought to what lay beneath that glassy water. Here, she knew, only too well!

Oh, My River, they've cut off your legs... amputated you below the waist and left you to live out your days a disfigured paraplegic! She sees a rock separated from the main wall in the shape of a lizard's head—but only the head?—the entrance to Lost Eden. *Dear God, is it that deep already? Jesus! It's got three hundred more feet to go. There won't be anything left. I can't, I won't go in there!*—to find the deep pothole that once held her prisoner. Now it was drowned in a much deeper prison... forever.

Being two hundred feet higher changes all contours, and those that are somewhat familiar have changed color; everything is purple, pink and blue, reflecting more blue; no varied shades of green for contrast, no whites, no banks of flowers, no yellows.

Seeing some arches that look familiar, and a chipped trail up the slickrock, she knows it must be Shock's old trail and the cave with an Anasazi ruin. She has a longing to see, before it all goes under, the old Swede miners' names they chipped in the rocks. The reservoir scum has licked up to the kiva's foundation rocks once, and been drawn down again some twenty feet. As she cuts the motor and glides in, her wake bangs the chine against a slanting wall. She isn't used to this sort of non-river landing—no place to tie up, nothing to tie up to. About to climb out and take the bow rope with her, she looks up and sees—MARGO & WAYNE—in silver spray paint on the face of the Swedes' rock. *S-S-Shit!* She pushes off, waiting for the current to take her far away.... But she sits in water that's dead, silent and unmoving. She finds the silence disturbing... unnerving.

...Makes my ears ring. We're so used to sounds that we need them to tell us we're alive.... Silence is golden only when it has the edges knocked off.... On my river there was stillness beside the river's murmur; in this place where nothing is familiar the silence is sinister, like before a storm.

She pushes the starter.

The miles go by in a dream. She sits on the seat back, steering with her feet, like Buck, feeling like a stranger in a strange land. Time after time she is thrown off by inlets that weren't there before and fooled into calling the canyons wrong. *Won't get lost, huh...? That honky fisherman may have been right after all.*

The motor drowns out every sound but the *ping-and-swish* of water rushing beneath her boat. She's afraid to drive close to either the right or left walls for fear of hitting or scraping rocks lying just beneath the surface; her wake writes on the bland reflecting glass mid-channel.

A few water-skiers pass by, coming from downstream. 'Down what?' she asks aloud. 'Down reservoir...? Down marina...? What the fuck is *up*, here...? Up canyon? What did we call our directions on Mead? To Boulder... to Pierce's Ferry?' She thinks of Lilly again, how she would love this glassy-ass reservoir for her ski boats. 'Not me, baby.'

She is bored to tears with this ugly place; bored and angry, miserable... and lonely.

Goddammit, Buck, why do you have to be so stubborn? I know you want to be with me again; you're scared, that's all, scared you'll be trapped. Hell, I don't like traps any more than you do...! You couldn't stand to have a woman underfoot all the time any more than you could fart neckties!

Coming hard onto the Rincon's crumbled edges, where they had often hiked together, has made her think of him again. She pushes the gears to neutral and sits rocking quietly in the wake... wondering...

After the two nights when they had been locked together in North Wash, she'd learned the true reason for his backing off from her; not through any conversation, but by the way he made love to her: Softly... gently... eagerly, yet holding back... caressing, whispering, touching, burying himself in her, then retreating... not using words, only his actions, over and over again, that told her he cared for her... hopefully, like no other.

She sees the arch near the inner cap that they had hiked to, now only a few feet above the present water level, and decides to camp there for the night. There's no wood, just beer cans and people's trash. She hauls her air mattress and bedroll to the lower end of the arch, is too tired and disheartened to cook on the gas stove, so she opens a can of beans, eats them cold, brushes her teeth, snuggles into her sleeping bag and drifts off under a deep star blanket and a moonless sky.

৵৽

CHAPTER 18

Hidden Passage — Dangling Rope

Shan wakes but doesn't move because something heavy is resting between her feet. Asleep in the night, dreaming or for real, she felt a pressure on her back and tried to rock it off; now she wonders if whatever it was has decided to stay. Hoping it's not a snake coiled on her bedroll, she cautiously lifts her head... The cottontail leaps two feet in the air and hits the ground running.

'Ho, Bunny! Hope you've got a home way high up.' She tries to picture how all the critters are managing with flooded burrows—understanding now what Jason meant when he told her of the hundreds of beaver that had died in the canyons: *They cut every tree and sapling, frantically trying to stop the flow.... Their food rotted and their homes floated on the still water—some of them sitting, bewildered, on top the woven sticks.... And the deer, once forced up a side canyon, couldn't swim out because of the driftwood, or if they did manage to get to bedrock, it was too steep to climb and they either starved or drowned.*

She struggles with coffee, bacon, egg and tortillas over the small burner, cursing most of the time, pining for the old driftwood fire and grate that made it almost fun to prepare a meal in the open. She tops off her gas tank—so much oil, so much gas— packs up and sets out on the longest straight stretch in the old river, now something like a cement trench. The hanging canyons that had always intrigued them looked like open gutters pouring in from both sides.

She had planned to boat a little way up the Escalante River, a bit over thirty miles down-canyon from Hoxie, but when she gets there, it is so clogged with giant swirling driftwood she doesn't dare try to enter. Where the San Juan enters the Colorado, she finds the highest walls in the river canyon stunted by a third, and the reservoir more than a mile wide from wall to wall. She feels like one of the bewildered beaver, sitting on top of her floating home. Yet, only a couple miles from the San Juan is the one canyon she's determined to enter, a favorite of all the river runners. Hidden Passage.

Major Powell's name for it is now utterly invalid. The entrance, no longer hidden, is agape and uninteresting like all the rest, scummy and clogged with drift. After many years of walking, climbing and swimming around curve after curve in this sinuous canyon, now, a hundred feet above on flat water, she has no clue as to what part she boats over. In the flotsam she notes that the ubiquitous beer can vies for equal billing with motor oil and plastic containers. 'Pigs!' she spits, inching her way through the mess.

Trees poke from the muck, looking as if they'd been stripped by locusts. Cutting throttle, backing, going around a submerged tangle, she tries to get away from the smell of sick water and exhaust fumes; still, up ahead cottonwoods beckon, brilliant in their fall golden colors, so she cuts the motor, takes an oar and tries to paddle ahead. Twenty feet from the bank, she gives up. 'Christ, I couldn't get through there with a crowbar.' Ready to turn back, she hears the trickle of living water and the song of a canyon wren. Her heart leaps to the familiar call and she shouts, 'I *will* get up there and out of this puke. I *will*, goddammit!'

She strips and crawls over the side, takes the rope and winds it around a tree that's anchored in the mud; ooze clutches at her legs and she sinks to her hips, but bedrock stops her—she emerges a gooey fish-smelling mess. Once on solid ground she races up Hidden Passage and washes off in the first clear pool.

A warm breeze drifts down. She walks and runs, splashes through the stream, talks to it, drinks thirstily of the crystal water, wiggles through each shallow, plants her toes and fingers into Moki steps, same as the Anasazi who made them a thousand years ago, and slows only for her city-tender feet. A redbud tree in full green leaf—the tree of a million emerald hearts—her favorite Glen tree, stops her. It hugs the slickrock as they do, up these narrow, not-always-sunny slopes, at times growing right out of a crack in the rock... in springtime splashing it with pink-purple blossoms. Shan reaches for the leaves, brushes them across her cheek and says, 'Thank you for your splendor, my beauty.... May you be lucky enough to rise above the deluge.'

She turns down-canyon, gathering dry wood to take aboard, determined not to cook on the gas stove. In tune with her whole-ness once again, intoxicated by the dynamic, living canyon, she fails to hear the sound of voices as she rounds the bend coming in sight of her boat.

'Wow-ee!' a voice rings out with an all-too-familiar connotation.

Startled, she drops the wood and looks up to see two men and a woman fishing over the side of their boat. She neither runs for cover nor feels she is out of place.

'Hey, lookit the babe with no clothes,' says one of the men. The other snickers. The *woman* looks away.

'Looks like we invaded a nudist camp,' says the snickerer 'Wonder what'cha gotta do to belong?'

Shan smiles, thinking of the poet Frank Townshend, '... *Then they fled, with cries and twittering/ Like a lot of doves disturbed by a snake./ Yet we were of the same race/ And I meant them no harm...*' but says nothing as she picks up the wood and moves to her boat.

In a nasal, scolding tone the woman says, 'Young lady, you'd better get some clothes on.'

Shan stops, muck and water to her knees, and blandly asks, 'Why?'

'Well now, just a minute. This is a public place. You could be arrested!' They look apprehensively behind her as if expecting her to be joined by others.

'Really? Am I bothering you? Are you being molested in any way? Besides, this is a very *private place*'—she raises her voice and bites out her words—'and I will take my clothes off *here* any god-damn time I please!'

The men reel in their lines. 'Now look here... we...'

'I'm looking—and I see three maggoty-looking slobs in a boat with a titsy-poo awning over it so they won't get any sun on their white flab, plus several beer cans and candy wrappers floating

around, known as *litter,* and *that is* against the law!' She slams the
wood on the deck, extricates herself from the mud and points her
rosy bum at them as she wiggles over into the pilot's seat.

'We're going to report you to the… to the…'

'Try the Mermaid Society,' she smirks, pushing the starter
button.

Unable to make a grand sweeping exit through the debris, she
veers as close to them as possible, leans over and sneers, 'You poor,
sick, dirty-minded old farts. Get a life!'

Shan slogs through the deadwood and drift of Hidden
Passage's entryway, her stomach churning. The few loving hours
she has spent in the live canyon and stream have been submerged
in the aberrations of the reservoir. Finally, free of scum and tangle,
Screwd River emerges from the tarnished walls in a burst of speed.
It is noon.

Music Temple, across the way, yawns uninterestingly beneath
the crown of its identifying hat. Wary of another encounter close
on the heels of the last—there are people in these aborted canyons now—she passes it by. 'I'll catch you on the way back, my
beauty—when I'm sure there are no turds bobbing about.'

The wind raises goose-bumps, making her reach for her
clothes. She dresses as she passes many familiar canyons, heading
for her next target, eight miles downstream: Forbidding Canyon…
once the start of a five-mile hike to Rainbow Bridge.

When the boat passes buoys that mark the way to the Bridge,
she slows, looking down into the water where ruins, now disinte-
grating, line the undercut, and follows more buoys that mark the
turn into Aztec Creek and Bridge Canyon. The water changes to
murky green, a salt belt girdles the pink walls and oil slithers over
the surface. She motors up to the marina, now resting in the canyon's narrow throat, and grumbles, 'This is insane!'

She knows no one here, or wants to. While the attendant—
who looks like a teenager—fills her gas cans, she checks cables,
battery, prop and shear pin supply. 'Lost one in Hidden Passage
and will probably shear more before this fiasco is over…. I should
have a saw-blade for a prop with all the lumber floating around.'
She goes into the makeshift store for some cans of oil. When

paying the man she smiles, recalling another missing part of the river days: no money ever need change hands.

'You all alone, lady?' asks the gas kid as she steps into *Screwd River.*

'Yes, I am.'-

'Hm-m, interesting name, your boat. Goin' up to the Bridge?'

'No.'

'Oh, you should see that—quite something t' see, and easy t'get to now; just a short walk up a good trail. Over twenty-five thousand people have signed the register, and...'

'My *first* signed number is 9,366—and you couldn't pay me nine-thousand three-hundred and sixty-six dollars a *step* to go up there now, kid. Once, years ago, I slept on top of it.... Sure am glad nobody can do that now, or there'd be a bloody hotel up there. Thanks anyway.' She smiles at the memory as she motors away from the dock.

The youth scratches his head. 'Another one a' them hard-asses! Wonder what makes 'em so damn touchy about this place—act like they own it.'

As she winds her way out of Forbidding Canyon a single cloud flits across the winding blue ribbon of sky above, momentarily darkening the murky water beneath her boat and curdling her thoughts.

'These know-nothing marina children make me feel like Fred said... like an old ghost. I feel as if I've risen from the dead to take a ride over my own grave.'

Back in the main trench, she almost passes one of their favorites—Cascade Canyon. She spins a loop and returns. The entrance walls are inundated, of course, and the canyon narrows as she slowly winds her way in, each turn the same as the last, no identifiable features. The sound of her motor reverberates irritatingly off the walls... where once reigned beautiful stillness.

An odd shadow appears in the water and she slows to five knots, eyes drawn to a mark on the wall where it stops twenty feet above her. At its base is an arch large enough to put her boat through. The 'fluct,' her name for fluctuation, has left it plastered with dead algae. 'Oh-h-h... must be our little eye-in-the-sky that was two hundred feet up.' Driftwood fills each concave, and the float stretches wall to wall until there's no hope of getting to the arch. Carefully, she turns and moves back toward the main canyon.

She has perceptive moments about Jason's need to prepare himself for this parade of horrors. What she can't understand is how he can still be here, still take trips, still operate the marina, but she knows well enough why Buck is leaving and wishes to God she was with him. She is almost numb to the destruction—this flagrant making of a new kind of desert in a sandstone trench.

'That's what this is, *a desert!* No green thing. No birds. No tracks. No moss, ferns or flowers. No sound but the slurp of...'

A speeding outboard cuts a curve at the edge of sunlight. The driver, momentarily blinded, bears down upon her. She yells and swings *Screwd River* toward the wall. There is a bang and scraping as it hits, but the speeding boat zooms on without cutting throttle, passengers waving as they disappear around the next bend, a three-foot wake curling up the walls behind them.

Shan throws her boat into neutral and leaps to the foredeck to stave off. Her wrists take the shock. She winces in pain, slumps down on the rocking deck and moans: 'You were right... all of you... Buck, Jason, Step, Bennett and even old Windy.... There's no sense my being here. It's gone, like you said... all gone.... Even the sky doesn't look like sky... just a white sheet over walls dripping blood... blood spilling into a pig's trough!' She grits her teeth, then gives in to hugging her sobbing, shaking body.

Her final destination, the one she most hates to witness, because she named it—Dangling Rope Canyon—is about four miles away. Curiosity propels her to look at the place the Park Service intends to plunk the most isolated marina in the states, or so Fred Bennett had told her. Seven years ago, she, Step and Jason had put that name in their journals because a frayed rope dangled from near the entrance. Jason said, *'It's a shortcut from here to the Klondike Trail, a trail that supplied the placer gold miners who worked on Klondike Bar during the late eighteen-hundreds. It goes up through the Entrada and Carmel formations to the Kaiparowits Plateau, where their stock and supplies came from.'* Shan had gone for the rope, but when she jerked on it a slither of rocks almost hit her on the head. Jason had pulled her back, saying, *'Nix, Miss Intrepid Explorer, that rope's too rotten; there are three forks, we'll just try another one.'* And Step had agreed.

Half an hour after leaving Cascade, she sees a white marker floating somewhere to the right of middle—right bank is still right bank to her, river or not. As she comes within reading distance she bursts out laughing.

'Jumping Jesus!' Slowly she circles the buoy, making it bob in her wake, and reads:

DANGLING ROPE CANYON
Rainbow Bridge 8 mi.
Last Chance Gas

'Why name it, then say: 'Last chance gas'...? Two gas-ups eight miles apart...? That's ridiculous.... Unless they plan to haul the floating dock at Rainbow Bridge down here.... Furthermore, Dangling Rope isn't *here*, it's way the hell gone under, and over *there.'* She is over the benches that the rope led to, and at this level can see parts of the Klondike Trail.

Bobbing around in the wake of her own circles, she must decide what to do next. It is now late afternoon and cloud formations have the look of frozen tundra, glacial and sparkling under the setting sun. Deep shadowy cervices divide them into an eroded white skyscape, delicately tinged with pink and violet. As always, the upstream wind has increased, so she searches for a place out of it, in what she decides must be the middle fork of the three. She finds a shallow, secluded cove beneath melting chocolate people, their shoulders slumped, hats askew, some with babies on their backs, also melted... The Carmel formation.

Still determined not to cook on the gas stove, she hikes over gravel bars and sandstone caps looking for firewood. Drift is thinly scattered in the drawdown but is caked with salts and un-burnable. As the sun flares out on the rim she drags back some horse-weed, black-bush and a few snap-weed stalks—barely enough to cook a steak. When she goes for water she's surprised to find it warmer than the air; not surprised that it tastes flat, mildly saline, and will make a lousy cup of coffee.

To keep warm and to help her sleep she mixes some rum with hot water, honey and lemon juice. Looking up, she toasts the Carmel People's disheveled ranks, who stare at her suspiciously from beneath their floppy hats. 'We never took booze on our trips,' she tells them. 'We were high on the scenery, on life and each other.'

She cooks her steak and eats listlessly. The night is oddly still—only *Screwd River*'s intermittent scratching against the slick-rock is audible. The clouds in their arctic rigidity seem to have disappeared…. The air feels weighted and smells fishy, unpleasant, not of the earth, not of the river; even smoke from the small fire is rancid. 'E-yuk… this poison must be contaminated!' she snorts, using one of Buck's favored phrases.

She mixes another drink, this one stronger than the last, and stumbles around laying out her air mattress and sleeping bag. 'You were right, Fred, there was no point in leaving our name *here*.'

Overwhelmed by a terrible loneliness, she flops on the bag and cries long, rending sobs. 'Why did I come… against everybody's advice…. Why do I have to torture myself? And Buck… you're heartless and mean for not helping me through this part…. I could take it, even enjoy some hikes, if you were with me… *and so could you!*' Her hand no longer itches to slap him. 'Du-doesn't love me because I'm sour on the world…. You been sour on it longer than me…! That's ju-just an excuse! You too, dear Jason, you've let me down, and Step… all of you… think I'm so tough, that I'll come smiling through, no matter what…. Bullshit…! My mush is softer'n alla your muh-mushes put together!' Looking up at the ragged group on the skyline, she whines, 'Dear me, Chocolate Folks… aren't we feeling sorry for myself…! Yes we am… an' why not…?'

She crawls into her bag and swirls to sleep with drunken blubbering.

In the night, oblivious to all and every, a member from the Chocolate Folks loosens itself and comes hurtling down off the cliff, bouncing over shelf after shelf of rock, and rolls to a stop beside her sleeping bag.

ᔆᔆ

CHAPTER 19 .

The Storm

Shan wakes at sunup shivering with cold. She looks to the south-west and far away, behind Gunsite Butte, sees layers of pearly orange; like fog banks that roll in from the sea, they reflect sunlight and reach high into the atmosphere. As she raises on her elbows, a surf of pain rolls across her forehead. She shakes her head and notices that one of the chocolate folks came to visit her sometime in the night.

'Jeez...! Any closer and we'd have been bedfellows. Ooo-ie, my head.... Coffee... coffee.'

A pot of the elixir brews on the Coleman stove as she stumbles about, hurriedly packing her gear, all the while keeping her eye on the awkward looking sky.

'What is it...? A storm...? Wind...? Sa... Dust storm...! Oh shit!' She drops what she's doing and climbs a twenty-foot knob of sandstone above her camp for a better view. It now looks more like a landscape than a skyscape; strata of brown and yellow layered with the orange. 'What to do...? Stay...? Too open here.... Go...? I'm sixty miles from Hoxie Crossing... that's three hours. I can probably make it—if not, I'll hole up in one of the side canyons like Jason said.... Hope it's a quickie.... *I'm ready to leave this latrine!*'

Half an hour later, gear stowed and tied down, gas tank full, she's underway. Zipped in a parka and jeans she stands on the seat looking over the windshield, the better to read the shallows—now's not the time to ding her prop on some submerged monolith. The early morning sun still shines here so she can read beneath the surface fairly well. Still, she stays dead center in the wall-to-wall water, not daring to open full throttle in case she has to cut back suddenly.

She passes Forbidding with the surface starting to ripple. The orange glow behind her has turned a murky red and seems to be gaining on her.

Three miles later, passing Twilight Canyon and fairly sure that she can't make Hoxie before it catches up, she plans to cut into Mystery, where the walls are high and protective.

Three more miles.

'Life jacket... better get that bugger on!' She reaches under the deck and steers with her feet as she buckles it. Cutting across the bend at mile seventy-three, she sees the mouth of Mystery ahead and pushes the throttle forward.

The sound of a screaming jet fills the canyon.

Before she realizes that's not what she's hearing, her boat rises on a swell. She turns to see a hump the size of an ocean breaker riding down on her before a cyclonic wind. Looking frantically for a place to run and seeing none, she turns *Screwd River* into the blast, hoping to ride the hump before it collects, breaks and tumbles her into its frothing fury.

The boat rises, hesitates on the lip... and plunges down the back side of the wave into a wind tunnel of sand and water. The fiberglass hull screeches on impact and she is thrown from the wheel to land astern beside the gas tanks. Walls are blotted from view... the water coated with red spirals that spread and sink... spread and sink beneath the driving force.

Shan's reaction is one of surprise—surprise that she's in the boat at all, and that it's still afloat. Suddenly it lurches. Automatically she high-sides, pulls herself forward, turns the wheel and comes about into the gale. The terror that leaped in her throat is gone now. She's not part of this event, but watching it—her mind ticks away what her eyes see, weighs it instantly, puts her body into action and takes on the next problem. Big waves streak across the bow.... She must play the throttle, not let it idle or stall... stay clear of the walls! Wind is cold... water warm as it strikes her full in the face, crashing over deck and windshield into the cockpit.

There's no way she can bail..... One thing about these ski boats is that they float, upside... or down. Somehow she doesn't care. Beyond fear, she feels a kinship with these wild elements, remembering those in her camps that tore the shore to pieces as she stood beneath a storm-born waterfall.

The motor sputters and dies as it falls off the stern-block and sinks in a trough, popping the gas line, swirling gas into the air and blowing it upriver. She pulls off her sneakers as the boat rises on a wave, skids, leans to port, wallows in the trough and rolls over. She pushes off the high side and momentarily goes under. When she surfaces the bottom of the boat is ten feet ahead of her.... On the next wave it's twenty.... Something whips between her legs and she grabs the stern rope... pulls herself closer... goes down again rides the next wave... reaches the boat and holds on.

Now comes the rain.

It hits the water in horizontal sheets, making mud of the dust it mixes with, turning the rain into blood, the atmosphere to purple. She can hardly breathe it's so dense.

Screwd River's stern suddenly drops. The nose rises and sways like a fighting fish at the end of a sportsman's line, then disappears over the wave's crest, skidding the rope through her hands.

If this were a storm on a natural river there'd be a rhythm in the waves, a current toward one bank or another and Shan could use the river's power against the storm to get herself aground. But in this freakin' teacup there's no symmetry. Waves ricochet off waves, thickening the air with spume, blinding her. She knows there are no banks, only vertical walls to smash into or be pulled away from. As she feared, those walls rise in dim outline above her, streaked by the russet falls that gush from their lips. Despite all effort, she is being washed toward them. Her strength ebbing, she tightens her Mae West and curses: 'You stone-headed river killers! I hope this busts your fucking dam wide open!'

A massive wave lifts her toward a break in the cliffs, then curls over her. When she emerges choking and gasping for breath, another lifts her and slaps her against the cliff beneath a cascade. Her last conscious thought is of Buck—greeting him... her arms entwining his neck, legs scissoring his waist... and his hands around the cheeks of her bottom, holding her to him.

She is smiling.

∂∾∾◌

Jason's truck growls uphill in first gear.

He tops out on Clay Hills Pass above the multicolored cones of Chinle Shale as the sun climbs over New Mexico into southern Utah. Ahead, the western sky looks as if it's been beaten—a sick yellow, blotched with deep purples.

'Hm-m-m. Never saw that before.'

But Jason is used to the weather's tricks, and drives his careful, moderate speed over the rutted, dusty road on his way to Hoxie Crossing, where he's supposed to find Shan and go up-canyon with her for a few days.

Kinda glad I had those meetings to go to. By the time she gets back from the lower canyons she'll be over some of the shock and I can relax a little bit with her... maybe.

He'd known all along he could never witness her initial distress, her *lake sickness* he called it... and he needed time. Time to comprehend the new Shan, the one he'd seen in Chicago—above all, the one who'd written him a month or so after she'd left her boat with him last year. One sentence in that letter had left him confused and adrift.

'I'm tired of beating my wings against the egos in this business. I want somebody to look after ME for a change, pay some of the bills, LOVE me... I'm thinking of getting married.'

'Married! Dear Joseph!'

Not a hint, not a clue that this had been in her mind. Love her? My God, didn't they all love her? What else could she want?

A month or so later (he still hadn't been able to answer), she wrote from New Jersey asking him to come for a visit when they tied the knot and found a house. New Jersey! She *hated* the east... Lord, why was she doing this...? Because the river was gone and there was nowhere for her to turn? She wasn't that unrealistic. Or was she? What could he say? What could he do? He couldn't take care of her. He could sympathize with her, and try to help; he could share the river with her.... Ah-h... not anymore.

Six months later another letter came:

'...gave up the idea... the man's an impossible jerk... I'd end up taking care of him. Who needs it? So-o-o, back to the salt mines. But not like before, Jason... I've changed direction... only doing concerts now. No more clubs or coffeehouses. I've a new booking agent and several concerts already lined up in colleges and for non-profit organizations... and I think I'll try the Rotting Reservoir come fall in my own boat, since nobody wants to take me in theirs—not even Steps in his new Chris Craft.'

Jason understands that they've grown apart since Chicago, mainly because of her attitude toward the reservoir. He has accepted it because he has to, but she never will. She was right about the 'new breed' though; fishermen who drink more than they fish; people who've never camped out, loading their boats to the gunnels with unnecessary items, who know nothing of lakes, rivers, oceans or motors, piloting them for the first time. And rudeness...! as if he were some sort of lackey: *'Whaddya mean, ya don't sell liquor...?' 'Where the hell's the cigarette machine...?' 'Don't you have anything in this store...?' 'Two bags of ice? We need ten...!' 'How much longer do we have to wait for gas...?'*

Occasionally old river friends will take him off for a few days of hiking up the side canyons. They give him a sense of performing a worthy service, turn his thoughts to better days and salve his ulcer—but they are few and far between, and don't like the reservoir any more than Shan, really.

He has left the truck for a moment to relieve himself, and looking westward, has become very concerned about the strange color of the sky. His thoughts return to Shan-of-the-present.... 'Hope we're not in for a big windy... she's out there all alone.' He slams the door, and picks up his speed toward Hoxie.

As he tops another two miles of up-hill climb something rocks the truck, and it's nothing on the road. 'Wind! It *is* a blow. Gosh, I hope she's holed up safe somewhere; there's no way to get to her if this is a bad storm.'

He races for Hoxie in the paint-removing sandstorm.

As he kills the engine a low moan comes up-canyon. His employees are dashing about, dragging equipment off the ramps, throwing it into the store, the gas shed, into trucks and station wagons. Nowhere is there a concerted effort to lash things down or get boats that are anchored to buoys into the cove.

The low moan turns to a shrill whistle.

Jason runs for Step's Chris Craft in a nearby slip, starts it and speeds toward the cove. At full throttle he skids around the end of the dock to open water. At the turn-in he meets the advance wave that Shan slid over, twice its size now. It lifts the pleasure craft thirty feet in the air, over the boats on buoys, over the gas dock, the store, the slips, like a tsunami wave and deposits it inside the dry dock fence on top of a two-hundred-thousand-dollar yacht.

Jason is still at the wheel.

❧

Three days after Shan blows him off the stick, Buck has his truck packed, along with *Rintintin* on its trailer, has bought his supplies and said his last goodbyes.

He puts the key to Windy's trailer on the counter of the Fry Canyon store and says to his friend standing beside him in the cold light of dawn, 'Sell it, Orvil, and bank the money for me until I send you my Mexico address.'

Orvil picks up the key, thoughtfully flips it over in his hand. 'It don't take you long once you make up your mind, does it.'

'Hell, ain't nothing t'stay here for now…. But I'm leaving *my* trailer here with you, case I should decide, against all odds, t'come back…. For once old Windy has the right idea.'

'Looks like you'll beat him to it.'

'Not by a whole lot; he's only got one more load.' Buck zips up his parka, they smile, shaking hands. 'Well, don't fall down any shafts, and keep yer pecker up—I'll be thinking about you when I'm out there in the clear, warm waters of the Sea of Cortez, droppin' a line off my boat.'

'Better goose that truck to the flatlands, ol' buddy, looks like we're gonna git some wet—funny lookin' sky over southwest indicates a slight movement of the atmosphere.'

Buck gets in the idling pickup and turns east on the main road, his boat trailer shivering over the corduroy as he heads for the Cedar Mesa turnoff and the Isobella Dugway he helped build down at the old uranium mill at Mexican Hat. When he arrives at the lip overlooking Monument Valley, the rising sun strikes the tops of those imposing cliffs—molten gold poking through a dusky purple haze. Usually from here he can see all of southeastern Utah clear into Arizona, but this morning a curtain drops across the valley; a curtain that changes color as the sun rises. He stops to check his boat and trailer before descending the serpentine drop of two thousand feet, is puzzled by the strange looking sky and wonders if Shan might still be on the reservoir.

'Ah, shit! That crazy woman'll probably be standing bareass as the newborn, jumpin' up and down in the rain.' He smiles and shakes his head. 'Boy, was she ever pissed at me!—I needn't worry; she can take care of herself.' Yet, the longer he looks westward the less convinced he is. There's violence going on down in those canyons.

About an hour later, after he's crossed the Utah/Arizona line, he feels the back end of the truck skid into the left lane and turns to see the trailer wrench free and blow off the road in a blast of tumbleweeds, flying red earth and sage. He slams into third, the truck fishtails crazily on the sand-coated asphalt and rolls, landing upright in the soft hummocks beside the road.

The motor coughs and dies.

He drops his hands from their brace against the cab roof, gingerly rubs his head and ear, and reaches for the back of his neck. *Nothing serious.* Outside he can hear sand blasting and the tarp ropes over the truck bed drumming against the leeward side. A few seconds later great drops of rain smear to saucer size against his windshield.

'Good. That'll harden up these little dunes and maybe I can get the hell out of here after all.' He turns the key... the engine starts. Knowing he can't get out to salvage anything until the blow is over, he turns it off, pours a cup of steaming coffee from his Thermos and leans back against the gun rack. The cab rocks violently, spilling the coffee on his hand and leg.

'Christalmighty! What is this... a fuckin' tornado...? Shan on the reservoir? Surely she's not still there.' He starts ticking off days on his fingers, trying to remember what Fred told him about her trip down canyon. He'd gone to the Crossroads after all, to make his excuses about the night before; still not ready to admit he'd been the sonofabitch she'd said he was, just wanting to see Fred and Helen before he left for Mexico. They'd given him an uneasy feeling that night, especially when Fred, the old philosopher, started putting ideas in his head, like: *Shan's in the wrong frame of mind to be out there by herself.... She's not as tough as she seems.... Should have company...* and stuff like that.

'Sure didn't sound like she wanted any when I last saw her!'... He's added up the days.... 'Holy shit. She must still be there!'

Again the wind blasts the truck—feels like it could tip over just sitting there. 'Where the hell's my boat and trailer?' He looks out into the fury but can't even see the truck's nose. Putting the top back on his Thermos, he reasons, 'My God, if she *is* out there on that fuckin' puddle of piss... if it's anything like this, she's just as good as drowned!'

His heart bangs hard against his chest. All the memories, passion and dreams he has immured for the last year break through the dam he thought was so solidly built, leaving him awash in an ocean of questions... with only one answer.

He brushes the sleeve of his parka across his eyes and says to the Monuments that are beginning to show themselves dimly against the western sky, 'I got to go see if I can find her... if she's still afloat.... But how in hell am I gonna get out of here... before it's too late!'

He's totally helpless in the rocking cab, frustrated that he can't move, and has to sit there and wait out the furry... an hour... two hours... more.... Who knows?

ॐ◌ॐ

CHAPTER 20

After the Storm

'I'll be a glass-balled ape!'

Windy's bright, beady eyes dart about surveying the wreckage. 'Never seed such a goddamn mess!' Standing beside his tired truck, lower lip clamped in his teeth, he rubs the stubble on his chin. In the gauzy after-light of the storm the Crossroads look more trashed than usual, with patches of brush and puddles of muddy water slimed with gasoline.

'Sum'bitch!'

Incredulous, he stares at the gas pumps—one down, the other leaning from the cement base. The two light fixtures overhead look like someone has tied a knot in them. To the west of the pumps, his thousand-gallon water tank sits topless, right-side up and half full—but the fifteen-foot platform he built under it is *gone*.

'Shee-it!' he yelps with a mixture of awe and dismay. 'Where the hell's my platform?'

Somehow, to him the place seems oddly uncluttered, and clutter is what gives Windy a sense of security—*big* clutter—of all his things around him. He pulls in his shoulders, feeling uncomfortable, not knowing why. Early yesterday he took a load of stuff to Cortez and sold it to a junkman; stayed overnight with a friend and missed the storm altogether. Now he's back to packrat whatever odds and ends he might use in Alaska, considering himself lucky to have gotten back at all with the roads as rutted and slushy as they are.

'Shitamighty… place looks like a Topeka Tornado smacked it.' Slowly he turns his head to peer toward White Canyon, bringing his eyes to rest on…

…nothing. He spins, loosens his hardhat, grabs it as it tilts over one eye, pushes it back and whispers, 'Sweet suckin' Jesus… they're gone!'… A fenced area of old tires and car parts, a shed full of gas and oil drums, a house-trailer and a flatbed. Gone.

Windy's first reaction—that of the habitual underdog—is to feel a rush of self-pity; injustice foisted on the innocent, tragedy that can befall a man who's only trying to make things better for himself and others. He drops his jaw and stares hollow-eyed before the bolt of realization strikes him.

'Yipes!' He leaps in the air, kicks his heels together and knocks himself off balance to sprawl in the clay, were he sits pounding his boot heels in the mud, howling with laughter.

'Yiiieeee-ha! They're all gone! And they ain't mine no more! I done sold them fuckers to an innocent pardy an' the whole mess of shit blowed off inta White Canyon. Fer once ol' Windy got the tit'n his mouth b'fore she went dry!'

He pushes to his feet and prances around the half-deserted plot, kicking anything that's loose. 'Take that, you poor asshole… 'n that… 'n *that*. There ain't no water on this side neither, 'thout ya gotta haul it from the spring five miles… an' in a dry year, Ya-hoo, there ain't no spring.'

One thing Windy has managed to keep to himself is who he sold his land to. Fearing adverse sentiment among the canyon people about his choice of a buyer, he plans to be long gone before they find out.

He bounds over the uneven ground, around the bent junipers to the edge of the White Canyon Narrows, and peers into its gloomy storm-ravaged depths. Strewn along the benches are pieces of metal, wheels, sundry car parts and a trailer window frame, glass unbroken, that winks faintly from behind a cedar. Over on the *other rim* lies the sheet-metal cover for his water tank. The bottom he can't see, but he knows the trailer is down there, accordion pleated, scrunched between the canyon's stony jaws.

'Wheeeww! That wind musta blowed through here like nothin' seen since the Pleistocene.' He hustles back to his truck.

'Bet that lake's a mess of crap and corruption. I better jingle my balls outta here b'fore some good Samaritan comes along thinkin' I'm another one, and hauls me down there t'look fer a carload of bodies. Them poor 'n separated pissers got no damn bidness out there in them little punkin' seed boats on that wall-to-wall puddle, nohow.'

The starter *er-err-errs* for half a minute before it catches.

'Hey... what about Shan?' He shrugs. 'Ah... she probly got out the day she got in…. She kin take care of herself…. Anyhow, Jason's with 'er by now... they'll be okay.'

He skids through mud onto the graveled road.

'I sure got the laugh on them land-grabbers—Jock somebody, and that other guy—same bastards come messin' round Buck's cabin—b'fore he done them the favor of excavatin' it. They was so hot to have my place within commutin' distance while they run the new Hite Marina…. Hee-haw! I'm gonna write her 'n Buck… tell 'um who bought it…. They'll be real pleased with ol' Windy, leavin' them such a cleverly planned and good, goodbye present.'

⁂

It is six o'clock the morning after the storm.

The sky to the north of Hoxie looks as if it has exploded, leaving cinnamon clouds rolling in its wake, with the billow's tops tinged in red from a rising sun.

Buck paces back and forth in front of his truck while Carl Blacktop's dozer clears boulders from the road leading down to Hoxie Crossing's once-upon-a-time boat ramp, floating like a cork atop the waves. The jumble of boats with bottoms up, high and dry, or bashed clear in, cover fifty acres of what used to be the marina. Below he sees a place where he can slide *Rintintin* into the water, regardless of the destruction, *if* he can get his truck and trailer down to it.

A few of Jason's employees wander about, still dazed, as if they don't know where or how to start the cleanup. Only two boats are upright in the water, one being bailed and possibly serviceable—if a working outboard is found to power it. In the bailing figure he detects a familiar movement, gets his binoculars from the truck and focuses… on Jason.

Buck shouts over the rip and roar of the dozer, 'Hey, Carl, how much longer before I can get down?'

'If the engine don't sputter and die on me, maybe half an hour, Buck. I think she's coughing water outta the gas and...'

'Then I'm going to walk down and help Jason bail. Give me a blast on the horn when you're done.' He climbs over the rubble and hikes downhill, his faint shadow bobbing over the slickrock.

'I could help you with that knee-bending exercise you're doing there, Jason, if I could find another bucket; otherwise, why don't you just give me that one?'

Jason turns to the familiar voice and stares blankly before answering. 'Well for heck sakes, Buck, what are you doing here? Aren't you supposed to be on your way to Mexico?'

'I only got by one border and one Mexican—the one with the Hat,' he says with his tight little grin. 'I was stopped short by a cyclone that blew me clean off the road. Hadn't a been for Honoshay heading for Kayenta, who stopped and helped me dig my boat out, I'd still be there.'

Jason climbs from the hull, looks down at his soaked boots and rolled-up pants legs, unable to respond at the moment. His eyes are moist when he raises them and asks in desperation, 'You've got a boat with you that *floats?* And a motor that's *working?*'

Buck starts to answer, but Jason's words, edging toward hysteria, tumble over each other, and he realizes the man is still in shock.

'...Lord, Buck, you can't imagine what happened here! Only five boats in the whole place were operable and they're all out on rescue.... They've sent ambulances all the way from Salt Lake to take in those we've found still alive, an'... and left us body... body bags for others.' He swallows, hard. 'I... we haven't... no word yet about...'

'I'm going after Shan, Jason—got a feeling she's still out there and needs help—soon as Carl gets that road cleared...'

Jason chews his lower lip and shakes his head. 'No... no, Buck... I couldn't,' he says shakily. 'I wouldn't be any good to you, if we, found... found her....'

'Not you, *me*.... I'm going to look for her. She's probably high and dry somewhere and not feeling too good; hell's fire, after hearing what happened to you...'

'That was a fluke. I don't know what the Lord is saving me for, but He sure went out of his way.... I should'uv been with her.... I should have gone. She begged me and Step a hundred times.... I didn't want to see...'

'Jason! *Jason!*' Buck shouts, trying to snap him out of it. 'You shouldn't be down here working. You need to go home, get some rest. Come on up the hill with me. and when Carl's done clearing the road...'

'Three of my workers... gone, Buck.... And Bill... he went out in the ambulance last night all broken up.... There's no...'

'I'm having Carl take you to town. Now c'mon, let's get outta here.'

Jason walks quietly to the foot of the old trail before the flood of words begins again, telling Buck the terror of the last twenty-four hours—a two-hour storm that funneled into the former Glen and seemed to concentrate all its power there. Buck understands well enough after being on the periphery and tries to inject some of his own story to get him to slow down, but Jason jangles on:

'Shan was right, you know.... This kinda thing is not for me. I don't have the business head to run a marina, not even with the partners who do.'

'Especially with *one* partner who does,' Buck mutters.

'How in the world will we ever get this place back in working shape again? It sure will take more money than *I'll* ever have.... Should've sold out to Carl like he wanted me to before this happened. Now I'll have to work like the devil to get it in shape so he *can* take over.'

'I've got an extra Johnson motor in the truck I can leave here to put on that boat you were bailing. I'll pick it up...'

The dozer horn blares, echoing against the truncated walls.

'Road's clear now, Jason.' Buck takes his arm, steering him toward Carl's van. 'You get in and I'll send Carl over to drive you home after I have a talk with him. The sooner you get the hell out of here, the better!'

When he reaches the dozer he finds Carl tinkering with the carburetor. He thanks him for moving the rocks, then tells him about Jason's condition. 'He could flip out if he doesn't get home to a hot meal, a hot shower and a warm bed. How soon can you take him in?'

'Damn, I just got here a couple hours ago, an' look what all I got left to do.' Carl swings his arm in a circle. 'Can't you ferry him?'

Buck's anger rises. 'Then get one of your boys to do it, god-dammit—the man is sick! Mine's the only workable boat here now, and I'm going after Shan.'

'Hell, we got rescue boats out, an' it don't take 'lotta brains to figure Shan's probably lost and gone, down there,' he points at the water, 'in the Jewel of the Colorado.'

'In the *what?*'

"Jewel of the Colorado'... That's what Floyd Dominy calls Lake Powell. Purty nice, huh?'

'Well, Carl, since you're asking me, if you want to call this fuck-ing sewer a *jewel*, maybe brains don't run in your family.... Maybe they just crawl.'

ᔐᘏ

The sun seems to rise almost painfully.

Hazed over from yesterday's storm, it leaves almost no shad-ows on the rolling mounds and creases of sandstone that sur-round Navajo Mountain like a billowing skirt. Reservoir Powell's dull glint lies like a rusty butcher knife between blood-streaked cliffs. The great wind and rain have passed on, leaving untold destruction.

Mega waves have rolled up side canyons, scattered tons of driftwood like straw, splattered boats against walls, killed and drowned many. In some of the narrower passages the watermark is a hundred feet overhead. No marina is still afloat. The only boats saved are those that were so far up side canyons that the waves played out before reaching them, and by freak accident—lifted on the foaming tongue and spit out intact, as was Step's Chris Craft with Jason aboard.

Such a wave has lifted a slight, unconscious form from the rag-ing reservoir, over the twisting convolutions above Music Temple, and deposited it, belly down, in a tangle of orange and blue, on a slope some fifty feet above the streambed. The head lies down-slope, with a ribbon of water and vomit stains below it.

The figure moves... then lies still again.

Some minutes later her cold, blue hands push against the stone as she tries to sit up. Cliff walls reel about her head.... Nauseous and shivering she sinks back down, closing her eyes. She tries again, raises on one elbow, is dizzy, can't steady herself and rolls over. The parka squishes under her, the bulk of the life jacket over it blocks another roll, leaving her on her back.

Pain shoots through her whole body when she pushes up on her elbows.

Slowly, she moves her head left, then right. Walls fix their position and she looks around, half welcoming, half rejecting what she sees—the familiar crown of the hat-rock above Music Temple. She seems to be almost under it. Haltingly, her ragged mind shifts a gear.

'How'd I get way up here...? 'N how'd I get into Music Temple...? I was three miles downstream when...' The surface of the reservoir is not visible, only the upper part of Music Temple canyon.

Nothing in Shan's makeup has ever allowed the possibility of a death wish—fighting has always been her way out of a tight place—but in the last month or so, intensified these last few days, a sense of hopelessness has risen. What, after all, is there to fight for? When she wakes to her continued existence and a body that's weak, cold, sick and sore, she flops down again on the slanting stone and covers her face with trembling hands.

'Why...? Why keep *me* around?' she asks the great unknown. 'It was so easy going down like that... so easy.' Recalling her last thoughts in the deluge, she asks, 'Where are you now, Buck...? Across the border in sunny Mexico?' Then, she sinks into a great backwash of self-pity, forgetting that this familiar place will be covered in time, same as the great Temple below her is now. 'Okay... Tarzan, you can run, run, run your lovely balls off looking for another Eden that's anything like this... this river and our canyons.... There isn't one... not in this whole wide world... an' you know it...! We could run the river, and live here....' She tastes salt in her mouth, unaware that she's been crying—her head buzzes, reality returns and thoughts trail away. She drops her hands and relaxes, face up to the sun.

Her stomach growls. She fumbles for the buckles on the Mae West, finally releasing them. Her next try at a sitting position is successful—she lets the Mac West drop behind her—now she can unzip the slushy parka. Inside one pocket is a waterproof capsule of matches and a small flat tin of chocolate nuts and dried fruit. The tin has leaked, but no matter, she eats half and waits to see if it stays down.

Her bare feet are cold. When she pulls them to her, one knee protests and a streak of blood starts down her calf from a reopened wound. She sees the jeans are ripped clear to her thigh and the gash is deep enough to keep bleeding unless she stops it. The pocket knife at her belt. Gone. With teeth and cold, sore fingers she tears strips from the denim to bind the cut. 'Good thing this leg was uphill or I'd have bled to death.' That done, her survival instincts return full-blown.

It is still early morning... not warm... first things first.

'I need to get dry before a wind comes up. How...? in Music Temple with everything soaked? Ah... the cave, upstream... not far.... Lots of wood we left there over the years... if nobody's found it.'

Still dazed, she inches down the slope on her bottom and one leg—stops once beside a clear, settled-out pothole for a long drink—finds a stick on the canyon floor to use as a crutch, and limps beside the swollen stream, painfully easing her bound leg over fallen trees and piles of driftwood. Abrasions sting her bare feet and there are barks on her shin when she finds the cave, a couple hours after sunup. The cut below her knee has stopped bleeding.

There is wood piled near the back, beside the untouched foot-prints of the three who discovered it some years ago and have con-tinued to visit. She stares at them, her mind shifting gears again.

'Jason! Oh, God...! Did you set out to find me...? Did the storm find *you*...? Poor, dear Jason... backed into a corner you can't get out of... burying your heart, making concessions—own-ing one...! Always ready to compromise, or compensate.... Those things will kill your sweet soul if the reservoir didn't do it already.'

She sees Step's prints close to the rear wall where he always left food for the mice. 'Fetchit! You ol' procrastinator... funny, slow, wise, artful and somehow detached from it all, yet warm and caring. You would've liked the storm, Step… if you could'uv watched it from afar.'

Shan builds a fire and dries her clothes. She looks for cattail stalks to chew on their tender bottoms, finds some, bent to bedrock and silty, but edible… like their salads were after a dust storm.

A sound like boulders tumbling from on high fills the canyon. She hobbles out, naked, sees a helicopter slapping the air above the reservoir near the mouth of Music Temple and for no reason she can remember later, hobbles back in the cave. To hide? The chopper makes a circle, then flies down canyon.

Another rattle of her groggy brain brings her to the cave's lip, thinking: *Dumb of me to do that…. I should try to be visible if they're out to rescue people already…. I s'pose it's about mid-morning… better get up on the cap where I can be seen.*

Clothes dry, she begins to dress, but as she painfully tugs on her one-and-a-half-leg jeans, she shakes her head— still full of water—and feels sick again.

'Urgh…. I'll just lie down a few minutes… until the dizzies go away.' She looks around for the life jacket to use for a pillow, and swears. 'Oh, shit! I left it on the slope!'

Stiffly easing down beside the small fire, she rests her head on one arm and within seconds is asleep.

࿐࿐

Buck's Mercury can push the light aluminum hull of *Rintintin* along at thirty knots or more, but he can't open the throttle for all the floating wreckage. Shan had told Jason she wouldn't go past Dangling Rope, but that was sixty miles down canyon. Under normal conditions he could do it in three hours, but having to make his way in and out of more than a dozen side canyons before he even gets to the San Juan would double that time, so he opts to begin the serious search near Iceberg Canyon, about seventeen miles from Hoxie. The Escalante and San Juan he won't worry about either, because he's sure she'd pass them up. He can stay four or five days if he has to; has plenty of food and gas, and for those still afloat awaiting rescue, he has extra first aid supplies and a few rations.

When he enters narrow side canyons that he's spent some sixteen years hiking in, exploring for ruins and ferrying supplies for the uranium miners, he is dismayed and angered beyond what he expected. Buck hasn't been down river… down canyon… since the fall of '63, and the water level, only after a year, is way past what he imagined. Even the high natural lake in Iceberg that he and Shan would swim across (no matter how much he hated it) to get to ruins on the other side, is about to be inundated with drift from the storm.

In the main canyon across from Hole in the Rock, a few feet up on a narrow bench, something bright catches his eye. As he approaches, he sees that it's a striped awning flung against the rock. That's all. There's no boat under it. Then he hears a croak and looks up thinking to see a raven, but in a lean hollow three figures stand frantically waving their arms—two men and a woman.

'Oh, shit, more,' he mutters, cutting throttle. He's been stopped twice before this and done what he could—left matches, flares and first aid kits with those stranded; told them to hang tight, rescue boats are on the way—always asking if they've seen a woman alone in a fiberglass boat with the name *Screwd River* on the side.

This time one of the men nods and answers, 'Yeah, I think so, two days ago, maybe…. Hell, I kain't remember, so much has happened…. Our boat…'

'Where?' Buck's heart takes a flip—he searches the three faces, imploring more information—'Do you remember where…? When? Was she going toward Wahweep or Hoxie…? Any of you talk with her?'

The woman squints down at him and with a Midwestern twang says, 'Oh I remember where, all right. According to the map, it was in that canyon they call some kind of Passage. She was right uppity… and she was *neked!*' Buck is unable to suppress a smile. 'Yes, ma'am, that's probably the person I'm looking for. You saw her before the storm, right…? Day before yesterday?'

The man answers, 'Yeah—it was in the morning, wasn't it, Mert? And we saw her up at the *end* of that canyon. We was fishing in there and she went out before us. We don't know which way she went…. We didn't see her again.'

Buck nods as he backs away from the wall. 'I'm much obliged to you folks for the information.'

What to do with it, he ponders. Doesn't tell him anything but the fact that she was in Hidden Passage days ago... no need to go inside... and she has to be somewhere below Hidden if she was determined to get to Dangling Rope.

What little sun burns its way through the haze tells him the time is around noon. Giving the motor a burst of throttle, he checks Llewellyn Gulch, passes the San Juan, and turns into what they called Horse Canyon, just below the San Juan on the right. He chokes up, looking at what's happened here. A snaking trench of nothing but wall-to-wall water where there used to be curve after curve of greenery; redbuds, flowers, fern, small cataracts, Anasazi ruins in arch-cut walls and the prints of wild horses in the sand—the reason for the name. He half expects her to be here at the end of this known route up to the Kaiparowitz Plateau. She isn't.

He decides to take a short rest at the last cataract, eat lunch and try to think like Shan—what she'd do out here on this puddle... alone. He tries not to feel helpless about finding her before dark, and worries what another night's exposure can do to her if she has survived.

☙⚬❧

CHAPTER 21

Above Music Temple — Same Day

Shan scoots backward on her arms and bottom, up the mounds of Navajo sandstone, dragging her wounded leg over the last high dome where she rests, then totters across the cap and stands looking down at the reservoir from a cliff that once rose twelve hundred feet above the river—now more like eight hundred. The atmosphere has cleared a bit, allowing the sun to look at itself in water now splotched with the storm's debris.

She has slept a couple hours, yet still feels nauseous and feverish; regardless, she must get to a place that's visible to the rescuers. Up here, off the rim, are the Moki steps where they made their way up and down to the river, and without thinking whether or not she can navigate them, she hobbles beside the drop-off in that general direction, dragging her blood-stained parka and stopping often to wipe perspiration from her face and neck with the tail of her shirt. It isn't that she can't walk on the injured leg, it's that it starts bleeding whenever she takes a normal step with it.

In trying to move over a jagged rise in the sandstone she stubs her toe. Earth and sky twirl, her good leg gives, tumbling her forward. She braces against stiffened arms, head hanging, water running from her nose and mouth, the taste of sour chocolate rises in her throat. With great effort she pushes back from the cliff's edge into a small hollow and watches Navajo Mountain and the high humps at the San Juan confluence change places. She shuts her eyes. When they open, an unusual form on the skyline fixes them—she squints the object into focus.

'My fish!' Slowly she gains the rise to inspect it.

The sharkish form hasn't altered a grain in the three years since she first saw it. She strokes the smooth back and tail. 'After hundred-fifty-mile winds and shredding rain, you're still here... untouched. Incredible!' She lifts it from its base of saturated sandstone. The base crumbles. As she holds it aloft to look beneath, the tail drops from the body and rolls to her feet.

Tears fill her eyes. 'Why did I do that? You've survived a million storms, but you can't survive *me... us...*! Like this canyon... billions of years to form... gone... in one black second of man's interval. Oh, fuck! Why do I care...? I'll be gone from this puke pool forever as soon as they find me... and somebody will. C'mon, fish, I need you to remind me how unrelenting gross the human race is. You can be my guiding light.'

She stuffs the body into the sleeve of her parka, the tail into a pocket and presses on toward the Moki steps.

From a bald knob she looks down at the first flat shelf, fifty feet below her. Past the first six steps she can see no more—they drop steeply from her vision into space, but she remembers them well. After that drop of thirty feet or so, there's a resting place, and below that it's not as steep. She can then butt-crawl to the edge of the shelf and be seen by anyone on the reservoir.

Shan looks to the west. Even though it's early afternoon, this time of year the sun is about to be eaten up by the very high Kaiparowitz Plateau, making her realize she'd better not wait much longer to make up her mind what to do.... Sitting up here in the late afternoon when it gets cold is not an option. From somewhere comes the faint whine of an outboard engine, solidifying her decision.

She carefully removes her fish, tucks it under a ledge, pulls on the parka and eases down the part she had formerly danced over while Step sat above her muttering, '*Oh, Christ, I hate these drops!*' Where it falls off, she stops. Somehow, it doesn't look the same. The steps angle off, hiding themselves under a slight bulge, and those below the bulge, thirty or more feet to the resting place, look more like a hundred.

'Oh, damn. I may be crazy, but not crazy enough to try getting down there by myself this time of day... afternoon,' she sighs.

Twisting around for a hand brace to shove herself backward to the top again, the five steps loom above her—spaces between them a leg's length or more. It was easy enough to slide down, but both arms and one leg, even two if she had them, won't push her weight up that kind of gradient. She can't turn around without the danger of slipping. When she tries for the first step above her, she slides off her parka back to the narrow ledge before the drop.

Trembling, she leans back against the wall and stares out over the water.

'Oh, Christ! I've rimmed myself.'

෴

Buck emerges from Horse Canyon with deep worry lines creasing his tan forehead as he measures the pros and cons:

'Well, goddammit, other people who can't beat their way out of a wet paper bag are still afloat, why not her? She knows the canyon and that's sure a big help.... She has a life jacket and b'sides, she's a good swimmer.... Big deal...! Weissmuller would'uv drowned in the hell they had here.... *You Tarzan, me Jane.*... Aw, Shan Lu, I'd better quit moaning and start looking seriously into every slice of slickrock.'

He knows there are only two or three canyons she might have ducked into within five miles of the Passage—canyons he hasn't seen since the reservoir took them; canyons that had white sand beaches with willows and cattails at their entrances, or rabbitbrush dotting the talus slopes at the base of their low cliff walls. Now they could be slits in the wall, or open water for half a mile—confusing... frustrating... spooky.

'She wouldn't be coming back to Hidden Passage after being there once already.... And Music Temple... she probably looked in there too. Below that, she might have tried Mystery. Guess I'll head for that.'

He is confounded when he gets to the mouth of Hidden Passage, so choked with drift that nothing and no one could get in or out of it. Across the way he expects to see the same kind of mess, but the Temple's small entrance curls back from the path of the storm and looks to be unclogged. He slows.

'If the water's up past the spout, I might could get in there. The upper canyon wouldn't be flooded... yet... maybe. It's the kinda place she'd go... if she could get in... *if* she got there before the storm hit.'

He turns the canoe in.

Around the second bend he starts battling drift. A big log twenty feet away sets him to swearing because it blocks the whole narrow passage to the upper part and looks like it's jammed in there. Coming closer, he sees it's not a log but the bottom of a boat. Under water, where the rust coat ends and the pink paint begins, he can make out the wavering gold letters.

'Oh, Jesus Christ! No!'

His first thought is that she's under it. Frantically, he looks for something to flip it over before logic tells him there's no way he can do that. This time of early afternoon, the sun slants down the dome's east wall, reflecting enough light for him to see under the boat... *if* he gets in the water. 'Saints above, preserve my gonads! Okay, Jane... here we go!' He strips and eases over the side, issuing the sounds of a man in a medieval torture chamber.

Nothing is under the boat. No life jacket, no gas cans or gear. Even the motor is gone, the cables dangle free. He surfaces.

'Okay, woman, where are you? You're not below the falls or you'd be floatin' by now.'

Blue, shivering and only half relieved he crawls into his boat, rubs himself down with a piece of old tarp, and pulls on his jockey shorts. There's nothing to put in them.

'Wonder if a guy ever swallowed his own nuts.' He smiles, recalling Shan telling him one time—'*The angle of the dangle is in direct relation to the heat of the meat, Tarzan*'—'And maybe a frozen lizard heads for the gizzard,' he adds. Trivial thoughts. Those of least importance often flood the brain, giving it time to find and measure the best solutions to the more serious problem at hand; calming it down with ripples instead of waves that may roll over what a viable solution would be. Finding humor in the most dire of situations often keeps sanity from losing its grip.

Buck works to maneuver *Screwd River* out of her private slip so he can pass and proceed into upper Music Temple. The four-hundred-foot dome that once echoed music to the river is over half inundated. There is only a narrow convoluted passage for access to the canyon's upper reaches. This passage was made by the stream, which is still here but not running heavily now, so he is able to wedge the narrow canoe some few feet to the near end where water pours over the lip level with his shoulders. He stuffs his parka with first aid supplies, some food and a flashlight, ties the bow rope to his belt and looks up for cross-bedded ridges to climb the sandstone. When he clears the crevasse and stands in the stream, he finds a boulder, snugs the canoe and looks around.

Catching the sunlight on slanting walls fifty feet away, and almost as high above him, lies a faded orange Mae West. He's about to climb for the life jacket when he notices a barefoot print in the mud beside the stream, and then another... and another.

Relief floods over him like a warm bath. 'You're here somewhere... but I'll just make sure.' He hikes up for the jacket which is proof enough; stenciled on the back is 'Hoxie Crossing Marina,' along with a dark stain of dried blood. He traces the intermittent drops back to the stream, where they disappear in the sand. Apprehensive again, he begins following footprints upstream where the canyon widens out; stepping over flooded brush, tumbled rock and tree branches, and some places where she'd stepped on rocks or the sandstone bank, he sees more drops of blood in the afternoon light.

Buck knows this canyon—has been up and down the high Moki steps a couple of times with Shan, but that was several years ago, and of course he doesn't know it like she does—doesn't know about the cave. With her, he always hiked the middle view from the very top of the Mokis, across what resembles a landscape of muffins, rolls and loaves of bread, until they end for any climber without suction cups. He's never hiked the bottom part, going upstream, before now. When he realizes he hasn't seen any footprints for several yards or holes poked in the mud beside them—easily read as a stick she was using for a crutch—he stops.

'What the hell...? Did I miss where she quit the stream...? Or did she take to the rock...? Kinda steep here for anybody with an injury to climb... even her.

'Oh, man, how'm I gonna track her on slickrock, especially barefoot. I'm sure no match for my old Navajo friend Honoshay.'

He turns back, walking the low shelf beside the stream she'd most likely climb out, intently looking for scraped-off ridges or mud where it doesn't belong. The years they've hiked together and hypothesized various escapes from tough situations helps him fit the land, and marks upon it, to her way of thinking. After a few meanders, he finds mud clots on the wide level bench where he should have been looking all along, instead of down beside the water. Her route from there is obvious; he sees a small, low arch on a wide, protected shelf, just shy of the next sharp twist in the canyon floor, and smells a latent tang of spicy juniper smoke.

His expressed relief as he rushes forth, bounding up the rise onto the smooth, wide bench at the mouth of the opening, is more like a gargle of laughing and crying at the same time:

'Shan Lu...! Oh, Shan Lu...! I just knew you were here somewhere, felt it in my bones..., Oh, Little One... thank God you're here!'

The cave is empty.

Buck sits at the lip of the ruin, head in hands, without the slightest tinge of guilt or embarrassment, and asks the canyon walls: 'Why...? Why didn't I go with her when she wanted me to...? Why am I so fucking dumb that I don't want her to know how much I care for her...? So dumb I don't even want *myself* to know...? So dumb that when I made love to her in North Wash I wanted more than anything to keep us together... somehow.'

What he just blurted without thinking has finally proven it: *Little One.*

Buck Watson hasn't uttered those words to her—actually, Jason's careful words for her—or to anyone else in his entire lifetime. Pamela was his one and only *sweetheart*—another word he hasn't used for other women along the way, because Buck hasn't been in love with anyone but Pamela after all these years, or admitted that he could be...

...Until now.

≈≈

Golden leaf-shade from the rugged old cottonwood dapples the pool and plays over Shan's bare body where she lies at its edge, too lazy, too content, to roll over into the sun—unusually warm on this early October morning. The scratch of leaves, clicking of branches, the croak of a fingerling toad tucked under a ledge and the musical notes of water tumbling into the pool are the only sounds. A light breeze ruffles the pool, pushing a golden armada to the far end, only to be doused and sunk by the waterfall or rained on by a nearby seep.

She folds her arms beneath her head and looks at the waterfall, smiling.

The top is a perfect drawing of a woman's vagina—water ripples over the clitoris, moss-green hair surrounds the vulva, and at the moment, shadows and the rock's formation accentuate creases where the legs join the rump then spread open, heels resting on the bench above.

Shan sighs. 'Fantastic! No wonder men think of Glen Canyon as a woman; fair enough… the river is a man.'

Sunlight reflecting off the water makes weaving, dancing patterns against the slanting rock of an overhang. It has the hypnotic effect of a full-screen kaleidoscope and reminds her of Jason's description: Music on the Walls. Her gaze wanders to the south rim where an arch peeks over the horizon, keeping an eye on paradise… for as long as it lasts. The sun, full upon her now, makes her sweat. She wants to take a shallow dive into the pool, but can't. A clean thick bandage and dressing is wrapped around her left leg, with a splint back of her knee so she can't bend it and open the wound again. Various parts of her body are painted with mercurochrome, like maybe she's been in a war dance.

'Make love… not war,' she chuckles. 'Did we really make love for three hours?—looks to be coming on noon. What was it he said this morning when I was half asleep and reached for him…?'

'You keep that up and you'll soon have my undivided attention.' So, she had, and then his next remark—*'Thank Christ I've still got'um… wasn't sure they'd ever come back.'* 'What?' she had asked. *'Never mind, it's between me and that stuff that rots your skin.'* She twists around, easing the upper part of her body into the pool and lies back, hair floating about her head, water lapping over

her breasts... rotting her skin, of course. With ears underwater, she listens to the *pings and pops* of aquatic life; a muffled *durping* from the waterfall, the seeps *blurp-blurping* and a *r-r-ratchet* from the toad.

Something tickles her nose.

'Ahoy, mermaid! Come ashore.'

Buck stands before her with something wrapped in a sweat-shirt. He gives her a hand up, sits down and puts the bundle in her lap.

'Aw-w-w. My fish! How'd you find it?'

'Last night in your nut-headed state, all you could mutter about when I toted you down the slickrock was about some stoney damned fish, so after I checked out the boat, I went to look for it.'

'But still...' she is amazed... 'how did you know where...? I stuck it under a ledge somewhere if I remember...'

'Hellfire, m'dear Shan Lu, I been lookin' under ledges most of my life for things far more important than this.'

'Hey. This is *very* important, as important to me as the *cha-muhia* is to you. This fish is going to keep me sane in my darkest hours. I'll look at *him*—yeah it's a him, see that there thang?—and it'll call up this picture, right here, Music Temple... with a gold and blue ceiling, painted by autumn.'

'I thought we were goin' to Baja.'

'We are, but we have to come back. You know that as well as I do.'

'Hm-m, someday maybe. But we aren't goin' *anywhere* until that leg heals. I left a note in *Rintintin* for whoever comes by—to deliver the message that we're okay, and that we'll be at Hoxie in a couple days.'

'I can walk on this leg, Buck, it doesn't hu...'

'No, ya can't. That gash is almost a half-inch deep and won't take much more abuse. B'sides, I want to sit here where nobody's going to bother us and discuss vicissitudes.'

'Who?'

'It's not a *who*, it's a *what*.'

Shan laughs. 'Okay, what vicissitudes?'

'Like you don't intend to spend the rest of your life in front of a bunch of TV cameras, warbling in bars and...'

'No, I sure as hell don't. Ol' Fred Allen said it for us all, y'know—'Television is a device that permits people who haven't anything to do, to watch people who can't do anything.' He could have gone further and said: *'The viewer becomes a know-nothing authority, and as such is polled... Programing is then dished up for the appetites of Mr. & Ms. Know-nothing Fats.'* So, I've moved out. Concerts... that's for me. They don't have to come if they don't like the performer, are chained to the chair and can't talk or smoke.... They can only applaud... heh heh.'

'What if they boo?'

She gives him a baleful look. 'They haven't yet, smartass.'

'It's that easy, huh? Just skip over to another arena.'

'It'll take time; changes always do, but it'll work. My new motto is: 'Don't be affected by the many, be directed by the few."'

'You weren't singing this song a couple of years ago.'

'I hadn't stared that bony hollow-eyed critter in the face then; it can give a lass pause.'

'I know.' Buck squints his eyes closed and rubs his crew cut.

'I know you know. I'm sure glad you quit working with a pick and shovel in those goddamn holes.... Now all ya' gotta worry about is spilling acid on your pecker, or some other valuable place.'

'Don't think there's much chance of that. I'm near done with mining in any and all forms. Since you're only going to be with me part-time, whenever we can and want to, like we agreed, I'm thinking I'll base my camp in the house trailer at Fry Canyon, and you can stay there with me whenever you come by. I'll be going in with Rex, building roads on the reservation. He's been after me for a couple years to join him, and the pay's lots better than hole-digging.'

'That sounds really good to me, Cowboy.'

They had finally talked it over and had come to the conclusion that the two of them could never live together full time and still retain the loving relationship they now have... and want to keep.

'Actually, my coming in with him will be kind of a bonus. His kind of construction always needs someone who knows the delicate business of setting dynamite charges.'

She gives him a know-it-all look with one raised eyebrow, and in slowly measured words, says, 'And Buck Watson is the perfect man to do it... and do it *right*.'

He pulls back, quickly, and stares at her. 'What's that supposed to mean? There are plenty other guys in this area...'

A big clown smile spreads over her face. 'Fred told me about your cabin poofin' up in the middle of the night... how cool!'

'When did Bennett tell you about that?'

'Windy's farewell party at the Crossroads, when you peed in everybody's Wheaties.' She lays the fish down and smacks his leg hard with her fist.

'Aw-w, I went and apologized. You were right about that, but dammit, Shan Lu...'

'Sh-hhh.' She puts her hand over his mouth and pushes him gently back onto the slickrock. 'Who's on top, Tarzan?'

His hands cup her bare bottom, pressing her down against him. 'Looks like you are, Jane.'

CHAPTER 22

— The Mid-Seventies and Beyond —

Shan lasted in Baja almost six months before she got antsy and returned to the concert circuit. Couple months later, Buck finally fished himself out, packed up the camp trailer and came back to Fry Canyon.

After having dug himself out of small, dark and dangerous holes, he began working outside with his contractor friend, Rex, under mostly clear skies on the Navajo Reservation. They repaired the old roads and built new ones across the shifting orange sands of northern Arizona and southern Utah. Rex and his wife owned a trading post outside of Kayenta at a place called Baby Rocks... so Buck could be found there on occasion, taking care of the post whenever Florence and Rex hied themselves off to parts unknown. In season, sometimes out of it, he'd be off hunting elk, deer, birds, rabbits or rocks with Leo or one of his local Moki hunting friends.... Could even be found cowboying during spring and fall roundup for the public lands ranchers in the area.

Shan semi-settled into a kind of home base in Sedona, Arizona, when she wasn't touring.... Actually rented a house, had an address and a phone. They stayed as close in touch as possible, considering the distance in time and space that separated them, but whenever she had time—much oftener now, and for longer— she'd take off for Fry Canyon.

Sometimes Leo would pop in from Kansas and the three would go hiking in the upper ends of canyons that once drained into the river. A standing rule about those hikes was that the minute they smelled the stink of the reservoir they'd turn back, retrace their steps or find a more interesting way out along the benches.

They knew from the Bennetts that Myrna Nelson, Tammy and the baby had moved from Blanding to the Midwest, where Brad's parents lived. On a visit to Dove Creek, Fred told them:

'She stayed in Blanding until she got some sort of USGS government pension sorted out for Brad's accidental death while on duty—don't know how much it was, or if it carries her through, but we sure were relieved when she moved back with family and friends who could look after her—she shouldn't be out there all alone with two children.'

Then Helen added, 'Jason kept an eye out whenever he came in from Hoxie Crossing, which wasn't too often, and we visited her whenever we could, you know... but it's a really a long way from here to there for old folks like us to drive.'

'Would you give us her address, Helen?' asked Shan. 'We want to keep in touch with her... at least let her know we think about her and the kids.'

Fred tilted his head, looked at each of them from under his hawk-wing eyebrows and smiled. 'Seems like you two made up while you was down there in Baja... what with all this *we* stuff...'

'Oh, we made up all right,' nodded Buck, pulling Shan in close to him, and sticking his tongue in her ear. 'Made up for lost time.'

Fred's grin covered half his face. Never, in all the time he'd known Buck, had he seen the man display his feelings, nor would anyone else be witness to them. Fred was close—more like a father to him than his real dad, and Buck wanted Fred to *know* how he felt about Shan—the rest of the world needn't have a clue.

⁂

At times when she came to be with Buck she stopped to see Jason. Jason, who faded back into the dull fabric of Mormon small town life after selling his interest in the Hoxie Crossing Marina. At least he'd ceased to water the thirsty crevasses in small minds about his river trips with Shan and Step... the trips that were no more. Gentle Jason. Always glad to see her—never reproachful, ever helpful. Whenever she came to cry on his shoulder about anything and everything, he'd always be there for her. When he first learned she was going to Baja with Buck, he hugged and held her long... telling her how much he liked Buck, and how happy he was that she was going with a man he knew darned well would take good care of her. Shan knew she was fortunate beyond words to have a friend like Jason.

Step trotted the globe with his cameras, his slow poke and his wife—she was an intense botanist and birder—almost as tall as he, sturdy and always smiling. Shan thought if anyone could, she could probably out-walk him, no matter the terrain. They also hiked the canyons, but Step and Shan, with or without Jason, never hiked or ran rivers together after they left the Glen... or more precisely, after the Glen left them. Neither knew why—it seemed when one zigged the other zagged... yet they'd talk about their hikes whenever they got together, and vow their timing would be better the next year. It didn't happen.

For Shan, there was never a way to give up. The fight for her river would continue until she herself was gone from the planet. She started writing stories for non-profit organizations that had fought the dam. Essays about what had been lost in the Glen. These turned into a published book... two books. Her concert bookings evolved into reading with songs, and she became quite well known among river lovers and dam haters throughout the southwest.

A decade passed before she ran rivers again—the San Juan, the Green and Yampa—rivers that still carried their color with them. But those rivers never sang or talked to her like the Colorado had, never seemed intimate or gave up secrets that astonished her—maybe that was the reason Buck never joined her on those trips. It was as if she'd had one truly great love and no other could fill the void. He took some of the immediate sting of her loss by being just who he was, of the river, someone who cared for her and knew exactly how she felt because he felt it too—and being her lover added to the depth of feeling. Their togetherness was like the river—in springtime rising, then in passionate flood; in summertime languidness, storm or quiet eddy, always flowing, never dammed.

Buck, unused to having a lover he felt at ease with, found himself not anchored like he thought he'd be, but tethered on a lengthy rope that he could stretch, or break, at will... giving him less reason to do so. He knew she spent time—even a bed now and then—with other men. How could she not? Her profession wrapped her in the company of show-business people, singer, musicians, writers... and she tended to turn heads. Yet, he felt his stratum more secure than others, because of the river that had brought them together, and kept them engaged... thus far.

As for Shan, she adored the looseness, the ease with which they came and went to each other, as if no days or weeks had passed since their last meeting—no pushing, no pulling, no demands. Nor did she know, or really care, if he had other lovers—but she doubted it. The closest she ever came to wondering was one afternoon in Blanding when she and Leo met him at the Elk Ridge Cafe for a hike they were going to take in Rhodes Canyon. All the waitresses knew Buck, of course, and their server that day even knew Leo.

When she picked up her money along with couple of dishes, she said to Buck, 'Liz and I went over to Fry yesterday to visit with you, but you weren't there.'

'Uh-huh... Orvil told me.'

'Where were ya?' she asked, a little frown clouding her face.

'I wasn't there,' said Buck, the corners of his mouth tucked into his tight little smile.

Shan looked down at the Formica, barely able to turn a laugh into clearing her throat.... Leo nodded.... The waitress shrugged and took the dishes to the kitchen.

By the late sixties telephones had replaced the old and very uncertain radio contact in the faraway pockets of southeastern Utah, so Shan would often call Orvil at Fry Canyon Trading Post to ask if he knew where Buck might be. She'd sniff him out, working within a radius of a couple hundred miles of Fry—sometimes rounding up cattle, driving the stock truck or supervising the road crew. He never wanted, or had, a phone, regardless of where he lived all the years she spent time with him... or after.

She was heading north from Sedona one warm spring day, zipping along in her T-Bird through Monument Valley, when she was flagged down by road workers a few miles past Goudling's Trading Post. Almost certain that Buck was part of that crew, she pulled to the side and walked past the few cars ahead of her to find they were blasting straight through three hundred feet of sandstone to cut off a sharp curve—more than one person had been killed or injured when they'd rolled or catapulted over that particular ledge.

She walked up to the flagman. 'Hi there. Do you know if Buck Watson happens to be working with this crew?'

He looked at her and smiled. 'Yes, Ma'm, he sure is. I think he's up there with the boss. We're about to blast some rock, so you'll have to wait until he comes down.' He looked back at her Bird and added, 'I'm lettin' these few cars through, so you can go along over to the other side. I'll have Rex tell him to meet you over there.... Is that okay?'

'Oh, sure, that'll be fine.... Thanks a lot.'

She drove around with the others, pulled over on the side, got out, sat on the back fender and waited, swinging her legs and singing. She was dressed a-la-canyon in shorts, halter and sandals.

Ten minutes ticked away before Buck thumped down the slag pile and walked to her car. She jumped from the fender, about to encircle his neck, when he reached for her hand and shook it. 'Goddammit, Shan! Every sonofabitch in Utah's gonna be blabbin' about the fancy dame in the T-Bird, who stopped to see the foreman....'

'Bu-bu-but...'

'No buts, ya hear? Just act like this is some sort of business deal, or you're goin' grocery shopping for whoever... whatever. Get in the car and *go!*'

'Wh-h... Are you going back to Fry tonight? I've got a few days off, and I was going to...'

He took her arm, walked her to the driver's side, and opened the door. 'I'm gonna get the razzin' of my life 'less'n I figure out a way to pass you off as somebody's wife.' He shook her hand again, half pushed her into the seat, smiled a big fake smile for the crowd—oh yes, they were watching—and said, 'Steaks are in the fridge.... Warm up the bed.' Then he walked back to the crew, shoulders braced for what he knew was coming.

That same night, they set the truck to rocking and squeaking where they slept in its bed under a blanket of stars.... Set them laughing too, because the rocking reminded them of how it all started that wild night in North Wash in Windy's trailer. Then, Buck turned serious, pulled her close and murmured in her ear, 'You've no idea how hard it was that night not to tell you...'

'Oh, I do *indeed* know how hard it was that night... like right now,' she interrupted, reaching for his impressive and expressive love-making tool.

'...Sh-h-h! I'm about to make a confession.' Squeezing the breath from her to shut her up, he continued. 'You know how lame I am about confessions, so it's best you listen while I'm in the mood. You also know how seldom I use the key word... love. I'm suspicious of it and its many meanings.... I wanted to tell you I loved you that night... only I'd programmed myself not too care that much because I knew you wouldn't stay with me full-time, and I was too dumb to know that the stayin' part didn't really matter, so long as we had prime time like this.'

'Ah, Buckle, I knew by the way you made love to me that night... the gentle way you kissed and held me, that your feelings were deeper than you'd admit.... And if it's any consolation, after you said the you wanted me, I was close to wondering if it wouldn't be very nice full-time with you... until you said it was only going happen once.'

'Looks like I blew it, darlin'. But those months in Baja showed us a thing or two about long term. I'm damned happy you stayed as long as you did.... And your leaving let me know how much I missed you.... Still do when you're gone too long.'

'Me too, Tarzan.'

They stopped talking and lay spooned together draped in starlight, listening to their favorite coyote chorus—the generator at the Post long shut down. The occasional flash of some faraway car's headlights would skid across the buttes west of them, and they would bet each other—truck or car?—before it went by many minutes later on the road far below them.

Every time she came back to Buck's trailer she'd head straight for the bookcases with the tilting glass fronts that stood beside the couch; the ones that held his found artifacts and the prized *chamahia*. It drew her like a magnet. Carefully, she'd lift it out, run her hands over the smooth surface of its strange shape and beauty, trying to imagine what its history could be... who formed it... which strata of rock it may have come from, and where. And the biggest mystery... what purpose had it served those many centuries ago? Leo had kept it in Kansas while Buck was in Baja, but brought it back to the high desert, where he'd always felt it belonged.

'I ain't gonna be moving it 'round no more,' he told Buck. 'Officially, the *chamahia* is yours from now on.'

Shan felt that having it was more than just an ego thing with Buck... a connection of some kind, beyond being a real find. Not many of the Moki hunters came up with something as rare. More than once she'd tried to trade him out of it... even tried to shame him into taking it to a museum, where she told him it belonged— though she didn't think so either—but nothing ever worked.

'No way, Sugar. They'd just plunk it in the basement along with the other trillion artifacts they got; at least here it gets seen by a few folks who can truly appreciate it.... B'sids,' he asked, looking her up and down, 'what you got to trade?'

'Hm-m... I don't have it on me, but how about the Bearcat? You've always said you'd take the Ruger back whenever I got tired of playing with it.'

'Oh, no, baby. That's not what I said. Whatever I give to someone is theirs to keep. I don't take things back. B'sides, you'd best have it by your bedside in case some Geronimo climbs in your window some night.... Keep it loaded, so you can shoot his balls off.'

With her small vessel of friends she made long, two-week backpack trips into the multi side canyons off Glen—two or three canyons a year over a period of ten years. Buck would not go with her, and she put it down to the fact that he didn't know all those people—he was a loner after all—so she never tried to press him into going. Yet he'd be eager to hear about her adventures on returning... especially if they'd found any ruins. They still continued their short day or two hikes; would drive in the Jeep or truck to places he'd discovered over the years—hike canyons to bridges, animal trails to ridges, hollows and caves she'd never dreamed existed.

She came to Fry Canyon one day in the late seventies with her T-Bird loaded, nearly dragging the ground and pulling *Screwd River,* also bloated like a beached whale. When Buck came out to give her a hug, he lifted his chin at the loaded boat and asked, 'What's all this?'

'My mom died, Buckle, and I...'

'Ah, Shan Lu Baby... I'm so sorry.... Bad things seem to...'

Struggling not to cry, she sniffed, 'Not all bad.... Mom left me a little money... so I'm moving to Aspen. Gonna take up skiing on snow instead of water like my sister-in-law does.' He took her in his arms and held her close as she struggled on with more. 'I'll sell the *Screw* and take up kayaking.... They've got some undammed rivers up there running into the old Colorado where the water sparkles, an... and you can see the rocks goin' by on the bottom.

Still holding her close he warned her, 'You'll freeze your darlin' ass up there, Baby.... That place is cold.'

'You could come along,' she offered, and smiled. 'I can make you a fur-lined jock strap out of the tail of my old mink coat. What could be better'n that?'

'You, stayin' here, and making me the jock... or better yet wrapping your legs around me; it gets cold here in wintertime too, ya know.'

'I'll always come to you... winter, summer, spring, whatever, Buckle. Some day you could return the favor.'

'Too many fancy people up there. B'sides, I don't think skiing will keep my fabulous chest muscles and hard-rock belly in the shape it's used to.' He released her, pounded his chest and added, 'Me Tarzan.'

They spent a couple days just lolling around, not even going on a hike, instead, she told him of a plan that her Aspen friends had dreamed up to hike Dark Canyon, not too far from Fry. 'It'll be a two-week hike, and I already know you won't go. I told them I wouldn't go either, because it drains into the latrine, which I know is well up past the old river entrance to the canyon. You and I have been up it from the river at least a mile, and we always wanted to see more of it… and you know it's full of ruins. This time we'll be hiking it from the top down. I thought, well… shitamaring, you've still got the supply boat you go fishing in now and then. You could meet us at the end and haul us to the Hite Marina. I could just close my eyes and pretend I was on Lake Michigan or somewhere.'

'Better hold your nose too. Anyhow, I never go to Hite Marina, I put in off the Farley Canyon road. And what about timing? How the hell do you know exactly when you'll get to the res? I might have to wait there for…'

'No you won't! We've done lots of hikes together, the six of us; we know how to get to a designated place on time.'

'Sounds dicey to me.'

'Leo'll be unhappy if you don't.'

'What's he got to do with it?'

'He's coming with us… right after his Moki hunt with you.'

'He's… com… What! Why in hell didn't he tell me that he…?'

"Cause I told him not to. And I think he knows why you won't go with us, but it's something I've never figured out—long hikes don't seem to appeal to you anymore—why?'

'Lotta people… too much shit to carry, and…'

'Uh-huh… same song, twenty-fifth stanza.'

The hikers got there when they said they would—Buck only had to wait half an hour before he heard their voices echo down between the narrow cliff walls. He was lucky to get through the thick, gooey silt to a ledge covered with driftwood where their hike ended. Right away he cornered Leo and had a quiet chat with him in the back of the boat. Shan watched Leo hand him a perfect spear point; watched Buck shake his head and pull in the corners of his mouth in his tight little characteristic smile.

Shan closed her eyes for a little way, but mostly held her nose. The intoxicating, musky river smell was gone; the latrine smelled like a latrine. The cave in Narrow Canyon they had hiked up a hundred feet or more to get to during the rainstorm that September of '62 was less than ten feet above the water. *If this sewer comes up much higher the flatwater fuckers will be driving right into it, over ruins and all. What do they know about us, or the ghosts that came long before us? Nothing. What do they care? Even less.* She closed her eyes again until they passed Hite Marina and entered over the once bubbling spring at the now wide mouth of Farley Canyon.

It was late November of '79. Buck had gone over Mancos Mesa to Red Canyon to help round up some cattle. She waited for him on the steps of the trailer, wondering how he was going to take the news she had to deliver.

Probably just like always... no matter how he really feels.... Tell me it's a great idea... now's a good time... before I get too old... I know how to take care of myself... and so on... and so forth.

෧෨

CHAPTER 23

May, 1981

Shan took her backpack and circled the globe. She was gone a year and a half, and returned to what she wouldn't have expected in a hundred more of those years.

That last day when she saw Buck at Fry Canyon, she had tried to get him to come with her, but there was no way she could pull him into her game. It wasn't the expense, they both had enough, but he'd told her that long trips to faraway places just wasn't his thing. A few of his letters she picked up at *poste restante* windows where she'd spend a few weeks before going on to her next destination. One said he'd left Fry Canyon for good and moved to Winterhaven, California, down by Yuma near the Mexico border.... *'It got too damn cold for me there without you to warm up the bed every now and then, so I collected my pension and social security and went where the sun always shines, like any old retire-e-e.'* Another, months later, said he'd gone home that fall for his usual visit with the family and stayed longer than he'd expected: *'I spent a few weeks in the vet's hospital, 'cause I had a problem with my pecker and wanted to get it all tuned up for you, if you ever come home.... Sure do hope they did the right thing!'* She laughed until tears dampened her cheeks, then cried until they rolled down to wet her blouse, thinking of how different things might be in the future.

Typical of Buck, he hadn't told her the true reason for his seven-week stint in the hospital: two serious operations on his feet. He could barely walk. His years in the mines—especially that near-death experience at the Hideout when his boots were buried to their tops in heavy boulders—had torn muscles and done extensive nerve damage. Had he been less stubborn and paid more attention, he could have saved himself those operations. At the time, he was able to endure the intermittent pain and discomfort caused by the rock fall, unless the hike lasted for many days.

Shan returned home the first of May, 1981.

The solo trip around the world had altered her horizons considerably. The jagged, playful, youthful rocks of the canyon country had smoothed down to a long, wide, valley draining toward a lonesome future without a mate; just friends and part-time lovers... like Buck. She didn't go abroad looking for someone to live with—far from it. She'd spent over a decade of her adult life engaged in two short marriages that mostly wasted her time, and one five-year marriage that could have lasted forever, except he died. The other years she'd lived alone, producing songs, music and written works, and traveling 'the road' to make her talents known to others.

When she went abroad, she went looking for adventurous places, not people. She found plenty of both—from jungle trails to sea caves, dune deserts to tropical paradises—and made many friends among those who lived in those enchanting places. They made her welcome, gave her a place to stay, insisted that she return, enjoyed her company and wanted her to go with them on more adventures. Of course she had complied, pleased with the variety of their interests, the conversations she held with them, their hospitality and warmth.

One in particular.

A kindred soul had stepped from behind a backdrop of wild, lonesome country; a man of the outdoors, free and independent—similar to Buck in some ways, unlike him in many others. He would soon be following her home—sometime in July—to live with her for a long time, she hoped.

How Buck would take this news she wasn't sure, or even if she could find him to let him know. Regardless of how he took it, she could see his china-blue eyes light up when she began sharing with him the wild places she'd been and the incredible sights she'd seen. He, of course, still had no phone, and she didn't know which trailer court in Winterhaven he'd chosen to live in. A postal address, yes, she had that, but would rather they were together when she told him. Other ideas and solutions pooled in her head, but answers to them failed to join in the swim.

She need not have worried. Similar to many unexpected happenings in her life, the situation solved itself.

She'd been home a couple of weeks when she received a phone call from Buck's cousin—a person she'd never met and knew nothing about. He seemed to know about her, but didn't know if she had returned from her trip. He'd taken the chance that she might have, and was pleased to find her home.

He spoke hesitantly, as if unsure of himself or worried about her response. 'I'm sure my news is not the best you've heard since your return, Miss Farran,'—a deep breath—'but I have to let you know that Buck passed away the first part of February, at a Yuma hospital. We've found no one to contact but a couple of his mining friends, now deceased, and we only discovered their names and yours through some correspondence we found, just recently, in his trailer-home. That's how I got your address and phone number.'

She choked over a sob. Big hot tears spilled through squeezed tight lids and dripped off her chin. She could only shake her head and burble through her sobs... *No... no... no! Buckle... no.*

The cousin remained quiet until she found words.

'Wh... what happened...? How did he...?'

'I understand how you must feel, just like the family. None of us knew a thing about it. We finally learned from the park manager that he'd fallen down the trailer steps and couldn't get up. She called 9-1-1 and said when the ambulance came he handed the team a plastic bag with his wallet, some papers and I.D., and told them: *'If anything happens to me, everything you need is in this bag.'*

She took in a sobbing breath and asked, 'Nothing else...? Nobody knows why he fell...? If he was sick...? Or hurt himself in the fall...?' She well knew about those trailer steps; she'd fallen down them once herself. She could picture his falling, but his not getting up didn't screen... unless he'd hit his head on something when he fell.

'Miss Farran... Shan, if I may call you that—and by the way, my name is Dave—the circumstances are bizarre. We didn't even know of his death until three weeks ago.'

'Three weeks...! My Lord...! But that's more than two months since...'

'I said bizarre. I'll try to tell you what has taken two months—with the help of lawyers, county and military officials—to partially find out what happened. Certainly not all of it.'

'Oh, my God.... This is so sad.' She could not stop crying.

'Shan, I know it's hard, hard for me too, but I have to tell you.... So, it seems the ambulance delivered him on January 28th to the Yuma Regional Health Center. He checked in with his wallet, checkbook, glasses and various papers. They left his glasses and the plastic bag by his bed. Those items were never seen again!'

'His ID, everything gone? I can't... believe... this!' She was choking.

'Obviously they were stolen by someone—but to go on. He was in the hospital for three days, during which time he was interviewed by a public fiduciary who determined he was indigent, since Buck told him he had no living relatives or friends except a sister in St. Louis—a sister he never spoke to, by the way.'

'*Indigent!* Holy Mother of God! Why? Buck would never say he had no relations or friends... unless he was drugged out of his mind.'

'That's what I think, but it gets even weirder.' Dave was blinking back his own tears now. 'He died in the hospital February 3rd, and was sent to Kammann mortuary where another public fiduciary did some research and found that he'd been in the military. As a result, on the 5th of February, his body was taken to the National Cemetery in Cave Creek, Arizona, and buried there as an indigent.'

Shan was howling now, howling in pain, in frustration, in anger and a great avalanche of sorrow.

Dave let it roll... until a breathless moment when he offered, 'I should've come to see you, Shan. I'm so sorry I didn't pursue my hunch and do just that. It's taken these last couple months to find, and *legally* get into his trailer, where we found your rat-eaten letters.'

'I... I... I can't remember the date I last heard from him... in Athens, I think, where I was visiting a friend.... Wh... wh-en,' she hiccuped, 'was the last time you...?'

'The last any family member heard anything was early November—he phoned his brother—we don't know from where, or whose phone. When no one heard anything at Christmas time, we believed something was wrong.'

'I wonder why he quit writing to everybody?' Then she remembered how he was. Of course. If something was wrong with him he'd tell absolutely nobody, especially his family, so they wouldn't worry—never considering that it might turn out to be something like this, making them even sadder. She knew that stubborn streak first-hand. Through her jumbled thoughts came Dave's voice:

'Miss Shan, when we finally got to his trailer we rescued a few things, and some of them we don't know what to do with. There are some decorated Indian pots, glued together, some ladles, arrowheads and chips. I'm wondering if I might come now, belatedly, and visit... bring them to you. I know you went exploring with him, so I thought even if you didn't want them yourself, you'd know what to do with them. Sorry, I had to read your letters to see if there were any clues to...'

'It's okay, Dave. I understand, and yes, I'll be happy to do whatever I can. Buck is... was... very special, no matter how goofy he seemed sometimes.' Blinking tears from her eyes, she nearly smiled, remembering: *The cabin.... His blowing it up.... The shower.... Giving her the Ruger Bearcat.... Finding her in the storm.... The Wolverton Mill trip....* Rintintin *on the river.... The accident at the Hideout.... Sleeping in the bed of the truck.... Fry Canyon.*

Through her reverie she heard Dave say, 'Yes, he was quite different from the rest of the family.'

They spoke a bit longer, arranging a time for his visit; she gave him her address and directions to her place, took his phone number, then said goodbye.

Five days later she opened her front door to a middle-aged, soft-spoken man in the six-foot range, who resembled Buck not at all, though why she expected him to, she couldn't say—maybe wishful thinking, a reminder of him. He carried a large cardboard box under his arm, resting on his hip—a water-spotted file folder lay on top and something that looked like a sword and scabbard poked up from one corner. She recalled the sword with a stab to her solar plexus—it had stood beside the glassed-in bookcases—Buck had traded one of his small Anasazi bowls for it, because he thought the sword might have been of Spanish origin, lost along an ancient trail somewhere.

Dave set the box down on a side table, took both her hands and held them. They stood looking at one another for a long minute without saying anything.

He released her hands and said, 'I can see why Buck regarded you as one of his close friends. I don't think he had many—especially women—but you look like you'd be plenty strong, and healthy enough to keep up with him.'

She didn't know what to say, so she asked him if he'd like something to drink. 'A beer, some coffee, tea?' forgetting to ask him to sit down and make himself comfortable.

'No thank you, Shan. Just had lunch.' He reached into the box and handed her the folder with her few letters. Smiling at her rather sheepishly, he said: 'I felt like a Peeping Tom when I first found them and knew I had to look to see if there might be some information pertinent to his demise—then I wished the rats hadn't shredded the others, because they contained remarkable stories and...' Embarrassed, he cleared his throat and looked at his shoes. 'He never told the family anything about his life out West y'know, except that he worked in a uranium mine and ran the river in his boats.'

She took the folder, laid it on the arm of the chair and chuckled. 'Not to worry, Dave. I most certainly would have done the same thing. I'll look at these later, when I'm in the mood to reminisce. Let's see what we've got there.'

Knowing that what was in the box might choke her up, she took a deep breath, bent over and lifted a large bowl off the top. She'd not seen this one before. Under it, a ladle with the handle intact, cracked on one side.... Didn't know that one either. She pulled out a plastic bag full of chips and shards, some large stone knives and two cereal-size bowls that had been in pieces when he found them—he had glued them together. All of these items were hand decorated, and she recognized most of them, running her hands over their surfaces, before she set them down on the chair cushion. Toward the bottom was a whole bowl of woven reeds from the Basketmaker period—people who came before the Anasazi, so the archeologists said—it even smelled like the earth it came from. *Ah-ha! I knew you'd go back to that Basketmaker site and start digging.... Only reason you didn't while we were there was 'cause Leo was waiting for us down canyon.* A big grin spread across her face.

'Must be something special about that piece or you wouldn't have that big smile,' said Dave, who had been watching her retrieve all the treasures.

'I'm almost sure where he found it—I was picturing him going back for it. The big smile was because he had to swim a lake to get to it, and he hated the hell out of that. 'Guess you didn't know he was allergic to cold water—river water, spring water, any kind but hot water under a shower.' ·

'Not the sort of stuff he'd tell anybody about, was it?'

Shan giggled. 'You got that right.... You'd have to watch his antics trying to avoid it in order to understand.'

Shaking a head full of those pictures, she reached in the bottom of the box and picked up a sandal.... Still looking in the box, she opened her eyes and mouth wide, let out a scream and dropped the sandal on the floor.

Poor Dave didn't know if she'd found a scorpion, was laughing, crying or both.

'Ah-ah... Oh, Buckle, I don't believe it...! What could be more fitting?' She reached down with both hands. Shaking slightly, she slowly lifted the venerable and alluring foot-long wedge of cool, golden stone and brought it to her cheek, letting the laughing, crying tears spill over its silken surface.

The *chamahia!*

Looking up at Dave, who stood wide-eyed before her emotional display—probably wondering how his taciturn cousin ever got involved with someone so expressive—she shook her head and whispered, 'Why did I not think about the *chamahia,* or even imagine it might still be with his artifacts. How could I forget?' She handed it to him. 'Careful, it's heavy. Feel how thin and smooth it is—an ancient ceremonial piece that was probably used by a Shaman in some kiva long, long ago—we'll never know—but sacred to the Anasazi, I'll wager. And sacred to Buck too, I think. He felt a special attachment to this piece, above all others.' Her memory flared. 'I saw him running his hands over it one time, and I swear, he was talking to it.'

'H-m-m, really? Doesn't sound like Buck.' He weighed it slowly up and down in both hands. 'Yes, it is heavy, isn't it? What kind of stone, do you know?'

'Jasper, I think, but I'm not sure. I'm no archeologist, but a friend of mine who is says they found a few, similar to this, in Glen Canyon when they excavated as many sites as they could before the reservoir came up and drowned everything.' She told him of the times she'd tried to get Buck to trade or give it to her, and how amazing that it should end up in her hands after all.

Taking it back she smiled. 'Dave, I think he would be pleased to know the *chumuhia* has ended up here with me, after all.'

Like wind chimes, Shan's emotions blew about with a breeze of joy one minute, next, a hot wind of sadness—her new man's entrance into her life, and Buck's sad, oh-so-sad, exit. With the joy came a bit of apprehension. Trying to look into the future was a job for wizards, and she wasn't one. She was certain that she loved this man, and he, her, but living together was not the same as the few weeks they'd spent playing house, and they both knew that. His coming to stay would test both their desire and tolerance for compatibility. Next month she would be driving to Denver to meet and share her new life with him.

The loose and lazy relationship she'd had with Buck would not work here. She'd had affairs with other men since she'd met Buck—he knew that and let it pass when he'd finally told himself he couldn't handle a full-time relationship either. The days of 'musical beds' were over for Shan. She was ready for one man only.

But the way of Buck's passing continue to weigh heavily on her heart. She read her chewed up letters Dave had left with her, trying to place them in their time slots—get a feeling for her thoughts back then, looking to see if they had changed. It was interesting. Some emotions were identical, others had altered considerably. *We do change through the years, physically, mentally, yet emotionally and creatively we seem to stay much the same.* One thing for sure—Buck had been a golden part of her life, and she would always treasure that. He was gone, but she could not erase the nagging feeling that there was something she must do to rest his spirit. As many Native Americans feel about the passing of their loved ones, she felt Buck's spirit was restless and needed an anchor, a homing place—*querencia*, the Mexicans called it—where it would be at peace.

A few days after Dave left and the paroxysm of tears had lessened, she gathered together the letters he'd written to her over the years, feeling that now she might re-live the past with him, not crying, but smiling and laughing, pulling visions, memories—even lessons—from what could only be termed their 'romantic friendship.'

From the first to the last, she read…. A few choked back tears, but mostly she smiled, even burst out laughing. In the midst of them she found the answer to her dilemma.

'…never showed that place to anyone else, not even Leo, and haven't any smart idea why I took you there. You must'a ragged my ass until I got tired of listening to your bitchin'.'

৵৹৶

CHAPTER 24

Early June, 1981

June in the high desert is a magical time.

The canyons seemed to flag her by as she passed close to cliffs and outcroppings. On the horizon, trees looked pasted to a turquoise sky, in the foreground they were lacy and delicate, smelling of sap as they leafed out. The air was fresh and tangy, streams were beginning to take on the color of the run-off; patches of wildflowers trimmed the road on both sides—penstemon, prickle-poppies, paintbrush, poppies, asters—their perfumes tickling her nose through the open windows.

On this Monday morning there was little traffic— weekend drivers having taken their exhaust fumes with them back to work. Driving the route she often took when she went to visit Buck at Fry Canyon, she began to recall past trips—even remembered what she had been thinking when she passed a certain outcrop, side road or signs… especially 'Falling Rock'!

Everywhere she turned there was a memory of secluded trails, roads that climbed and switched back, roads that hung on ledges, far back in nearly impassable country—roads she hadn't learned until years later that Buck had built for the mining companies he'd worked for. And off those roads were hikes and camps. The entire landscape bristled with secret places, and some of the things that happened in them brought tears… then smiles… then laughter.

The closer she came to Fry, the more she wondered what to do about it.

Shall I stop and see who's there? Go in the store?

Driving east the store was hard to see from the highway, and she was almost upon it before she saw the turn, and swung in.

What in the world is all that...? Good lord! They've built motel units.... But there's no more gas pump... and the store's closed. Why is it all shut down? Looks like a ghost town.

She looked up where Buck's trailer used to be and saw one old weather-beaten shack that once housed oil drums and sundry tools. Empty. She made a slow U-ie in the trackless dust and returned to the highway.

That should teach me not to go looking for ghosts.

Shan wound and twisted beside White Canyon and the many magic side canyons she'd hiked that entered it, then turned south on Cedar Mesa, heading toward the Isobella Dugway, another switchback road that Buck had helped to build.

Two- to five-mile patches of country once thickly covered with piñon pine and junipers—one of the easiest places in the high desert to get lost—had been chained, along with hundreds of archeological sites, and was bare as a skinned rabbit. This devastated her, but did not put her off her mission. There were sections of this vast mesa she'd roamed with Buck, and well remembered how to get to them, knowing further they would damned well *not* be chained. The highway—dirt when she first drove it—twisted and looped across its forty miles like some sniffing reptile. Two-wheel tracks took off of it every few miles, probably looking like a centipede from the air, but were she was planning to stop she was sure there would be no tracks.

On the seat beside her, wrapped in a towel, lay the object of her mission.

At a spot near the middle of the mesa, she pulled onto a pad of Navajo sandstone that came up to the very edge of the road; drove over this and behind a thick clump of juniper that expertly hid the car from the highway. She got out and stretched, took the bundle from the seat and started walking toward an outcropping about a mile away.

Animal trails were everywhere; mostly deer, but also javelina, coyote, mountain sheep, skunk, badger, rabbit, lizard, squirrel, snake and chipmunk, to name a few, had left their tiny and large messages scrawled in the sandy soil. To keep herself on track, every fifty feet or so, she'd check her intended direction with the Bear's Ears—the most prominent landmark in the area—a method Buck had taught her to keep from getting lost in thick piñon-juniper forests, outside of using a compass.

Now and then through the twenty- to thirty-foot-tall trees, she would sight the outcropping. For desert walkers this was an easy one, since most of the animal tracks bore in the outcrop's direction because of a small seep at its base. She had only been there once before.

Sure hope to hell I can find my way past that seep... and if I do, if there are no rock falls and it's still climbable...

The forest thinned. Bare sandstone and potholes appeared—then the rim of the mesa. She looked down two thousand feet into a maze of side canyons, and fifty feet up to the outcropping's top where she stood alongside it. Rock falls and talus mounds, along with ledge after ledge of dead-end impassable drops, met an eye trained for trails in places such as this.

The inclination for anyone looking for a way down this mass of drop-offs would be to walk to the right, skirting the rim until they found a crevasse, a log, a rock fall or cave-in that would let them descend to the next ridge wide enough to walk on. Buck had found a way, in the *opposite* direction, at the base of the outcrop. If you stepped across the seep, there was a fourteen-inch ledge she could walk along with her back against the outcropping wall and the two-thousand foot drop at the end of her toes.

Shan unwound the towel from the *chamahia*, tucked it in the pocket of her jeans and crossed the seep. It curved around, fifty feet or more, to a crevasse that had minute Moki steps down its wall. None of this could be seen from the rim, and the ledge snaked around so nothing was visible from the far side either.

At the bottom of the Moki steps, a ledge led to the right, ten feet or so, to a rock fall that let her down to yet a third level—this one's width about ten feet, and running twenty feet or so before it dead-ended in another drop-off.

Three small granaries were tucked in a twenty-inch crevasse along the base of the rear wall, just as she'd last seen them. Untouched. She could never figure how Buck had found this spot.

Neither from the valley floor, nor the rim, could it be seen, even with binoculars. But then, she was never a pot hunter, and she knew that they had eyes trained to the rock, to the ways and means of the many hundreds of Anasazi who had lived on Cedar Mesa, nine hundred to a thousand years ago.

Above the granaries she removed a loose piece of slate-like Navajo sandstone, took the *chamahia* from her hip pocket, laid it against her cheek one last time, then pushed it into the slot where the slate had been. It blended completely with the shape, color and thickness of the slate above and below it. She smiled, satisfied, speaking to the *chamahia*, and to Buck:

'I've no idea if they found you on the mesa… neither one would ever tell me… but you belong with the ghosts of your people and Buck belongs here with you. This is all I can do. Buckle. You were a treasured island in the river of my life…. I'll be forever grateful to have known and loved you. Rest your troubled spirit here with the *chamahia*.'

She climbed up the rock-fall crevasse and the Moki steps; returned to the spring, picked up the towel and followed her footprints through the forest, back to the car.

As soon as she turned onto the highway she began to sing. She sang Buck's favorite songs… sang to him past the mines, through the desert, into the redrock country, past arches and canyons, winding beside the Colorado River, all the way up into the pines…. Singing, singing his spirit home!

❧

ACKNOWLEDGMENTS

This story has been pieced, patched and fitted together by my dreams, my desires and actual happenings over a period of fifty years. Many folks who at one time or another read all or parts of the old manuscript and gave helpful advice have long been on the 'no breakfast forever' list. Ed Abbey told me to '...chuck it, and write from your journals.' Almost as numerous as those dear departed ones are present-day friends, very much alive and kicking. Those I forget to mention should return the kicks to me!

As with all my books, CDs, DVDs, etc., my longtime friend Diane Rapaport—herself the author of a dozen books—stays at the helm, guiding me through the snaky world of contracts, publishing and recording. Her new book, *Home Sweet Jerome: The Death and Rebirth of Arizona's Richest Copper City*, is being published in the spring of 2014.

Sue Ring deRosset is a writer, writing teacher, organizer and activist. A person who makes a difference. She floated into my life on the wings of an interview assignment—after which, she asked to read my unfinished manuscript and help. Her assistance proved invaluable! She spent many hours untangling tenses, clarifying punctuation, showering praise here and there, and forever urging me onward.

At times I seem to live on serendipity alone. Kurt Florman, a mere acquaintance and follower of my work, came out of the blue offering to edit the finished story—the very thing I needed at the precise time I needed it. A blessing way beyond friendship!

Jody Drake, Chautauqua performer, playwright, director, organizer, fund-raiser, producer and founder of the Blue Rose Theatre in Prescott Valley, has been more than a friend for many years—she produced my *Ballad of Gutless Ditch* as a play, hired me for singing gigs, publicized my gigs, and through the years has done more for other Arizona musicians, storytellers and singers than anyone can tell. She also has a ghostly hand in this book.

George and Leslie Walker helped tremendously with the ending of this tale by supplying actual details and presenting me with a gift box of letters and artifacts from a family member.

Thanks to the folks at Northern Arizona University, Cline Library Special Collections, where the 'Katie Lee Archives' reside. Had it not been for Karen Underhill and Richard Quartaroli there would be no Archives. They deserve crown jewels.

No way could I have gotten all this together without my longtime— almost 'assistant'—friend and webmaster, Noel Fray. Computers and I are not exactly friends, so Noel is the peacemaker, go-between, helpmate and fixer.

Charles Seiverd, publisher of *The Noise*, a monthly news and arts magazine, Clarkdale, Arizona, has published several of my pennings over the years. Under the title 'Hidden Passage Sunk' are parts of Chapter 18 of this book. Sarah Gianelli—Arts editor, interviewed me for it.

Naturally, friends of the river have been my most faithful supporters. Heading the list is Lynn Hamilton, Executive Director (and a whole lot more!) of Grand Canyon River Guides. She has no idea how many times she's cleared the deck, pointed the way and revved me up to continue whatever I was doing, or will be doing in the future … as long as it lasts. Lynn knows more about the river people than she would ever tell! www.gcrg.org.

One way or another, these fine folks in Flagstaff, Arizona, have helped to push this project along: Richard Jackson—Hance Editions, Purveyors of Exquisite Photography; Helen Ranney— Associate Director of Philanthropy, Grand Canyon Assn; Tom Martin and Hazel Clark—Vishnu Temple Press; Brad Dimock— Fretwater Press; Julie Sullivan—book designer.

From far and wide: Lew and Gail Steiger and Amy Hale Auker; Myra Perrizo—my old editor at Johnson Books, Denver, Colorado; Barry Scholl—Robbers Roost Bookstore, Torrey, Utah; Andrew Gulliford—Professor of History and Environmental Studies, Fort Lewis College, Durango, Colorado; Beth and

George—Gage & Gage Film makers, Telluride, Colorado; Mark Meloy—Ellen Meloy, Desert Writers Foundation; and the Aspen, contingent—Bruce Berger, author, Su Lum, journalist, and Steve Skinner, river/radio man, KDNK, Carbondale, Colorado.

Jerome, Arizona, February 7, 2014